"Just who is it we're looking for?" Damian braced himself with a hand against the dashboard as Ann showed the Astra's accelerator pedal no mercy.

"All of them. The streets are filled with prospective mothers and daughters searching for one another. It's as if someone's opened the door to the nut house and let everyone out all at once."

So goes another case for Detective Inspector Ann Treadwell, the senior-most female detective in her division. When a kidnap victim is found in an abandoned mine on the outskirts of a small town just north of London, Ann must find the kidnapper before he can strike again. But her investigation is hampered by an eccentric boss and budget cuts which have left Ann with a series of misfit temporary partners.

As she delves deeper into this case and the victim's past, Ann uncovers an elaborate scheme spanning two decades involving men of wealth and power. In a desperate attempt to catch the man responsible for it all, Ann puts her life on the line and comes face to face with some of her most disturbing memories.

A Squirrel's Breakfast

KATHLEEN RUDOLPH

abbott press®

A DIVISION OF WRITER'S DIGEST

A Squirrel's Breakfast

Abbott Press books may be ordered through booksellers or by contacting:

Abbott Press
1663 Liberty Drive
Bloomington, IN 47403
www.abbottpress.com
Phone: 1-866-697-5310

ISBN: 978-1-4582-0765-4 (sc)
ISBN: 978-1-4582-0764-7 (e)

Library of Congress Control Number: 2012924086

Printed in the United States of America

Abbott Press rev. date: 1/17/2013

I would like to thank Clare Chaffey, Chris Chapman, Barry Murphy, Barb Shields and Kevin Davis. Special thanks to Olivia Cronk, who is an amazing teacher and helped me more than I could ever have hoped.

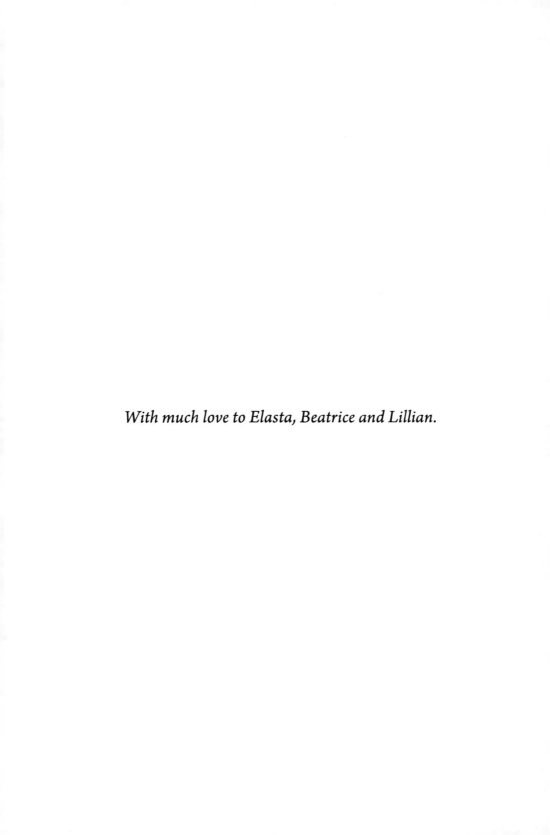

With much love to Elasta, Beatrice and Lillian.

CHAPTER 1

D URING HER FIFTEEN YEARS AS a police officer, thirty-seven year old Detective Inspector Ann Treadwell had worked every sort of crime imaginable. As the highest ranking female detective in her division in a small town just north of London, whenever there was a case involving rape, she was usually the first one called. The call this time came at five-thirty in the morning. It was a bad one. The victim had been found in an abandoned mine on the outskirts of town. She had been held prisoner for an indeterminate period of time and was suffering from so many injuries they wanted Ann to come to the hospital to talk to her while that was still possible. When Ann arrived at St. Pritchards Hospital she was met by Detective Sergeant Patrick McGinty. Patrick was thirty-two, tall with blue eyes and blonde hair – longer on top and short on the sides – that made him look more like a California surfer than a cop, and as always impeccably dressed. His appearance was in sharp contrast to Ann's, who had large brown eyes, shiny auburn hair just past shoulder length and, at five-foot-eight, one-hundred twenty-five pounds, stood half a foot shorter and weighed four stone less than her junior officer.

"What've we got, Patrick?" Ann said in the hallway outside Accidents and Emergencies.

"A woman, approximately in her late-teens or early twenties, found in a cage barely large enough for her to fit inside," Patrick read off his notepad. "Doctor says she's been beaten about the face and torso, suffering from concussion and badly dehydrated, among other things."

"Raped?"

"They don't know yet, but I got the doc to say as much. Here's the photos. Glad we took 'em while she was still unconscious." Ann couldn't hide her revulsion at what she saw. There was a cut held together by dozens of stitches down the right side of the young girl's face, six stitches near the corner of her left eye, four – or was it five? – on an angle above her right eyebrow and about three times as many in her chin. Both of her eyes were black, the left one twice as dark as the right. She looked like a monster. The rest of her was even more gruesome. There were deep bruises everywhere in shades of black, purple, yellow and green, and the left side of her torso was sticking out.

"Do we know who she is?"

"No," Patrick said. "There was no identification on her, not surprisingly, and she hasn't uttered a word since she was rescued."

"Where was she found?"

"Old pit building just east of town. Most of it's been torn down except the kitchen block."

"Any personal belongings?"

"Just the clothes on her back, and they were in no fit state. And, well, see for yourself." Patrick held up a large plastic bag containing the victim's clothes. "They're men's."

"Even the knickers?"

"They're womens' but..." Patrick used a pencil to lift a bra and underpants from the bag. "Both are far too big for someone her size."

"Why would she be wearing those then?"

"I've been wondering that myself. Can't have been comfortable in them."

"What's this?" Ann asked as she stared at a small, dark object at the bottom of the bag.

"Not sure. Looks like a braided leather bracelet."

"Did you run her prints?"

"Yeah. Nothing there either. One of the paramedics said she mumbled something in the ambulance. Nothing coherent, but he detected an accent. American. Or Canadian, perhaps."

"God," Ann said while she looked at the photos again. "What sort of person does this to someone?"

"She doesn't know how bad off she is, does she?" Patrick said.

"I really don't think she's aware of anything at the moment. But she's going to come out of it sometime. Hopefully she'll be able to tell us who did this to her."

Ann handed him the photos. "What about known sex offenders?"

"Nothing so far," Patrick said as he slipped the photos back into the envelope. "We don't know who brought her there or why. No one's filed a missing persons report so we don't even know how long she's been missing."

"What about ransom demands?"

"If there were any, no one's notified us about it. I don't understand. When she was found the door to the cage was unlocked and no one else was there. Why didn't she just run away?"

"In her condition? I doubt she had the strength. By the way, how did we find her?"

Patrick flipped through his notebook. "Phone call. Anonymous."

"Anything on the caller?"

"Erm…no. We weren't able to trace it beyond where the call originated. A call box. Dozens of prints on it. And I've been told the tape isn't very useful, either."

"I'd like to listen to it."

"Why? What do you think you'll find?"

"I don't know. Maybe something in his voice, something that will tell us whether he's a good samaritan or the kidnapper himself. With any luck, perhaps she'll be able to identify him."

"You think she can?"

"I have a feeling his is a voice she won't soon forget."

Ann saw a doctor exiting the examination room. "How is she, doctor?"

"Eh? Oh, yes. Well. Where to begin...," he said while consulting the chart in his hand. "She's been beaten literally from head to toe. Her eyes are burnt, not from fire but from the intense lights she was subjected to. Nothing permanent, we don't think, but her eyes will need to stay wrapped for a day or two. She has rather a large gash to the back of her head which required several stitches to close. We've removed a dozen or so splinters," he said, handing Ann a small plastic bag. "Some have rotted, so I would hazard to guess she was struck with rather an old piece of wood. A board, perhaps. The wound itself is an older one, at least in comparison to her other injuries, a number of which are quite severe. By the bruising pattern, they appear to have been caused by a fist."

"He did all this with his bare hands?"

"It would appear so. What else...Ah, yes. Her ribs are badly bruised. Some may even be broken. We're still waiting on the X-rays. She has multiple abrasions on her arms and legs and—Oh, yes. This one is most disturbing. Her skin is red and raw from indentations running down the length of her back, from her head to her heels. Not quite sure what that's from."

"The cage. She was confined in a small cage."

"I see. Well it must have been quite small indeed. The indentations are rather deep in some places. Would've taken days to work their way that far into her skin. We're doing a blood screen, but I'm almost certain she's been drugged. Shows all the signs. Also suffering from dehydration and a slight case of malnutrition."

"God," Ann said under her breath. "Is there anything else?"

"Oh. Right. If you want to know if she was raped, the tests haven't come back yet, but her injuries do seem to be consistent with that."

"I want to be sure about this, doctor. I want to make sure there's no chance it was consensual."

"Anything's possible, Inspector, but if she consented to this, then she has a different problem altogether. She would have to be deeply disturbed to invite this sort of behavior. Oh, hang on. There's a note here on her chart. According to this, the tests were inconclusive."

"What does that mean? That she wasn't raped?"

"It means that we cannot say with any degree of certainty whether she was or not. Could be her attacker wore a condom. She does have bruising on her inner thighs, which is not uncommon in rape victims. The rest of her injuries are so severe it's difficult to say what the motivation of her attacker was. Only that, whoever did this, it was almost certainly done out of pure rage."

"What do you mean?"

"That this is more than just a simple kidnapping, if there is such a thing. Over the years I've treated many victims who have been beaten, stabbed, shot, even burnt. But this one, it's almost as if he made a game of it. I mean, how many blows to the head are enough? How many punches to the ribs? How many days without food and water? This is a case of someone doing all he could to destroy his victim. It's as if he kept inventing ways to torture her." He thought for a moment. "Inspector, is it possible that more than one person did this to her?"

"We won't know until we talk to her. Any idea when that might be?"

"Not for some time, I should think. She's keeps drifting in and out of consciousness. More out than in."

"Are any of her injuries life-threatening?"

"Surprisingly, no. She's young, which is in her favor, but it'll take some time for her wounds to heal completely. Physically, she should recover. Mentally, well, that's another matter entirely."

It was approaching the middle of the day and Ann went to the vending machines to grab something for lunch. As Ann ate, she couldn't help wonder what was stirring in the mind of this town's most dedicated slackers.

CHAPTER 2

Seven days earlier.
Forty-seven paces.

THAT WAS THE DISTANCE FROM the end of the alley to the fire escape. Danny Acre knew this because he had counted it out not once, not twice, but no less than three times. Twenty-two paces from where the ancient cobbles started at the edge of the alley behind Shepard's Road, situated in a run-down section of this town just north of London, to the skip behind the chemists. Then, after a brief rest, a further twenty-five paces to the back of the old Woolworth building, now abandoned. That's where the fire escape was, where Danny spent most of his semi-waking and fully unconscious hours, from sunrise until dusk, seven days a week. He was less certain about the nights, only that he awoke each day – a miracle in itself – in a heap on the bottom of the escape.

Fifty-one paces. He'd forgotten to count the drain, the one that cost him at least two paces after his foot got caught in the grating and forced him backward, and the crates of empty bottles stacked one on top of the other, which made it necessary for Danny to alter his route once more. The climb onto his perch was a difficult one, requiring him to pull himself up on large cast iron pipes, in place since Victorian times, then hope he didn't catch himself on the electrical wires, a more modern convention, draped along the walls the length of the alley about fifteen feet above ground, before lifting his leg precariously across to his intended destination, the crumbling sill of a barred-up window. An exhausting endeavor, one that would be made simpler if only he knew about the pull-down ladder at the bottom of the escape. Fifty-two paces, actually, counting the puddle, the one he had to sidestep so as not to trod on the rummies and addicts who lined the alley like decaying carpet in this land of lost souls.

It was important for Danny to know such things. He had put more thought into this than anything else in his twenty-four years and everything, every last detail, was critical if this was going to work. It *had* to work.

He was sat on the ledge, legs crossed, and neared the end of his second Sovereign Black cigarette when he noticed how dark it was in the alley, even now, in the middle of the day. His watch told him it was just past three. He took one last, long pull on his fag and tossed it onto the cobbles below, then tried blowing rings out of the smoke escaping from his lungs. He was following a partially formed one as it slipped between the rails when he spotted him, wearing that same oversized gray coat he always wore, collar turned up to ward off the cold breeze that regularly whipped through this narrow alley like a wind tunnel. Danny's fingers did their best to tighten their grip on the length of four-by-two resting tenuously in his hands. He drew in a shaky breath, then silently coaxed his prey down the alley: Come along now...A few more steps...Nearly there...

Danny remembered the kidnapping in bits and pieces. He remembered lying on the floor of the alley, his victim out cold not five feet away. His forearms ached from dragging him into the car he had nicked just for the occasion. He scarcely remembered driving him back to where he now stood, inside a derelict pit building in the middle of an abandoned mine, all the while hoping none of the pieces of the battered red Citroen C2 JWRC that were falling off every few feet were not vital to the operation of the vehicle. But now he didn't see his victim. He was about to begin searching when he spotted him, sat on a wooden chair at the table across from Danny, head tilted to one side, blood dripping down his face, off the V shaped end of the large handkerchief tied around his eyes and hanging limply over his nose and mouth. But it wasn't the blood that caught Danny's eye. It was how much shorter the man looked in person than he did from under a fire escape.

Danny lit another cigarette. Anxious to have a look at his prize Danny tried to undo the knot, but his hands were too unsteady so he turned his attention to the lights. All of them were on since Danny hadn't worked out yet which switches operated which lights. Another attempt brought him no closer to solving them, so he had another go at the blindfold. This time, his fingers didn't betray him. With the top part of the handkerchief still in his hand, Danny walked around to the side of the chair . The handkerchief fell to the floor as Danny was finally able to get a glimpse of him. This wasn't the man who reminded him so much of his father. This was a girl! A scrawny, scruffy girl! Danny squeezed his head between his hands and silently cursed his luck. How could this have happened? he wondered. How could his carefully thought out plan have unraveled so quickly? His first thought was to dump her back in the alley, but what if she saw him? What if she looked up just before he struck her?

He quickly replaced the blindfold and in his haste, tied it too tightly. His heart jumped as she began to stir. His eyes grew wide and his breathing stopped as he watched her try to pull her wrists apart, then raise them until the rope connecting her wrists to her ankles became taut. She winced, then sniffed the air a couple of times. The cigarette! Danny had forgotten about it until it was now just moments away from burning the first two fingers of his left hand.

"Who are you? Why did you kidnap me?" Her weakened voice broke the silence in the large room and made her human to Danny, who took a small step back.

"If you're expecting any ransom for me, you're wasting your time. I don't have any money. I don't know anyone who has." Danny blinked and he was jolted as his lungs rapidly filled with air. He stood frozen in place until the cigarette charred the first layer of skin on his middle finger and he shook his hand until the cigarette dropped. He silently recoiled in pain, then grabbed a bottle of beer from the table and poured its contents over his injured fingers, and increasing his pain.

"You haven't done anything yet. Let me go. I won't tell anyone," she said.

Danny sensed an air of desperation in her voice that struck a nerve within him, a primitive one that relaxed him and left him feeling empowered. He lifted the beer bottle at the neck and had a long swallow while he looked her up and down, his eyes settling on her jumper. He fantasized about what was behind it. Then he noticed the rest of her. Five-foot-five or six; seven, eight stone; short brown hair, ends tucked behind her ears; small, round nose; lips just right, not too full or too thin. She had on black trousers, a long gray coat and zip up cardigan over her red jumper. *Take forever getting her out of all that,* Danny thought. He pulled out a chair from the table and sat with the back facing her, leaning back until the front legs of the chair were off the ground, and studied her.

"Why were you in the jennel?"

"I was working.".

"Workin'? You a workin' girl then?"

"I'm a bounty hunter."

"A bounty hunter? You?" The laughter exploded out of him.

"What's so funny?"

"A girl bounty hunter! That's what's so funny! Tell me," he said as he tried to catch his breath, "what sort of criminals have you hunted? Pocket pickers? Shoplifters? Not the cunningly devious litterbug?"

"Anyone who's got a price on their head. I'd be coming after you if anyone was dumb enough to pay money for you." Danny stopped laughing and again eyed her lustfully.

"What's your name?"

She was silent for a long time, then finally, "Melinda."

He played that name through his head for a moment. He liked it. It suited her.

"You still haven't said why you kidnapped me." The room fell silent with the exception of an almost indiscernible whistling sound emanating from Danny's nose. "You don't know *what* you're doing, do you?"

The fantasy broken, Danny again turned to the bottle as she suddenly seemed ordinary. "Let me go! There are people who are going to start missing me!"

"Yeah? You someone important, are you? Wait. Don't tell me. Is it the Duchess of Doncaster? The Princess of Penzance? Oh, I know. It's the bloody Queen herself! So sorry, your majesty. I didn't know it was you I had tied up, there, on your royal throne, in middle of Buckin'ham Palace."

"Royalty aren't the only ones who take revenge on their enemies!"

"Yeah? And you must be the daftest person I ever met!"

"Let me go, and I'll pay you whatever you want."

"Really? I thought you said you haven't got any money, don't know anyone who has."

"I can get it."

"Can you now? Well, maybe it's not money I'm after." He made the intent of that remark clear by running his hand along her inner thigh, but that gesture also betrayed him. His hand was trembling.

"I wouldn't if I were you! I'd kill you before you got the chance!" Caught off guard, his hand was off her in an instant.

"Kill me, is it?" Danny regained his composure. "And just how do you reckon with your hands bound? Your feet as well? And anything else I may decide to tie up. I know lots of ways to tie someone up."

"Use one more piece of rope on me and I promise before I leave here, you'll be wearing most of it!"

Danny's hand tightened around his beer bottle until it nearly broke. Then he smashed it on the floor next to her, glass fragments and beer glancing off her legs. Then he slammed his fist into the side of her head with enough force to topple her from the chair. But before she could fall he grabbed her by her collar and pulled her close.

"I'll tie you up any time, any way, I so choose!" he said through clenched teeth. "As for these friends of yours, there's no one comin' to rescue you, so you may as well get that idea out your head. What time you eat, sleep, drink, go to the toilet, it's all up to me now, not these friends who don't exist!"

"They *are* looking for me and they will find me! And you! Just something for *you* to think about!"

Indecision briefly clouded Danny's mind, but with his next breath he struck her across her face with the back of his hand. He saw the corner of her mouth split open from the ring he wore on his right hand and a stream of blood trickle down her chin and he felt inspired. He shoved her up against the wall behind her and her head hit hard, rendering her even more defenseless .

"Now, just so you don't go gettin' any ideas," he gasped while he stood over her, "we're somewhere in the middle of nowhere. There's no one who can hear you, no one who can help you. And I'd advise you to keep that blindfold on at all times. Oh, and, if you're real nice, I'll introduce you to my mates. You'll like my mates, but not as much as they're gonna like you. Right. Up ya get."

He pulled her roughly to her feet, then cut the rope connecting her hands and feet. He turned her to her left, pushed her ahead a few paces, then down to her knees. Then he grabbed her by the back of her collar and forced her to crawl forward until she was inside a cage. She used the heels of her hands to move forward, but the bars dug deeply into her palms. She stopped momentarily, but a push in the backside from Danny's boot got her moving forward again. Now fully inside, her back brushed up against the top, giving her little room to move, so she lowered herself until she was lying flat on her back, knees up.

"This is where you'll stay when I'm not here. And I don't plan on bein' here a lot," Danny said, his face hot, sweat beading up on his forehead.

His heart raced and his ears pounded as if they were about to burst, and his legs nearly gave out before they could take him back to the table. His confidence in the healing properties of beer waning, he treated himself with a joint instead. It calmed him, allowed him to forget his failings on the day.

But it also made him think. What if she *was* telling the truth? What if someone *was* looking for her? If they were, they'd never find this place. Danny was confident of that. It was a veritable island in a sea of dust that kicked up even in the slightest breeze and filled the air with swirling bits of shale and coal dust.

But it kept him dry when it rained and warm against the cold. Only the shower and canteen block and the kitchen were still standing. There was a bathroom through the door in the corner to Melinda's right, along the same wall as Melinda's cage, and a hallway to her left which used to lead to the workshop, but it had been torn down and now formed a tunnel that led outside. The top floor was gone, too. All that was left were some loose boards, bits of slate and columns of bricks rising a mile in the sky. It was Danny's favorite part, when the wind wasn't blowing. The kitchen was the only part not covered in dust. The only part that still had four walls. As for the rest, there was nothing but the flattened pit tip, the spoil heap and bits of the old headgear. There were still some vents sticking up from the ground and tracks from the disused railway. This part of town was so deserted, even the police didn't come round anymore. So Danny took it. Claimed it as his own. No one apart from Danny had been to the colliery since it had been abandoned more than a decade ago. No one but Danny and his mates.

HE COULD COPE WITH THE dirty floors, the grease streaming down the windows, the chipped plates and bent silverware, even the frequent visits by the local health authorities. But Danny didn't fancy seeing Pablo and Juan today. But there they were, in Beaumont's Restaurant at their usual table in back. Pablo had on a green army shirt, a white shirt with long sleeves underneath. Danny had been tempted to tell him how daft it looked, but you don't tell that to someone who stands six-foot-four and weighs somewhere in the neighborhood of two hundred forty pounds. Much the opposite of Juan, who was nearly invisible when he stood sideways. Always wore sleeveless shirts, as if he had something to show off. At the moment he was staring down a fly while Pablo was working on his wood carving on the table top. Danny was dreading this. He had made the mistake of telling them about his plan and he knew they'd want to know all about it. Still, he was glad they were here. At least with them, he knew he would get some intelligent conversation.

"Me nephew, he got accepted to Lilleshall last week," Pablo said, his nose not two inches from his knife as he flicked a piece of table that just missed Juan, who didn't flinch.

"That little prat? The one's always got left shoe on his right foot?" said Juan, who could hardly hold his head as high as his pint.

"Sod off, Juan," Pablo said matter-of-factly as he continued carving. "We're quite proud of him, we are."

"He's that good, is he?"

"Got brilliant foot work, him. Runs like the wind, too."

"How's his leg?"

"Kicks the ball like it's comin' out of a cannon. It's his grades that has me Aunt Iris worried. She reckons he won't be able to keep up if he spends any more time with his football."

"We gonna talk about your cousin or nephew or whatever it is all night?"

"My nephew, Dan, " Pablo said as if his feelings were hurt. "He's me nephew. Neil's his name."

"Oi, Dan," Juan said facetiously. "So how're things in motel hell? Holdin' up under all the torture, is he?".

"Yeah, Dan," Pablo added. "This bloke remind you of your old man as much in person as he did from your little ledge?"

"Yeah, well…I've decided to go about this a bit differently."

"What d'ya mean, different?" Juan asked.

"I mean, I didn't kidnap the old bastard. I got someone else instead. Someone better."

"Who?"

"A lass."

Juan's mouth fell open. "You mean you've had a bird locked away in that dungeon of yours all this time and ya haven't seen fit to share her with yer mates?"

"That's not what she's for, Juan. She's there to listen. That's all."

"That's all? Odd, that."

"What's that supposed to mean?"

"Nothin'. Just that, if I had a bird there all alone like that, I'd've done more by now than just talk."

"So tell us, Dan," Pablo said while digging his blade into the table, "Has it all been just talk, or have the two of you—"

"I told ya, that's not what this is about! I don't care what you tossers think. It's my business what I do or don't do. She's mine to do with whatever I please."

"So what's pleased ya so far?"

"I just told you, ya—!"

"Relax, Danny boy. Here, have a pint," Juan said, then pushed his half empty glass across the table as Pablo sat back and took a good look at Danny.

"You're quite jumpy today, Dan. Never used to be that way, did he, Juan?"

"No, never used to be that way," Juan mimicked.

"What're you two on about?"

"You, Dan. Look at ya. Drummin' your fingers on tabletop, fidgetin' with your keys, tappin' your foot against the chair leg. You're just a bundle of nerves, ain'tcha?"

"Don't be daft. It's you lot that's changed."

"Aye. Must be us, eh, Juan?" Danny took a drink, then slammed his glass on the table, sloshing beer all over Pablo's art work. "Easy, Dan.

All I'm sayin' is, me and Juan, we ain't never known you to hurt no one, especially not some girl. I mean, you didn't even work your way up to it. You went from bein' a somewhat decent bloke to a full-fledged kidnapper. And now here you are, havin' a drink with your mates, and all the while she's sat there by herself in that cold, lonely building. Don't expect she's havin' any fun, do you, Juan?"

"No, don't expect she's havin' any fun," Juan repeated.

Danny sighed. "Christ, what is it with you lot? We never talk about anything normal anymore like before."

"That's because things ain't like before," Pablo pointed out. "You saw to that. She's your responsibility now and we don't think you're livin' up to your responsibility, do we, Juan?"

"No, we don't think yer livin' up to yer responsibility," Juan echoed. "You took her on, now ya gotta look after her. Ya gotta feed her, wash her, clean up after her, then buy her a uniform and send her off to school. Then one day, you'll have to give her away at her weddin'!" Danny hunched over his beer and bristled as they shared a hearty laugh at his expense.

"So, Dan. What've you told her so far?" Pablo said before polishing off the rest of his Abbots.

Danny fidgeted with a large chunk of table top that had landed nearby. "Was *gonna* tell her, ya know, about my parents, how they mistreated me, left me behind. How they thought I killed my brother and sent me to that hospital."

Pablo looked at Danny, who did his best to avoid eye contact. "That's a load of bollocks, ain't it? Apart from the mental hospital."

"Some of it might be bollocks, but it's only because she made me stretch the truth a bit!"

"A bit?!"

"What, you're sayin' it didn't happen?"

"Us? Course not. We was there. We saw how hard you took it when they left you and went travelin' round the world. On business, was it? Ya just didn't cope with it as well as ya do now."

"Meaning?"

"Meanin', me and Juan, we might've heard your sad stories once or twice before. All I'm sayin' is, my old man knocked me about a bit when I was a boy and I turned out alright. I got no plans to kidnap anyone."

"Yeah, well it wasn't the same for you as it was me. I wouldn't have minded if all he did was knock me about, but it were all the mental abuse."

"Yeah, all ya had was all that money they gave ya," Juan smiled behind heavy eyelids. "I'd put up with an unkind word or two for that amount of dosh."

"I told ya, it ain't about the money!"

"No, but ya did take it, didn't ya?" Pablo said, then checked the sharpness of his knife by running the blade across his tongue. "So, Dan," he said while he resumed carving, "has she been sympathetic to your plight?"

"No, she's no different than the rest. She don't behave properly, her, not the way someone who's been kidnapped ought to. It's as if... It's almost as if she was laughin' at me."

"Laughin' at you? I wouldn't take that from no one, Dan, especially not some bird. Here you've gone to the trouble of kidnappin' her, tyin' her up and leavin' her in a damp, dark pile of rubble and now she won't even make the effort to understand you and all your assorted problems. That's one bird I wouldn't want to be the mother of my children."

"No, but I'd sure like practicin' with her!" Juan said before bursting into a fit of laughter.

"That what you lads think?" Danny said over the noise, his even tone masking the fraying ends of his patience.

"Me? I think she thinks you're a great big baby who can't wipe his own arse unless his mum is there to do it for him," Pablo replied.

Their laughter faded in the distance as Danny left Pablo to his wood carving and Juan to the dream state he had slipped into. Danny sought refuge at the mine. He sat amongst the rubble on the roof above the kitchen and savored the cool, refreshing breeze, the stillness of the night, the taste of the first of a half-dozen freshly rolled reefers and thought about how much he liked it there, more than he did home. There was no one there anymore but his brother and they didn't get on like they used to despite his brother's assurance that he bore no grudge. But Danny knew he did even if he didn't understand why. After all, they were able to pump most of it out of his stomach before it killed him. The doctor said he was right as rain now, except that problem with his eyes, and the occasional bout of asthma. Then there was that difficulty with his hearing, but the glasses, inhaler and deaf aid took care of all that.

Danny's thoughts were interrupted by a twinge of pain. He reached behind him and discovered the source of his discomfort: His stash of pot, still in the zip bag. Somewhat lighter, he noted, since Pablo and Juan found it. Instead of putting it back under some loose bricks, they left it out in the open where the elements could get to it. Danny couldn't risk walking the streets with it, what with the police always stopping him for one reason or another. He thought about flushing it, but then another idea came to mind. His conversation with Pablo and Juan had convinced Danny that she had to go. He wanted his old life back, a life he no longer had since she'd been here. He quickly formulated yet another plan, one that would reluctantly involve his two best mates.

Danny rang them and told them to meet him in the high street near Beaumont's Restaurant. He waited nearly a half hour before he spotted Pablo coming out of the sweet shop several doors down, his nose in the white bag resting in the meaty part of his palm. Pablo acknowledged Danny's wave, but that didn't make Pablo move any faster.

"So? Is she a ravin' mad lunatic yet?" Pablo asked while he picked through the bag.

"I haven't given it to her yet. Haven't got enough dope, thanks to you and Juan. Where is he, any road? There he is. What's he doin' over the way? Oi! Juan!"

"Did ya give it to her yet?" Juan asked after barely surviving another slow-motion dash through traffic.

"No."

"And?"

"And what?"

"Did it work?"

"I haven't given it to her yet!"

"Easy, Dan. Ain't his fault ya didn't get her sorted yet," Pablo said in between bites of the slab of chocolate he pulled from the bag. Juan staggered past Danny, who followed him with his eyes until Juan's progress was halted by a rusted bit of metal sticking out of the side of Danny's car which snagged his trouser leg. It was all that stood between him and the pavement.

"Yes it is his fault," Danny shot back. "Yours as well."

"How do you reckon?" Pablo said through blackened teeth.

"Because you lot stole my dope the other night! That's why I've none left for her!"

"What're you on about? That were our dope. You'd already done yours, remember? Juan had to do his community service the next day and I had to work that night haulin' slate, so we kept ours for later. You were out cold when we left. No one stole anything from you, ya idiot." Pablo put the chocolate away, wiped his hand on his shirt, then pulled a plastic bag from his pocket. "Here." He poured the contents of the bag in Danny's hand. "I just got these. Haven't tried 'em yet, but they should do the job."

"These're Allsorts," Danny said.

"Eh?" Pablo looked at Danny's hand, then took another bag from his pocket and dumped five white pills on top of the licorice.

"What're these, then?"

"LSD. Well, not really LSD, but near enough. That's what Vlad said, any road. Said it's even more powerful than LSD. That's why I haven't done 'em yet. I don't normally do acid."

"Then ya don't know how strong these are or what they'll do?"

"No. That's what I want her to find out." Danny looked at the pills and the Allsorts.

"Just put it in her food, then?"

"If you break it up small enough, she'll never even know it's there.

The subject of the conversation finally made it's way through Juan's thick skull. He freed himself from the car, walked on his knees to Danny and pulled Danny's fingers open.

"No! Ya don't wanna do these, Dan! They're vicious little bastards!"

"You sure this'll work, Pablo?"

"I know it will."

"No, don't do it, Dan!" Right on cue, Juan hit the pavement face-first.

"So, Dan," Pablo said as he picked through the bag of sweets again. "On the phone you said you wanted to get her sorted so she wouldn't remember you or the colliery, yeah?"

"Yeah."

"So, if she can't remember, that means you could do anything you want. Anything at all, and she wouldn't be able to tell anyone a thing about it."

"Yeah. Erm, yeah. Right."

"When ya goin' back there? Tonight?"

"I don't know. Why?"

"Thought maybe I'd go with ya. Haven't been there in ages. Just wonderin' what the place looks like these days."

"I don't think so, Pablo. Not today."

Pablo shrugged and headed for his pickup truck parked at the end of the road. Danny waited until he was gone, then helped Juan to his feet. With more than a little regret he had Juan run an errand, then waited for him at the colliery. When an hour passed and he still hadn't arrived, Danny went looking for him and found him lying flat on his face again, this time in the tunnel leading into the kitchen.

"Finally!" Danny took the paper bag still clutched in Juan's outstretched hand and brought it to the table. "What took ya so long?"

"Wasn't my fault," Juan said after dragging himself inside. "Long line at takeaway shop."

"What did ya get?" Danny opened the bag and was hit square in the face by a blast of fragrant, hot air.

"Chinese. You can hide anything in Chinese."

"I can see it's Chinese, ya prat. What sort of Chinese?"

Danny dumped the contents of the carton onto a paper plate. He still didn't know what it was, and he didn't care. He took the bag of Pablo's pills, crushed one and dusted the top of the food with it.

"Make sure ya mix it in good so she can't taste it," Juan advised.

"I know–Oi, don't eat that! That's for her, that!"

"Just the bean sprouts. I love bean sprouts."

"You *are* a bloody bean sprout!"

"Go on, give it to her! I wanna see what happens!"

"No! Go on, get out! I don't want ya givin' it away with your stupid laugh! I'll let ya know what happens!"

* * *

BY HER COUNT, IT HAD been three days since Melinda had been kidnapped, three days since Danny locked her away in the cage. She'd spent that time thinking about the things Danny said and some of them were starting to worry her, causing her mind to drift in all the wrong directions. As it did, she could feel herself starting to slip away. It had been so long since she'd heard anything. No sounds of life other than her own heart beating. At first she tried keeping track of time, but he kept the lights on all the time. It came right through the blindfold and never changed, and she wasn't sure anymore if it was night or day. Or the last time she ate. She was always too hot or too cold and her body ached where it didn't bleed. Her coat helped cushion her from the bars but no matter what position she got into, it wasn't long before the circulation got cut off and she had to move as much as she could until it returned. Then she waited for another part of her to go numb and did it all over again.

Enough of her senses had returned now for her to realize she wasn't alone. Danny. She could smell the tobacco that had become one with his clothes, the alcohol that leaked from every pore. But through it all, there was another smell. Food.

"Hands!" she heard him say.

She raised her hands, he cut the ropes, then passed something to her. A paper plate, folded in half so he could get it through the bars. Melinda was so hungry, she didn't even mind that the food was soaking through the bottom, or that it burned her hands. She found the plastic spoon he left on top and did her best to push the food into her mouth. She didn't know what it was, but it smelled good. It was as if every bite was bringing her closer to living than dying.

But it came at a price. At first the food revived her, but as it went down all she felt was pain as it passed through what she could only imagine was now a tangle of twisted bones and organs. The food sat in her stomach like a pile of rocks, then it churned, as if it was trying to reject the very thing that it needed most. She heard Danny walking around the cage. That didn't help her digestion, but she didn't think anything short of medical attention could at this point. But there was something else. The food. It tasted bitter, and she realized he must have put something in it. She didn't know what to do. If she kept eating, it might kill her. If she didn't, he might do it himself. She stopped eating but Danny remained silent, and she thought maybe she was wrong. The bitter taste could have something to do with her condition. All the blood she'd been coughing up, the headaches…She couldn't keep her mind from wandering. She couldn't remember things from one minute to the next. But she had to. Either she kept her wits, or she'd lose her life.

CHAPTER 3

THE SCREAMS THAT AWAKENED MELINDA were her own. It scared her more than anything else so far. Why had she screamed? Was it a nightmare? She couldn't remember what she had dreamed, or if she had dreamed at all. Something was happening to her. Images were racing through her head, most of which she didn't recognize but frightened her just the same. Was this it, she wondered? Was she dying?

"Shit, Juan! I thought ya said ya knew how to do a proper ear piercin'!"

Melinda, who had worked the blindfold down to a single layer while she was alone, peered through it and saw three men sitting at the table: a big man with short ginger hair, a skinny man with long stringy blonde hair, and Danny. Danny's friends at last. She couldn't see what they were doing, only a small flame flickering in the middle of the table.

"I told ya, Dan, ya can't do a proper ear piercin' with a sewin' needle even if ya do hold it over flame first," the one with the stringy hair said.

"Leave him alone, Dan," the big one said. "It's only a small gouge, this. You'll be as lovely as ever in a few days time. Anyway, after what ya done to her, I shouldn't think such a small amount of blood would bother you."

"Sod off, Pablo!"

"Christ, Dan. It ain't half bright in here," Pablo observed. "You could light the whole of Wales with these."

"Yeah, well, those're the only bulbs I could find, aren't they?"

"Oi, Dan! Look! She's awake!"

"Leave her!, Dan said.

"Don't ya wanna see how she is?"

"No!"

Melinda saw the skinny one pick up a needle and start hurting Danny's ear again. The big one walked toward her.

"How you gettin' on in there, miss?" Melinda smiled, then grimaced through the pain as the obvious answer to that came to mind. Obviously, apparently ,only to her. "Don't worry. Dan won't hurt ya. He's not that sort." Melinda started to laugh, but the pain ended it. "I'm Pablo, by the way. Well, it ain't really Pablo. Me and Juan – it ain't really Juan, either – we just call ourselves that after famous Colombian drug lords. We owe quite a lot of who we are to them. Danny there, he didn't want one. Just as well. Couldn't think of another one."

"Pablo…Is there water?" Melinda said barely above a whisper.

"Water? Oi! Dan! She wants water, her."

"Get it yerself! I'm busy—Ow! Shit, Juan! The ear, not the neck!"

Pablo disappeared, then returned and carefully pushed a paper cup through the bars into Melinda's trembling hands. It hurt to swallow, but the water felt good as it went down.

"Dan here tells me he's been takin' good care of you—"

"Help me!" Melinda whispered.

"Oi, Dan," Pablo said without taking his eyes off her, "I thought you said you was lookin' after her."

"Leave her and come here!"

Pablo returned to the table, plopped himself on a chair and said, "So, Dan. Whatcha reckon?"

"What about?" Danny replied.

"My pills. Think they're alright for us to try?"

"You've just been chattin' 'er up the last ten minutes. Why don't ya ask her? Ask her if she sees cars flyin' at her or fruit runnin' towards her or—"

"What do you think, Juan?"

Juan was half-sprawled on the table, his head facing the cage only because that was the direction it landed. "Oi! Juan! I said, whatcha think?"

"I think we should have a party, just me and her," Juan said, smiling broadly.

"Drunken sod. I mean whatcha think about the acid? Think it's alright for us to try?"

"Course it is. She took it and she looks alright."

"Juan thinks it's alright to try. Come on then, let's have it."

Danny hesitated, then took a plastic bag out of his trouser pocket and tossed it on the table. "Oi! How come there's only one?" Pablo said after counting.

"Well, how many were ya plannin' on doin'?"

"More than one."

"That's just daft, that is."

"Yeah, but," Pablo held up the bag, "where's the rest?"

"Where? Look, it doesn't matter how many are left. All that matters is how it works. Now we know it only takes one hit of LSD to get high."

"It ain't LSD," Pablo corrected.

"What? I know it's not LSD! I'm just callin' it that because you don't know what it *is* called!"

"So—right. So, she took more than one, yeah?," Pablo asked.

"But that's just her, isn't it? Probably doesn't get sorted regularly so takes twice as much for her to get high as it does us."

Pablo looked at the bag. Then Melinda. Then the bag again. "No, one won't do. I gotta have more."

"But ya ain't never done LSD before," Danny said. "Ya want to take care."

"It ain't LSD."

"I know, I know!" Pablo took another look at the bag, then turned toward Danny, who didn't hesitate this time. He took a second bag from his pocket and tossed it toward the table. Without taking his eyes off Danny, Pablo caught it. The count this time was more to Pablo's liking. Danny flinched as Pablo reached across the table for a bottle of beer. He studied Dan for a bit, then said, "It's her, isn't it" Pablo asked with surprising calm. "That's what this is about, not to get back at your old man by boring some old poof to death with tales or your sad, pathetic life." Pablo sat forward and said , "So, Dan. Have ya done it yet?"

"Done what?"

"Her. Have ya done her?"

"Yeah. Course I have."

Pablo shifted his eyes toward Danny. "That's another lie, ain't it?"

"Yeah? Go and ask her then. Go on!"

"What, her? She won't say anything for fear of what you'll do to her if she does."

"She don't have to say a word. All ya have to do is look at her."

"Yeah? And just what is it I'm meant to be lookin' for?"

"You'll know when ya see it."

"What, like the glow of sheer and utter contentment that comes across a bird's face after she's been in the lovin' arms of one Danny Acre?"

"Get stuffed!"

"That's why you've been keepin' her here all this time. A man can't go as long as you have without havin' it off. It ain't natural, that."

"Yeah, well…Well, look at her! How am I supposed to go near her when she smells like that?!"

Pablo put a firm hand on Danny's shoulder and said, "You'll never have a better chance, mate. Go on. Do ya a world of good."

Pablo got up, grabbed Juan by the collar and dragged him outside. Moments later Melinda began to stir. Her vision was hazy and the blindfold didn't help, but she could make out a figure standing at the end of the cage silhouetted by the light.

"Get out," Danny said in an ominous tone.

Melinda heard the cage door open and she tried to move, but she was too weak. Danny's hands clamped down on her legs just above her ankles and she braced herself in anticipation of again being violently dragged out for another beating. But this time he slid her out gently. Then he helped her to her feet and led her through the door in the corner to her right.

"Ya got ten minutes," his voice echoed off the walls. "Mind, I know every inch of this room. There's no way out."

She heard the door close, then lifted the blindfold. She was in a bathroom, with three stalls to her left, a row of urinals on the wall in front of her, and four basins to her right. The lights were on but it wasn't nearly as bright as it was in the kitchen. She made her way to the basins. The mirrors hung over them were covered with dust, and Melinda's arms were too stiff to reach far enough to wipe them off, leaving her to only imagine what she must look like after all these days.

The tap squeaked as she turned on the cold water. She let it run until it was clear. Then she cupped her hands and drank as much as she could. It revived her, like before. On the side of the sink was a small bar of soap that was so dry it was cracked. She picked it up and held it to her nose. After days of nothing but stale beer, cigarette smoke and wet jeans, it smelled wonderful. She held it under the water, hoping to get it wet enough to lather. There was none as she rubbed it on her arm, but she felt it sting as it touched her raw skin. She used the last paper towel in the dispenser to dry off. Then she ran the towel under the water and carefully pressed it to the back of her head. That made it throb. When she looked at the towel, it was bright red. Feeling the need to use the toilet while she had the chance Melinda turned to her right. But when she turned she gasped as she saw Danny standing behind the door watching her.

"Go on. Wash." It wasn't a request, it was an order. "Look at ya! Go on, look! You're disgustin', you. Don't know how you can stand it."

Melinda stood frozen in place. Her heart was racing. He came toward her and she saw the rage in his eyes. He shoved her against the wall between the urinals. He pulled her coat down, pinning her arms to her sides. Then he tried to undo her trousers. Panic started to set in until Melinda noticed he was struggling with her zip.

"You've never done this with a girl before, have you?" Melinda improvised, her voice suddenly even and clear and pugnacious as it had been that first day. "Don't worry. I won't tell your friends. It'll be our secret."

Momentarily stunned, Danny took her by the arms and pulled her close, and for the first time she could see his face clearly: Short, dark hair; a nose that had been broken more than once; and bright red lips. His deep set brown eyes burned through her, but there was something else. His anger. It was almost primitive.

Melinda waited for the inevitable beating. But instead, Danny released her and turned away, giving her the opportunity to zip up her trousers. In that instant, with her guard down, Danny spun and landed a solid punch to her jaw. Her head hit the wall behind her and she heard a loud pop. She could feel herself passing out, but she didn't dare. Danny grabbed the top of her jumper and tried tearing it off. But she bit into his hand, then lifted her knee into his groin. He tried not to let go of her, but his hands were needed elsewhere at the moment. This time, it was her looking down at him as he writhed in pain on the floor. It was the first thing she had enjoyed since she'd been here. She started for the door, narrowly avoiding the hand he sacrificed from his crotch to use to reach for her ankle. He missed, and she hurried unsteadily down the tunnel. But in her eagerness to escape she slipped on the rubble and fell. Suddenly, the light was gone. She looked up and saw someone coming toward her. Pablo.

"Here, where you off to then?" his voice boomed off the walls while he lifted her by her arms.

"Help me!"

"What's this then? What's our Dan been up to? He hasn't tried anything funny, has he?" Pablo brushed her off, and Melinda wondered if he had come to rescue her. He wasn't trying to hurt her, like Danny, but he wasn't letting go of her, either. Her thoughts were interrupted by a sound coming from behind her. She turned just in time to see Danny, bent over, his hand still soothing his sore crotch as he rushed toward them.

"You bitch!" Danny uncoiled his fist from behind his ear, but Pablo caught it and held onto it as Danny sank to his knees and searched for air.

"Christ, Dan. Whatcha been doin' to her in there?"

"That little bitch kneed me in the balls, that's what I've been doin' to her in there!" Danny said, bracing his hand against the wall and struggling to his feet.

"Yeah? Well, maybe you deserved it. That it, miss? He deserve it?"

"Here, give her back, you!" Danny lunged toward her.

"Easy, Dan," Pablo said, holding Danny back with a hand on his chest. "She says she don't want to go back."

"I don't give a toss what she wants! She's mine! I'm the one brought her here! I'm the one says when she can go!"

"What, you're sayin' she belongs to you? You own her, do you?"

"Yeah!...Yeah, that's right! I own her!"

"Tell ya what, Dan. Why don't we let her decide? Well, miss? You want to go there, inside that cramped, lonely cage, or would ya rather come with me, out there, in the fresh air?"

"NO! I'm not gonna let you take her!" Danny pushed toward her but was again easily repelled by Pablo.

"Whadda ya mean, you ain't gonna let me?" Pablo inquired with some amusement.

"I know what you'll do to her and I won't let you! Not this time! Not her!"

"Not her, is it? Like she's someone special? They were all special, mate, each in their own way." Danny tried one more time to reach for her, but Pablo threw him aside with one hand. "Well, miss? What's it gonna be?" Melinda knew it didn't matter what she wanted, that they would ultimately decide for her. But before another word was spoken, Melinda heard glass breaking. She instinctively put her hands up to shield her face, then opened her eyes to see Danny holding the top half of a wine bottle. The rest of it was in pieces in Pablo's hair. She watched as Pablo sank to one knee, blood dripping down his face. "Alright!! She's yours!! Ya flippin' idiot!"

"No!" Melinda let escape.

Pablo staggered back down the tunnel, moaning and holding his head as he made his way outside. Melinda started to go after him but Danny took her by the throat and pushed her back inside, then threw her to the floor. Her head hit hard and she saw a splash of light. She was on the verge of blacking out, but Danny put his hand around the back of her neck, dragged her back to the cage, stuffed her inside and slammed the door shut. All these days she had done her best to show him he hadn't hurt her, but she could no longer deny he had worn her down. The battle now wasn't for her body. It was for her mind.

DANNY STORMED OUT OF THE colliery in the face of yet another failure. He could have gone back and tried again, but getting his life back to the standstill it was in before he came up with this caper took priority and he went to a call box several miles away to ring the police. He picked up the receiver but before he could press nine, a constable took the phone from his hand.

"Right, Danny. What'cha you up to today?," the first of two Bobby's asked.

"Just makin' a bloody phone call!" Danny replied with appropriate belligerence.

"Come along then. Step out." It sounded as if he knew something. About her? But how? "Right, then. Empty your pockets." Danny breathed a premature sigh of relief.

"I haven't done nothin'! You cops think you can harass me just because—"

"Yes, yes. Be a good lad then, eh, Danny? Don't make us do it for you." No sooner had Danny reached into his pocket than the constable pulled his arm behind his back and shoved him face-first against the wall next to the phone box, his face scraping against the bricks, and pulled a plastic bag from Danny's pocket. "Well, well. Looks like we've got more than enough to hold you this time."

"That ain't mine, that!"

"Just holdin' it for your gran, is that it? Right. Let's go."

Several hours after he was arrested, Danny was finally allowed to make a call. He rang Pablo who, it was widely known, had just a fraction of an ounce more brains than Juan, and told him to say he was Danny's solicitor so they'd let him come see him.

"Oi, Dan. What's up?" Pablo said after arriving nearly two hours later.

"What's up? Do you not know where you are?"

"Well, what did you ring *me* for? You know I don't like bein' here." Danny was struck silent by Pablo's suit. Red and brown plaid, and a bow tie! The trousers were too big, the waistcoat too small and the jacket went out of style ages ago.

"Nice suit. Right. I need ya to do somethin' for me," Danny said in a low tone. "Call that bastard solicitor of mine—number's here on this paper—and make sure he's comin'. I gotta get out of here right quick."

"Right," Pablo said as if he understood.

"Then I want ya to look after her. Ya know? Her?"

"She's in a bloody cage. Where's she gonna go?"

"Shhhh! Mind your voice, you! Just make sure she don't die. Give her some food. Just enough to keep her alive, but no more. None of them ten-course dinners like the ones you fancy. Just throw somethin' in her cage. She'll eat it."

"Right."

"After you've done that, ring the police. Tell 'em where she is, but for God's sake, don't tell 'em your name like ya done that last time."

"That weren't me! That were Juan!"

"Just do it, yeah?"

"Yeah, sure. But you're gonna owe me one hell of a favor when you get outta here."

ONE MORE DAY, AND SHE still wasn't dead. But Melinda awakened to find she had company. Pablo was seated at the table, a half-empty wine bottle in front of him. He seemed oblivious to the loud thud and subsequent moan that came from the tunnel behind him and didn't even bother to look when Juan appeared a few moments later, his clothes covered in dust, gashes on both knees. He walked past Pablo and sat cross-legged on the floor next to Melinda.

"Bet ya'd like to come outta there, wouldn't ya, miss?" Juan said through a toothy grin.

"Yes," Melinda whispered.

"Yeah, course ya would. Here, what's happened to yer jumper then? Looks as if someone's torn it. That it, miss? Someone tear yer jumper?" Juan looked over his shoulder and grinned at Pablo, who was busy opening wine bottles from the shelves. "Oi! Pablo! Give us the key!"

"I haven't got it!"

"That's alright" Juan smiled at her again. "We don't need no key, do we?" Pablo lifted his shirt, revealing a small crowbar tucked in his waistband. He slid it along the floor toward Juan, who stopped it with his hand, then attacked the lock and opened it in seconds.

"Here, that's no place for a nice girl like you," Juan said as he eased her out of the cage. "Me and Pablo, we never did like the way Danny treated ya. We told him he should let ya go, didn't we, Pablo?" Melinda tried to get up, but Juan stopped her with a hand on her shoulder. He scrambled to the table and grabbed two of the bottles Pablo had just opened, then hurried back and offered her one. "Go on. It's good for ya, this. Make ya forget things that've happened. Things that're about to happen. Right, Pablo?"

"Shut it, you!" Juan took the bottles and went back to the table. Melinda again tried to get up, with more urgency this time, but she was too weak. All she could do was lie there as they sat drinking as much wine as they could hold, laughing and taking long looks at her. Then Juan had one last drink and lifted himself out of his chair. But after only a step or two, he found himself in a familiar position: face-first on the floor. Undeterred, he crawled towards her, his eyes riveted on her. Just as he arrived alongside her, Pablo struggled to his feet and stumbled toward them. Juan raised himself up, swung his left hand over Melinda and clumsily fell on top of her. She opened her mouth to scream but nothing came out. She could see Pablo's silhouette move toward her. She closed her eyes and mercifully passed out.

When Melinda awoke, she was alone. The table was empty. There was no one by the table. And she was back in the cage. The door was slightly ajar, but she couldn't move. She convinced herself she had to try and somehow summoned the strength to wrap her hands around the bars. She was about to try to pull herself forward when suddenly, out of nowhere, the room began filling with people rushing in from every direction. They were shouting, and they had guns. Some gathered around her, disrupting the bright light that had been searing through her eyes all these days. One of them crawled inside the cage and reached a hand toward Melinda. His fingers pressed lightly on her neck. He turned his head and yelled, "She's alive!" Other voices called for an ambulance.

CHAPTER 4

ANN AND PATRICK HAD JUST returned to the station when they were called to the office of Chief Inspector Owen Clarke. Owen had just recently passed his fiftieth birthday and held his trim, six-foot frame proudly. He had a full head of gray hair and a mustache with eyebrows two shades darker. He used to lead this sort of investigation but two years ago his foot was crushed under the wheel of a car driven by an ex-girlfriend during an ill-fated parallel parking lesson. Despite his protests he was promoted and forced behind a desk. The ensuing inactivity had affected his mind, but not his mindset. He wanted to remain as involved in each case as he was when he was a DI and Ann was his Sargent. An independent person, Ann liked the arrangement. But that ended when Patrick was promoted.

Fortunately, the amount of Patrick's contribution to a case was such that it never interfered with Ann's preference of working alone. He was useful to a point, though he seemed to enjoy the more high profile aspects of the job than the investigative end. But at least Ann knew that, with Patrick, there would be few differences of opinion since he rarely bothered to form any. But Owen insisted she have someone to back her up, and Patrick was the perfect physical specimen to fill that role. Ann had already observed the extent of Patrick's protection, which had more to do with the safety of his Armani suits against the threat of hostile mud than watching his partner's back. Normally, Ann wouldn't have to rely solely on him. She would have the benefit of a team of detectives and uniformed officers, but they seemed to be in short supply today. Ann and Patrick sat opposite Owen at his desk.

"Have Dunn and Needham arrived yet, sir?" Ann said.

"No, and I don't expect to be seeing either of them any time soon," Owen replied.

"Not them as well, sir."

"As of yesterday, Dunn's off to his mother's in Falkirk and Needham's off somewhere testing his new motor. A Jaguar, no less."

"How on earth can he afford a Jaguar on sergeant's wages?"

"Can't. It's a beat up old wreck he and his brother bought for next to nothing. They've been trying to get it to run for months, as I've been informed by his daily updates. Can't say as I'll miss those."

"How long are these layoffs going to last?"

"Until the people who are in charge of such things figure out a way to find enough money to staff a proper police force. Damned fools! Don't they know you don't lay off cops? Dustmen, yes. Police, no." Owen calmed a bit. "Well, no use moaning about it. We'll just have to press on as best we can with who we've got."

Owen interrupted the proceedings by interlocking his fingers behind his head, holding his breath and trembling for the next ten seconds while Ann did her best to pretend there was nothing unusual about Owen's recent foray into the world of isometric exercise as he held onto the slim hope of returning to the streets one day. Owen blew the air out of his lungs and without missing a beat said, "Now. Am I to understand correctly? You don't know who this girl is, who did this to her, why, or for how long? Just what *do* you know?"

"That she was held captive in a derelict pit building," Ann said, trying not to sound as intimidated as he sometimes made her feel. "She was beaten, quite possibly raped and nearly starved to death."

"I already know all that from the preliminary report," Owen said, report in hand. "What I need are more than just dry facts. I need a story, all nicely pieced together from the information you and McGinty here have gathered during the course of your investigation. Now. Have you been able to assemble any of those pieces yet?" Patrick slid down in his chair and turned his attention to his manicure while he waited for Ann to bail them out. As usual.

"Well, sir, without being able to speak to the victim it's rather difficult to learn just what did happen. Perhaps by tomorrow we'll know more," Ann offered.

"Fair enough. But I expect you to have more than what I can get from a simple report. Her name might be a good place to start, wouldn't you agree?"

"Patrick's run her prints. We've drawn a blank there as well."

"I see. I understand she might be American, perhaps Canadian. You're looking into that?" A short jab from Ann's elbow loosened Patrick's tongue.

"Yes—Erm, yessir," Patrick slid back up in his chair. "I've faxed her fingerprints. Just waiting for them to get back to me."

"Well, don't wait! You get back to them!"

"Yes, sir," Patrick said, then hurried out of the room. Owen got up and paced, one of his many mannerisms when he wanted to think. Because of his injury, his limp was pronounced. He wiped the corners of his mouth, then said, "What's your best guess, Ann? What have we got here?"

"No record of who she is, no one who reports her as missing…I don't know what to make of it. Could be she was living rough."

Owen picked up one of the photos of Melinda from his desk. "How does someone go missing this many days and not have anyone who cares enough about them to notify us?"

"I don't know, sir."

"What puzzles me is, if there's no one to report her missing, then there's no one to pay her ransom. So why bother kidnapping her in the first place?"

"Could be it wasn't about money," Ann theorized. "Could be it was about something else, like revenge. But whoever did this they did it over a period of days, yet didn't kill her. That would seem to indicate they knew her and they were punishing her for something."

"I see," Owen said, the pain in his foot necessitating a return to his chair. "Are you basing your opinion on past experience?"

"Sir?"

"A young woman, kidnapped, tortured. I just wonder if this case might not be too much for you."

"I am perfectly capable of handling this or any other case I am assigned to," Ann said more defensively than she intended.

Owen clapped his hands together and said. "Right! I understand the only lead we've got is a phone call telling us where to find her. What about that, Ann? Who made it? A passerby?"

"I don't think so. It's a remote area. I haven't heard the tape yet, but I think it's possible it could be the kidnapper himself."

"He doesn't contact anyone about ransom money, yet he rings the police. Why? Why tell us where she is and not ask for anything in return?"

"Maybe he wanted someone to stop him before he *did* kill her."

"A sudden burst of conscience, is that it? And if he wasn't the one who made the call?"

"Then we're lucky we got her back alive." Owen spent the next few minutes at his desk re-reading the preliminary report, as if it would reveal something on the twenty-fifth read that it hadn't on the twenty-fourth. Ann sat patiently, wishing Patrick were here, fidgeting and acting generally disinterested until Owen threw them both out. After what seemed like an eternity Patrick returned and discretely as possible sat next to Ann.

"Well?" Owen said without looking up.

"Oh, erm, well, nothing yet," Patrick replied. "Hopefully they'll have something for us soon."

Owen's eyes raised. "By then, he'll have done this again. He's already had enough time to kidnap someone else. I don't want this to become a daily nightmare for us. I don't want to have to keep sending a steady stream of detectives to hospital to interview one victim after another while he's out there terrorizing the entire town. I'd at least like to know who it is we're dealing with. And since that girl is the only one who can tell us, you've got to make her talk, Ann."

"Yes, sir."

"Only, you're going to have to do it without Patrick here." Owen turned his eyes toward Patrick. "You've been reassigned to the Lombard case. It's too important and I don't want Williston and Hartag to bungle another case."

"Yes, sir," Patrick said, his posture straightening and his face lighting up.

"Sorry, Ann, but with this latest round of budget cuts on top of the ones they made last month, it's all I can do to find enough detectives to keep this place going." Ann was still trying to get over the reassigning of Patrick to a case as important as the Lombard murder. It was very high profile and Ann understood the pressure Owen must be under to get it solved especially after Williston and Hartag had made so many errors in their previous case that it resulted in a man who had all but confessed to attempted murder being set free. But Owen apparently wasn't aware of Patrick's shortcomings when it came to the investigative process. Ann sometimes wondered why she was the only one who knew that.

'HERE, BE CAREFUL WITH HER!'

'Get round to that side. Count of three, lift her out. Slowly, slowly… Mind her head!'

'It's alright, miss. It's the police. You're safe now.'

Apart from the tubes leading from her arm to IV bags hanging on hooks and the wires that cascaded out of the top of her gown into machines with monitors, what struck Ann the most about Melinda were the number of bandages holding her together. Ann stood at the end of her bed and said softly, "I'm Inspector Treadwell. I'll be investigating your case."

Melinda stirred, then suddenly stopped. She gasped and put her hands to her face, then tried peeling off the tape that secured the gauze pads over her eyes.

"No, you mustn't take them off!" Ann warned. "There's been some damage to your eyes, but the doctor says you'll be able to see again in a day or two." Melinda's hands relaxed. "Can you tell me your name?"

"Melinda," she said weakly.

"And your last name?"

Melinda lay motionless.

"Can you tell me what happened? Who put you in that cage?"

"Cage?"

Melinda's brows knitted and her face contorted, and Ann wondered if she wasn't there again, back in the colliery, in that cage, being terrorized again by her captor, helpless once more to stop him. "Is there someone you'd like us to contact? Your family? A friend?"

There was a long silence, then Melinda whispered, "Terry."

"Terry? Terry who?" Melinda turned her head away. "Where can I reach him?"

Melinda wiped her nose with the side of her hand, then said, "The pub. The Black Knight."

The Black Knight Pub was probably very charming in its day, but it was now in a desperate state of disrepair. It dated back to the sixteen-hundreds and had a long and colorful history with thieves and royalty alike having frequented the place. The bar was the only part that was clean enough to eat off of.

When Ann arrived there were only three people in the pub, including the barman. He was in his early forties, his short, dark hair only slightly receding. He showed signs of having once been a boxer, most notably from his eyelids, which were thick with scar tissue and sagged at the outer corners, and a nose that had been broken more than once. His barrel chest filled his white shirt, which was open at the neck. Ann sat at the bar and cleared her throat, causing the barman to close the X-rated magazine he was 'reading' and stuffed it on a shelf under the bar.

"Inspector Treadwell." Ann showed him her warrant card.

"Mack," he said with some embarrassment. Ann showed him a photo of Melinda's battered face. It wasn't pleasant, but it was the most recognizable one she had.

"Do you know this girl?," Ann said as she sat on a barstool.

"Aye," Mack said, his eyes wide. "That's Melinda, that. Terry's Melinda."

"Who's Terry?"

"Don't know his last name. Used to come round all the time. There," he said, nodding to a vacant table in the corner to his left near the windows along the front of the pub. Ann turned to her right, shielding her eyes from the bright midday sun. "That's where he sat, every day, noon 'til late at night."

"How late? You close at eleven, yeah?"

"Aye, but Terry and the owner did a deal. Most nights he'd stay 'til well past closin'. I was to leave along with rest of the punters, what there was of 'em, and leave Terry and his lot here on their own. But Terry'd pay me a few quid to stay on and pour drinks for him and his lads."

"How is it the police didn't close you down? Surely they must have known you were in violation of the law."

"Wasn't, though. The owner, he got an order of exemption for permitted hours."

"How did he manage that?"

"Don't know."

"You said Terry *used* to come here. Does that mean he no longer does?"

"Aye."

"Any idea why?"

"One day, just stopped comin'"

"How long ago?"

"At least a week, I reckon. Perhaps more."

"Do you know where he lives?"

"No. Don't want to know where the likes of him keeps himself."

Mack had an obvious dislike for Terry, and Ann wanted to know why. "What can you tell me about him?"

"Nasty piece of work, is Terry. Always into some sort of caper."

"Such as?"

"This last time, claimed to be a bounty hunter. Yeah. Said he'd already brought in so many marks – that's what he called 'em, marks – he never had to work another day if he didn't want to."

"A bounty hunter? Is that true?"

"I reckon he could've caught someone on the way here, but once he arrived he hardly ever left that table. Never spoken of it, either, about catchin' anyone, and Terry's quite the talker."

"Tell me about Melinda. Did Terry say who she was?" Mack held up a glass, but Ann politely waved him off.

"Never a word," Mack said as he drew himself a pint of Boddingtons. "In he comes one day and there she is, just behind him. Didn't notice her at first. Terry's a big bloke, easy to get lost behind, especially if you're as small as her."

"Was she related to him?"

"Not likely."

"Why not?"

"'Cause of the way he treated her."

"How did he treat her?"

Mack plunged his upper lip into the foam, wiped his mouth with the side of his thumb, then said, "First time she comes here, Terry goes to his table, same as usual. But he makes her sit by herself at that table there, in the corner near his."

Ann again shielded her eyes as she looked to her right. "Why did he make her sit there?"

"Don't know, do I?"

"Anything else you can tell me about her?"

Mack shrugged. "Quiet, she was. And her eyes. Always looked so sad."

"Didn't anyone ever wonder who she was or why she was with him?"

"Aye, but ya don't ask Terry such things."

"Right," Ann sighed. "So this girl who no one seems to know just appears one day with a man who, as far as anyone can tell, isn't related to her or—"

"Aye. Night after night she comes and sits there without a word while he holds court with all them yobs he's got round him. There she'd be, sat at her table, just shakin'. I thought she were cold so I brought her a drink. Thought it might help her stop her shakin'."

"Did it?"

"No. That's how I knew it weren't from cold."

"What did you suspect it was then?"

"Fear. That girl was afraid of somethin'."

"What of?"

"Bounty hunts, more than likely."

"Terry sent her on bounty hunts? Who did he send her after?"

"Yobs mostly. When she first started comin' here, she was right scared. Then one day, Terry calls her to his table. A word in her ear, and she's out the door. Each night after that he'd send her out, and each time she'd come back more frightened than the last. Then one night, she changed. Wasn't frightened anymore. Even heard her tell one of Terry's hard boys to sod off. I thought Terry would show her the back of his hand, but he just laughed."

"Did you ever see Terry hit her?"

"No, but someone must've. Always came back lookin' worse than when she left. Clothes was always in tatters, but Terry kept sendin' her. Don't know why. Not as if she were any good at it. Never did catch anyone."

"When was the last time you saw her?"

Mack took another drink. "Last Sunday, it was. This bloke comes in, dressed all in black. Sits at Terry's table and the two of 'em get into a row. Then Terry calls Melinda over. A word in her ear and out she goes, same as before. Don't think she wanted to, though. Looked as if she were cryin'. Must've been no more than an hour before she comes back, dirty, bruised, blood all over her. The whole place goes dead quiet as she makes her way to Terry's table. She says somethin' to him and Terry, he grabs her arm so tight she cries out. Never seen him so angry, which is sayin' a lot."

"Why was he so upset? If she'd never caught anyone before, what made him think this time would be any different?"

"He was right angry, but not just because she made him look a fool in front of everyone. The way I heard it, this fellow in black paid Terry to go after Mitchell Stropman. To kill him, that's what I heard."

"Are you saying Terry hired himself out for, what? Contract hits?"

"Aye. Contracts."

"Who was this man in black?" Ann asked.

"None other than Cervantes Roschine."

Ann cringed at the name. Along with Stropman they controlled most of the drug and prostitution business in the area. Both were very dangerous men with unpredictable tempers. Roschine had a shorter fuse and loved flaunting his wealth while Stropman was more flamboyant and spent most of his time immersed in sexual pleasures, which didn't seem to interfere with his ability to run his empire. He lived much the same as he did before he became the leader of such a notorious gang, except he no longer conducted operations from the cellar of his parents' house. Their rivalry often led to disagreements which usually ended in violence. Lately things had been heating up and the result of their feuding was starting to wash up on nearby beaches.

"Mack, why would Roschine hire Terry to kill Stropman? Why not use one of his own men?"

"That lot? Nothin' but drunkards and addicts and halfwits. I reckon even Roschine's got enough sense not to give 'em any weapons."

"Yes, but why Terry?"

"Odd, that. 'Til then, Terry never did anything more dangerous than collect loans, that sort of thing. Never murder, and no one near as dangerous as Stropman. I reckon Terry's ego got the best of him. Ego, and greed."

"What did Roschine do when he found out Terry hadn't killed Stropman?"

"When Melinda came back that night and hadn't done the job, Roschine told Terry he'd better carry out the contract by week's end or he'd take care of both of 'em, Stropman *and* Terry. Terry, he doesn't want to get killed and wasn't keen on givin' the money back, so he blames Melinda. Tells her it's all her fault, that if she'd done what he told her to do his own life wouldn't be in danger now. Tells her if anything happens to him, there'd be no one to look after her. She'd have no choice but to live with Roschine, that they'd already done a deal. My stomach turned when I heard him say that. Roschine would've had her workin' the streets soon as he got his hands on her. Terry left her no choice but to try again."

"What happened when she failed this time?"

"That last time, she never did come back. Next day Terry comes in round four. Right furious, he was. Wants to know, have I seen Melinda. I told him I hadn't. I wouldn't've told him if I had. He pounds his fist on the bar, orders me to line up three shots of whiskey, then pours 'em down his gullet one after the next. He smashes the last glass against the wall behind me, then storms out."

"Did you ever find out why Melinda didn't return?"

"Ever since I learned what Terry was up to, I always knew there'd come a day when she wouldn't come back, that one of them louts would kill her. Or worse. When Terry said she hadn't returned, that's what I feared happened."

"And Terry?" Mack again shrugged.

"He must've gone after Stropman. Must've finally realized he'd have to do his own dirty work for a change."

"Did Terry ever came back after that day?"

Mack took a long drink, set the glass on the bar and said, "Ah, he never should've gone after him. Damn stupid, that, one man against Stropman's boys. They make Terry's lads look like saints. I did hear someone say they heard Stropman warn Terry he'd kill him before he got within ten feet of him. I reckon that's what must have happened."

WHEN HE REASSIGNED PATRICK TO the Lombard case, Owen assured Ann he would find her a new partner as soon as possible. Unfortunately, he was a man of his word. The next day Owen presented her with a temporary partner, one Morten Cutler. It was his first assignment since being promoted to Detective Constable and it showed. Ann tried being patient with him, but their partnership lasted all of two days. Unfulfilled by a mere kidnapping case, he asked to be reassigned to something more challenging. Ann didn't stand in his way. She knew this was less than an ideal match when she spent their first twenty minutes together going over every detail of this case and he replied by complaining about the coffee. Then came grievances with the degree of swivel in his chair, the location of his desk, and some problem with the height of the urinals in the men's room. Half-unzipped, Morten went directly from the toilet to Owen's office and let his feelings be known. With the manpower shortage in mind, Owen made an impassioned plea for him to stay. But there was no stopping Morten, who transferred to London where he was promptly laid off. Once again, Ann would have to go it alone.

WHERE HAD SHE COME FROM? According to Mack, Melinda just appeared out of nowhere one day. But someone had to know who she was. Where to begin? Terry seemed like the most logical starting point. Since he had seemingly vanished without a trace, Ann decided to check the morgue. She had done this many times before but she disliked viewing dead bodies, especially ones that were in such an advanced stage of decomposition. But it was part of the job and she was willing to endure a little nausea and miss a meal or two if it meant solving a crime. She prepared herself in the usual way, with a large slug of antacid from the bottle she kept in the glove box of her car. It was still making its way down her digestive tract when she was notified by the attendant that the body was ready.

She followed him to the viewing room, to a metal table containing a large body covered with a white sheet. The assistant removed the sheet, revealing the body of a man who, Ann was told, had died of a massive coronary. He had been stricken while walking to or from some unknown destination and had been found two days ago. It could be Terry, but the time line didn't fit. The attendant then opened a drawer containing the body of another large man. He had the beginnings of a beard and mustache and even in death had an air of cruelty about him. There were a number of bullet wounds in his torso and limbs. Taking into account the nature of his profession, Ann determined that this body was more likely to be Terry than the first one.

Mack had no objections to viewing the body, though he let it be known he was only doing it for Melinda's sake, and he instantly recognized the second corpse as Terry. He had been discovered by a constable in Addict's Alley, as it was known, behind Shepard's Road. The hands had been burned so badly they had been unable to extract any useable fingerprints. But as Ann thanked Mack for coming down, an idea came to mind: They couldn't get a print off the body, but what about the pub? Judging by the clutter, whatever was on Terry's table a month ago was undoubtedly still there. Ann rang the station and had a fingerprint technician meet her at the Black Knight. A few hours later he informed her he had matched a number of prints with one Terence Collier Royce. Unfortunately, Ann would have to locate him with the help of BT. That's because PC Everett Montaigne, her newly and temporarily appointed partner, had two more years to go before completing his computer course at University. Still, he assured Ann he would be able to retrieve Terry's complete records from the department data base and was now in his third hour of attempting to do just that.

From what the post-mortem had been able to determine, Terry was somewhere in his mid-forties and had been dead approximately five days, which was about the time Melinda disappeared. That would explain why he hadn't been looking for her. Ann was interrupted by PC Montaigne, who stopped by her office to tell her the computers were down – he swore he didn't know how – and that as soon as they were up again, he would have the information she requested. Ann just smiled, not believing for a moment she would see Terry's file any time soon.

According to phone company records, Terry lived in a flat not far from the pub. Either he hadn't been home for awhile or he wasn't too fussy about his housekeeping. Everything was covered with dust. Clothes – all men's and in very large sizes – were scattered everywhere, making the lounge barely passable. Empty beer bottles floated on a sea of papers. Ann uncrumpled a few, but they were so illegible she soon gave up and stuffed them into an evidence bag.

There was a couch covered in a garish print in the middle of the room. There were end tables to either side of it and a coffee table in front of it loaded with magazines, some spilling onto the floor where they formed new, less formal piles. Still others were lying on the floor waiting for the day when they, too, would have a table of their own to fall off of.

The only picture in the room was a cheap copy of a mountain landscape. Ann looked to see if the artist had had the guts to put his name on it. He hadn't, but she noticed he had substituted overly optimistic renditions of naked women for clouds and even managed to find a way to add detailed Formula One race cars in the valley.

On the wall facing the street were three large windows covered by a curtain made of material so heavy, light couldn't penetrate it. To her right was a half-wall bordering a hallway that led to a bedroom and bathroom. The bathroom was true to the flat's décor. There were only men's toiletries. If Melinda lived there, where were her things? Ann walked down the hallway to what was obviously Terry's bedroom, which was littered with even more dirty laundry. Among the debris she found were empty plastic film containers that smelled strongly of marijuana, and a half empty box of syringes next to the bed.

The filth and rancid odors finally forced Ann out of the bedroom. She was about to leave the flat when she noticed a door to her left. She thought it concealed a broom closet but when she opened the door she discovered a small bedroom. This had to be Melinda's.

There was one window, situated impractically high in the right hand corner and covered by a curtain made of the same material as the one in the living room. The decor was sparse, to say the least. There was nothing on the walls except a sickly shade of green paint. Along the wall opposite the door was a bed with a thin mattress and flimsy blanket on top. To the left was an unfinished wooden dresser with three drawers. In the top drawer was a hand knit jumper that looked as though it had never been worn. In the middle drawer was a nightgown and the bottom drawer was empty. Ann wondered where the rest of it was, the things that said somebody lived here. She didn't see any personal items, not even a comb or a toothbrush. There were no dolls or toys or anything else left from childhood. How long had Melinda been here? Had she only just arrived, or had she lived here for years? And if it was years, why didn't anyone know about her until recently? Where had she been all this time? In this flat? In this room? What did she do here all day, or at night when Terry was at the pub? Was sitting at that table, an almost invisible figure among Terry's circle of assorted thugs, the high point of her day? Of her life? Now more than ever Ann wanted to know if Melinda was related to Terry and if so, how. If she wasn't, then where was her family? And why didn't any of them care enough to look for her?

CHAPTER 4

IN SPITE OF HIS SHORTCOMINGS, Ann had really hoped Everett would work out. But after deleting several files of active cases – he swore he didn't know how – he quit the force and joined the family business. Something to do with side show work with a small circus in eastern Europe.

Ann didn't give much thought to losing another partner. Terry was dead, and now she had to find a way to tell Melinda. Ann stepped off the lift on the second floor of St. Pritchards and headed for Melinda's room. It was almost as if she was waiting for Ann to arrive.

"Where's Terry? When is he coming?"

Ann didn't know how much more Melinda could take, but she had to find out. "Melinda, I'm afraid I have some bad news. We believe Terry is dead." In an instant, the trembling stopped and Melinda lowered her hand from her face. Then Ann saw it: An almost imperceptible change in Melinda's demeanor. Her body relaxed and her eyes were alert. She was no longer the frightened girl who had stood before Ann just moments ago.

"Melinda, who was Terry? Was he your father? Was he related to you some other way?"

"Why do you want to know?"

"I'm just curious as to how you came to live with him. Were you close? You seem to be taking his death quite well."

Melinda's eyes grew wide. "I know what you're trying to do! You're trying to trick me! The guard in the hall? I know why he's there, to make sure I don't escape until you take me to jail!"

"What makes you think you're going to jail?"

"Because of the things I've done."

"What sort of things have you done?"

Melinda remained still for a long moment. "Terrible things. Things you could never dream of. I've caught people you'd be too afraid to even go after…"

Ann listened to this barrage of boasts that were as hollow as the look in Melinda's eyes, and she just sighed. She doubted the authenticity of the tales this incarnation of Melinda delighted in telling, but she also knew it didn't matter whether they were true or not. Melinda wasn't a suspect, she was a victim, one whose psychological scars were every bit as profound as her physical ones. But there just wasn't any more time to spend listening to grandiose tales of improbable proportions.

"…I've done things you could never imagine, caught criminals you could never hope to catch—"

"Yes, so you've said. Melinda, is there anything you'd like to know about Terry?"

Melinda paused. "Is he the one who told you where to find me?"

"We don't think so," Ann said gently. "The truth is, no one reported you missing. We didn't even know you'd been kidnapped until we found you in the colliery."

"Then how did you know I was there?"

"We received an anonymous phone call."

"When?"

"Two days. You were found two days ago." Ann took a tape player out of her bag. "We have a recording of the man who phoned it in. We were hoping you might be able to identify his voice." Ann's index finger was on the 'play' button. "Ready?' Melinda didn't react, so Ann pressed the button.

'Which service do you require?'

'Which…?Erm, right. There's—Go to—erm, uh, derelict pit building near—twenty miles east of town. Badly injured person inside. Come quick, or you're gonna need a body bag.'

'Hello? Which building? Hello? Sir? (click) Hello? Hello?'

Initially, Melinda had no outward reaction to the tape. But her face fell and the anguish returned to her eyes. Her newfound invincibility slowly melted away, all but confirming to Ann that the voice didn't belong to the mysterious Terry. And if it didn't, then surely Melinda must now know that what Ann said was true. Terry hadn't phoned the police. He hadn't been looking for her at all.

"Do you know who that man is?" Ann asked.

Melinda hung her head. "Juan."

"Juan. That's the name of the man who kidnapped you?"

"Yes," Melinda replied, then, overcome with emotion, "His—He had blue eyes...blond hair...He tied—hit me, tied me up and—Pablo, he tried to help me—"

"Pablo? Who's Pablo? Can you describe him?"

"He was big and...short hair. Red. He wore a—had a black shirt... striped, with white sleeves and...a white shirt...blue jeans...black boots...," Melinda said. "His hair was blonde and, red lips...He wanted to talk...He wanted to...I wasn't afraid because he knew if I...if my hands..." There was a look of discovery in Melinda's eyes as she turned toward Ann and said, "Danny."

"Sorry?" Ann said, doing her best to keep track.

"Pablo didn't kidnap me. It was Danny." So now there were three. Ann returned to her office and was greeted by a deskful of paperwork and a fairly quiet CID office as the shift change approached. The few daytime detectives still on duty were gone. To the pub. Or the restaurant, that new one that opened just down the road from the station that Ann had wanted to try. She put it out of her mind and concentrated on her notes. She tried to make sense of what Melinda told her, but she hadn't given her much and Ann soon put aside trying to work out the identities of the three men. She started on her desk, but tidying wasn't Ann's strong suit and, half an hour later, it was just as disorganized as ever. Ann kept at it until she was startled by Owen, who entered her office with hands clasped at waist level, his face a bright red.

"Are you alright, sir?" Ann asked.

Owen let out a rush of air and said, "What?"

"Oh. Sorry."

"I've been looking over your report, Ann," Owen said as he sat, "and I must say, I'm a bit puzzled."

"What about, sir?"

"To begin with, her identity. Any progress there?"

"I ran the name Melinda Royce through the computer and came up empty. In fact, there doesn't seem to be any record of her of any kind."

"What do you mean?"

"She has no driving license, no bank account, credit cards, has never paid taxes and has never been married or divorced, at least not in this country. It also seems she's never attended school, private or public. It's almost as if she doesn't exist."

"Well, keep at it." Owen took a moment to shake out his hands. "There's something else that troubles me."

"Sir?"

"It's this whole business about being raped."

"You don't believe she was?"

"No, no. It's just that, well, as much as I hate to say it, I don't think we can rule out that it was consensual."

"Consensual rape, sir?"

"The doctors found cuts and bruises on her inner thighs, plus a number of other injuries of that nature in and around that part of her body."

"And you believe she may have consented to that?"

"No, certainly not. I'm just saying the possibility exists that she may have agreed to it, at least at first. Could be her young gentleman took her to that building for an evening of, well, intimacy. Then these two mates of his show up and, before you know it, things got out of hand. She found herself in a situation that became more than she bargained for."

"But if that were true, it would still be rape. Unless she agreed to have sex with all of them."

"You don't think she might have done?"

"Three men? I don't believe for a moment she agreed to that."

"Date rape?"

"Not unless she was on a date with all three of them. The cage and the wounds on the back of her head suggests it was anything but a date, unless caveman etiquette has suddenly become acceptable behavior."

Owen grunted himself to his feet. "Any luck with the dusters?"

"No. Seems they wiped the place clean before we got there."

"Then our best hope is for her to identify them," Owen said as he casually glanced at Ann's notebook. "I want her to have a go at the mug books. I see she's given you descrip—Hang on. Do you notice anything odd?"

"Sir?"

Owen read from Ann's notes. "Pablo. Red hair. And Juan. Blonde, with blue eyes. Do these sound like descriptions of someone called Pablo and Juan to you?"

"I'll check it out straight away," Ann said, gathering her notes moments too late to hide her embarrassment over not having noticed that before.

"Oh, Ann. I've heard from upstairs. They feel this case has gone on long enough. I understand she hasn't been cooperating with the doctors."

"She's just having trouble coping. Hopefully the guard outside her door will be enough to reassure her that she's safe." Owen eyed her skeptically. "She just needs time, sir."

"Along with everything else they've taken from us recently, time is one of them. You've already had two days with her and what have you got? Three first names and some partial descriptions."

"Still, that *is* something. It could mean her memory is returning and she'll soon be able to remember more."

"Again I refer you to the issue of time. Now. Is this bit of nothing she's given you enough to lead to an arrest?"

"Hopefully. Once we distribute their descriptions, I'm sure someone will recognize them."

"You are, are you?" Ann hated how inept he could make her feel with just a look. "I'm afraid we can no longer wait. She has to tell us what she knows, and she has to tell us now."

"I don't know, sir. She's in quite a fragile state. I'm afraid if we keep forcing her to remember, she may not survive it."

"What are you saying, that she'll die from being asked questions? Can't recall that ever happening before."

"No, not—I don't mean survive, I meant—"

"Anyway, how much worse can it be than the way she is now? In the long run, I think it will only help her instead of keeping it all bottled up inside. It may upset her, and I suspect it will. But she can't go on the way she is or one day soon you may find yourself investigating her suicide."

While Ann didn't completely agree with him, she couldn't deny that something was impeding Melinda's memory. When Ann tried to question her, Melinda went through some sort of transformation that effectively cut short her memories. A remarkable ability, but not very useful as far as finding answers. Since she couldn't stop Melinda from adopting these different moods, Ann would have to work around them. But first she would have to understand them.

To that end, she turned to someone trained in the matters of the mind. The psychiatrist on call today was Ophelia Stanton, who just happened to be the Consultant Psychiatrist at St. Pritchards. A middle-aged dynamo packing one-hundred forty pounds onto her five-foot-two inch frame, topped by a mop of soft, curly blonde hair, Dr. Stanton sat at her desk on a high-backed chair and made Ann wait while she finished a phone consultation with an associate in Tibet or Taiwan or some other far off place. In the meantime Ann compressed herself onto the only other chair in the room, a square wooden one, the height of which left her barely above eye level with the top of the desk.

Ophelia moved the phone from her mouth and without missing a beat said, "You know, Inspector, you really should let us handle this. We're trained to cope with this sort of thing—Yes, that's right. That is the course of treatment I would recommend. Uh huh. Yes. I see. Well, if you have any further questions, do let me know. Yes. Good-bye now. Really, Inspector." Ophelia replaced the receiver. "If only you knew the complexities of extreme psychosis you would understand the harm you could do that girl by the utterance of a single misspoken word."

"I agree it would be better if your people treated her, but some of your staff have already tried and she has so far refused to speak to any of them."

"I'm sure she would do so in time."

"Time is something we don't have a lot of," Ann said while she tried to find a comfortable position in the narrow space between the arms of the chair. She was even less comfortable with Ophelia, who studied her through her oversized, clear-rimmed glasses as though she was a patient.

"I find it interesting, Inspector, that Melinda has been here for two days, yet you've only now taken the time to come see me."

"I've been busy with other aspects of this case," Ann said, trying once more in vain to sit straight instead of sideways in the snug chair.

"Oh? And why are you coming to me now then?" Ophelia asked, her index fingers pressed against her lower lip.

Ann lightly tapped the arms of her chair with open hands and said, "Excuse me, is there another—," but Ophelia quickly dismissed her request with a subtle shake of her head, her eyes closed. "It's her condition," Ann said. "Her mental condition. It seems to be changing."

"In what way?"

"Her behavior. At first she seemed confused. Terrified. But now she's behaving quite differently."

"How so?"

"She's...angry. But it's not just that. It's her whole attitude that's changed. Even her body language is different."

"Is she that way all the time?"

"No. That's what's even more puzzling. She goes from frightened to angry, confused to confident, all in a matter of seconds. It's as if she isn't the same person from one moment to the next."

"She isn't." Ophelia sat back in her plush chair. "Tell me, what had you been saying when this transformation first occurred?"

"I asked her if she knew who might have kidnapped her," Ann said, yanking the bottom of her coat out from under her. "Oh, and Terry. He was murdered recently. Apparently she was quite close to him."

"Well, there you have it. From what you have described I would say she is attempting to avoid things that are too difficult for her to cope with. She is trying to fend off your attempts to intrude upon those places which hold the most damaging memories. It's her way of holding onto her sanity which, I understand, is teetering on the brink at the moment."

"Could I have pushed her too far?"

"It would help to know exactly what you said and the manner in which you said it, but in this case, I shouldn't think so. My staff have kept me apprised. Considering the state she was in when she arrived and her lack of progress – compounded, I might add, by the absence of a trained psychiatrist to aid in her recovery – I believe her behavior was inevitable."

"Then it is your opinion that she would have reacted this way no matter what I said?"

"No, not necessarily. But I do believe that, for her to have had such an extreme reaction, the seeds had already been sown and, I would hazard to guess, long before this most recent event took place."

"You're saying she's been this way all along?"

"Most definitely. Probably buried deep within her psyche, but I assure you, it's there. That she's responded in the manner you've described indicates as much. When you confront her with things she's not yet ready to hear, she copes by calling upon another, stronger aspect of her personality. At those times she is only too willing to allow another part of her, a part which arose from and exists solely as a result of her own fears, to deal with the situation for her. By exaggerating her capacity to withstand as well as dispense such violence she's trying to create the illusion that she's much stronger, both mentally and physically, than she actually is to ward off anyone she feels poses a threat to her. That is most likely what you encountered."

"How can I get her to stop relying on this person she's invented?"

"She hasn't, as you say, invented it. It has been born out of necessity, out of a perceived attack on the very foundation of her sanity. If you persist, she's already let you know she'll only retreat further into this part of her that she's called upon to protect her. You must understand, this is her way of guarding secrets that she simply is not ready or able to reveal yet."

"The problem, doctor, is that I need to find who did this as soon as possible. So far all she's managed to give me are a few first names."

"Well, you can take heart that you did get through to her once and that she has given you that much, and that she did so of her own accord no matter what part of her told you. But you must be mindful that there are things that are simply too dangerous for her to remember. They are locked away in the innermost recesses of her mind for a reason, and you must respect that."

"If I did want to help her memory along, how would I go about it?" Ann was too busy repositioning herself to alleviate the pain in her hip to notice the piercing stare that met her rejection of Ophelia's advice.

"If you do attempt to delve into her past before she's ready, you do so at great risk. From what I've determined it will take years of therapy for that girl's mind to be put right. It would be a pity if the police chose to ignore that fact simply for the sake of an investigation."

"Please understand, doctor, I don't want to do anything that will cause her more harm. But it is vital we learn what happened because if we don't, this hospital may soon be dealing with a lot more Melindas."

Ophelia's eyes narrowed. "Alright, Inspector. Have it your way. Tell her things she's not ready to hear. Tell her you know about her private world, that you know she goes there to escape the things that terrify her so much she feels the need to go there in the first place. If you haven't driven her further away by then, you can consider yourself lucky. She may even begin to trust you. She may lower her defenses enough to allow you to enter her world and tell you what it is you wish to know.

"However, I must warn you, the exact opposite is more likely to occur. Her first reaction may be one of anger or resentment. She may even threaten you. If she does, it is important you remember she is not doing this for the benefit of anyone but herself. It is a device her subconscious mind has constructed solely for the purpose of protecting her. The subconscious mind absorbs things we cannot deal with on a conscious level, but it cannot erase them. It stores them where they cannot be easily accessed. It puts up a wall, a shield as it were, and this shield can take many forms. In this case, it has taken the form of the persona you encountered."

"So what are we talking about? Schizoph—No, erm, that other... What's it called?"

"It may be a form of dissociative disorder, but I cannot be certain until I or another qualified psychiatrist examines her. There are signs the untrained eye wouldn't notice, such as memory loss—"

"But she *has* lost her memory. There are large amounts of time she cannot account for."

"Ah, but that doesn't necessarily mean she's forgotten them. It may only mean she has chosen not to tell you. If it turns out those memories are indeed lost, then I would say there is a better chance she has a true dissociative disorder. That would be quite unique. It would take years to cure such a rare illness..." Ann was indeed noticing a change in personality, this time in Ophelia. Her eyes sparkled at the prospect of having a patient with such an intriguing illness to dissect.

"But surely she can't keep this up forever."

"Oh, but she can. I can take you through the wards of this hospital and give you living, breathing proof of that. But those are extreme cases. I believe, with proper care, she has an excellent chance of recovering."

"Yes, but again, there is the issue of time."

"Yes. There always is with the police. I have given you my opinion. It is up to you to decide which path to take."

CHAPTER 5

"AN AMATEUR?"

Ann blurted out the words, unable to contain her reaction to her latest temporary partner.

"Officer Graham Hatfield is *not* an amateur—Well, not entirely. He's had fully six months on the job," Owen said from his desk while Ann stood opposite.

"But, sir, a *Special*. I mean, I don't have anything against him personally. And I do believe in the Special program, but—"

"Granted, Officer Hatfield may be a bit green when it comes to investigating crimes of a more serious nature, but we looked into the barrel, gave it a right going over, and he was the only one come up trumps. Now I know it's not the ideal situation, but I'm afraid you're just going to have to manage until we can come up with someone more suitable. I've already found you several partners—By the way, what is it you do to them that they last no more than a day or two? Right then. Officer Hatfield will be your partner for the foreseeable future and that's all there is to it."

FOR MOST OF HIS FORTY-SEVEN years, Wallace Thornton had lived an ordinary life. Since being hired by the Monroe Bank and Trust some thirty years ago he had risen from mail room clerk to vice-president of mortgages and loans. He was a loyal employee devoted to his work. A typical family man, he had been married for twenty-six years to the same woman and had managed to emotionally alienate her and their three children while he pursued his career. He had also neglected himself to the point of becoming a strong candidate to drop dead one day from high blood pressure, low blood pressure, liver disease, bleeding ulcers, perforated ulcers, kidney failure, too much bad fat, too much good fat, high cholesterol, a heart attack or a stroke. He also had a balky prostate, an erratic thyroid and suffered from the early stages of emphysema. But on a clear, sunny, winter morning they were putting Wallace Thornton in the ground for none of those reasons. Poor Wallace Thornton had been murdered.

FOUR DAYS AFTER MELINDA WAS rescued a body was found in another alley by children taking a shortcut home from school. When the police arrived they discovered a middle-aged man lying face down in a pool of blood. He had been hit on the back of the head with a blunt instrument, and his shoes were missing. He had been dead less than eight hours.

Danny had been careful with Melinda. Or lucky. He hadn't left anything behind that could be traced back to him. But he made a mistake this time, a big one. He left clues all over the place. They even found a board with blood on it just a few feet from Wallace Thornton's body. Not only did it have fresh blood on it, it also had traces of old blood which, with any luck, would turn out to be Melinda's.

Ann spent the morning exchanging information with DCI John Traler and DS Ronald Causey, the lead detectives on the Thornton case, until they were interrupted by a call to go to forensics.

"Ann. How nice to see you again," said Adam Clement, a forensic pathologist.

"Adam. You're looking well," Ann said..

"I see you've an interest in this case?"

"There may be a connection to one I've been working on."

"Yes, the kidnapping at the colliery."

"Adam. Have you got something for us?" Traler asked with some impatience.

"Yes, I have. The victim was indeed killed by a blow to the back of the head, and with this board." He pointed at the blood-covered board resting on the table to his right.

"Erm, do you have anything new to tell us?," Traler said.

"The blood on the board is that of Wallace Thornton. In fact, his is the only blood on the board."

"What?" Ann said so softly that no one else heard.

"And the fingerprints?", Traler continued.

"Oh, those are Danny's. Danny Acre, to be more precise."

According to his record, Daniel Aloysius Acre had been arrested six times this year alone, all for minor drug charges, and each time the charges had been dropped, officially due to a lack of evidence, unofficially due to his wealthy father's influence. His address was his parent's house in an exclusive neighborhood, but he also had a flat in a less desirable part of town.

Detectives Treadwell, Traler and Causey brought enough officers with them to Danny's third floor flat to cover every possible escape route, an unprecedented amount of manpower in the face of the department's budgetary woes. Causey knocked on the door and identified himself as the police. When there was no response, he kicked the door in and police poured in from all directions. The shades in the sitting room were down but light was still finding its way in through their many holes, making the drug paraphernalia spread out on the table in front of the couch plain to see.

What wasn't quite so plain was what the room concealed in its darkest corner. There, slumped on the couch was Danny, a rubber hose tied around his left bicep, a syringe in his right hand aimed at one of the bulging veins in his left arm. He was about to inject himself when Causey slapped the syringe out of his hand and threw him face first to the floor while instructing him not to move. As his hands were being cuffed Danny tried to deny whatever it was he was being arrested for, but a shoe on the back of his neck prevented him from speaking.

He was abruptly lifted to his feet, roughly patted down, then taken downstairs to an awaiting panda car.

While that was taking place Ann was already looking for any evidence that would connect him to Melinda's kidnapping, but there wasn't much to see in the two-story flat. Along with the couch, there was a small television balanced on a wooden crate in the living room. The bedroom, which was littered with used tissues and other debris, contained a thin mattress and another crate standing on end, an ashtray and clock on top and some personal items inside. Ann used her foot to move the debris, looking for something worth risking tetanus for, but there was nothing.

"Well, looks like he's our boy," Traler said upon entering the bedroom. "Find anything?"

"Not yet," Ann sighed.

"Well, whether he confesses or not, we've got him for murder. And have a look at this." He held up a pair of black boots, identical to the ones Wallace Thornton's wife had given him for Christmas the year before. "I think these have eliminated any urgency on our part to interview him. He's all yours, Inspector."

When Ann entered interview room two she saw a different Danny than the one Melinda had been seeing in her nightmares. He looked average. Ordinary. Could this be the man who had masterminded a kidnapping, who had decided every day for, by all estimates, the better part of a week, the fate of a young woman who was helpless against him? He hadn't had time to fix before his flat was raided and at the moment he was going through some of the more unpleasant phases of withdrawal. Gravity was his enemy now and he struggled to stay on his chair. His forehead rested on his hands, which were flat on the table, and his eyes were closed. Ann sat across from him, her notepad on the table before her, and felt no pity for him.

"Danny Acre. Do you know why you're being arrested, Danny?"

"No—yeah—I mean, no, not sellin' it. Just usin' it for—For medical purposes…"

"No, that is not why you are in our custody." Ann said, replacing her pad for a mini recorder. "Why did you kill Wallace Thornton? Did you even know him or did you just choose him at random, like you did that girl?"

"No, not…There was no ransom—"

"Not ransom, Mr. Acre. Random."

Still unable to open his eyes, Danny grimaced as he raised himself up with the help of the heel of his hand, which he drove into his forehead, his elbow resting on the table.

"Why did you kill him?"

"Don't know. Bored…"

"You take a man's life because you're bored? Is that what you want me to believe?"

"No, that's not why I did it."

"Why then?"

"I had to, ya see."

"No, I don't see."

Danny's eyes opened halfway. "How much is your life worth? More than five bloody quid? If it was your life or the money, which would you choose?"

"But you didn't take the money, did you? He left his house with forty pounds and he was found with forty pounds." Danny's eyes popped open, then closed again as he shook his head over his latest blunder.

"Where were you on the tenth of October, Mr. Acre?"

"October…? No, I wasn't there—"

"Wasn't where? Come now, surely you remember. That was less than a fortnight ago." Ann waited for an answer but instead watched as Danny's head slipped off his hand and continue falling in slow motion until it hit the table with a thud. "Kidnapping, rape and now murder. Rather ambitious, aren't you?" Ann placed some of the photos of Melinda on the table near his head. "You know her, don't you, Mr. Acre?"

Danny raised his head just enough to see the photos. "No, don't know her."

"Of course you do. You kidnapped her, beat her, raped her, terrorized her for…How many days was it?"

"Raped her?" Danny's eyes again briefly sprang open.

"How did Melinda come to be your victim? Did you know her before you kidnapped her, or did she simply have the misfortune of getting within striking distance of that board?"

"What?—No, him! It was him she was meant to be! No, he was meant to be him—" Danny winced, the result of his ongoing struggle with his senses. "I only wanted to talk to him, but it was her came down the jennel instead!"

"You expect me to believe you mistook a six-foot-two, fifteen stone man for a girl half that size?"

"No, it weren't him I was gonna kid—talk to!"

"Who then?"

"Don't know, do I? Just some sod comes down jennel every day."

"Mr. Acre," Ann said, "do you mean Wallace Thornton, the man you murdered? Or do you mean someone else?"

"The blindfold…I took the blindfold off and…," he started to laugh, "…and it were this girl! This stupid, bloody girl!"

"Is that why you raped her?"

"I didn't rape her!" Danny said, the heels of his hands pressed over his eyes. "She wouldn't let me!"

"What do you mean, she wouldn't let you?"

"I mean—Yeah, alright," he dropped his hands from his face. "I wanted to. Rape her, as you say it. I tried! Christ, I tried every fuckin' day! But she made me hit her instead! Yeah. All I wanted was to have a bit of fun, but she'd say things. Insultin' things. Well, I had to hit her after that, didn't I?" Ann eyed him skeptically. "Go on, then! Ask her! Ask her if she didn't want me to!"

Once Danny had been identified, finding Pablo and Juan wasn't difficult. Michael Reeves, aka Pablo, had already been picked up, having been involved in yet another bar fight. Sidney Wallingford, otherwise known as Juan, was found lying face down in the middle of a busy street, backing up traffic for miles. The records for all three indicated their lives revolved around drugs. But kidnap and rape didn't seem to fit their profiles quite so comfortably.

"By the way, Sidney, which Colombian drug lord goes by the name of Juan?" Causey began in interview room one.

"Eh?"

"According to your record, you live in Bolton. What were you doing all the way out here on the tenth of October?"

"Visitin'," Juan slurred contentiously.

"Visiting who?"

"A bird."

"This bird's name wouldn't happen to be Melinda by any chance?"

"Me bird's name is Francine."

"This Francine got an address?"

"Don't know her address, do I?"

"But you just said she's your bird. How were you intending to visit her if you don't even know her address?"

"I know where she lives, just don't know the number. Ain't never been before."

"Really. Sounds like quite a hot and heavy romance you got there."

"It is. Hot and heavy," Juan said as his duty solicitor put his hand firmly on Juan's arm.

"Why is it you've never visited your girlfriend before? Was she afraid to have you in her home? Was she afraid you might try to rape her, like you did this girl?" Causey placed a photo of a battered Melinda on the table in front of him.

"Wasn't me did this." Juan flicked the photo back across the table with his index finger.

"No? Who then?" Juan sneered. "We know you were there, Sidney. Right now, you're our number one suspect."

"I told ya, I was with me bird when—"

"When what?" Even Juan knew enough to stop this time. "You may as well tell us. We're going to find out eventually." Causey leaned a little closer. "Come on then. If it wasn't you who raped her, then it had to be Danny. Or Pablo. You could testify against them, get the charges against you reduced." Juan glanced up at him. "If you cooperate, I'll speak to the prosecutor. But I can't offer you anything until you tell me what you know."

"Detective, I'd like a word with my client," Juan's solicitor said. With the possibility of getting a confession, Causey gladly stepped into the hall. After a reasonable amount of time, he returned.

"Well, Sidney? What's it going to be?"

"My client is willing to cooperate in exchange for complete immunity."

Causey's eyes bored through Juan's solicitor's over his unrealistic demand. "That it, Sidney? You ready to tell us what you know?" Juan shrugged. "Right. Let's start with who carried out the kidnapping."

His solicitor nodded at Juan. "Danny. It were all his idea."

"He's the one who kidnapped her? He's the one who raped her?"

"Yeah. All of it. It were Danny."

Meanwhile, in interview room 3…

"Right, Michael. Or would you prefer I call you Pablo?" Traler began.

"Yeah—I mean, what's this all about? I didn't do nothin'." Unlike his mates, Pablo was alert enough to be concerned.

"Detective, why has my client been arrested?" Pablo's duty solicitor asked.

"He hasn't been arrested. We just want to ask Michael here as to his whereabouts on the tenth of October. Well, Michael?"

"October...Yeah. Right. I was haulin' slate for Mr. Preston."

"And who might Mr. Preston be?"

"Colin Preston. He's a builder."

"And if I ring this Mr. Preston he'll verify this, will he?"

"Yeah. Yeah, sure he will," said Pablo, who had yet to make eye contact with Traler.

"Have a look at this." Traler showed him photos of Melinda. "She didn't deserve this, did she, Michael? Look what you did to her. Go on, look. Are you this savage, Michael? Are you capable of doing this to someone?"

"No, I couldn't do this to someone."

"Who then?"

Pablo wiped his mouth, his other hand in a tight fist on his lap.

"You know who it was, don't you? Why would you want to protect someone who would do this to a girl?"

"Danny," Pablo said without hesitation. "He's the one did this. "

Melinda however, wasn't as certain as Pablo and Juan, a fact she confirmed by failing to pick either of them out of separate lineups later that day. Word quickly reached Owen.

"Ann. Come in." Ann heard Owen's voice, but she didn't see him until she was a few steps inside his office. She found him in the corner to her left, his hands braced against the wall as if he was trying to push it over. Ann just smiled. She would never get used to his new exercise regimen. "I understand congratulations are in order," Owen said after righting himself into a more vertical position. "I hear Danny's confessed."

"Well, not exactly. With the evidence he left in the alley, we've got him dead to rights for the Thornton murder."

Owen put his uniform jacket on and buttoned it. Then he sat at his desk and gestured to Ann to be seated as well. "And the kidnapping?"

"He's implicated himself, though he still insists he never raped her."

"What about the other two? Any chance of getting confessions out of them?"

"Pablo and Juan say Danny raped her but that he acted alone. We're holding them but with Melinda unable to identify them and the tests inconclusive likely do to condoms, we can't charge either of them."

"What about their records?"

"All have been nicked on various charges. Drug possession mostly, though never with enough to lock them away for any significant amount of time."

Owen sighed as he sat back in his chair, profile to Ann. "How does it happen?" he mused. "How do petty criminals make the leap to kidnapping, rape and now murder?"

Ann didn't respond. She wasn't sure if she was supposed to.

"You know, most of the time, I understand why they do these things. I don't agree with it, mind, but if you give it some thought, you can begin to see how they might have arrived at the decision to carry out such terrible crimes. What I don't understand are the ones who haven't the slightest bit of remorse over what they've done. I know it's just human nature to take advantage of the weak and helpless, but I've never been able to tolerate that sort of thing. It just isn't civilized."

"Yes, sir."

"Well, since they've chosen to take the more difficult path, that'll mean a trial. Which means she'll have to testify, and she'll probably have to do it more than once."

"Yes, sir. About that…I'm afraid there may be a problem with parts of her testimony."

Owen's head turned sharply toward her. "What sort of problem?"

"According to Danny, in order to keep him from raping her, Melinda provoked him into hitting her instead."

"And just how is she supposed to have provoked him?"

"With, erm…She insulted him."

"She what, called him names?"

"That's Danny's version, anyway."

"Just when I thought I'd heard everything. I don't suppose Melinda will be able to confirm any of this?"

"I have little hope of that, unless we catch her in a rare moment."

"She wanted him to hit her?"

"Sort of like choosing between the lesser of two evils."

"Yes, but that's not how it'll sound to a jury. How in the world are we going to take *that* into court?" He rubbed his hand over his mouth. "Could be another one of his lies. Have you at least tried asking her about it?"

"Not yet. She's having more tests done this morning."

"You know," Owen said while raising himself out of his chair, "I'm beginning to think these memory lapses of hers are just a convenient way of not telling us what we want to know. Oh, I know there are probably things she's unable to remember but this is getting a bit tiresome, isn't it? She should be putting it all behind her by now."

"I know it's been slow, but she *has* identified Danny."

"That's not good enough, is it? He was caught purely by chance, because the damned fool decided kidnapping wasn't enough. He had to add murder to his list of crimes, then left behind enough evidence to get himself convicted without a trial. Even his solicitor went pale when he saw what we found at the crime scene. And that's just the start. She's told you next to nothing about what went on at the colliery. What I would like to know is, when is she going to tell us what she knows?"

"Soon. I hope…," Ann said, her voice trailing off.

"At this point I would be grateful for any amount of cooperation, though I can't say I'm confident that even if she does talk she'll be able to do the same in court in six months time. Six months! We should be so lucky." Owen shook his head. "I remember when cases were so much simpler. You had a victim who was more than happy to cooperate. An arrest would be made, the victim would testify, a verdict would be rendered and the guilty party would be locked away until they reached a nice, ripe old age. Nowadays everything has to be so complicated."

"Yes, sir."

"What's your theory on this memory loss?"

"I think what happened at the colliery is part of it, but I believe something else is blocking her memory, something to do with Terry."

"Yes. Must be difficult for her to cope with that on top of everything else."

"Yes. I think that's probably it."

"No, you don't. You've got a different take on this, don't you? Think she might know something about his death? Think she might have done it? Killed him?"

"No, I don't think she did."

"But it is possible. Perhaps this something else led her to take drastic action. Maybe that's what's been blocking her memory. She killed him, only now that he's dead, she has no one."

"I'm not sure she had anyone when he was alive," Ann muttered.

"What?"

"I don't know, sir. In spite of the way he treated her, she revered him. She relied on him for everything. That's probably just the way he wanted it, too."

"What do you mean, in spite of the way he treated her?"

"It's—Nothing. Just thinking out loud."

"Please confine your thoughts to the facts, Ann. Right. Since we have nothing else at the moment, let's assume something did happen to her before this. What do you reckon it was?"

"I'm not sure. Only, the way she's behaving, it's got to be something even worse than what happened at the colliery."

"Worse than being kidnapped and raped? What sort of abuse could be worse than that?"

"The psychological kind. I'm not saying it's worse, only that it can be every bit as traumatic. It's just harder sometimes to see the inner wounds than the outer ones. That could be why she's closed herself off from her memories of the pit building."

"So that's it then?" Owen said while he limped to the door. "End of investigation, we defer to her fragile psyche?"

"No, I don't want to do that, either."

"Well then, what do you propose we do?"

Ann shrugged. "Find out what happened before she was kidnapped. That's why I want to take her to Terry's flat."

"What on earth for?"

"Because I believe Terry was abusing her."

"I thought we already knew that. And what if he was? We can't prosecute a dead man, Ann."

"Yes, but if we bring her back there, to the very place where the abuse took place, she might be able to remember something that could prove useful in finding Terry's killer."

"Or it may just frighten her to death."

"I think she can cope, sir."

"Do you?" He sighed and looked off in the distance. "I can see it now. The door to his flat opens. She starts to see all sorts of things from her past coming at her from all directions. She panics, faints, is taken to hospital where she sits staring at the wall in a shock-induced trance while the Crown Prosecutor is in court staring at an empty witness box. Then the Chief Constable, Deputy Chief Constable and anyone else in a position of authority rings me and wishes me well in my new job. Something to do with expired parking meters, I should think..."

"Sir, you asked me what's next and, quite frankly, I don't know what else there is to do. I've already tried everything I can think of."

"Have you?" Owen said wistfully.

"If this doesn't work, if something happens to her as a result of going back there, I'll take full responsibility."

"That, Inspector, goes without saying." Owen again shook his head. "Alright. Take her back. But make it count. I'm only giving you this one chance. If this doesn't work, you drop both investigations and get started on your other cases. I just hope you know what you're doing."

"Yes, sir."

"Let me know when you get back." Owen took a rope from the top drawer of the file cabinet behind his desk and wrapped the ends around each hand.

"I thought maybe you could free someone up—"

"Why don't you take your partner?"

"I'm afraid I can't, sir. He's—"

"Just where is young Hatfield anyway? You haven't scared him off as well, have you?"

"Special Officer Hatfield is presently in jail," Ann said non-judgmentally. "He was found to be publicly drunk and disorderly early this morning. Arrested by another Special, I believe."

"Oh. I see…Oh, I don't know, Ann. You're an Inspector now. Don't bother me with such trivial matters. I'll leave that to you. Just don't take more than one car will hold. We're not paying for a whole fleet to transport one witness a handful of miles." Owen rose, held his arms straight out in front of him, took a deep breath, then pulled his hands outward until the rope was taught. As he stood there and trembled, Ann thought this was probably a good time to leave.

ANN HAD BEEN LUCKY. SHE had been spared the added burden of a trial. What would it have been like, she wondered, if the detectives investigating her ordeal had made her relive it just to strengthen their case? She didn't know but she was glad she never had to find out.

It had taken great courage for Melinda to face those men again, even from behind a two-way mirror. All of them were currently behind bars. Why, then, was she still so frightened? That led Ann to theorize that maybe Dr. Stanton was right. Maybe Melinda's life was already in shambles before she was kidnapped. Or maybe simply knowing their tormentors were behind bars wasn't the end of it for the victim. For them, it would never end.

It was a sad fact that some cases had no answers and some criminals were never caught. They just followed their victims to the grave unpunished, unless there really was a higher power that dealt more harshly with criminals in death than in life. That ran through Ann's mind as she sat in her car outside the station and sipped the coffee she had bought on her way back from dropping Melinda off at the hospital. She wasn't in a hurry to tell Owen the trip to Terry's flat hadn't unearthed anything new, which would be followed by a good five minutes of him telling her it was no surprise to him that it had been a complete waste of time. Then he would ask her what was next, skeptical of course that anything actually *was* next. Ann understood his side of it. With the department's financial situation the way it was, it was his job to use what personnel he had left as efficiently as possible. And having one detective linger over a case that had so far proven unsolvable while others waited patiently for her attention didn't seem very efficient.

Still, Ann wasn't willing to give up just yet. She sat at her desk and tried visualizing the alley, then put various scenarios into motion, but there were still too many missing pieces. Was there someone else there that day who may have wanted Terry dead? Based on who he associated with, the possibilities seemed endless. Ann could always try asking Melinda again, but she couldn't risk wasting valuable time while Melinda challenged her to a fight or wondered why Terry still hadn't come. Ann knew she shouldn't think that way. She knew Melinda couldn't help the way she was, but Ann was tired and that was merely a reaction by some of the less disciplined parts of her mind.

Lost in thought, Ann noticed that her foot had been pressed against a plastic bag wedged under her desk. The crumpled papers she had collected at Terry's flat. She lifted the bag onto her desk and began going through them one by one. She hadn't been able to make sense of them before, but after uncrumpling a few, she began to realize what they were. Some were nothing more than gibberish, but others appeared to be bets Terry booked on the horses. Finding confirmation of Terry's gambling activities was hardly an earth-shaking discovery. It was already well-known that he took bets on almost anything that moved. But if he recorded bets, could he have done the same with his other business dealings? Ann brought the papers to DS Con Walters, who had a talent for solving puzzles like this. Four hours later, she was back in his office standing by his desk, peering over his shoulder.

"I've had a good look at these and I think I may have found something," Con said. "Most are bets placed at various racetracks across the country. But this one here is quite interesting." He held a magnifying glass over the upper right hand corner of one of the papers. "You see this bit here?" Ann strained her eyes to see it through the glass.

"What's it say? Something about...It looks like the twenty-sixth of...September?"

"You have the date right, Inspector. Underneath that there's a mark, a dagger, which I believe is meant to represent the pound sign. There are three letters after that, a 'B' and two 'Xs'. Those are meant to be numbers. 'B' being the second letter in the alphabet, I would hazard to guess it means just that, two. The 'Xs' probably indicate how many zeroes to add to the first figure. In this case, the number would be two hundred pounds."

"What about this writing here?" Their heads touched as they again both tried reading through Con's magnifying glass, which he focused over a pair of words halfway down the paper on the left side.

"It appears to be the word 'CReek'. Odd, that. See how the first two letters are capitalized?"

"What do you make of it?" Ann asked.

"I'm not quite sure. Could be anything. Initials, perhaps?"

"Cervantes Roschine. Of course. That has to be it. What about the other word?"

"It looks like...'MiSter'. It's a bit like 'CReek', with a second letter within the word capitalized."

"MS. Mitchell Stropman."

CHAPTER 6

"IT MAKES SENSE, THE WAY you explain it," Owen said from behind his desk, alleged contract in hand. "But there are a few things that need to be sorted out before we go arresting people. First, there doesn't seem to be anything here that confirms that these symbols, or whatever they are, actually represent numbers or that they're pounds. If this is indeed a contract, it doesn't say who the intended victim is, who ordered the hit and who accepted it. They're just names, aren't they? Not even. Just words."

"The paper was found in Terry's flat, which automatically implicates him—"

"It implicates him only if you can prove this is a contract. I mean, this sort of thing is usually done with a handshake. There are no legal documents to sign, nothing written out."

"It's in coded form."

"I don't see the words 'kill' or 'murder' anywhere. For all you know, Royce was writing a note to a Mister Creek."

"With the letters capitalized like that? It would be quite a coincidence, those exact letters."

"Could be his natural writing style. I myself have a devil of a time with the lower-case 'R'—Hang on. This can't be right. Roschine paid Royce two hundred quid to kill Stropman? What was he running, bargain days that week?"

"I know it's not a lot for that sort of thing, but it's not the money Terry was after. It was the chance to impress Roschine."

"And all he got was a bullet instead. Several, from what I understand. And just why would Roschine go to Royce in the first place? Surely he could have dealt with Stropman on his own. He had the resources, if that's what you want to call that sorry lot he calls his gang."

"Perhaps he wanted to be more discreet than that."

"But to hire someone like Royce...It makes no sense. He was a con artist, a turf accountant. Not a murderer."

"That may have been why," Ann said. "No one would have suspected Terry of carrying out such a crime. Probably the same reason Terry turned to Melinda. But when Melinda failed to kill Stropman, Roschine threatened Terry, which is why Terry panicked and came looking for her at the pub the next day, not realizing Danny and his cohorts had already intervened with plans of their own."

"So if the contract was never carried out, that would make Roschine the prime suspect in Royce's murder. Well, as much as I'd love to nick Roschine for murder, I don't intend to proceed unless we're absolutely certain. He's gotten away from us too many times before. I don't want to give him another chance to make us look like fools."

"Yes, sir. But we do have Mack's account of what he saw. That would seem to eliminate any doubt as to who ordered the hit and who accepted it."

"But it's all just circumstantial, isn't it? It wouldn't take the brightest defense attorney to put more than just the tiniest bit of doubt into the minds of a jury that these words, letters, symbols, could mean almost anything. And unless we can link them directly to Roschine, we've got nothing more than speculation on your part."

"Circumstantial evidence can be quite effective if we have enough of it, and I believe we do. We have Mack, who can place Terry and Roschine together the night Terry sent Melinda after Stropman, the same night she disappeared. We have Terry turning up dead in the same alley Melinda was kidnapped from shortly after he came looking for her at the pub the following day. It may all be just one huge coincidence, but I think it's enough to pique a jury's curiosity no matter what a defense attorney might argue to the contrary." Owen grumbled, but a convincing argument eluded him at the moment. He shook his head, then sauntered over to the window and stared out.

"Let's assume for now Roschine wanted Royce dead because he failed to carry out this alleged hit. What about Stropman?"

"He must have known Terry was up to something after seeing Melinda follow him twice in one day."

"So all their paths just happened to cross in the same place at the same time. Extraordinary." Owen placed his hands on his lower back, stretched and yawned. When he finished realigning his spine, he said, "What about our three kidnappers? Have you asked any of them if they knew Royce?"

"They weren't all that forthcoming when they were arrested, and I've been informed that they're all presently going through various stages of withdrawal. At the moment they're incapable of telling us much of anything."

"As soon as they are, I want to know if they've ever had any contact with Royce. Even if it was as a baby, I want to know. Could be those three killed Royce. Surely there's enough there to suggest they may have taken part."

"For what reason? If they knew Terry at all, it was most likely as their drug dealer. Why kill him?"

"Why indeed. That's what I want you to find out." Ann lightly cleared her throat. "What? You don't agree?"

"They aren't angels, sir, but as far as we know, none of them are murderers."

"With the exception of Danny, of course," Owen responded. He sighed. "You will at least agree that *someone* killed Royce? And that someone must be held accountable?"

"Yes, sir."

"Right. As for this so-called contract, bring them in, Stropman and that other pain in our collective posteriors, Roschine."

Mitchell Stropman. His relationship with Roschine had always been contentious at best. Being in the same line of work just naturally lent itself to a generous amount of justifiable paranoia that required both of them to constantly look over their shoulders. If they actually were the big time hoods they aspired to be, they would have hired competent bodyguards to do the looking for them instead of relying on halfwits who, when armed, were more likely to put a bullet in themselves than in someone who actually posed a threat to their respective bosses. Neither had ever been convicted of murder, but it was widely assumed both were capable of it.

Ann could have brought Stropman to the station, but she decided he might be more cooperative on his own turf. If there was a more appropriate place for someone like Stropman to live, Ann couldn't think of it. The houses in this neighborhood were so decrepit that most had been marked for demolition. Most of the other residents had long since moved away, leaving behind only those who were too poor or too stubborn to relocate. It was suspected that Stropman paid them to be lookouts, which made it difficult for his enemies to enter the area without him knowing about it.

Stropman's house was the largest in Seaton Road. From the outside no one would ever have mistaken it for anything other than an aging building not long for the wrecking ball. Ann couldn't get over how quiet it was. The most prominent noise was the soft rustling of dead leaves that hadn't yet fallen off the trees that stood at irregular intervals down both sides of the street. That in turn opened her up to new sounds, like the banging of loose boards dangling precariously from the many dilapidated structures. She wondered where in this two-story brick-and-mortar building Stropman was, where his guards were, and if any of them had their guns trained on her right now.

Ann knocked on the door and waited, then gently pushed the door open. If this was a trap, it was one without much imagination. She shined her torch inside. After determining no one was lying in wait, she headed for a light coming from a room at the end of a long hallway just to her right and straight ahead. She cautiously peered inside and saw a scene straight from a cut-rate Roman orgy.

The room overflowed with bad taste. There were cheap Persian rugs with more loose threads than fringe hanging from them; pedestals topped with plaster statues of Roman gods that curiously all had Stropman's face, even the women, and were adorned with all sorts of intimate attire from the world of S&M; enormous pillows covered in paisleys thrown on the floor and currently occupied by people who were either unconscious or in the middle of group sex. In some cases, both. Adding to the décor were lava lights, inflatable chairs and blacklights aimed at posters of men with wide sideburns, mushrooms dancing with butterflies, and a VW van painted in psychedelic colors. Evidently Stropman's mother had saved all his stuff from the seventies. There were peace signs everywhere, on wall-hangings, paintings, medallions and in holes left by body piercings. Incense was burning and hookahs were present, though wisely not in use in Ann's presence. Lording over this surreal world was Stropman himself kitted out in a white dressing gown with strands of love beads filling the V-neck opening. He was sitting on a huge pillow in the middle of the room surrounded by his subjects, adored by those who hadn't yet lapsed into a coma and pawed at seductively by scantily clad women.

"Inspector Treadwell. Yes, I know who you are," Stropman said, then sucked the cream out of a cherry cordial, not at all bothered by the mess running down his chin. Apparently, that's what the sleeves of his robe were for.

"Well, well. You've got to be kidding," Ann said as she ran her hand through a curtain of beads.

"What, you don't like it?"

"It suits you, Mitchell."

"Don't call me Mitchell! Me mum's the only one calls me that!" Stropman's round, cherubic face turned bright red. What little remained of his wavy blonde hair was so thin, the redness of his scalp showed right through. But he was quickly calmed by his harem, who fed him more chocolates. In the meantime, Ann's attention was drawn to the sound of a door opening behind her. She turned to see a woman in bondage gear exiting a room partially concealed by loud wallpaper that continued uninterrupted over the entire wall. With Stropman preoccupied with his overattentive whores, Ann wandered over what little floor space she could find and looked inside the room. It was filled with state-of-the-art video equipment, including several cameras, dubbing machines, VCRs and monitors. An entire wall was filled with shelves of video tapes.

"Oi!" Stropman cried out. Holding his robe closed with one hand he rushed toward Ann and nudged her out of the doorway with his rotund belly. He found the key in his pocket and quickly locked the door. "Unless you've got a warrant, you've no right to search the place!"

"Why? Have you something to hide?"

"Does it look as if I've got something to hide?" Stropman took a deep breath. "It's merely a hobby, Inspector." He returned to his throne and, after dumping its contents – some unidentifiable creature weaving side to side to sounds only he could hear – was again attended to by his fawning minions.

"Well, Inspector? What is it you want?"

"I'm here regarding—" Ann was distracted by the many derelicts suddenly stirring from all corners of the room, like some impromptu re-enactment of the Living Dead. At times they moved in unpredictable ways, like a sea of spastic eels, which Ann found a bit unnerving. They tripped over each other and bumped into Ann on their short pilgrimage to their leader, causing Ann to blurt out, "Is there someplace else we can talk?"

"Why? Do my people bother you?" Stropman smiled with amusement. "Perhaps a bit of nourishment will help calm your nerves." He made a sweeping gesture to his left, toward a long table loaded with food.

"No, thanks. I've come to talk to you about Terry Royce."

"Terry Royce?"

"He was hired to kill you. He sent a girl after you the night of the ninth of October, and you sent her back with her face bloodied." Stropman smiled while he stroked the hookers who were draped over him, clinging to him as if he would float away if they let go.

"I don't know what you're talking about. I don't know anything about a girl wanting to kill me. Women love me, as you can plainly see."

"Are you saying you don't know her?" Ann held up a picture of Melinda that showed her at her most gruesome. Even the whores, no strangers to abuse themselves, gasped.

"As I said, I've never seen her before," Stropman said before dropping another cordial into his mouth. He took the photo from Ann while noisily sucking the chocolate from his fingers. "Rather nice, this one. Has a certain quality. I'll keep this one in mind. Very much in mind..." Ann pulled the photo from his sticky grasp.

"What do you hear from Roschine these days?" she asked.

Stropman's finger cleaning came to an abrupt halt. "Roschine? I've got nothing to do with him."

"Really? That's odd, what with both of you being in the same line of work and all, drugs and prostitution."

"That's a bloody lie!" Stropman quickly composed himself. "I'm a legitimate businessman."

"Who's this lot then, your nieces and nephews?"

Stropman looked around the room. "Yeah. Some of 'em—"

"Are you aware that Roschine put a contract out on you, that he hired Terry to kill you?" Stropman's face glowed red and he looked as if he was about to explode. But instead he flashed a sly smile. "I know the two of you are great rivals, but I daresay, I'm rather surprised Roschine would go to such lengths to rid himself of you."

"Terry wouldn't have tried to kill me. We had an understandin, us."

"So you did know Terry?"

"Yes, I knew him. He didn't exactly keep a low profile, nor could he have done with his enormous girth. But the only business we ever conducted was the horses. Made a fair bit of money, too. But it was that and nothing more."

"When was the last time you saw him?"

"I wouldn't know. I'm a very busy man. But I assure you no one tried to kill me, certainly not that girl."

All Stropman had done was raise Ann's suspicions even higher. She wanted to hear what Roschine had to say, though she doubted he would be any more forthcoming than Stropman. A career criminal, Roschine had a sixth sense when it came to avoiding the police. But he made things easy this time. He had been caught red-handed carving up some poor soul who failed to pay one of Roschine's whores after services were rendered. Ann watched him – dressed all in black, as usual – through the two-way mirror in interview room three while he ranted to his lawyer, a man who looked more like one of the vacant souls who occupied Stropman's place than a qualified member of the bar.

She saw Roschine unfurl his trademark smile and was riveted by the morbid spectacle of his yellow teeth against his unnaturally bronzed skin, made that way by the tanning bed he had installed in his home. According to ex-associates, Roschine used the bed several times a day. That would be followed by a good hour or so of strutting about in nothing more than his Speedos in the belief that his emaciated physique had been magically transformed into the second coming of Charles Atlas. But, as the story went, it was a fragile illusion. It took no more than a word or even a look to cause a dramatic drop in his self-esteem. The bare chest that only moments ago seemed so massive it had forced him to walk with his arms out to his sides to avoid his bulging lats instantly reverted back to the concave oddity that it was. That would lead him straight back to the tanning bed for even longer sessions and even more ridiculously dark skin tones. Ann took a moment before entering. She had dealt with him before. It was never easy.

"Mr. Roschine—"

"Look, love, I missed you too, but I can't be sat here all day. I got a business to run." Roschine sat on an angle, his bent right arm resting on the back of the chair. Ann sat opposite him.

"You fancy going out for a drink now and then, Mr. Roschine?"

"Is that what this is about? If ya wanna have a drink with me, love, you can come round to my place any time. Might want to tart yourself up a bit first." Determined not to let him get to her, Ann's voice remained even throughout the interview. It was the only way to get through it.

"I don't imagine you're the sort of man who likes to drink alone, are you?"

"I ain't the sort of man who normally does anything alone."

"Do a lot of your drinking over business, do you?"

"Sometimes."

"Ever have a drink with Terry Royce?"

"Sorry, love. Don't know him."

"Really? What about all those bets he placed for you?"

"That weren't business, that. That were just for laughs, just a bit of sport."

"You and Mitchell Stropman have been at odds for quite some time, haven't you?"

"Long as he stays on his side of the street."

"But he didn't stay on his side, did he? He began dealing drugs on your patch, then started sending his whores there as well."

"Drugs? Whores? You're jokin'. She's jokin', right?" His solicitor's eyes were fixed on the wall behind Ann, who knew an existential trance when she saw one. Roschine was now paying the price for failing to read the motto on his business card: Mediation through Meditation. "Like I said, I got nothin' to do with that sort of thing. I'm strictly a businessman."

"What sort of business would that be, if I might ask?"

"It's...imports. I import things. From all over the world."

"What sort of imports?"

"Whatever punters want."

"What did Terry want?"

"He had an interest in acquirin' certain, erm, merchandise."

"What sort of merchandise? Wicker furniture? Beaded car seats? Fine porcelain vases?"

"Whatever he wanted, love," Roschine smiled broadly.

"And if I look into it further, will I find any of that to be true?"

"I'm legit, me. Even got some cards made up. Here..." He began patting the pockets of his leather jacket.

"I'm not interested in your imports right now. Which is not to say I won't be later. What I want to know now is, what do you know about Terry Royce's murder? What do you know about what took place the night he sent Melinda out to kill Stropman?"

"Christ, how should I know? I wasn't there!"

"We have witnesses who place you in the pub the night Melinda disappeared. With Terry, who was found dead the next day, who we now know had been hired by you to murder Stropman." The smile tried to fade from Roschine's badly scarred face, but the muscles were too well trained.

"Alright. Maybe I was there. But I was preoccupied with, shall we say, other things." Roschine's full range of teeth were again on display as he suggestively rubbed his crotch.

"What about Melinda. Where do you suppose she went that night, after she left the pub?"

"I don't know, do I?"

"Then you wouldn't know whether Terry sent her for ice cream or if he made her go after a knife-wielding maniac who wouldn't have had the slightest remorse over cutting her face open with an eight inch blade? A blade, I might add, very similar to the one we found on you earlier today. The one you used to slice up that man in the car park on Morley Road?"

"Ya got me all wrong, love. That ain't my style."

"There's a man lying on an operating table who might disagree."

"I only carry it for protection. Streets are so unsafe these days. By the way, what're you lot goin' to do about that? Anyway, if it's Stropman she went after, what makes you think it wasn't him that cut her up?"

"Because you're the one who was holding the knife when you were arrested not five feet from your latest victim."

"Lots of people have knives. I hear they're quite common. And I ain't the only one that carries one. Stroppy's got loads of 'em."

"Stroppy?"

"Yeah. Stroppy by name, stroppy by nature."

"It won't take us long to match your knife to the cut on Melinda's face."

"Sorry, love, but I didn't cut her. How could I when, as you say, there were all them witnesses who saw her leave while I stayed at the pub?"

Ann was undeterred. "Tell me, Mr. Roschine, how do you think Stropman will react when he learns you hired someone to kill him?" Ann put a copy of the alleged contract in front of him and his smile retreated. "Look familiar?"

"No. Why? Anything important?"

"I think you know what this is. Are you going to tell me, or would you like me to tell you?" Roschine tried to revive his solicitor's interest. And pulse. When that failed Roschine lifted the top corner of the paper between the first two fingers of his right hand.

"Looks like bollocks. Doesn't make one bit of sense, this." He tried sliding the paper back toward her, but Ann held it up so both of them could see it.

"It makes a great deal of sense. This part here, where it says 'CReek'? Odd, isn't it, that both the 'C' and the 'R' are capitalized, as if they were initials. *You're* initials, perhaps?" Suddenly Roschine had trouble taking a drag from the cigarette he had just clumsily lit with one hand.

"Mine, or a million others with them letters in their name."

"You hired Terry, but then you found out he sent a girl to do the job instead of doing it himself. At first you thought it amusing, but when she kept failing you became angry. You didn't think Terry would ever carry out the hit. Is that when you decided to kill him?"

"I had no reason to want Terry dead because we had no such deal. It shocks and saddens me he'd send a young girl like that out into the streets. That's not the proper way to treat a lady."

"You would know all about the proper way to treat a lady. How much did you pay Terry? Two hundred pounds, was it?"

"I didn't pay him anything, apart from what I owed him for the horses."

"Where were you on the tenth of October?"

"Christ, that were ages ago. Do you know where you were a month ago?"

"I'm sure I would remember if I had been cutting someone's face open. Or murdering someone. Or does it happen too often for you to narrow it down to just one?" Roschine's jaw clenched. "You say you don't know if this is a contract calling for the murder of Mitchell Stropman?"

"As I've said."

"Then you would have no objections if I showed this to him, would you?"

Roschine's smile was short-circuiting. "Go on then! Show it to him! He'll know it ain't no contract! Just one of your cop tricks, this! God, what a stupid bitch you are!"

"Right then. I'll let you know what he says. Or perhaps he will."

"You're daft! I got no reason to want him dead! We're businessmen, us! We got no time for such rubbish!"

"I think he might find time for this, don't you?"

Roschine was no calmer by the time he'd been returned to his cell, but getting himself in and out of trouble was a full time job for the man in black. Unable to take care of this matter on his own, it was time to resort to his standard Plan B: Look for someone else to do the dirty work for him. It was vital for a man in Roschine's line of work to stay informed, so he already knew who the three young men were who were locked up in cells near his.

"I know you lot," Roschine said, his face close to the door. Danny was sitting on the bed in his cell, which was to Roschine's right. Pablo was standing against the back wall of his cell, which was directly opposite Danny's, and Juan was sitting on the floor propped up against the bed in the cell opposite Roschine's enjoying the lingering effects of his most recent drug cocktail. "I've seen you tossers before. At Beaumont's Restaurant. Yeah. Beaumont's."

"Who the fuck are you?" Pablo asked.

"I'm the one sees to it sods like you get yer daily fix."

"What're you on about?" Danny managed to interject between withdrawal pains. "We get our dope from Bravo."

"Yeah? And where do you reckon he gets his from?" The cell room went silent.

"What're you doin' here then?" Danny asked.

"Doesn't matter what *I'm* doin' here. What matters is, I know what *you* lot are doin' here. I know what ya did, and I know who ya did it to." Danny and Pablo simultaneously drifted toward the doors of their cells. Juan was still on the floor, his knitted brow indicating that, despite his diminished capacity, he had also heard Roschine's words. "So what was it like, eh? What was *she* like?" Roschine smiled at their silence. "Oh, I see. Ya don't wanna talk about it just yet. But ya will, ya see, because I seen ya in the jennel. I seen ya hit her with that board. Right nasty, that. Thought you'd half killed her."

Danny was the first to find his voice. "You saw—"

"Yeah. I saw."

"Why are ya tellin' us this?" Juan said, too stoned to be intimidated. "What d'ya want?"

"I got a proposition for you lads."

"What proposition?" Pablo asked.

"What proposition?" Juan echoed.

"The girl. The one ya kidnapped. I want ya to finish what ya started."

"What's that mean, finish?" Juan slurred.

"I want ya to kill her. That's what ya had in mind when ya took her to that colliery, wasn't it?" Roschine thought he might be able to explain away the alleged contract Ann threatened to show Stropman, avoiding a full-scale war between their two gangs. And he could pay off Mack to buy his silence. But Melinda was a bigger problem. If she was dead, she wouldn't be able to testify that she saw Roschine in the pub with Terry that night, or in the alley the day he was killed, thereby casting doubt over the credibility of Ann's assumption that Roschine hired Terry to kill Stropman. All Ann would have was her interpretation of Terry's rather vague and amateurish practice of keeping records.

"Why should we?" Pablo said. "You want her dead, go and kill her yourself."

"Why, when I've got you to do it for me? And ya *will* do it, 'cause I got enough on each of you to see to it ya won't be gettin' out of here 'til you're so old, even Viagra won't do ya no good." Roschine smiled at the sudden silence. "Now here's what you'll do. Now Danny's not gettin' out of here any time soon. Confessin' to murder was right stupid, mate. Ya should'a said you was innocent, then let 'em prove it in court. Now you'll never get out of here. But you other lads, I reckon you'll only be in here another day at most. That'll give us just enough time to go over what you're to do and how you're to do it. Oh, and if either of you thinks of backin' out once you're outside, I'll see to it the police find out about the colliery. They'll throw ya back in here so fast, you'll never even know you was out." That left Pablo and Juan with no choice. If they told the police about Roschine's proposal, there was little chance they would believe them. And even if they did and Roschine was put away for soliciting murder, they would always be looking over their shoulder.

"Alright," Pablo said. "Tell us what you want us to do."

Two flights up, Ann had just arrived in Owen's office to find him hunched at his desk, his hands underneath the center drawer as if he was trying to lift it. Ann sat and waited patiently until his face changed from a crimson red back to its normal color. "Well? What did Stropman and Roschine have to say for themselves?" Owen said while he did shoulder rolls.

"Stropman claims he didn't kill Terry and has no idea who did."

"Hmmph! And Roschine?"

"He said practically the same thing."

"I don't suppose we should hold out hope Danny will tell us who murdered Royce."

"Not likely. Even if he saw something I doubt he'd tell us. Actually, given his history of drug abuse, I'm surprised he had the strength to knock Melinda out with that board."

"Still, for what it's worth, my money's on Danny. As you say, drugs are all he's got on his mind and, I daresay, there's nothing he'd let stand in his way to get them, including murder. Seems predisposed to that sort of thing."

"Yes, sir...," Ann said, only half-listening. "Do you have their statements?" Owen handed them to her and she quickly read through them. "Here. In his statement, Danny never actually said he struck Melinda. He said he woke up on the floor and found Melinda lying next to him, unconscious and bleeding. The board was a few feet away." She looked at Owen. "What if he didn't do it? What if he was too stoned and someone else hit Melinda with that board?"

"What are you saying, that he had an accomplice? Pablo or Juan?"

"I don't think so. I think there may have been someone else in the alley that day who may have had reason to harm her."

"Who?"

"Someone wanting to get back at Terry. It doesn't seem as if Melinda had much chance to get to know anyone well enough to make enemies of her own."

"But if not Danny and his mates, then who?"

"Stropman and Roschine would be the obvious choices. They each had motive."

Owen ran a bent finger over his mustache. "Who else do we know was in the alley that day?"

Ann pictured the alley in her mind. She had been there many times looking for suspects who rightfully saw it as an ideal place to blend in with the comatose crowd of regulars. Then the missing piece came to her.

"Bravo. I'd wager he knows something."

"Right. Pick him up."

Addicts Alley had been in existence for as long as anyone could remember, but only earned its nickname with the arrival of Bravo. Well known in this part of town, Bravo had been dealing drugs and evading police for years, reducing law enforcement's role to making sure his operations didn't get any larger than they already were. He had the means to move his business into higher-priced digs like Stropman and Roschine, but that wouldn't have suited Bravo.

From his vantage point atop the wooden barrel that served as a place to sit and a place from which to conduct business, Bravo saw everything that went on. If he didn't see it, he heard about it from his small but well-trained band of foot soldiers. Unlike those that Stropman and Roschine employed, Bravo's men were experienced professionals – most were ex-police or ex-military – who did their jobs so well Bravo had never been arrested. The police tried sending in undercover agents, but all of those attempts had failed. Until recently, the only interest the police had in Bravo was finding his supplier. Now they needed his help to catch a murderer.

His skin a grayish color, the result of living in darkened alleys and abandoned buildings most of his adult life, Bravo had a lean build, years of being on the run and sampling his own wares keeping the weight off and the muscle tone down. At six feet tall, Bravo was lucky if he carried more than a hundred and forty pounds on his frame. He was a different kind of thin than Juan, more athletic, though his attention to personal hygiene was every bit as current. He was dressed in a mix of worn fatigues, his head covered by a navy blue knit cap. He had a drooping mustache amid several days growth of beard and scratched it so frequently Ann was certain something would fly out. His eyes were watery, deep set and so red they would give a mortician the creeps. They followed Ann's every move as she sat across from him in interview room two.

"Bravo. What sort of name is that?"

"Nickname," he said in his gravely voice.

"That's right. You were in the military, weren't you?"

"Army." Ann looked into Bravo's eyes. If she stared long enough, the red lines seemed to spin like pinwheels.

"As much as it disappoints me to say this, you are not under arrest. You were brought here to answer some questions and I thought you might be more comfortable answering them here." Bravo's eyes stayed on her. Ann knew he didn't like being inside, especially in a police station, and that gave her an advantage. She also knew that, as much as he hated the police, they did have common enemies: Stropman and Roschine.

"What do you know about Terry Royce?"

"Dead."

"Yes. Thank you. You were in the alley the day he was killed?"

"Aye."

"What can you tell me about the events leading up to his death?"

Bravo scratched his beard and said, "Afternoon, it was, but it were dark, as if it wanted to rain."

"What time was this?"

"Just past three, it was. Saw Stropman in the jennel. Never comes round no more. Got no reason. But there he was, big smile on his mug, lookin' over his shoulder. I look down the jennel and see what he's smilin' about. A lass."

"Melinda?"

Bravo nodded and his eyes appeared to be strobing, causing Ann to squint. "Stropman, he goes down the other end and hides behind a skip. Then Roschine comes up behind her, but she don't see him. Terry, he turns up further along by tattoo parlor, between Roschine and Stropman. All happened so fast—"

"Go on."

"I hear this noise above me. Danny, up on his ledge on fire escape. Always up on that ledge, him. Falls flat on his face, right in front of Roschine. That's when all hell breaks loose. Stropman, he comes out from behind the skip and starts shootin' at Roschine. Roschine shoots back, then Stropman fires at him while he runs across the jennel and takes cover behind some crates. All them bullets flyin'…One of 'em must've hit Terry 'cause next thing I know, he's in a heap against tattoo parlor, blood all over him, and he ain't movin'."

"Which one of them shot him?"

"Could've been either one of 'em, couldn't it?"

"What about Melinda? Where was she while all this was taking place?"

"She was stood there, same as before. Didn't move 'til Danny starts moanin'. She turns round, sees him rollin' on the floor like he'd been shot as well. Wasn't, though. I hear more shots so I duck behind a building. Next thing I know she's lyin' on the floor near Danny, both of 'em unconscious. That's when I knew she'd been hit."

"By a bullet?"

"No. A board."

"A board? By who?"

"Roschine."

"Roschine? I thought he was busy shooting at Stropman." Bravo took a roll of pep-o-mint Lifesavers from his pocket and placed it on the table. Then he slowly pulled the string and watched it cut through the foil, briefly mesmerizing Ann. "Why would Roschine hit Melinda with a board?"

"Knock her out, take her for his own."

"Why did he leave her there then?"

"Afraid of gettin' shot, I reckon."

"Where did Roschine get the board?"

"Danny. When he fell, he were holdin' a length of board. When she turned to see who was moanin', Roschine picks it up and takes a swing at her."

"Did you see if she was alright?"

"With all them bullets flyin'?"

"You've been shot before, haven't you?"

Bravo placed a Lifesaver on his tongue and sucked on it. "Falklands."

"What sort of guns were they firing?"

"Forty-fives, more than likely."

"Right," Ann sighed. "So Stropman was in the alley because Melinda followed him there. Roschine was there to kidnap Melinda. Danny was there because he's always there. Why was Terry there?"

"To protect what was his."

CHAPTER 7

"LYDIA. THE AFTERNOON COSTUME. THE one with the floral print."

Perhaps the other residents of this small Tyrolian village thought it strange that someone would choose to live as a well-off member of mid-1800s society, but Madame Peto, as she called herself, had grown fond of that time, of the elegance and gentility that seemed to have permeated the era, and had completely immersed herself in it. She had lived here, in a two-story building with overhanging gables in this former market town at the foot of the Alps near the German border by a river that wove its way down the mountains and narrowed through this closed-off part of the valley for several years now. But she had been born thousands of miles away in both time and distance.

She stood in front of her full length mirror wearing nothing more than a slip – her one concession to the twenty-first century – and a single lace petticoat. It was a daily ritual, spending hours in front of the mirror until she could decide who she would be that day. Staring at her reflection, she was transfixed by the non-stop changes in herself both inside and out, changes that were so minute only she noticed them. She watched herself alternate between tall and short, light and heavy, blonde and brunette. In the blink of an eye, she was a young woman again. The texture of her skin, the color of her eyes, the style of her hair, all changed. In reality she was of average height with reddish-brown hair and deepening lines in her face that didn't diminish her attractiveness even though she was approaching her fiftieth birthday.

Of all her visions, the one she had grown the most fond of was that of herself as a regal woman in the court of Franz Josef the II, the reigning Emperor of the Hapsburg dynasty. That was her time now, the time to which she had transported herself, to a world that hadn't existed in over a hundred years and may never have existed at all, at least not in the glorified manner in which she imagined it. When she was there, she enjoyed the privileges afforded someone based solely on their breeding. The irony was that if she had actually lived during that time, her social status would have been that of a commoner. But Madame Peto never let reality stand in the way of her delusions.

It didn't take much to trigger one of these regressions. A soft breeze coming through the window, the smell of something cooking a few houses down, a cloud momentarily dimming the sun's light. In a flash she became a lady of dignity, nobility, of a certain standing. She was someone to look up to, to be in awe of, to admire. Her fantasies would sweep her away, and she would welcome them. Embellish them. Twist them and turn them until they established the kind of world where she belonged. Once they started to take hold of her she always hoped that she would be able to maintain them and make them viable so she could live forever in this time gone by. She didn't know yet just how close she was to realizing her dream.

Most of her time was spent sitting in her parlor on her imitation Biedermeier sofa next to the matching writing cabinet, or the Thonet replica side chair, staring aimlessly out the window. She was oblivious to the activity going on around her and only her outer shell was available to the friendly greetings of her neighbors as they passed by on the cobbled streets below. They had become used to her silence, though there had been times when Madame Peto's real and fantasy worlds aligned long enough to compel her to wave back. Of course, it wasn't her neighbors she was waving to. They were noblemen, servants, peasants, serfs.

Lydia, Madame Peto's secretary, had long since gotten the desired dress from the closet. She had been standing a respectful distance away as Madame Peto completed her mirror gazing. Madame Peto's wardrobe was, to put it mildly, unique, but wearing such clothes in public was just the sort of thing Lydia was there to prevent. To that end, the hoop skirts, artificial cages, whale-bone corsets, knee-length drawers, lace pantaloons and full-skirted petticoats had all been deposited in the nearby landfill.

Lydia, who was in her early twenties, had worked for Madame Peto for nearly two years and would be accompanying her on her impending journey. These excursions occurred so infrequently that they were more or less an event, with Madame Peto making all the arrangements and Lydia converting her nineteenth century plans into their twenty-first century equivalents. Over time, Lydia and their neighbors had adapted to her eccentricities. If they only knew. In their wildest dreams, they could never have guessed the answers to the puzzle that formed Madame Peto's life, nor would they want to if given the chance. Hers was a story best left untold. Until a few months ago, Madame Peto would have been content to leave it there as well. But after recent events, that was no longer possible. Now, in the waning days of autumn, her days as a recluse were fast coming to an end.

CHAPTER 8

AFTER TALKING TO STROPMAN, ROSCHINE, Melinda and Bravo, Ann still didn't know who killed Terry. Now that she had been reduced to grabbing at straws, Ann remembered there was one family who hadn't been home when she canvassed Terry's building after his body was identified. Maurice Hendrickson and his family lived just down the hall from Terry. None of the other residents Ann had spoken to knew anything about Terry other than his physical appearance and that he was rather unpleasant. But they all thought he was up to something suspicious, though when asked what they thought that might be none dared offer an opinion, as if they were afraid he would somehow take revenge from beyond the grave. But what Ann found most interesting – and disturbing – was that all of them expressed horror that a girl of any age would be living with him. None of them would elaborate on those concerns. Perhaps Ruby Hendrickson would.

"Yes, I'm Mrs. Hendrickson." The door to the flat opened and Ann was greeted by the imposing figure of Mrs. Hendrickson. She was immensely overweight, her head swimming in a collar of fat. She wore a striped tent dress and slip-on canvas shoes from which sprouted barrel-sized calves. Every movement brought with it a labored breath and another stream of perspiration cascading down her face which she wiped away with the oversized handkerchief clutched in her hand. Behind her, Ann could see children's clothes hanging from lines stretched from one end of the living room to the other, and the floor was cluttered with toys.

"I'm inquiring about one of your neighbors," Ann said while showing Ruby her warrant card. "Terry Royce?" Ruby rolled her head back, then snapped it forward and spit something into her handkerchief. She would repeat that revolting bit of regurgitation for the duration of Ann's visit.

"Come through." Ruby rocked herself out of enough of the doorway to allow Ann to squeeze by. The floor boards creaked as Ruby waddled down the middle of the room, clearing a path as she did by pushing toys out of the way with her feet. She continued into the kitchen, filled a glass with water, then sat at the kitchen table to the strains of screeching metal struggling to support her weight. Ann sat on a matching chair to Ruby's left to far less fanfare. "You say you're askin' about Mr. Royce?"

"Yes. What can you tell me about him?"

Ruby's expression became serious. "Oh, I don't know..."

"Do you know what he did for a living?"

"No, but whatever it was he was doin' in there, it's not the sort of thing I wanted my children round."

"What do you mean?"

"The sort of people he had comin' and goin'," Ruby's eyebrows knitted. "And at all hours, too."

"What sort of people?"

"The sort that's no good," Ruby said with disgust. "My husband says they're nothin' but tearaways, that lot. Tearaways and troublemakers. That's why we're movin' house, to get away from all the drug dealers round here."

"Terry dealt drugs?"

"Didn't used to be that way. They didn't used to allow that sort in here, especially with so many of us havin' babies. But that didn't matter, not after he moved in. Not after he started showin' his money about, if you know what I mean." She took a moment to rehydrate.

"Mrs. Hendrickson, do you know for certain that Terry sold drugs?"

"I don't know anything for certain. I never saw him sellin' 'em, but you don't always need to see to know."

"Was there anything else that seemed out of the ordinary?"

"No. Well, not 'til that girl arrived. Thought that a bit odd."

"What girl?"

"Little bit of a thing, she was. Had short brown hair, just like my Gracie. She came home with him, with Mr. Royce one day, holdin' onto his hand as if for dear life. Terrified, she was. I remember because, as it happens, I had taken my Jonathan to the doctor for strep and we'd only just gotten back when I saw 'em comin' down the corridor. She was about my Jonathan's age, too. Or perhaps Winslow's, a bit older. I remember, she kept lookin' round as if she had no idea where she was. Come to think of it, she wasn't exactly holdin' onto his hand. More like he was holdin' onto hers."

"Do you know who she was?"

"No. Mr. Royce kept himself to himself. We've been here six years and I don't know that I've ever had a conversation with him. Not so much as a hello."

"Then you wouldn't know if she was his daughter, his niece or—?"

"Don't think she was his daughter. Didn't seem the type to have had any children. Might have been his niece—"

"Did you ever see her again after that day?"

"Just once. Mr. Royce, he left his flat every mornin' round seven or so, but I never once saw her leave. I thought, maybe she isn't there anymore. Maybe she's gone back to wherever it is she came from. Then one day I heard sounds comin' from his flat as I was on my way to take my Arthur to school. I knocked on the door quiet like. I knew Mr. Royce had already left, but you never know."

"Did she answer?"

"Not at first. My Arthur was getting a bit restless so I started to leave. Then I heard the door bein' unlatched. It opened just a bit, but enough so I could see her. What I saw shocked me like nothin's ever done before."

"What did you see?"

"It was that girl, that same girl I'd seen not a week earlier holdin' Mr. Royce's hand. Only she was in such a wretched state, I didn't recognize her at first. I pushed the door open a bit more. She didn't try to stop me so I took her by the hand and brought her out into the corridor so I could get a look at her in the light. It was worse than I imagined. I had to put my hand over little Arthur's eyes so he wouldn't see what I was seein'. That girl had been terribly neglected, Inspector. She was filthy, wearin' the very same clothes I'd seen her in that first day. They were badly wrinkled and dotted with white powder, as if she'd tried washin' 'em in the basin and hadn't rinsed 'em properly. But what troubled me most were her eyes. Even the dim light in the corridor seemed to bother them. Then I noticed the blinds in the flat were drawn and all the lights were off except for a small lamp near the sofa. But there was something else about her that just didn't seem right."

"What?"

"Well, for one, she seemed so terribly frightened. Didn't say a word when I asked if she was alright, if there was anything I could do for her. At first I thought, maybe she doesn't understand. But that wasn't it. She was afraid. Kept lookin' down the corridor as if she were afraid he'd come home and see her talkin' to someone and hit her again."

"Do you know that he hit her?"

"I never did see it, but there were bruises. Her arms, her face. And I'd wager other places as well."

"Did you ask her how she got those bruises?"

"Yes. I asked if Mr. Royce had struck her, but she didn't answer."

"Did you call the police?"

"I wanted to, but my husband wouldn't let me. Said he didn't want any trouble with the neighbors, especially that one."

"So you did nothing to help her?"

"Certainly I did," Ruby said with mild offense. "We're not all monsters in this building. I had Deirdre, my eldest, take Arthur to school, then I brought that poor child to my flat and gave her something to eat. She ate everything I offered, too, but she ate so slowly. It was obvious she was hungry, but it didn't seem as if she had the strength to eat."

"Did she say anything?"

"Not a word."

"What happened when she finished eating?"

"I asked if there was some place I could take her, to her mum's, perhaps? She just sat there. Then, without a word, she got to her feet. Had to use the table to steady herself. Then she walked straight back to his flat. Walked so slowly, too, as if she were goin' to the gallows. I'll never forget that, nor the look on her face as the door closed behind her. I had a chill run through me, as if I'd never see her again. Not alive, anyway."

"How long ago was this?"

"Well," Ruby held a chubby finger to her chin. "I was six months pregnant with my Vernon at the time. Rough one, it was, too. He was born two months after that. The eleventh of February. Four years come this spring."

"The eleventh of February. That's the day your son was born?"

"When I fed that poor child. Little Vernon came the ninth of April. Or tenth. No, that was Mavis. She was on the tenth. Of July, I believe it was..."

"Is there anything else you remember, Mrs. Hendrickson?"

"No—Oh! There was that one night. Oh, how could I have forgotten? I was up all night with my Cliffy. He was just cuttin' his teeth and I couldn't get him to go back to sleep. I remember, it was just a few days after she'd arrived. All those suspicious people comin' and goin'. I always thought that had something to do with it. But this one night, I heard sounds comin' from his flat. I was up anyway, but the noise bothered my husband. He doesn't like to mix in other people's business, but he was about to ask them to quiet down so he could get some sleep."

"What did you hear?"

"Loud voices, as if there were some sort of argument. Went on for quite some time. Just as the voices stopped, I could have sworn I heard a scream, and not just one. I'm not sure how many, my Cliffy was making such a fuss, but I'm certain I heard someone scream that night."

"And you say you didn't call the police?"

"As I said, my husband insists I not mix in the neighbor's affairs."

"Mrs. Hendrickson," Ann measured her words carefully, "you knew a young girl was staying with a man you yourself said was of questionable character. You saw bruises on her. Her behavior was unusual, to say the least. Knowing all that, didn't you wonder why she might have screamed?"

"I didn't allow myself to wonder. I knew what sort of person Mr. Royce was. Everyone did. But we just didn't want any trouble. My husband said if we interfered, he might come after our own children. I had to make a choice: that poor girl or my own flesh and blood. Mind, it was quite difficult not being able to help…"

Ruby started tapping her finger against the side of her glass and a wave of perspiration rolled down her forehead.

"Was it?" Ann asked.

Ruby hesitated, then said, "Just after the scream, I heard Mr. Royce and his mates leave. I opened the door just a bit and waited 'til they left. I thought it safe to have a look so I went to Mr. Royce's flat and — Oh, if my husband ever finds out—"

"What did you see, Mrs. Hendrickson?"

"First, I put my ear to the door and heard someone moaning, as if they were in pain. Then I heard crying. Soft, it was, so soft I almost couldn't hear. I was about to knock when Mr. Royce returned."

"What did he do?"

"Oh, he was very polite," Ruby said with derision. "Asked if there was something he could do for me. I said no, that I thought I'd heard a noise coming from his flat. He said what I'd heard was a tape recording of sound effects he had done for a friend who makes films and he must have forgotten to turn it off. He explained they'd made several recordings that night and what I'd heard was one of them."

"Did you believe him?"

"Not for a moment, but what was I to do? Fetch my husband and have him knock down the door so I could see for myself what I already knew? He had given me an explanation. It wasn't my place to interfere." Ann put her hands flat on the table and got to her feet. Ruby eventually got to hers, too, and cleared another path to the door.

"Was that the only time you heard screams coming from his flat?" Ann asked as she followed Ruby.

"Yes. I never heard another sound after that night."

"Thank you, Mrs. Hendrickson. If you remember anything else, please ring me." Ann placed her card in one of Ruby's chubby hands, the one without the crusty handkerchief.

"I will. Mind," Ruby said in a low voice, "not when my husband's home."

Before leaving, Ann decided to have another look around Terry's flat. She had been there before, but it was different this time. She knew a little more about Melinda now, about the circumstances of her life. Ann stood in the middle of Melinda's room and got a real sense of just how little she had. After a few minutes it was obvious there was nothing new to see and Ann decided to leave. She turned and noticed a small shelf on the wall behind the door. It was just an unfinished piece of wood balanced on two nails hammered into the wall. On it in a neat row were a dozen or so books, all in identical red binding. There were works from Shakespeare, Thoreau, D.H. Lawrence, Kipling, Hawthorne and Hugo. Perhaps Melinda had a place to escape after all. Ann flipped through one of the books and something caught her eye. A name, written across the top of a page. She rifled through another book. The name appeared again, on the same page, in the same place. The same was true of the rest of the books. All of which led Ann to wonder, who was Karl Wagner?

Police records indicated that no one named Karl Wagner had ever committed a bookable offense in the UK, and no one by that name had an address in the area. With few options left Ann turned to Boris, the latest person to occupy the desk across from hers, to see what he could come up with in the police data base. Boris was fourteen years old and had recently won a contest to be constable for a day. Little did he know he would be doing more than just sitting behind the Superintendent's desk, wearing his hat and posing for publicity pictures. Seeing him in his office, Owen assumed he was a recent transfer and assigned him to Ann. Boris was working diligently at his new post, his hours of playing video games coming in handy while he scanned the computer monitor before him. Ann didn't bother to ask. She just left quietly and returned to the hospital.

"Melinda, do you recognize these?" Ann said after placing two of the books on the table by her bed. "They're yours, aren't they? Do you remember where you got them?"

Melinda looked at the books with unfocused eyes. "Danny. Danny gave them to me."

"Danny?" That was hardly the response Ann expected. Could Danny have known her before he kidnapped her? If so, that would link him to Terry and bring Ann one step closer to finding a possible motive for Melinda's kidnapping and Terry's murder. But Danny said he didn't know Melinda before the alley. The way he told it, he didn't intend to kidnap her at all. She was just in the wrong place at the wrong time.

"Melinda, are you certain it was Danny?"

"He was in the other room with Terry," Melinda said with a blank expression. "He had something in his hand—"

"What did he have in his hand?"

Melinda's eyes closed. "A stick."

"A stick, or was it a board?"

"He held—leaned on it—"

"A walking stick?"

"I woke up, and I was wet," Melinda said anxiously. "But I have to stay here. I'm not allowed to leave when he's away."

"When who's away?" a puzzled Ann asked. "How long did he make you stay that way?"

"He opened the door...pulled me out...red eye—"

"Who pulled you out? Out of the cage?"

"He let me wash...use the toilet...It was so dark—"

"Dark?" By all accounts, it wasn't dark at the colliery. Just the opposite, in fact.

"He held me down...won't let me go...red eye—"

"Red eye? Did one of them have red eyes?" It was an odd thing to ask, but it had to mean something. "Melinda, did someone hurt you? Someone in Terry's flat?"

Melinda's distress melted away and her face relaxed. "No one hurt me. No one can." Ann instantly recognized the sudden change in Melinda. Her harder side had made an unscheduled appearance, all but answering Ann's question for her.

"Melinda, you said the man who gave you these books was Danny. You said he had a stick. But Danny doesn't use a walking stick, does he?" Melinda again retreated behind closed eyes. "The man in Terry's flat. Was his name Karl Wagner?"

"Karl?"

"His name is in your books." Melinda's eyes opened and she looked at the books with renewed familiarity. She reached a trembling hand toward them, then opened the top book carefully, as if it had been rigged to explode, and turned right to the page with 'Karl Wagner' written on it. "Who is he? Who is Karl Wagner?"

Melinda closed the book. Her eyes were wet and her face brightened a bit as she said, "My father."

"Where does he live?"

"In a big house, with vines growing on it."

"Where is this house?"

Melinda paused. "Where the lakes are."

"Cumbria? What part of Cumbria?" Ann asked to no avail. But Ann was tired and wanted to end this for the day. "Right. We'll try again later," Ann said as she took a step toward the door.

"A shop," Melinda stopped her. "I worked there. They were nice to me—"

"What's the name of the shop?"

Ann could see a light go on in Melinda's head. "Palmer-Atwood."

IT TOOK THE BETTER PART of a day to drive to western Cumbria, to the small town where Palmer-Atwood was located. It had been the only shop in town for more than a century before being joined by smaller shops in recent years as tourists found even the more remote parts of the Lake District appealing. From the beginning Palmer-Atwood catered to the moderately wealthy. They demanded quality and Palmer-Atwood provided it. Ann entered this part of the world of the semi-elite and asked to see the manager.

"I'm Howard Deagle. How may I assist you?" Ann looked down and saw a short, pudgy man with thick black glasses, a bad comb-over and a somewhat effeminate manner. He wore a three-piece suit that was surprisingly ill-fitting considering where he worked, and his face glowed with nervous perspiration. Ann showed him her warrant card, then Melinda's photo.

"Do you recognize this girl?"

"No, but I've only been here five months." He turned to his left and raised his hand high. "Miss Wainwright? May I see you for a moment?" Mabel Wainwright, Ann was informed, had worked at Palmer-Atwood since it was just Palmer. She had a long face topped with graying hair that was held back with hairpins. She was put together with thin, brittle bones under loose, aging skin, but she walked and spoke with the energy of a much younger woman. Ann showed her the photo.

"Do you know her?" Mabel put on the glasses that hung from a cord around her neck.

"Why, yes. That's Melinda Wagner. Remember, Mr. Deagle? That's the girl who disappeared so mysteriously that day."

"Oh, yes. I've heard about that. That's her then?" Howard maneuvered his stout body between the two women to get a better look.

"Do you know what's happened to her, Inspector? We're all just dying to know," Mabel nearly burst.

"Melinda Wagner? Do you know if she has any family?"

"Why, yes. Her father. Karl, I believe his name is. Odd, that. I remember when Mr. Wagner came here, but I don't remember a wife, and I certainly don't recall hearing anything about any children until she began working here."

"Did you ever ask her about her family?"

"Melinda was quite shy, Inspector. She rarely spoke. We tried to make her part of the group, invited her to go with us on the odd night out, but she never did. Didn't even bother making excuses. At first we thought it was the difference in our age. It was myself, Anabelle over in footwear, Hermione in young gentlemen's accessories and Betty in lingerie. We're all a bit older than Melinda – well, truth be told, quite a bit older – but we felt so sorry for her, we thought she could do with an evening out."

"Why did you feel sorry for her?"

"She always seemed so sad. A girl that age, her whole life before her...It just didn't seem right she should be so sad all the time."

"Do you know why she was sad?"

"No. As I said, Melinda rarely spoke."

"Miss Wainwright, did you ever see any signs of abuse?"

"No—Well, I wouldn't call it abuse as such, but Melinda was quite thin, Inspector. One might even say emaciated. Her clothes just hung on her. The sleeves on her uniform – we all wore uniforms until recently, thanks to Mr. Deagle—" Howard humbly accepted the compliment, oblivious to its irrelevance to the conversation. "Her sleeves were so long they covered her hands so it was difficult to know if there were any cuts or bruises."

"What about friends?"

"You mean boyfriends?"

"I mean friends."

"I never saw her with anyone, and no one ever called for her here. But that's not unusual. We do have strict rules against visiting with friends and family during business hours. Unless they've come to shop, of course." Mabel returned Howard's approving smile, then rolled her eyes the moment he looked away.

"What can you tell me about the day Melinda disappeared?"

"Well, I do remember, that last week her behavior was a bit odd. She wouldn't talk, not even to say hello. Stopped waiting on customers as well. All she did was fold clothes and put them on shelves. That's what she was doing that day. We had just gotten a shipment when this man walks in and asks to speak to her. American, I believe he was. Quite distinguished looking, not at all the touristy type. I directed him to Melinda. She was folding jumpers, in that corner there. He spoke to her briefly and the next thing I knew, they were gone."

"This man...Was it Karl Wagner?"

"Yes. I didn't know it at the time, but it was him."

"You said he was distinguished looking?"

"Yes. He was rather tall. More than six feet, I should think. Had a neatly trimmed beard, too. Ginger, it was. Hair as well. Oh, and he wore wire-rimmed glasses. Dressed quite well," Mabel said as Howard, who was now stressing over a shipping manifest, couldn't overhear, "too well to have bought his clothes here."

"Is he wealthy?"

"Oh, quite."

"How do you know?"

"His house. It's the most expensive one in town."

KARL WAGNER'S HOUSE FIT PERFECTLY in this part of Cumbria. It was a late-nineteenth century Cotswald cottage that was so unremarkable, it had avoided being Grade II listed. That had allowed Karl to add onto it more than once until it was now nearly twice as high and wide as its original dimensions. It still retained much of its original features, including the stonework, steep gables, sloping slate roof and prominent chimney near the front of the house. The low door and small paned windows had been replaced with larger, more modern counterparts. There were vines growing up the sides and a good sized lawn lined with wide borders which, at this late date, were devoid of flowers. Winding through the middle of the lawn leading to the front door was a flagstone path with remnants of creeping thyme growing through the cracks. The whole property was surrounded by unusually high stone walls and was obviously well cared for. Nothing out of place. Ann couldn't help think that places of such perfection didn't actually exist. They were merely the product of creative minds and fairy tales. The houses here were miles apart, giving each resident all the privacy they could want. Anything could be going on behind the locked doors of these ageless homes and even their closest neighbors wouldn't know a thing about it.

The sign next to the door read "Dr. Karl Wagner". Ann identified herself to the maid, then followed her down a long hallway to double doors made of oak. The maid opened them to reveal a large, paneled library crammed with books on built-in shelves that reached from the floor to the ceiling. The uppermost shelves could only be reached by a ladder which moved along on rails. There was a large picture window along the back wall. Centered in front of it was a good sized desk where a man, silhouetted by the daylight pouring in behind him, sat taking notes from a book.

"Doctor Wagner?"

"Yes?" The man at the desk looked up and squinted, then stretched his glasses around the back of each ear and blinked his tired eyes to try to get a better look at his visitor. Ever the gentleman, he stood and slipped his gray coat over his matching waistcoat. He was a tall, thin, scholarly looking man in his mid-fifties or so with a full beard and hair that was somewhere between the ginger Mabel described and the gray that had begun overtaking it.

"I'm Inspector Treadwell. I'm investigating the disappearance of a young girl from this area several years ago." Karl closed his eyes, pinched the bridge of his nose and sighed.

"Yes, I know her." Karl didn't even look at Melinda's photo. "Tell me, what's happened to her?"

"Dr. Wagner…You're a medical doctor?"

"PhD. I teach at the university." After apologizing for his manners, Karl invited Ann to have a seat on the solid white sofa to the left of the desk while he sat on a black oversized chair across from her.

"Can you tell me who Melinda is?" Ann asked.

"She's my daughter." Karl shook his head. "No, she is not my daughter."

"Who then?"

"That's not an easy question to answer, Inspector."

"Why don't you try?" He briefly held his hand over his mouth, then began.

"About twenty years ago I was hired by Delacon Industries, a company in Texas that makes parts for oil drilling equipment. The following year Scott Conover – he began at Delacon about the same time I did – and I were both sent to England when Delacon opened an office in Leeston. We both worked in marketing, but we knew each other only casually. Once we transferred here, we got to know each other better. We were the only Americans in our department and I suppose that was our bond. We'd stop for a drink after work now and then and we'd take in a movie once or twice a week. But the more I got to know him, the more I realized Scott had this other side to him. He was driven, almost obsessively so. Maybe that had something to do with it, the way he changed so suddenly. I first noticed it at work one day. He came into the office and didn't say a word. That wasn't like him. He was always very chipper in the morning. I thought he was just having a bad day, but this went on for more than a week. Then one day he asked me if I wanted to have lunch with him. I assumed he wanted to tell me what was bothering him. Well, he unburdened himself alright. What he told me sends chills through me to this day."

"What did he say?"

Karl took a moment. "I knew Scott was married, but I didn't know much more than that. During lunch he began telling me about his wife. I had no idea how desperate he was."

"Desperate about what?"

"Scott and his wife had been trying for some time to have a child. Then, recently, she had given birth to a baby. A girl. I told him that was wonderful, he was a very lucky man. But Scott said no, he wasn't. He said his wife, Claire, was ill and having a baby had only made things worse."

"What was wrong with her?"

"According to Scott, some sort of mental illness. He said she wasn't right before the baby came and now that it was here...I asked him what he was going to do about it, thinking he would say something like get her help or, at the very least, hire someone to look after the baby. But that's not what he had in mind. He said he would have done that if he thought it would make things better, but he didn't think his wife even wanted the baby anymore. She had completely stopped taking care of it and Scott couldn't stand the baby's constant crying."

"Who was looking after the baby then?"

"Scott said he was, but I could tell by his voice that he wasn't. Out of politeness, I again asked what he was going to do. It was a question I would soon regret asking."

"Why?"

"Because it was then that I discovered the true purpose of my free lunch. Hmph! Free. I found out nothing was ever free with Scott. He waited until after we finished eating. Then he told me he never wanted children. He never even wanted to get married. All he ever wanted was to be successful, to rise to the top of some large corporation. That's the only reason he got married in the first place. He said you don't find too many high-ranking executives who were single. Not at Delacon, you didn't. He said he never loved Claire, but she fulfilled his need for a wife. But he couldn't bring himself to want her. And now this baby had come along. He said he had been so careful. He'd been giving her birth control pills without her knowledge. That's why she had gone so long without becoming pregnant. But somehow, it happened anyway. And, given Claire's mental state, he said he didn't push the abortion issue too hard. Of course I was sympathetic. I thought he just wanted to talk to someone. I should have known he had something else in mind. Scott *always* had something else in mind."

"What did he want from you?"

Karl stared out the window to his right. "I've never told anyone this."

"Go on, please." Just then the maid brought in a tray and set it on the coffee table between them.

"Please, Inspector, have some tea and biscuits." Ann picked up a cup of tea and had a sip of the citrusy blend and watched Karl grow more anxious. "He proposed a plan in which he would make it look as if the baby had been kidnapped. A suitable ransom would be asked for and paid – by him, of course – but the child would be found dead," Karl said, his voice catching at the end.

"Why did he want her dead?"

"I asked Scott that very question. I asked him why he didn't just give her up for adoption or leave her on someone's doorstep. Anything would be better than that. But Scott wouldn't even consider it. The only thing on his mind was, what if someone found her, found out what he had done? What would the executives at Delacon think? If someone had taken her and killed her, at least they would feel sorry for him and his chance for promotion would be that much greater. I know, but that's the way Scott's mind worked."

"What was to be your part in all this?"

"He wanted me to find someone to...," Karl put his hand over his mouth again, then lowered it and said, "I didn't have much of a connection with the underworld, but I did know this one fellow. Terry Royce. I think that's why Scott involved me in the first place, because of Terry."

"How did you know him?"

"I had placed some bets with him. Terry was a small time bookie back then. I'm not much of a gambler but when I first arrived here, when I was still trying to find my way around this country, I got caught up in all the different sports, the football and rugby matches, and I placed a few bets. Just for recreational purposes. Most of the bookies wouldn't take such small bets. Then one of them told me about Terry, that he could accommodate the casual gambler like myself. I found him to be a very likable fellow. We even struck up a kind of friendship. He seemed very curious about America and would ask me all sorts of questions. I told him about Scott's plan and I asked him if he knew of anyone who might be interested in helping. He said he did. Him."

"Terry agreed to kill her?"

"I only asked him as a last resort. I had no idea he'd be so willing to participate in a scheme that included murdering a child," Karl said, then drank his tea in one large gulp.

"Forgive me, Dr. Wagner, but hadn't you already agreed to it?"

"No. Not to murder. I thought all Scott wanted me for was to find someone to help him carry out his plan, but Terry had other ideas."

"Such as?"

"I started telling him the details, but all he wanted to know were the monetary arrangements. I told him Scott said he would pay each of us five thousand pounds with the one who killed her getting an extra three. I told Terry, as I had told Scott, I didn't want any money, and I certainly wasn't going to kill her. But Terry said, since he didn't know Scott, I was to act as the go-between. That way if Scott didn't come up with the money, I would have to pay Terry out of my own pocket. And if I went to the police, Terry would make sure they knew I was involved. Even if I backed out right then and there, Terry said he would implicate me. That left me with no choice. I had to see this through."

"Right," said Ann, who resisted the urge to comment further. "So Scott just gave you his child?"

"No. Scott decided to wait until Claire was asleep one night and bring the baby to me. I followed his instructions and waited for him at the end of a quiet road. While I was waiting, I had time to think. I thought, I can't go through with this. Why was I even considering it? I had a decent job, living comfortably in a very exciting part of the world. I came this close to getting in my car and driving away. But then I thought, that wouldn't change anything. Scott would just find someone else to kill her. That's when I realized I was this baby's only hope."

Ann had one last sip, then put her cup back on the tray. "What happened after Scott brought you the baby?"

"He arrived about twenty minutes after I did. I remember, I could hear my heart pounding as I saw his car approach. He got out and handed me the baby, then drove off without a word. Then I looked at her. As soon as I did I realized this would never work."

"Why?"

"Because my first thought was, he forgot to bring any baby things. No toys, no diapers, no change of clothes. Just her pajamas and the blanket she was wrapped in. I even started to call after him. I wanted to ask him what her name was. Tell me, Inspector. How was I supposed to give her to Terry after that?" Very noble, but Ann wasn't about to waste any sympathy on him.

"Isn't that why Terry was brought on board, to kill her?"

"He was. I snuck the baby into my flat and put her on the couch. I had nothing prepared for her because, as I soon realized, I hadn't really thought this through. I guess I thought Terry would just take her somewhere and...Anyway, Terry came by soon after. I remember my heart dropped when I opened the door and saw him there. It was then that what he had come to do became real to me. I suddenly saw him in a different light. He was a large man, over six feet tall and quite heavy. For the first time he seemed imposing when the circumstances of his visit were taken into account. Without saying a word he walked over to her. He leaned over to take a closer look and said, 'Is that it?' Then she broke out in a big smile. The next thing I knew, Terry was playing with her. He was holding her in the air and making faces and baby noises at her. They were both smiling and laughing like they were father and daughter. I thought, could he be so kind to her one minute, then kill her the next? I just stood there waiting to see what he would do. As I did, I realized I didn't really know Terry. I didn't know what he was capable of. Finally I said to him, We can't do this. We can't kill her. He said, 'Karl, old boy, I don't know about you, but I never intended to kill her. All I want is the money. All we have to do is make it look like we killed her so your mate will hand over the extra three grand.' I can't tell you how relieved I was."

"So you kept the baby?"

"Since neither of us wanted to kill her we decided we would raise her ourselves. We worked out an agreement. I would take care of her until she was fifteen, then Terry would take her until she was of legal age. He explained he didn't want to deal with diapers, mumps, that kind of thing."

"No one ever questioned why you suddenly had a baby living with you?"

"I didn't stay long enough for any of the neighbors to find out. Before the week was out I had moved up here. The house had been offered to me for next to nothing by a Delacon executive who had to get rid of it for tax purposes. It was the perfect size, just right for two people, and the neighbors were far enough away that they wouldn't know she was here."

"How was that possible? Surely someone must have seen her when she went to school."

"I'm afraid I couldn't allow Melinda to go outside."

"What, never?"

"Believe me, I wanted to send her to school. I wanted her to have friends. God, that was so difficult. When Melinda was little, she noticed other girls her age in their school uniforms. She asked me where they were going and if she could go, too. I wanted to send her, but it was too dangerous. What if they asked to see her birth certificate?"

"What did you tell her?"

"That she was exceptional and because of that, they couldn't teach her anything at school. Only I could, here, at home."

"You educated her?"

"Yes. I'm perfectly qualified. I taught her the basics, reading, mathematics, writing. Then, as she got older, science and history. Everything she needed was right here," he gestured toward the crammed book shelves. "Most of her education was about America. I wanted her to know about her heritage. I know it sounds silly, but I didn't want to take from her who she was."

"Yes, but if she was born here, in England, then she's a British citizen. At the very least, she would hold dual citizenship."

"I know, but since Scott was from Texas, I felt I could at least do that much for her, give her some sense of her past, of where her family came from." Ann could feel a headache coming on, one originating from the stupidity of a supposedly intelligent man.

"But surely she must know she's British as well as American."

"She only knows what she's been told."

"What about when she went to work at Palmer-Atwood? She must have noticed the difference in the way she spoke compared to the rest of the employees."

"Yes, I suppose she must have. But if she did, she never mentioned it. I think, in time, she simply accepted it."

"How do you know she did?"

"She just did," he said with an icy stare. "I don't expect you to understand, but it wasn't easy for me, either. It wasn't easy raising Melinda. She was a difficult child."

"Was she?" Ann said with mock surprise. "Did you ever have to punish her for being difficult?"

"Of course. You can't expect a child to go their entire life without misbehaving now and then."

"What sorts of things was she punished for?"

"Well, there was the time she went into a part of the house where she wasn't allowed to go."

"Where had she dared stray?"

"Here, in the library. I couldn't have her standing near windows. Someone might have seen her." Ann looked out the window. She saw the lawn, the stone wall and a dense cover of trees ringing the property. It would have taken a low flying plane or someone with a strong pair of binoculars and innate climbing skills to see inside.

"What sort of penalty was Melinda made to pay for that indiscretion?"

"I don't remember. It was a long time ago."

"Did you ever strike her?"

"I punished her. I can't recall if I ever hit her."

"Did she cry or scream when you disciplined her?"

"She didn't do such things."

"Didn't she? Children do cry, doctor. And scream, when they have reason."

"Well, she didn't."

"What would you have done if she had?"

"She wouldn't. She knew I wouldn't have tolerated such outbursts. You have to understand, Inspector, I came from a family that didn't express their emotions. We showed them in other ways. We channeled them into our work, our studies, to make ourselves better."

"Is that what you taught Melinda to do, channel her emotions?"

"Yes. It worked for me, didn't it? I'm a well-respected doctor of economics."

"Just like Melinda," Ann said under her breath.

"What?"

"Why did you finally allow her to take a job?"

"Shortly before she turned fifteen, it began to occur to me she wouldn't be here forever," said Karl, his remorseful tone returning. "I knew the day was coming when I would have to let her go and I wanted to prepare her for that. I have an acquaintance on the board of directors at Palmer-Atwood and I asked him if he could find her something."

"How did you explain her to him?"

"I told him she was my daughter, that her mother and I had divorced before she was born and I didn't know she existed until recently when her mother contacted me. She had fallen on hard times and could no longer care for Melinda, so it was decided she would live with me. It worked, too. Everyone in town believed it. After that, things became much easier for me."

"What about Terry? Wasn't he supposed to take her when she turned fifteen?"

"That was the deal we made, but he never came for her. It was just as well. By then, I didn't want her to go. I had grown quite fond of her. I guess you might say I even loved her. Not quite as if she were my own daughter, but we had developed a bond." Ann wasn't quite sure what he meant by that. "Just before she turned fifteen, the possibility that she might soon be gone started to become very real to me. Melinda knew nothing of our arrangement, of course, or Terry. On the day of her birthday she was so happy, like she was every year on that day. But I'm afraid I couldn't share in her joy. I know she sensed something was wrong, but we celebrated her birthday as we always did. As the day went on, I began to feel better. I didn't know why at first, but then I realized what it was. The phone. It never rang. I thought, maybe Terry had forgotten. Maybe he decided he didn't want her after all. It had been such a long time, and I hadn't heard a word from him since that night when I brought Melinda to my flat. But Terry hadn't forgotten. He phoned the day after her fifteenth birthday and said, in accordance with our agreement, she now belonged to him for the rest of her life.

Her life, he said, not just until she turned eighteen. My heart sank. I knew once he had her, he'd never let her go."

"How long ago was this?"

"Four years."

"Then she's only nineteen?"

"Yes."

"What did you do about Terry?"

"There was nothing I could do. We had an agreement and I had no choice but to honor it."

"Surely he could have been persuaded."

"I did offer him money, but he turned it down. Things had changed for him in fifteen years. He wasn't just a bookie anymore. He had branched out into other things, though I have no idea what. But whatever it was, money didn't seem to be an issue anymore. He wanted Melinda and no amount of money was going to persuade him otherwise."

"Any idea why he wanted her at that particular time?"

"No. I wondered about that myself but when I asked, he said it was none of my business."

"How did you tell Melinda that she would be living with Terry?"

"I didn't. Terry had it all worked out. He told me to take her to the train station in Kendal. He said to have her there the next day at one o'clock. I told him Melinda worked and wouldn't be able to get there that early. Then he reminded me Melinda no longer needed a job. I thought about taking her away somewhere and starting over, but there was no way I could win. If I didn't give her up, Terry would come after me and I would be on the run the rest of my life. I had to resign myself to it. One way or another, I was going to lose her."

"What did you do?"

"I went to Palmer-Atwood and told her to come with me. She didn't even ask where we were going, which was just as well. I don't think I would have been able to find the words. We drove to the train station. I took her by the hand and led her inside, to a row of chairs, and told her to wait for me there. I had avoided it up until then, but I looked in her eyes. I could tell she was frightened. I remember, it was so hard letting go of her hand."

"So you just left her there, and Terry collected her?"

"I passed him on my way out and told him to take care of her. He didn't say a word. Didn't ask me anything about her, what she was like, what her favorite foods were. I waited for a train to come and lost myself in a crowd of commuters. I never saw her again after that."

"Dr. Wagner, where is Melinda's father? Her *real* father?"

"Scott? Oh, he got his promotion alright. Landed somewhere in the Middle East. He'll have been missing nineteen years come February."

"What about Claire?"

"Poor Claire. She's disappeared as well."

"Would you have any photos of Scott and Claire?"

"I might. They used to hire photographers for some of the more formal affairs Delacon so famously threw." Karl removed a gold embossed album from one of the shelves, pulled two photos out and brought them to Ann. "That's Scott there, third from the left."

"And Claire?" He showed Ann the second photo.

"Here, by the door."

"Thank you for your cooperation, Dr. Wagner." Ann started for the door.

"Inspector. Is Melinda alright?" Ann stopped in her tracks and considered his question. "Is that why you've come? Please tell me. I raised her since she was a baby. I've worried about her every day since she's been gone. If something has happened, please. You must tell me." His eyes widened with alarm. "Is it Terry? Has he done something to her?"

"Surely you're not shocked by that," Ann said. "You knew the sort of person he was, yet you still allowed him to take her. A fifteen year old girl, alone with him in his flat. What did you think would happen?"

"I knew he wasn't a saint, Inspector, but…She was just a child."

"That's right, doctor. She was."

CHAPTER 9

ANN LEFT KARL'S HOUSE ALONE. She thought about arresting him, but she wasn't sure that what he had done was technically kidnapping since, if he was to be believed, Melinda's father had given her to him. And, since he had lived in the same village and had been gainfully employed at an institution of higher learning for the last eighteen years, Ann knew where to find him if she wanted him. She also intended to have the local police keep a watch on him.

Before leaving, Ann decided to have another look around the property. She stood at the entranceway to the back garden and finally realized what bothered her about this place. While the land wanted to be less predictable, evidenced by the rolling nature of the meadows and fields throughout the area, this property was rigid, forced flat against its natural habit.

Ann's observations were interrupted by a cloud of dust coming down a winding, hilly road just beyond the front of the house. In the middle of it was a pickup truck, its shock absorbers so worn that even the slightest bump lifted it in the air. It pulled up near the barn and Ann could see the words McQuaid's Landscaping painted on the side. A young man with the sort of build that comes from manual labor jumped out and started unloading fifty pound bags of top soil. He had on faded blue jeans, high-top work boots, a green and red plaid wool coat and a navy blue knit cap. He had just slung a bag over his shoulder when Ann approached him, her arms folded against the cold, her chilled hand holding her warrant card.

"I'd like to ask you a few questions." The man looked at the card, then let the bag drop to the ground in what Ann deemed a gesture of silent defiance. "You work for McQuaid?" said Ann, who realized she might have started with a better question. He took an exaggerated look at the side of his truck, then said,

"Yeah. That's right."

"How long?"

"Five, six years," he said, his arms folded to mirror hers, his gaze downward as he moved the dirt with the toe of his right boot.

"Do you know who lives here?"

"Lecturer. Teaches at university," he replied.

"Anyone else?"

He thought for a moment. "Yeah. Used to be a girl lived here as well."

"Do you know who she was?"

"No. Only saw her once or twice. Up there in that window." He nodded toward a window on the top floor overlooking the back garden.

"When was the last time you saw her?"

"Don't know." He pulled on the black work gloves that had been hanging out of his back pocket, then hopped onto the bed of the truck, threw another fifty pound bag over his shoulder and jumped uncomfortably close to Ann before dropping it.

"I don't believe I caught your name."

"Ian."

"Just Ian?"

"Harding. Ian Harding."

"Did you ever speak to the girl, the one in the window?"

Ian rolled his eyes. "It were ages ago."

"Try."

He exhaled hard. "Each time I came round I'd see her, up there in that window. And each time, she'd draw the blinds."

"Was there anything unusual about her?"

126

"Just a girl lookin' out a window," Ian shrugged. "I did think it odd a girl her age bein' home durin' the day. Should've been in school, shouldn't she? And her clothes. Always wore the same thing."

"How could you tell from down here?" Ian stopped, then lifted himself onto the truck bed, his legs hanging off the back, his head again down. "You spoke to her, didn't you?" Ian swung his legs. "How did you meet her? I understand Dr. Wagner was quite strict with her."

Ian removed his cap, ran his hand through his short, light brown hair, then replaced the cap. "First time I came here, he said I wasn't to go in the house. Didn't say why. Not long after, I was workin' here one day. It was right hot. Hose wasn't workin' so I went inside. Didn't think he'd mind." He pulled at the fingers of his gloves. "I didn't notice her at first. She was stood in the doorway of the kitchen while I had some water. I said hello but she didn't answer, so I did most of the talkin'"

"What did you talk about?"

Ian lightly shook his head. "Her name, was she the old man's daughter, but she didn't say. I was about to leave, and she says, 'Melinda.'"

"Is that the only time the two of you talked?"

"We talked every time I came round after that. She never did have much to say, but, I don't know. Maybe it was all the mystery about her, but I fancied her."

"Did you continue to pursue a relationship with her?"

"Wasn't any point, was there? Not with her old man about." Ian hopped off the truck, then turned his back to Ann. "Anyway, I'd just started this job. I didn't want to risk losin' it."

Ann eyed him with suspicion. "You're lying, Mr. Harding. You didn't stop seeing Melinda, did you?" Ann showed him Melinda's braided leather bracelet. "You gave her this, didn't you?"

Ian wiped his forehead with his gloved hand. "I was gonna end it, but I couldn't. I know her old man didn't allow her to see anyone, but I couldn't stop thinkin' about her. I had to see her again."

"Where did you take her?"

"Nowhere at first. Then after a time, for short drives. Not in town, though. Couldn't take the chance her old man would find out."

"How long before the two of you were intimate?" Ian's eyes shot in her direction.

"Yeah, alright," he flung another bag off the truck. "We had sex."

"Consensual, I presume?"

"Yeah. That what this is about?"

"Where did this consensual sex take place?"

"Different places."

"Different places each time?" Ian took a shovel from the truck and walked to an empty bed a few feet away.

"I don't remember every place I've had sex, Inspector. Do you?" he said, then began turning the soil.

"Try to remember where you had it with Melinda."

Ian stopped digging and sighed. "Her room. His room. The sitting room. My truck."

"Why did you stop seeing her?"

"Because Melinda wasn't—She didn't know much when it came to makin' love. I wanted her to do certain things, but she had no clue. Could'a paid a twenty quid hooker to do more."

"So you ended it because she wasn't good in bed?"

"Yeah," said Ian, who dug into the dirt with emphasis.

"Something else happened, didn't it?"

Ian again stopped. "She tell you that too?"

"As a matter of fact, she did."

"What did she say?"

"I think it would be better for you if you told me, to see if your stories match."

After a long moment Ian plunged his shovel into the dirt. "Ask him."

"Who?"

"Him. The Lord of the Manor." Ian pulled his gloves off and stuffed them in his back pocket. "He must've really hated that girl."

"Why do you say that?"

Ian got into his truck and said, "Ask him." With that, he closed the door and drove away. Ann headed home with Ian's cryptic words running through her head and a better understanding of Melinda's childhood, but she couldn't deny that Melinda was drifting further away from reality and not making much of an effort to find her way back. Each time Melinda survived one of her memories, Ann hoped it would be for good and she would be able to maintain her grip on reality. Then again, maybe she would never fully regain her sanity.

On the subject of losing one's sanity, Ann had just stepped off the lift on the second floor of St. Pritchards when a nurse informed her that Dr. Stanton wanted to speak to her. Ann sighed. She knew this wasn't going to be pleasant. Ophelia didn't seem to be in any hurry. In fact, it took another ten minutes before she finally came thundering down the hallway. Ann couldn't help notice that even her walk appeared angry. Ann was about to speak, but Ophelia walked past her and picked up a chart on the desk, then discussed several points with a nurse who seemed puzzled by Ophelia's sudden interest in a patient who had been admitted for a bowel obstruction.

"Dr. Stanton...," Ann interrupted the doctor's ongoing recitation of every drug she had ever heard of to the poor unfortunate nurse who hadn't had the foresight to make her escape before Ophelia arrived, "Have you been to see Melinda?"

Ophelia finally placed the chart on the counter and faced Ann. "Yes and, quite frankly, I'm rather concerned about her condition. What exactly did you say to her?"

"Just discussing the details of this case."

"I see. And how did she respond to that?" Ophelia's stare was again making Ann feel more like a patient than a cop.

"She listened, then seemed to nod off."

"Nod off? Inspector, she is now in a semi-catatonic state. Whatever it is you said to her has pushed her into an even deeper state of psychosis than before. I'm sorry, but I'm afraid I can no longer allow you to see her."

"You can't allow me? We're in the middle of a murder investigation."

"While she is here she is *my* patient and I shall do whatever I deem necessary to ensure her well-being including barring you and anyone else who may prove detrimental to her recovery from seeing her. I think you'll find I'm rather well connected. Really," Ophelia said with disgust. "I look at that child and I can only imagine the harm you've already done her. This is a perfect example of why things like this should be left to professionals."

"With all due respect, doctor, may I remind you of your own success with Melinda? How many times have you tried talking to her? Five? Six?"

"No fewer than nine, between myself and the members of my staff. All failures, thanks to the police."

"Yes, well, I'm sorry about that," Ann conceded to keep their latest disagreement from deepening, "but surely you can appreciate the importance of our having access to the only witness in a kidnap and murder investigation."

"And how do you intend to pry that information from her? More of your heavy-handed methods?"

"What are you implying, that I'm the cause of Melinda's condition?"

"Inspector, I blame you for that as I have always blamed you for that."

Ann took a deep breath. "I have to be able to speak to her."

"I don't think you realize just how ill that girl is, Inspector."

"I do realize. And I'm very much in favor of her receiving the care that she needs. But since she's the only one who can tell us who kidnapped her, I must insist I be allowed to question her."

"And what? Hope that she will somehow tell you what you want to know?"

"Yes."

"That is the difference between you and I. I know from my vast experience with such patients that she will indeed talk, but only if she is placed in the right setting."

"What do you mean, the right setting?"

"I want to take her to the Menninger Institute." Ann hoped she wasn't serious. The Menninger Institute was virtually a maximum security prison used mainly for the criminally insane. "It's an isolated facility. Nothing for miles around. Patients are rewarded for cooperating. Those that don't soon come round."

"Doctor, I understand this has been a very trying case. For all of us. But I hardly think Menninger is the answer."

"I'd think it over, Inspector. I've gotten some wonderful results there with patients who were even more stubborn than she."

"You know why I can't allow that. She must remain accessible to us. She must also remain lucid enough to answer questions. To that end, I want you to stop drugging her into unconsciousness."

Ophelia's round face turned a deep shade of red. "Until you present me with your medical degree, Inspector, I don't believe you are qualified to voice your opinion on that or any other matter relating to my methods. Unlike the police, my concern is for my patient, not some case she may or may not be able to assist you with."

"I don't mean to tell you how to do your job," Ann said. "I just wonder if less sedation would work just as well."

"I'll be the one to make that judgment and no one else." Ophelia wrote something in Melinda's chart with a broad stroke, then snapped the cover shut. Ann had no desire to be drawn any deeper into yet another irrational debate but she couldn't help thinking that, if Melinda ever did get to the point where she needed to be institutionalized, Ophelia could easily qualify as her roommate.

"Doctor, based on your experience, how serious is her condition, this catatonic state? How long will it last?"

"My experience." Ophelia savored the moment. "Yes, that does count for something, doesn't it? That is something only Melinda can tell us. It could be days, weeks. Months, perhaps. What I *can* tell you with a great deal of certainty is that the police have only slowed her recovery. But she is in my care now, which means she will finally get the treatment she so desperately needs. I'll have my secretary ring your superior when she recovers. *If* she recovers. If you still wish to speak to her then, perhaps we can work out some sort of an arrangement."

WHEN HE WANTED TO, OWEN could be quite forceful. When Ophelia challenged the police over access to Melinda, he sprang into action. He immediately phoned the Chief Executive of St. Pritchards, who expressed his surprise and regret that Ophelia had delivered such an edict. He assured Owen that the police could see Melinda whenever they wished, and that he would personally speak to the good doctor and let her know such decisions would be made by him, not her. A triumph for Owen, a sense of relief for Ann, and a bitter loss for Ophelia, who did not take defeat well. Or without taking some measure of revenge.

The Chief Executive also informed Owen that the hospital would be releasing Melinda in the next day or two. It had been determined she could heal just as well at home as she could at the hospital. The fact that she didn't have a home didn't seem to matter. According to hospital records Melinda's last address was Terry's flat which meant, officially, she had a place to stay and the hospital was covered from a legal standpoint. Owen turned to Ann, who remembered Mack's offer of a job after he bought the Black Knight recently, an offer which also included a room above the pub.

* * *

THE FIRST THING MELINDA NOTICED about the pub was the exterior, which had recently received a fresh coat of paint. The door and the trim were still red, but the color wasn't what Melinda remembered most. It was the door itself, the same door she had gone through so many times before when Terry sent her out on those so-called bounty hunts. He insisted she leave that way, passing every table on her way out, then again when she returned, enduring every remark, every taunt on her way to Terry's table.

"Looks a bit different, doesn't it?" Ann said. Nudged back to reality, Melinda now saw the pub as just another collection of bricks and wood and glass. She saw people going in and people coming out. None of them seemed afraid. She looked at Ann, who smiled reassuringly. "Come on. Let's go see Mack."

Melinda followed Ann inside and stopped in the doorway. The place was so clean now. In fact, it bore little resemblance to the way she remembered it. A crackling sound drew her attention to her left, to the fireplace in the corner. There was an occasional popping sound as the fire hit a piece of green wood, which pulled Melinda deeper into its spellbinding display. But this time, she was able to bring herself back. She took a look around and realized it wasn't Terry's pub anymore.

"Right. I'll show you to your room. That it, then?" Without waiting for an answer Mack took the paper bag containing Melinda's meager belongings and started up the stairs. Melinda followed, as did Mrs. Wanda Hudson, the social worker assigned to her case, while Ann stayed at the bar. She belonged to them now, to Mack and Mrs. Hudson. Ann didn't plan on abandoning Melinda. She had never done that with any of the victims she had worked with and she didn't plan on starting now. But police work was police work and social work was social work. And Ann was confident that, in time, Melinda would learn to trust Mack and Mrs. Hudson. But it was no use. The way Melinda was behaving, the fear she was conveying, Ann couldn't ignore that it was more than just apprehension over moving into yet another strange place. Ann drew on her own experience along with what she knew of Melinda and that was enough to give her an insight into what was going on inside of Melinda at the moment, and it was more than Mack and Mrs. Hudson could possibly imagine.

Mack took a set of keys out of his pocket and unlocked the door to Melinda's room. "Bedroom and bath are back there," he pointed to the right. "There's a place to heat the kettle over there. Here," Mack placed the key in Melinda's hand. "Now if you ladies will excuse me…" With that, he left. Melinda stood there and took it all in. She had spent so much time alone, in the hospital, at Terry's flat and Karl's house before that. But, unlike those places, this one was hers. There would be no one locking her in every day, no guards outside her door. She was free to come and go as she pleased. There was no reason for her stomach to be tying itself into knots, or for her hands to be trembling. This was her home. Mack, Ann, Mrs. Hudson all said it was. It just didn't feel that way.

"Well? What do you think? Don't you just love it?" Mrs. Hudson beamed.

"Yes," Melinda said softly.

"Right. Shall we go downstairs and see Mack? I'm sure he'll want to explain your duties to you." Mrs. Hudson left but Melinda was stopped by a wave of dizziness. It soon passed and she followed Mrs. Hudson down the stairs.

"Melinda just wanted to tell you how pleased she is with her room," Mrs. Hudson bubbled to Mack. "And how grateful she is to you for giving her this opportunity."

With the conversation stalled there, Ann got up and said, "Right. Well, I have some things to attend to."

"I'm off, too," Mrs. Hudson said. "Seems everything is under control at this end so I'll leave you two to get reacquainted." She handed Melinda her card and said, "I'll be stopping in from time to time but if anything does arise, anything whatsoever, you can ring me at this number. Oh, except…" She took the card back and with her teeth pulled the cap off the pen she had just taken from her purse, then proceeded to scratch things out and write things in. "…Except Mondays. On Tuesdays and Thursdays I'm only available in the morning. Friday is half a day as well and weekends, well, weekends are a complete nightmare as far as pinning me down to an exact time. There you are." She smiled as she handed the barely legible card back to Melinda. "Anything at all. Don't feel that because something is small, it isn't important."

CHAPTER 10

JASPER WESLEIGH COULD BARELY SEE his possessions let alone pick them up. He didn't have many, at least not the kind most people would want to keep. He gathered them up as best he could, then walked out of the police station after serving his sentence for drunk and disorderly conduct. Jasper, who smelled like a distillery and wore a mismatch of all the old clothes he had collected over the years, made his first stop the local liquor store. He wasn't picky. He'd drink anything as long as it contained alcohol. But he had no money so, for the second time today, he was shown the door. After exchanging a few choice words with the proprietor of the place where all the money he scrounged through panhandling, selling junk and lifting the occasional wallet ended up, Jasper staggered down the street and headed for the one person he could always count on for a handout: Mitchell Stropman.

This wasn't a particularly good day for Stropman. Informed by what passed for his accountant that his business wasn't turning the kind of profit he expected, he flew into a rage and personally roughed up two of his prostitutes. Then one of the derelicts who occupied space in his shrine to the psychedelic era had died. Such an occurrence wasn't unusual, but Stropman made that discovery seconds after he lowered himself into his hot tub along with a handful of whores he had personally selected to soak with him. So, when Jasper showed up at his door a short time later, Stropman was in no mood to be charitable. But Jasper didn't know any of that and probably wouldn't have understood if someone had explained it to him.

"What do *you* want?" Stropman growled while he waited for his Jacuzzi to be drained, disinfected and refilled.

"I got this pain, me. It's me teeth. I need somethin' for the pain, to make it go away," Jasper said.

"Yeah? What do you want me to do about it?"

"Eh? It's me tooth. It's got a hole. See?" Jasper pulled his upper lip back with his thumb. "Police knocked me gold tooth out when they nicked me this last time."

"Gold tooth? You pawned that years ago, for a fifth of cheap whiskey. Go on, get lost!"

"What, so, ya want me to go then? Yeah. Alright. But, how's about a couple a quid, so I can get somethin' for me teeth? For the pain?"

"A couple of quid? It's gettin' so every rummy in town thinks this is the bloody Salvation Army. Someone get him out of here!" One of the lost souls grabbed Jasper by the arm and roughly escorted him to the door.

"Roschine wouldn't treat me like this! Said he'd give me money soon as he got out!"

"Wait, what did he say? Bring him back here!" Stropman's henchman dragged Jasper back to his throne. "When he got out of where?"

"Jail. Told me he would when he got out of jail."

"And when was that?"

"Today—Yester—Erm, two days, I think it were. They said I were drunk and…drunk and disorganized. But that weren't true. I was only tryin' to get rid of the pain, here, in me tooth—"

"Roschine's in jail?"

"Was when I left. Ya gonna gimme some money now?"

"Oi! Old man! What's he doin' in jail?!"

"Jail?"

"Roschine, you idiot! What's he in jail for?" Stropman screamed, his entire head a bright crimson.

"Don't know. Gonna murder someone. Heard him talkin' to some blokes."

"What blokes?"

"Don't know. I was tryin' to sleep because of the pain. It's me teeth, ya see, this one in back—"

"Who is it he's plannin' on murderin'?" Stropman said through clenched teeth.

"Who?"

"Roschine!" Stropman exploded. "Who is it he's going to murder?!"

"Erm..." Stropman grabbed Jasper by the collar of his flimsy wool jacket.

"How'd ya like me to take care of those teeth of yours all in one go? Now. Who is Roschine going to kill?!"

"I—I don't know the name!" Jasper replied. "He told them other blokes to finish what they'd started! That's all I know about it!" Another sharp tug on Jasper's collar had a remarkable effect on his memory. "Someone—it were someone they get their drugs from! Yeah! Yeah, that's it!"

Stropman and Roschine were both driven by ego and an unending thirst for power, and those ambitions left open the possibility that Stropman was Roschine's intended victim. It didn't matter that Stropman had been told this by someone who was too preoccupied with his teeth and too dependent on cheap alcohol to be an unimpeachable witness, but Stropman wasn't a deep, analytical thinker. On the contrary, he tended to react first and think later. And the only way he knew to respond to a threat of violence was with a similar reply.

This was also becoming a trying day for Pablo. In the last half hour he counted twenty-seven people who had passed by the corner he had rooted himself to and none of them were Juan. Juan had been delayed because he was practicing with the gun Roschine's men left for them in the alley behind Shepard's Road. Roschine wanted to make it as easy as possible for his two newest hitmen to find it and it stood to reason that even they might have a chance if it was in a place where they spent most of their waking hours.

Juan had only fired a gun once before, but that gun wasn't nearly as impressive as the Glock 36 he now held in his hand. He tucked it in his waistband and practiced his fast draw. Roschine only provided one six-round clip so there were few extras to play with. Juan headed for a field and carried out make-believe gun battles against various objects. He pretended to shoot at trees, planes, tin cans and some children who were riding their bikes off in the distance, and he could feel himself becoming more comfortable with it. With the awesome power of just holding it. He loaded the magazine into the handle and smiled. He was ready.

"Where the hell ya been? I've been stood here nearly an hour," Pablo said after Juan finally arrived.

"Had to wait 'til me old man left so I could nick this." Juan pulled a portable CD player from under his shirt.

"Shit, your old man's gonna kill ya when he finds out it's gone missing."

"Don't care. I ain't goin' back there. I tried goin' back last night to get me jacket. Look what the bastard did to me." Juan lifted his shirt to reveal purple and black bruises along his all along his torso.

"Where ya gonna go then?" Pablo asked.

"Don't know."

"You ain't gonna do a runner, are ya? You ain't gonna leave me here to face charges on me own?"

"There won't be any charges, not after we kill her." Pablo jammed his fists in his pockets, shrugged his shoulders and stared at the ground. "We *are* gonna kill her, ain't we?"

"I can't," Pablo shook his head, his face twisted apologetically. "I want this to be over, but I can't kill someone."

"But if we don't, we'll go to prison. I don't want to go to prison." Juan took a pack of cigarettes from his shirt pocket and tapped it lightly on the back of his hand. "She don't know we raped her. How could she? Her eyes was shut. And even if she says it were us, it's her word against ours. If they'd found somethin', they'd've nicked us by now."

"Then we *did* do it?"

"Yeah. Course we did."

"We were there, I remember that much. But I don't remember that part."

A sly smile came across Juan's face. "I do. Every satisfyin' moment."

"Yeah?"

"Yeah. Ya want details?"

"Yeah. I want details." Juan dropped, picked up, then cooly lit a cigarette. "Well?"

Juan blew out a long stream of smoke, then said, "I've decided to keep them happy memories to meself."

Pablo rolled his eyes. "Shit, doesn't matter whether we did or didn't. Only matters what she tells 'em. And she'll tell 'em, I know she will. But I'm no killer, me. We should just do the time we got comin' and get it over with. It's our first offense. We might only get probation, maybe community service."

"For rape? Not bloody likely! We'd spend years in prison, maybe rest of our lives. I'm only twenty…three. I ain't gonna spend me best years locked away in some fuckin' prison." Juan took another drag, then said, "We gotta do it. If she's dead, they'll have nothin' to arrest us for. We won't spend a day in jail."

Pablo spun on his heel and took a swing at a sign advertising the day's specials in front of the bakery behind him. "Christ! She's all ya talked about when she was in that cage! Now all ya want to do is kill her! Why?"

"For the dope," Juan said.

"What dope?"

"Roschine's dope."

"He gave you dope?"

"No. But once I'm in his gang he will."

"He ain't gonna give you dope. Why would he?"

"'Cause of this favor I'm doin' him. And a great big favor it is, too."

"You think someone like Roschine is gonna let you be in his gang? You?"

"Yeah. Me. I reckon he could use someone like me, someone willin' to kill for him. Just so long as he pays me a fair price. A fair price in dope, that is."

"We don't need his dope. We got Danny's checks. His old man's crawlin' in it. He don't know Danny's been nicked."

"But I won't need Danny's money, will I? I hear Roschine takes good care of his lads."

"That's what you want then, to be one of Roschine's mindless zombies?"

"They was that way from the start." Juan pointed to his head. "I'm startin' off with a lot more up here than them."

"Yeah, you're a bloody genius, you are." Pablo shook his head again. "You won't last. You won't want to do that rest of your life, killin' people, spendin' all your time with them tossers."

"Won't I? What then? I can't go home. I can't get a job, what with me disability and all. Anyway, I've always fancied workin' for someone like Roschine. I think I'd quite enjoy it. Might even be good at it. Might just end up bein' somebody. What about you?"

Pablo ran his hand over the back of his neck. "I can't. I can't kill someone. Not someone I know."

"Ya don't know her. Just another bird, ain't she? Could've been anyone in that cage. Anyway, it was just a bit of fun. Never did say a word, did she? But she will now. She'll tell 'em what we did."

"Yes, but what exactly did we do? Why can't I remember?"

"It were all that cheap wine. Never seen ya drink so much. You wasn't nervous, were ya?"

"Nerv—? Shit, you know me with the lasses. Why would she be any different?" Pablo wiped his face with his hands, then said, "I can't."

Juan snuffed out his cigarette against the building. "Then I'll do it meself."

IT HAD ONLY BEEN THREE days, but it was the end of the pay period and at the conclusion of her shift Mack presented Melinda with her first paycheck. She stared blankly at the slip of paper until Mack took it from her.

"Here, I'll cash that for you." He took some money from the till and put it in Melinda's hand. "Now go and buy yourself somethin' nice. Anything ya want. And don't come back 'til you've got it all spent." Melinda changed clothes, then went out alone into the streets for the first time since Terry sent her out that fateful night.

In her entire life, Melinda had never gone shopping. Not for clothes, not for food, not for anything. Now, on a cool, clear autumn evening, she was taking in the sights and sounds of the high street, of the lights and activities visible through shop windows, of the people who strolled from shop to shop or continued on their way to some other destination. Who treated this just like any other day. One thing Melinda had yet to learn, however, was that, while she could see more of the world from here so, too, could the world see more of her. Caught up in the atmosphere, she didn't notice the man who was watching her from across the street. He followed her step for step, making sure he didn't lose sight of her.

"Oi! Melinda!" Melinda turned to see Pablo, who had crossed the street and was only a few steps away. His right hand firmly gripping the vial and syringe in his pocket, Pablo grabbed her by her arm and rushed her between buildings.

"There's not much time, so listen carefully! Someone's gonna kill you! You hear me? Someone's gonna kill you, and I can't stop it! I tried, but I can't! Here." He pressed the vial and syringe in her hand and wrapped his hands tightly around hers. "Fill it to the top, put the needle in your arm, then press this part down 'til it empties." She stared wide-eyed at him unable to speak, unable to look away.

"It's better this way. You won't feel anything. You'll just go to sleep." He took her by both arms. "Look, I've been shot before. The bullet, it went in here...," he pointed to the left side of his chest, "...ricocheted off me ribs, then stopped here," he pointed to his lower back near his right kidney. "Maybe you'll get lucky and it'll kill you straight away, but maybe it won't. You might bleed to death before someone finds you. I don't want you to die that way." A small group of people walked by and Pablo lost himself in the darkness down the passageway.

Her evening's shopping cut short, Melinda returned to the Black Knight, the vial and syringe still in her hand, and went straight for the stairs.

"Melinda. How was shoppin'?" said Mack, who was behind the bar adding up a customer's tab.

"Fine," Melinda said, stopping dead in her tracks, her eyes avoiding his.

"See some nice things, did ya?"

"Yes."

"Didn't buy anything then?"

"No." Mack became distracted by another customer and Melinda hurried up the stairs. She didn't bother turning on the lights. She sat on her bed, her hand resting on her lap, then slowly opened her fingers and looked at the vial and syringe. Pablo had given her two choices. It was now up to her to decide how her life would end.

While Melinda contemplated her future, Ann sat at her desk diagramming a kind of family tree of suspects. She hoped that by writing it out it would somehow reveal something that had so far eluded her discovery. But she had barely gotten started when she was interrupted by the last person she expected to see: Karl Wagner.

"Dr. Wagner. To what do I owe the...pleasure?" Ann said as she discretely hid the diagram from his view by sliding it under other papers on her desk.

"I'm here for Melinda. I've come to take her home. Since we spoke I've been looking into what's happened to her since she left. I had no idea what she had been subjected to."

"And what exactly is that?"

"Her being kidnapped. Surely Terry had something to do with that?"

"What? Are you saying it's possible for someone to have been involved in not one but two kidnappings? And both times involving the same victim?"

"That's not what I meant. I know the type of person Terry was. I have no doubt he was mistreating her."

"Dr. Wagner," Ann said wearily, "if you know something it would be in your best interest to tell me."

"Best interest? All I know is, she needs to come home. She needs to be where she'll feel safe again so everything will be like it used to be."

"How did it used to be?"

"What?"

"I'm afraid that's not possible."

"What do you mean, not possible? She's my daughter. That's her home. It's where she belongs."

"First of all, Melinda is not your daughter. Remember how she came to be with you, or have you conveniently forgotten?"

"But that was so long ago. She doesn't know anything about it. She doesn't know who her parents are. I'm the only father she's ever known."

"She doesn't know who her parents are because you took her from them."

"I told you, they didn't want her."

"That's your story. Perhaps it's true her father didn't want her, but what about her mother? You said she was mentally ill. Incapable of looking after a child. How do you know Scott was telling you the truth? Are we to take the word of a man who would hire someone to kill his own child? Perhaps if you had used some of that intelligence you profess to have and looked into Claire's mental state before taking her child from her you might have found she wasn't ill at all. Perhaps she was just suffering from depression following the alleged death of her child, or something else that was treatable."

"No! Scott wouldn't have lied to me about that!" Karl took the handkerchief from the breast pocket of his brown tweed coat and dabbed the perspiration from his forehead. "Please. Let me see her. Let me take her home."

"I find it odd, doctor, that you haven't mentioned anything about asking her first."

"Of course I intend to ask her, but that will be merely a formality. She'll want to come home with me, and once she's there, it will put everything right again."

"There wouldn't be a need to put things right if you hadn't put them wrong in the first place," Ann said. "I don't care if it was Scott who started this, it was you who had the power to stop it. Instead, for the better part of fifteen years you held that girl prisoner in that house of yours. Locking her away and indoctrinating her in your own unique view of the world was hardly in her best interests."

"I told you, I had no choice! What was I to do? Was I supposed to have done nothing, then waited until I read in the newspapers that a baby had been found murdered? I wouldn't have been able to live with myself."

"At the time you may have thought what you were doing was right, but you did have other options. Why didn't you go to the police when Scott first approached you? He would have been arrested and Melinda would have been taken from him and perhaps adopted by someone who did want her."

"*I* wanted her. I took care of her the best I knew how. I went out of my way to make sure she had everything. I doubt there was another child her age who was better provided for. She always had food, clothes, a warm bed. In spite of what you think, I gave her a good education.

She knows more about the relevant parts of the world than any child her age. Maybe I was wrong to have helped Scott instead of going to the police, but I do care about her. I saved her life."

"Dr. Wagner," Ann rubbed her eyes against her impending headache, "I can only point to the way she is now. You are not solely responsible, but you can take a great deal of the blame. She's never had much of a life, you can at least admit that much. You only have to see her to realize that." Ann had done exactly what she wanted to avoid, gotten into an argument with someone who tried to brazenly justify his own actions by twisting and turning them into misshapen representations of the truth. "You have confessed to the unlawful detention of a child. No matter what good you may have done in the ensuing years – and after spending time with Melinda I can tell that you and your cohorts have done little of that – the fact remains you committed a crime. No amount of convoluted logic is going to dispel that. You took part in her abduction, then gave her to someone you knew was a criminal. What did you think he would do? Give her a proper home? Or did you think that maybe, just maybe, he would use her for his own personal gain?"

"I suppose, somewhere in the back of my mind, I knew." Karl's lips trembled. "Of course I knew. That's why I offered him two-thousand pounds if he would let her stay with me. He took the money and said he wouldn't sell her, but he still intended to take possession of her per our agreement. I agreed, thinking he would be involved in something else by then. I was right. By that time, he had gotten into pimping. I think that's why he came for her when she was fifteen. He was waiting until she was ready." Just then Owen walked up with two constables in tow.

"Karl Wagner?"

"Yes?" Karl said, adjusting his glasses so he could get a better look.

"You are under arrest for suspicion of child abduction. If you'll come along with the constables here—"

"What?! That was twenty years ago!"

"Yes, yes. Now if you'll just come along quietly…" Karl straightened into a dignified posture, and the PCs led him away. "Another loose end all nicely sewn up, eh, Ann?" Owen gloated. Ann, however, was too tired to care that Karl was being arrested too many years after it really mattered. Alone again in her office, she was just starting to get some work done when the phone rang. It was Mack, and he was frantic.

"It's Melinda! She's taken ill!"

"How do you mean?" Ann asked.

"She didn't come down today so I went upstairs and knocked on her door. There was no answer so I used my key. I found her still in bed. I asked what was wrong but she didn't say."

"That sort of behavior isn't unusual for Melinda, is it?"

"That's what I thought at first, but somethin's not right! What should I do? Should I get a doctor?"

"No. I'll be right there."

While the doctors at St. Pritchard examined Melinda, Ann bided her time by strolling the halls and reading posters warning against the spread of almost every conceivable disease known to man. She particularly liked the art work on one of the posters, a joint effort of The Post Nasal Drip Society and the Deviated Septum Association, which featured the profile of an enormous nose with scaffolding inside and men in overalls hammering and sawing away. The bottom of the poster was torn so the point of all of that activity wasn't clear. Bored, Ann sat down and waited a further twenty minutes before a doctor finally emerged from the examination room.

"How is she?" Ann asked as she caught up and he slowed down.

"Physically, she's right as rain. Her temperature and blood pressure are normal. Slight headache and nausea, but we've given her something for that."

"Then what's wrong with her?"

"Well, for one, she's suffering from exhaustion. But then, aren't we all. She also seems quite distressed about something. When I asked what was troubling her, she didn't answer. You're the one who brought her in?"

"Yes."

"When did you start noticing a change in her normal behavior?"

"Doctor, this *is* her normal behavior."

CHAPTER 11

MELINDA DIDN'T SEEM TO CARE one way or another that she was back in the hospital. But Ophelia cared. She sat at her desk and perused the list of newly admitted patients this morning to see if anyone of importance had been admitted. Nothing stood out until she read the name at the bottom.

To those who knew Ophelia it was common knowledge that winning was everything to her, especially in her chosen field. It was no secret that she was driven, and that one of her aspirations was for her name to one day become synonymous with mental health. Melinda had challenged her authority from the very first day. That was three weeks ago. Traumatized or not, never before had a patient held out so long. Sooner or later, Ophelia made them talk, and it didn't matter how much time or how many drugs it took. She had a reputation to maintain, locally, nationally, even internationally. In the early part of her career she would use all of the standard, established methods to treat her patients, but that ended after a busman's holiday in Africa. It was there that she discovered the curative power of drugs from a doctor who had lost his license years earlier and had set up shop in the darkest part of a continent where medical boards and other disciplinary bodies could no longer reach him. Or find him.

Upon learning that Melinda had returned Ophelia immediately ordered her old room vacated, which meant displacing a lifelong agoraphobic who had finally been coaxed out of her house and into the only available bed in the psychiatric ward. Ophelia hovered over Melinda like a predator waiting to pounce on her helpless prey.

"Just set it down there, nurse." Drowsy from the drugs administered as routine by Ophelia's staff, Melinda's eyes were closed, so she didn't see Ophelia enter, or that the 'it' she asked the nurse to set on the table next to her bed was a metal tray.

"Thank you, nurse. That will be all." Ophelia waited until the nurse left, then leaned over Melinda, the smell of lavender soap and spearmint permeating the air.

"Well, my dear," Ophelia said in an ominous tone. "We've had our fun these past few weeks, haven't we? But we're going to do things my way now." She sat on the edge of the bed, then took Melinda's left arm and pinned it between her right arm and her side. She rolled Melinda's sleeve up and tied a piece of rubber tubing around her upper right arm until the veins bulged. Then she stopped and reflected. "If you only knew what a privilege it is to have me as your doctor. I've won awards. Been brought in for consultation by the finest doctors in the world. Treated like royalty both here and abroad. Understand, I am trying to help you but you are pushing me beyond my limits. I have taken it upon myself to see to your case personally and I do not intend to have my reputation tarnished by someone who, if not for the police, would presently be playing her little games in the charity ward of a lesser hospital." Melinda tried to pull away but she was too weak.

"The trouble with you, my dear, is you've been pampered too long," Ophelia said as she yanked the tubing even tighter. "The police have treated you like someone special and now you're convinced that you are. It's time you learned to show the proper respect. I'll show you what happens to patients who think they can make a fool of me." She leaned closer and said in Melinda's ear, "Think about it, my dear. What do you suppose will happen to you should you go on refusing to cooperate? Don't you see that your fate is in my hands? I can keep you here forever, or I can throw you out in the street. You'll be on your own then. And if you're thinking of going back to the pub, do you really think they'll take you back once they learn why you're here? Why you're *really* here? How long do you think you'll be able to manage once people discover you've been confined to a mental ward? No one will care about you. No one will help you. Certainly not the police. Once they find out you know nothing about the murder, they'll have no more use for you. You must put all your trust in me. Right now, I am your only hope." Ophelia turned at the waist, took something from the tray and held it up to the light. Then she turned back, her hand hidden from view, and again mused,

"No one knows of my ultimate ambitions, not even my own staff. When they released you, I thought I'd missed my chance. I thought you'd become the first patient I couldn't cure. And with the police involved, there would be official documentation, documentation that would be difficult to refute. There would be doubts, suspicions, my own people whispering behind my back. Surely you can see why I could never allow that to happen." Ophelia rubbed an alcohol-drenched cotton ball over the inside of Melinda's elbow. "Now here you are, as if someone has given me another chance. And I assure you, it is a chance I shall not let slip from my grasp a second time." Ophelia placed the cotton ball on the tray, then revealed what she held in her hand: A syringe.

"Now, when I instruct you, you are to count backward from one hundred." Melinda struggled in vain as Ophelia brought the needle ever closer until it punctured her skin, then pressed the top down until the liquid inside disappeared, just like Pablo said.

"Count. Do you hear me? Count!" Ophelia said through gritted teeth. Melinda tried to keep her eyes open, but the poison was doing its job. Her heart wasn't beating as fast as it was a moment ago, but she knew she was still afraid. She just couldn't feel the fear.

"You cannot win," Ophelia said. "Now I am going to ask you some questions and you will answer them." Melinda turned her head away. "You cannot resist me. The injection I gave you won't allow it, so you might as well cooperate. In time, you won't be able to do anything else. Now then, I want you to tell me what happened in the alley behind Shepard's Road the day Terry Royce was murdered." Melinda kept fighting the sodium pentothal. She knew if she didn't, Ophelia would have no reason to keep her alive.

"You may have fooled the police, but you don't fool me. I know you saw something in the alley that day. You saw who killed Terry Royce. You know who fired the fatal shot and I want to know who that person is. Then I can go directly to the Chief Constable and tell him I have learned in one afternoon what the police could not in nearly a month's time." Melinda started to fall asleep, but Ophelia jammed her thumbnail into the base of Melinda's.

"It would be a pity, my dear, if your heart suddenly stopped beating, or if you somehow cut yourself and bled to death before anyone could help you, now wouldn't it?" While her exterior conveyed a dream-like state, Melinda's mind was alert. She was convinced her time was short. Ophelia would see to that. She had to get away. If she didn't, Ann would find her lifeless body and wonder who ended her life. But how? She had only one connection to the outside world: The guard in the hallway. If she could get to him, then he would be able to tell Ann how she died. Mustering all of her remaining strength, Melinda tried to sit up.

"See here! Just what do you think you're doing?!" Ophelia jumped up and took a step back just as Melinda's feet hit the floor. She fell forward, pushing Ophelia into the table and knocking it to the ground. Melinda tumbled over her, landing just past her, and in desperation crawled toward the door, glass digging into her palms. She used the end of the bed to pull herself up but before she could take a step, Ophelia grabbed her ankle and she fell hard just as PC Weston burst into the room.

"Blimey!" he said. "What's happened here?! Doctor?"

"Nothing, constable, nothing at all," Ophelia said with a nervous laugh. "I'm afraid she's had a bit of an accident, trying to get to the loo all on her own. Silly girl. Not quite ready, I'm afraid." PC Weston lifted Melinda onto the bed and she fell back, the heat of Ophelia's stare inescapable as the constable helped the doctor to her feet.

"Do you need help? Should I fetch someone?" PC Weston asked Ophelia.

"That won't be necessary, young man. I assure you I have everything under control."

"Yes, ma'am, but I'm to report if somethin' out of the ordinary occurs."

"Yes, yes, of course you are. Of course you—Tell you what! Why don't you stay here 'til the nurse arrives. I shall be back shortly. I have, erm, another patient to attend to. I'll have someone come round and see to this mess." Melinda stirred and tried to speak. While PC Weston saw to her, Ophelia picked up the bottle and syringe and slipped them into the pocket of her coat. Melinda saw it, but PC Weston did not.

"No, don't let—!"

"There, there, miss," PC Weston gently restrained Melinda. "Doctor'll be right back. Said so herself. Just lie back and rest for a bit."

"So even Bravo can't enlighten us as to who killed Royce?" Owen said to Ann from the other side of his desk.

"No. All he said is Stropman and Roschine were shooting at each other and that their guns were likely forty-fives. The bullets found in Terry were thirty-eights and nine millimeter."

"How many times was he shot?" Owen sat back and surveyed the ceiling.

Ann read from the ME's report. "Eight. Once in the left arm, twice in the right shoulder, twice in the back, once in the chin, once in the abdomen and once in the right knee."

"Does it say which one killed him?"

"Abdomen. From the angle they entered his body, most of the other bullets hit him after he was already on the ground. It also says they found shotgun pellets in his stomach."

Owen's head swiveled toward her. "Shotgun pellets? Are any of the suspects known to have a shotgun?"

"Bravo didn't mention one."

"Right. So you have Roschine at one end of the alley shooting at Royce and Stropman. You have Stropman at the other end firing from behind a skip, then again as he's running across the alley." He paused, then started for the door. "Let's go. And bring the file."

On his way out of the station Owen recruited two Detective Sergeants, two PCs and a WPC to join him and Ann in the alley behind Shepard's Road. He positioned WPC Jenkins and DS Williams at one end of the alley to play the parts of Melinda and Roschine. Then he sent DS Bender to the other end and had him crouch behind a skip just as Stropman had done that day. PC Gibson, who stood six-foot-four and weighed fifteen stone, played the role of Terry and was positioned near the tatoo parlor. PC Phillips, a wiry young rookie, climbed onto the fire escape near the old Woolworths, the same escape where Danny had been lying in wait. Once Owen had everyone in place, he guided them through the events of that day using witnesses' accounts as his script.

"Right. Melinda enters the alley..." He nodded at WPC Jenkins, who walked forward until Owen held up his hand. She stopped even with the fire escape, within striking distance of a four foot length of board wielded by an unsteady and unstable attacker.

"Then Roschine comes along..." DS Williams followed the same path WPC Jenkins had just taken and was directed to stop a few paces behind her. Owen moved closer to get a better perspective of where they stood in relation to each other and to PC Phillips overhead.

"Danny takes a swing at Melinda and falls..." He motioned to PC Phillips, who lowered himself from his perch and crouched to simulate Danny's fall following his apparent failed attempt to strike Melinda.

"Terry enters from down there..." Owen pointed and, on cue, PC Gibson came around the corner of the tattoo parlor until Owen again held up his hand. Then he walked to PC Gibson and stood next to him to get a better idea of Terry's usefulness as a target.

"Stropman fires at Roschine, and Roschine fires back..." His limp even more pronounced, Owen gestured for DS Bender – aka Stropman – to go across the alley. Owen was stumped. Based on the ME's report, he already knew the possibility of a ricochet had been ruled out since the bullet that had been removed from Terry's stomach indicated it hadn't hit anything before settling there.

"Ann, do we know if Bravo owns a gun?" Owen asked as he walked toward her.

"No. But he doesn't need to, not with all those bodyguards."

"What sort of guns did you say Stropman and Roschine were firing?"

"Forty-fives, according to Bravo."

"But he doesn't know for certain, does he? Most people don't know a starter's pistol from a magnum."

"Bravo's had some experience with weapons, sir. He's army."

"Yes, well, he's not army anymore, is he? Several years removed, in fact," Owen grumbled. "He could've been mistaken. And just why is it they're allowed to roam the streets carrying guns? This isn't America."

"It's only because we've never been able to catch them with their guns. They're too clever for that."

"Yes, yes. That's a subject best left for another time." Owen then dismissed the others while he and Ann stayed to make sure they hadn't missed anything. Owen walked halfway down the middle of the alley, down the damp gutter that ran its length, and said, "Well, I'm fresh out of ideas." He started back and said, "You don't suppose Melinda didn't see either of them that day, that she only said she saw them here?"

"Why would she do that, sir?"

"To find a convenient place to lay the blame for Royce's death. I'm still not convinced she didn't have something to do with it," Owen said, still refusing to give up on his pet theory. "Who knows what went on during those years she spent with him. And I'll wager more went on in Cumbria than Doctor Wagner is letting on. Perhaps she decided to take matters into her own hands and tried to rid herself of everyone who tormented her."

"Then why is Karl still alive?"

"I don't know. Maybe she just hasn't gotten to him yet."

"I don't think Melinda killed him, sir."

"Neither do I." Owen scratched the back of his head and sighed. "Which of them do you think did it?"

"I don't know."

"Just between you and me, just so I'll have something to tell the grandchildren. Just give me a name. Just one name."

"Well, Terry sends Melinda after Stropman, then goes looking for her the next day when she doesn't return. Or, could be it was Stropman he went after, to carry out the contract, and gets himself killed instead."

"So you're saying Stropman did it?"

"No, only that he's a strong suspect. As is Roschine."

"If she never caught anyone before, what made him think this time would be any different? Why send her in the first place?"

"I don't know, sir. Some sadistic pleasure, I should think, watching her come back all battered and bloody."

"Well, if that was his game, I for one am glad we no longer have to deal with the likes of him." While he spoke, Ann started down the alley. It made sense when Bravo gave his version of what took place that day, but now that she was here, something just didn't feel right. She stopped at the corner of the tattoo parlor and gazed up at the bricks.

"Bravo said Terry came here to make sure Stropman and Roschine didn't take Melinda, right?"

"Right," Owen replied.

"And Mack said Terry went looking for Stropman when he realized Melinda hadn't killed him, hadn't fulfilled the contract Roschine had taken out with Terry."

"Your point being?"

"Terry comes into the alley from here..." Ann started toward the street. It was mid-afternoon, but the alley was already filled with shadows from the adjacent buildings. It was even darker between the buildings, which absorbed light like a black hole. Ann shined her torch on the ground along the side of the building and saw faint blood smears. She looked higher up on the wall. There was blood there as well.

"Sir! Here!"

"What is it?" Owen joined her and looked closely at where she was shining the light. "Well, I'll be!"

Ann continued down the building. There were more blood stains, darker and larger the closer she came to the street, starting approximately four feet up the wall and ending in drip marks frozen in place, clinging to the rough bricks at various intervals. Two feet from the front of the building the blood was smeared in a wide pattern, the kind someone would make if they had used their arms for balance. From that point to the pavement, there was no blood.

"Sir, what does the ME's report say about the gunshot wound to the abdomen?" Ann asked Owen, who was still gaping in amazement at the blood on the wall.

"What? Oh..." Owen read from the report clutched in his hand. "The bullet entered the abdomen from in front...no exit wound..."

"Any powder burns on the skin or clothes around the wound?"

"Yes. Yes, there were." Owen again gazed at the wall. "What are you getting at, Ann? What does this mean?"

"That Terry was dead before he ever reached the alley."

Owen's head turned sharply. "Before?"

"I think he was killed out there, in the street. And by someone he knew."

"By who? And why?"

"According to the ME's report, the bullet to the abdomen was a straight shot fired from fairly close range." Ann again shined her torch on the wall where the blood started. "Terry was probably shot just as he reached the passageway. To get that close to someone who had as many enemies as Terry, he had to have known the shooter."

"Any witnesses who might have heard a gunshot before Stropman and Roschine began firing at one another?"

"No, but I don't expect anyone would find the sound of gunshots all that unusual in this part of town."

"So Terry's already been shot and he's bleeding heavily, as these marks tell us. Why didn't anyone find these before?"

"Probably because it's so dark. Terry was found in a pool of his own blood at the back of the building. They probably thought he'd been hit in the crossfire and died there."

"Damn shoddy police work," Owen muttered. "How did he manage to get all the way back there with a bullet in his belly?"

"His size, and his desire to stop those two from getting their hands on Melinda likely kept him going."

They were interrupted by a call on Ann's mobile.

"Ann! Where are you off to?"

"Hospital!" Ann said as she hurried to her car.

"Why? What's happened?"

"I don't know yet!"

"We've got a meeting with the prosecutor for four!"

When Ann arrived at the hospital she was met at the elevator by a very nervous PC Weston. He had been restraining Melinda under the assumption that someone would return to sedate her, but instead he had been asked by a nurse to help with a patient who had become violent. After being reassured that Melinda would be fine, PC Weston left. A short time later Melinda dressed as quickly as she could, then exited down a back stairway.

"How long ago did she leave?" Ann didn't stop on her way to Melinda's room, and PC Weston wisely followed.

"I don't know for certain. When I got back, she was gone."

"That wasn't your assignment, was it?"

"I was only—No, Inspector, it wasn't."

"When did she go missing?"

"When? Erm, twenty minutes ago. I called you straightaway, soon as I found out." Ann opened the door to Melinda's room and was met by the remnants of the confrontation between her and Ophelia.

"What the hell happened here? What's all this on the floor?"

"Well, erm, glass, mostly," PC Weston replied.

"I can see that. How did it get here?"

"How?"

"Constable, am I going to have to guess or are you going to tell me what happened here?"

"No, erm, right. One of the doctors – Dr. Stanton – and a nurse came in round an hour ago. Next thing I know, I hear a loud noise. I go runnin' in and see the doctor and that girl on the floor, broken glass, bottles, syringes, surgical instruments all over the place."

"Where are they now, the bottles and syringes?"

PC Weston looked around the floor. "I—I don't know."

"Where was the nurse during all this, the one that came in with the doctor?"

"She, erm, she left, before any of that took place."

"So it was just Dr. Stanton and Melinda in here? Weren't you at all curious as to why a psychiatrist would be bringing surgical instruments to see a patient? And why was Dr. Stanton here to begin with? Melinda isn't her patient."

"Well, erm, way I heard it was, she got called in by another doctor. A Dr. Posthelwaite."

"Why?—No," Ann raised her hand. "Don't bother. Just tell me what happened."

"Well, I was out there, in the hallway, at my post, when all of a sudden I hear all this commotion. I run inside and see her – Melinda – lyin' there, on the floor, near the bed. She's – Dr. Stanton – sat up against the wall, just there. I go to help her – Dr. Stanton – to her feet. I thought she'd see to the girl, but she runs off instead."

"Why didn't you ring me then?"

"They – the nurses – seemed to have things under control. I didn't want to disturb you if it wasn't necessary."

"Constable, next time, you are to disturb me."

"Yes, Inspector."

"You're certain no one else was in here with Melinda before you arrived?"

"No. Just her. And the doctor – Doctor—"

"Stanton?"

"Erm, right." Ann stood, hands on hips, and surveyed the room, but there was nothing more to discover than what was obvious: surgical instruments, broken glass, and a metal tray.

"You screwed up, constable, but I haven't the time to deal with that at the moment. Right now, I want you to haul your...self outside and start looking for her. And I want all of this collected and sent to the lab for identification."

Ann spent the next hour questioning hospital personnel who were involved in or witnessed what went on in Melinda's room. All that did was to reinforce her desire to speak to Dr. Stanton, who seemed to be conveniently out of the building at the moment. With the lingering possibility that the fallout from his failure to do his job might result in his dismissal, PC Weston had been lurking around the hospital hoping to find inspiration that would lead to Melinda.

"What are you still doing here?" Ann said wearily.

"I thought I might be of some help," he said as he again followed her down the hallway. He'd never know it, but Ann didn't blame him for Melinda's disappearance. She knew there was little he could have done to stop her.

"You're sure she didn't say anything? A name? A place?"

"Sorry, Inspector. I've been goin' over it in me head, but she never did say a word." With nothing left to do at the hospital, Ann and PC Weston started toward the elevator. When they walked by the waiting room a voice caught Ann's attention. She wandered toward the TV on a shelf high in the corner of the room and gazed at the screen in utter amazement. There in all her glory was Ophelia, on a live daytime chat show, which she had made her own. What was supposed to have been a five minute interview touting her new book had turned into The Ophelia Stanton Show where chaos reigned. To the host's dismay she had invited four unsuspecting members of the studio audience to join her on stage and was making unsolicited evaluations of their mental state, leaving them confused, shaken and outraged.

The show turned into a free-for-all and the host announced an unscheduled commercial break, which again had Ann doing a double take. It featured Ophelia hawking her own creation, the ProBar: Prozac in a low-fat chocolate bar in four delicious flavors: almond, caramel, peanut crunch and vinegar, the latter for those who were too depressed to care what they put in their mouths.

"Find out where this is being broadcast from, then go there and bring the good doctor to the station," Ann said to PC Weston.

"You want me to arrest her?"

"If necessary."

CHAPTER 12

THERE IS A TIME WHEN a person contemplating suicide either finds their way out of their hopelessness or gives in to their despair. To live or end the fight. Simply by reaching that point, living becomes less of an option. The appeal of death is a sense of peace, of relief. Of hope that the pain will finally end.

She still had the key, the one she had taken from the drawer where Terry routinely left the contents of his pockets each night. It was a daring move, taking something that was his. But it was *all* his. Melinda put the key in the lock and turned it. The door made a familiar creaking sound as it opened. It was a sound she knew all too well. It meant *he* was home. The room was dark, dusty and the air rancid with the smell of cigarettes and beer that had soaked so deeply into the furniture it was unlikely to ever come out. But to Melinda it was home, the place where she spent so many long, lonely days, forbidden to leave for months on end. She had been here once since Terry's death, with Ann. But now, here on her own, she didn't have to suppress the fears and anxieties that had been part of her life for so long. Resigned to the inevitability of it all, Melinda had been inexorably drawn to a place where she could meet them alone. Where terrifying thoughts seemed to fit comfortably. Where her memories were.

"INSPECTOR TREADWELL? IT'S MRS. HENDRICKSON. We spoke the other day about Mr. Royce and the goings on in his flat?"

"Yes. Of course. Mrs. Hendrickson...," said Ann, who had fallen asleep on her couch until the phone woke her. She checked her watch: Eight-thirty. P.M.

"I can't say for certain, but I think someone's in his flat."

"When? For how long?"

"I'm not—Oh, hang on." Ann yawned deeply as she heard Mrs. Hendrickson discipline one of her countless children. "…and I shan't hear anything more about it!" Then, into the phone, "As I was saying, Inspector, there's something odd going on in there. You said his flat has been empty for weeks?"

"Yes?"

"Well, when I was coming home after collecting my Lowell from piano lessons tonight, I thought I heard something."

"What did you hear?"

"Sounds."

"What sort of sounds?"

"Human sounds, they were. I couldn't quite hear, my Lowell was making such a fuss, but it was a sort of whimpering sound, as if someone were crying."

"Did you bother seeing if anyone was inside?"

"No, but I know I heard something. I thought about knocking but my Lowell had gone on ahead and was bothering his sister so I had to see to that. I was going to ring you earlier, but I had to wait for my husband to leave for work."

"Thank you, Mrs. Hendrickson." Ann made the half hour drive to Terry's flat in twenty minutes. She stood by the door and listened. Not a sound. Then she tried the door and discovered it was unlocked. She took a step inside and stood in total darkness with the exception of a few rays of moonlight filtering through holes in the drapes, illuminating wisps of dust that hung in the air and floated aimlessly on their way to nowhere. Ann was about to turn on a lamp when she heard a sound coming from behind the couch. Her eyes soon adjusted to the dark and she saw a figure slumped in the corner where the wall with the bookshelves and the half-wall met.

"Melinda?" Ann came closer and saw Melinda curled up facing the half-wall to her left. "Melinda, what are you doing here?" Ann crouched in front of her. "How did you get in?"

"I can't testify!" Melinda whispered, her eyes wide with panic.

"You don't have to think about that now."

Melinda's eyes met Ann's. "Are you going to kill me?"

"Kill you? Why would I kill you?" Ann said. "Melinda, why don't we go—"

"No, I have to—I haven't finished yet."

"Finished? Finished what?" While she wondered what this was all about Ann's head turned just a fraction, just enough to catch a glimpse of light reflecting off something on the table next to the couch. A bottle and syringe. Ann picked up the bottle and read the label. "Melinda, where did you get this?"

"I don't want to see him again!"

"Who?"

Melinda's eyes darted wildly around the room. "I can't go back there! I can't—!" she said, her arms wrapped tightly around her.

"Melinda, you said you hadn't finished yet," Ann said, then showed her the bottle. "Is this what you meant?"

Melinda looked at it, her eyes wet, her voice calm. "I have to. It won't hurt if I do it myself."

"Who told you that?"

"Hurts to get shot. Pablo doesn't want me to get hurt—"

"Pablo gave you this?" That would take care of him for the foreseeable future. But ever since she first stepped foot in this flat, Ann suspected something happened to Melinda. She had lived here for four years under mysterious circumstances. She had never been allowed out. Then there was Mrs. Hendrickson's account of what she had seen and heard. But if something horrible did happen to her here, why had Melinda come back? Ann didn't know it, but she had the answer clutched in her hand: Because this time, she had a way out.

"Melinda, just after you came here to live with Terry your neighbor across the hall thought she saw bruises on you. Do you remember how you got them?"

Melinda shivered. "I have to wait here until he comes back."

"Why?"

"I heard them…talking—"

"Who did you hear talking?"

Melinda buried her face in the wall. "He looked after me," she said softly. "He never let anyone hurt me."

"But someone did hurt you, didn't they?"

Melinda paused for a long moment. "I waited for him to come home, but I fell asleep. I heard voices in my dream. Then they left my dream."

"Where did they go after they left your dream?"

Melinda choked back tears. "My bedroom."

"How did they get in your bedroom? Did Terry let them in?"

"I closed my eyes and pretended I was asleep but Terry… I saw them. I saw Terry…" Tears began running down Melinda's face. Her nose dripped but she didn't bother to wipe it.

"Who else was with Terry?"

"They talk—kept talking…red eye…it won't stop—"

"Those men…What did they do while they were in your room?"

"They—He was standing over me…He had a cane and…red eye… it's watching me—"

"What does that mean, red eye?" Ann asked, but again received no answer. "Melinda, who were these men who hurt you?"

In an instant, all of the emotion drained out of Melinda and her face relaxed. "No one hurt me."

"What you just told me? Those men in your room?"

"No one came in my room."

"What about the one with red eyes?"

"What?"

"You said one of them had red eyes. Don't you remember?"

"No one came in my room. Nothing happened. Nothing."

"Why are you so upset then?"

"I'm not upset."

"Then why are you crying?" Caught between her harder and her more vulnerable sides, Melinda shut down. Ann saw the hollow look in Melinda's eyes and hoped her image of Terry had been changed forever. Would she finally allow herself to see Terry the way he really was, or would she funnel that reality through her own unique thought process and color him so favorably that it would alter her memories of him until he fit the image she desired? She had made him into such a perfect person with no human faults, perhaps necessitated to mask his equally unforgivable qualities. Even when he sent her on impossible missions, her devotion to him had been unwavering. She had shown a propensity for taking the truth and twisting it in such a way that had enabled her to survive some of the worst crimes imaginable. And Ann knew she could easily do it again.

Ann arranged to have Melinda readmitted to the hospital, this time under a false name on a different floor, and Owen had Dr. Horgaarth, a police psychiatrist, take over her case. Then Ann turned her attention to the man with a cane Melinda mentioned twice now. The first person that came to mind was Roschine. He was known to carry a black cane with a gold handle in the shape of a lion's head, not because he needed it but as a status symbol. It was part of his image, as was bragging about his accomplishments. The bigger the accomplishment, the more he bragged. Ann was counting on that as she had him brought to interview room one.

"Have a seat, Mr. Roschine." He complied, then lit the first of an unending chain of cigarettes.

"What is it now, love?" Ann sat opposite him. Owen entered the room and stood against the wall behind Ann.

"When I spoke to you before you told me you deal in imports. Would that include drugs?"

"Drugs? What's she on about?" he said to Owen, hoping to find an ally in another male.

"You also told me the only business you had with Terry Royce was the horses."

"That's right."

"You never had any discussions with him concerning other matters?"

"Look, we gonna go through all this again?"

"Again and again until you come to realize you're not as clever as you think you are. No, you're not very clever at all." Roschine's smile momentarily faded before reemerging in all its glory.

"This about the jennel again? I already told ya, I don't know nothin' about that."

"This isn't about the alley. Rest assured, we'll find out about that soon enough. No, we don't need that to put you away for a very long time." Owen came forward, his eyes burning with anger, and tossed a folder on the table. It kicked up a puff of air and slid to a halt in front of Roschine.

"What's that?"

"That, Rosco, is a list of all the crimes you have committed throughout the course of your miserable life," Owen said. "It's only a list, not a detailed account. For that, we'd need half our computers running non-stop for the next forty-eight hours to print it all out." Roschine smiled proudly while Owen returned to the wall.

"It may interest you to know you are facing some very serious charges," Ann said.

"Yeah? So what else is new?"

"What's new is, we've got enough evidence to make them stick this time." That was enough to diminish Roschine's smile. He looked back and forth between Ann and Owen, who stared back unwaveringly.

"Alright. Let's do a deal."

"What could you possibly offer that would lead to a lesser sentence, especially considering the nature of your crimes?"

Roschine wiped the perspiration from his brow. "Well why don't ya just charge me then? Ya haven't arrested me, so there must be somethin' ya want to know."

Owen again approached. He leaned his fists on the table and said, "Yes, there *is* something we want to know. The only problem, Rosco, is you're credibility. You've lied to us before and I have every reason to believe that you will lie to us again."

"Me? Lie? Ya got me all wrong. Go on. Ask me. I'll tell ya whatever it is ya want to know."

"Tell us about your interest in Melinda," Ann said while Owen again retreated.

"Melinda? I got no interest in her."

"What, none at all?"

"Not at first." His smile returned. "But once I saw her, I knew she could be an asset for my business."

"You're import business?"

"Erm, yeah. Imports."

"And here I thought you were going to be honest." Roschine lit another cigarette, striking a match across his stubble and grimacing over the nasty friction burn it caused. "Tell me, how did it feel, after Terry invited you to his flat, to see him and another man, perhaps Stropman, trying to do a deal for her?"

"You're havin' me on, aren't ya, love? Terry'd never do somethin' like that. Not if he wanted to go on livin'."

"Really?" Ann waited, but there was no indication from Roschine that he had heard his own words. "But surely, once Stropman learned you wanted Melinda he would have done anything to acquire her, if only so you couldn't." Roschine shifted in his chair. "Then you agree it is possible?"

"What, Stropman makin' an offer behind me back? Bastard would've loved tryin' somethin' like that."

"And that's why you wanted him dead. To eliminate the competition."

"I already told ya, I didn't want him dead. Not for that, any road," he muttered. The door opened just enough for a Constable to fit inside. He handed a note to Owen, then both left.

"Still, you knew he wanted Melinda. You expect me to believe you stood by and did nothing while Terry and Stropman were doing a deal for her?"

"Believe whatever ya like. Any way, I was the last person to talk to Terry after Stropman left without her."

"Mr. Roschine, I realize that in that demented brain of yours rape and other forms of sexual abuse are considered socially acceptable behavior, but I can assure you the law sees it differently. It may interest you to know that what you did is a crime, the kind that should see you behind bars hopefully for the rest of your life."

"Why? It was strictly a business arrangement between two consenting adults. Me and Terry."

"Last time. Did you rape Melinda?"

"Have I not already answered that?"

"Mr. Roschine you are, at best, a con-artist and a liar. You change your story as it suits you but I, for one, don't believe any of it. It isn't likely that you will ever see the light of day again from anywhere but the inside of a prison cell. But in the event you somehow do get out, or if any of those pathetic louts who make up that gang of yours goes near Melinda you will be sent back and this time, I'll see to it you never set foot outside again."

Roschine's smile fell apart in stages. He had run out of avenues of escape. "You said somethin' about a deal?"

"I'll speak to the prosecutor. But first I'll need you to sign a statement admitting your part in the rape."

Roschine smiled once more. "Sorry, love, but there was no rape."

"I'm getting tired of this—!" Roschine stopped Ann in mid-sentence by getting to his feet, undoing his trousers and dropping them to the floor. Then he stood, hands out to either side and let Ann see what should be there but wasn't. Too stunned to speak, Ann couldn't help but stare at what looked like a medical experiment gone horribly wrong.

"I should think any attempt to charge me with rape would be a waste of time, don't you?"

"How…How did it happen?"

"It's funny, this," said Roschine, who zipped up then casually sat back down. "You've been doin' this a long time, yeah? I reckon ya think ya know all there is to know about people like us. Well, when I started out, I didn't. Back then, I was workin' for Menchini. I watched how he ran his business. All he did was send hookers out and collect the money when they returned, rough 'em up a bit when it needed doin'. I thought, I can do that. So I went off on me own. But a few days later some of his lads jumped me. When I woke up, I was stuffed in a skip. And it was gone. Cut off. But I was lucky, me. Menchini wasn't the sort to hold a grudge, so he had his doctor stitch it back on. But it turned black so he took it off again."

"Then what—erm, what's the…that…thing?"

"This? That's the doc's idea, this. After he took it off, Menchini told me if I promised to behave meself, he'd put things right. That's the sort of bloke Menchini was. Could've left me a lass, but he had the doc bodge me a new one from other parts of me. Lookin' back on it, I did some things I shouldn't have done. Stole his money, his whores. Would've been well within his rights to finish me off. But I was young and he knew it was just a stupid mistake. Menchini could be quite cruel to his enemies, but he looked after those who were loyal to him even if they did stray from time to time. So he gave me another chance. He had the doc give back to me what they'd taken away."

"You call that looking after you?"

"He could've let me bleed to death, couldn't he? If it'd been anyone else, they'd have been dead. And Menchini's lads, they never killed anyone fast. But he spared me that. He let me live."

Ann cleared her throat and said, "Is it—Does it…work?"

"Not like it used to. Let's just say I've had to find other ways to satisfy the ladies. Or, should I say, they've had to find other ways to satisfy me. But they're right talented, them. They know how to make me feel like this never happened. And if you're wonderin' if I can still get 'em pregnant, the answer is no. See? Things couldn't have worked out any better." Ann knew there were certain codes that criminals lived by, but this was a new one even for her.

"Mr. Roschine, in spite of obvious impediments, you will be charged with the sexual interference of a minor, plus a number of other assorted charges that will probably take me the better part of the afternoon to sort out. If I had my way you would be locked up in a nine-by-nine concrete, windowless cell for the rest of your natural life, but there is the legal system to consider."

"I told ya there was no rape, yet you refuse to believe me. Why is that, Inspector? Do I not have an honest face?"

Ann slowly pulled out her chair, then sat at the table. "Who else was at Terry's flat that night?"

"Hmmm...Let me think. There was Terry—"

"Obviously. Who else?"

"Who else, who else...Really, Inspector, it was such a long time ago."

"Who else?!"

"Fancy that. I can't seem to remember," said Roschine, who sat back and draped his arm over the back of his chair.

"The man Terry was arguing with when you came to his flat. You know who he is, don't you?"

Roschine turned serious. "The CPS first. Then I'll give ya all the names ya want. Maybe even a few ya hadn't bargained for."

CHAPTER 13

OWEN WAS NEVER MORE DANGEROUS than when he followed his own instincts. When he left interview room one, he did so secure in the knowledge that Roschine had all but confessed to raping Melinda. He hurried back to his office and rang the crown prosecutor, who was understandably delighted. Then Owen sent word for Ann to see him as soon as she was finished with Roschine. In the meantime, he sat back and reveled in his triumph.

"We've got the bastard. Got his confession…," Owen said, popping up on his good foot the moment Ann entered his office.

"Well, not exactly," said Ann, who sat in her usual place.

"….finally got enough to lock him away for good. No revolving doors this time."

"You heard what he said?" Ann said.

"Oh, yes. I heard."

"Then, you know he didn't rape her."

"What? Nonsense. Of course he did. He's as good as convicted."

"I don't think so, sir."

"Why not? Makes perfect sense. That's the trouble with this case. We're always looking for the most complicated solution when the answer is right there under our noses."

"He couldn't have raped her."

"Why not?"

"Because he, erm…doesn't have one."

"One? One what?"

"It…It's gone."

"What's gone?"

"His—He's... been castrated."

"What do you mean, castrated? You mean...gone? Nothing?"

"According to Roschine, Menchini did it, then had a doctor make him a new one, sort of, as a gesture of...that there were no hard—I mean, no ill will between them."

"Are you sure this isn't just another one of his lies?"

"I'm sure, sir. I've seen it myself."

"Eh? How did you—No, never mind. It's probably best I don't know." Owen eased himself onto his chair. "But, if it's back on, that means he still could have raped her."

"It—Well, it *is* back on, but it's...It doesn't, erm, work, quite the way it used to." Owen appeared puzzled, then winced.

"What about prison? Didn't he do six years? How was he not—"

"His gang, sir. There were enough of them in prison to protect him from...that sort of thing."

"Good Lord," Owen said, wiping his face with his hand. "Right. That eliminates Roschine from the list of rape suspects, though he's still every bit as guilty as everyone else who was there that night." They were interrupted by PC Weston, who stuck his head in the door and informed Ann that he had retrieved Ophelia.

"I would've brought her in sooner, Inspector, but she kicked up quite a fuss," PC Weston said as he and Ann walked swiftly toward the interview rooms. "Wouldn't leave 'til she signed all her books. No one even wanted 'em. She was forcin' people to take 'em, shovin' 'em in their hands—"

"That's fine, constable."

"She gave me this." He showed her a ProBar. "Then she told me to wait for her solicitor."

"Yes, perhaps you should do that. I've a feeling she'll be needing legal counsel, and not just in this matter. Oh, and I shouldn't eat that if I were you."

Ann entered interview room four and saw Ophelia sitting with her back to the door talking on her mobile.

"Sorry, doctor," Ann said, taking the phone out of Ophelia's hand and snapping it shut. "That will have to wait."

"Young lady, do you realize what you've just done?! That phone call was about my most recent discovery, one which will revolutionize the world of mental health!"

Ann sat across from her and said, "Yesterday you had occasion to visit Melinda in hospital."

"I was asked by a colleague to evaluate her, yes."

"You and a nurse entered her room, and the nurse left shortly thereafter. Perhaps you would like to tell me what took place during the time you were alone with Melinda." Ophelia responded with a smirk and a penetrating stare. "According to the guard, several minutes after the nurse left there was a loud noise. When he entered the room he found you and Melinda on the floor in the midst of broken glass and other items the nurse who accompanied you brought in with her on a tray."

"Lies like that will only bring you more trouble, my dear."

"He also said there was a bottle and a syringe, both of which seem to have vanished at the same time you left the room. How do you explain that?"

"I don't have to explain anything. I am the Consultant Psychiatrist at one of the most prestigious hospitals in all of Britain. I am highly respected the world over. I—"

"Right," said Ann with the weariness of someone who had heard it all before. "Now would you care to tell me what went on in that room?"

"You do not seem to understand that for every moment I am detained here there are countless patients being deprived of my services. That, my dear, shall be on your head."

"You'll get out of here a lot quicker if you answer my questions."

"Alright. If you must know, I was in the process of examining her. I was shining my torch in her eyes when she lunged at me and knocked the tray over. Next thing I knew, I was on the floor and she was trying to stamp on me as I attempted to get to my feet. Just as your guard came storming in, she slipped and fell on the mess she had created. Apparently your man thought I was the one at fault when it was that girl. In my opinion she needs to be brought back to the hospital, sedated and placed in restraints."

"That's it? That's why she became upset, because she took exception to you shining a torch in her eyes?"

"If you knew the disturbed mind as well as I do, you wouldn't be so skeptical. To answer your question, yes, it's quite possible that something as harmless as a routine examination could evoke that sort of response. If something else led to her inappropriate behavior, I'm sure I wouldn't know what that might be."

"But isn't it your job to know? Aren't you supposed to be the best in your field?"

"*Supposed* to be?" Ophelia bristled. "My dear, I *am* the best. Come to my office sometime. I'll show you the accolades I've received, the awards, the outpouring of appreciation from colleagues and patients alike. I am indeed well-respected by everyone, save for the police."

"Doctor, no one is questioning your expertise or your accomplishments. I asked you a simple question, and I am not satisfied with your answer."

"I see," Ophelia said as she sat back. "I have told you the facts as they occurred. I'm sorry if they do not fit your preconceived notion of what took place. I suppose I could embellish it for you, turn it into something the scandal sheets would be proud of. Let me see...What can I say to make it more interesting for you?"

"You can cut the sarcasm, doctor. Unfortunately I can find no legal reason to keep you here. Not yet. However, I intend to file a report about your conduct with the hospital board, the health ministry and any other organizations I can think of. Your reputation is about to take on a whole new look."

Ophelia sat forward, her piercing gaze reaching across the table. "How dare you speak to me in that manner! I daresay, I could file charges of my own against that girl. Assault charges for one. But I have accepted her attack on me as an occupational hazard. Why can't you?"

"Because I think you want me to believe it happened that way so I'll forget about it. But I assure you, I won't forget. Not this incident or any of your past behavior in this case."

Ophelia half-smiled through tight lips. "You. You're always so quick to judge me. I suggest, Inspector, that instead of trying to blame me for your failures with that girl you take a good hard look at yourself. Perhaps that's where the source of all this anger lies."

CHAPTER 14

ONSIDERING THE PERFORMANCE OF HER recent partners, Ann didn't expect to like Detective Sergeant Damian Dillon. He was thirty-two with brown eyes and dark, tossled hair. He wore button-down shirts - today's was white with blue pinstripes – and black trousers, both of which seemed half a size too big for his five-foot-ten inch frame. But despite his youth, or possibly because of it, DS Dillon was proving to be her most capable temporary partner yet. Temporary. Ann would gladly have that changed to permanent for anyone who showed even the slightest amount of competency.

So far, Damian held the most promise. In the two days he had been working with Ann he hadn't complained about anything, hadn't deleted anything and hadn't postured for promotion. He also listened while Ann brought him up to speed on this case and didn't mind if she did the driving. However, that didn't mean he always agreed with her. Like today. He was prepared to work on the Canavan Street assault case, especially after Owen called them into his office and said he expected them to give it their full attention. But Damian soon learned that Ann didn't always do what she was told.

Damian had just settled in at his desk with a large cup of coffee and the Canavan Street file when Ann walked past him.

"Inspector? Where you off to?"

"Leeston. Coming?"

"But the Super wants us to work on the assault case."

"You're perfectly welcome to stay here and work on that if you like," Ann said as she buttoned her coat. Damian sprang to his feet, then stopped suddenly.

"Wait. I have to be in court this afternoon. The Cooper trial."

"Next time."

LEESTON WAS LOCATED BETWEEN YORKSHIRE and Durham, not far from the eastern edge of the Yorkshire Dales National Park. The closer Ann got to her destination the more the landscape gradually transitioned from lush meadows to vast patches of brown grass dotted with larger and larger tangles of dead trees. She had expected to see more of the storybook English countryside tourists flocked to see, not a post-apocalyptic wasteland. That's what Delacon Industries had done to this area. It was now a far cry from its origins as a farming community. There were still some farms in the area, worked for generations by the same families. But those that remained were not only locked in a daily struggle to keep their farms going, they also found themselves in a constant fight with a number of companies who were determined to fill the area with one pollution-spewing factory after another. So far, they had managed to keep all of them out. All but Delacon.

When Delacon chose this quiet area in which to build their plant, it was so unassuming and blended in so well with the landscape that no one gave it a second thought. But company executives soon decided the building was too small for their needs. They made a deal with the local council and promised jobs for everyone who wanted one in exchange for permission to add on. But the deal they so shrewdly negotiated didn't include a limit on expansion. The company had taken advantage of that loophole and bought up so much land that the townspeople had to resort to suing the corporate giant to stop them from swallowing up the entire area. But even though the locals objected to Delacon's presence, by now it had become too important to their economy. They reluctantly resigned themselves to the harsh reality that Leeston as they knew it was gone forever.

Ann continued on to Duffield, the next town up the road where the only hospital in the area was located and where Melinda would have been born. Duffield was a small village that would have been much happier being lost in time rather than forced into the twenty-first century by a corporation that would just as soon bulldoze the few acres it occupied and use it for parking. In spite of the turmoil, Duffield had managed to maintain most of its charm. Thatched houses with picket fences wound throughout the village, but there was an odd blend of country and city, with men in business suits walking alongside those dressed in much more casual attire. Ann sensed a kind of tension, one that was more noticeable each time the two sides crossed paths. Clearly, Delacon had split Duffield in two.

Ann arrived at the hospital and noticed it wasn't so much a hospital as it was a clinic. She sat in his office a good half hour before Dr. Edwin Edgerton, a husky, energetic man closing in on his sixties, arrived. The only doctor at the clinic, he was dressed in surgical attire and explained that he had been helping a Mrs. Crawford deliver her baby.

"Inspector. How can I be of assistance?" Dr. Edgerton said as he sat at his desk and dried off his meaty hands with paper towels.

"I'm inquiring about a couple who had a baby here some nineteen years ago. Scott and Claire Conover?"

"Hmm, yes. I was here at that time. Been here—Good Lord! Going on thirty years now. Where does the time go…Conover, you say? I'm afraid that name doesn't ring a bell, but that's not all that surprising. I must have delivered hundreds of babies since then."

"You may remember this couple. They were from America."

"That's not unusual either. Since the factory opened up, we get people from all parts of the world. Asians, Africans, Eastern Europeans—America, you say?"

"From Texas, I believe."

"Yes, of course. I remember them quite well."

"Because they were American?"

"Because, even though there was just a few of them, foreigners were rare back then. Plus, I hadn't seen Mrs. Conover until the day she came here to have her baby. Most unusual. I asked if she wouldn't rather have her own physician deliver it. She said no, that they'd only just arrived in England and hadn't had time to find one—No, that's not right. It was him that said they hadn't found one yet. As a matter of fact, I don't recall her uttering a solitary word. Odd, that staying with me all these years—"

"How did she seem otherwise?"

"What do you mean?"

"Did she seem as if she had been abused in any way?"

"Not that I can recall. Mind, it was quite some time ago." His curiosity piqued, Dr. Edgerton asked his secretary to get the Conover file. They hadn't yet entered the computer age so it took awhile to retrieve it from the attic, where non-current files were stored. In the meantime, Dr. Edgerton had tea brought in for Ann and a cup of strong coffee for himself in anticipation of another busy afternoon. "So what's this all about, Inspector? We don't usually get visits from the police way out here."

"Doctor, what can you tell me about Delacon?" Ann asked before she sipped her tea.

"I can tell you most people in town don't want them here. I personally don't share that opinion. If there was no Delacon, there'd be no need for me."

"What I meant was, what can you tell me about the people who work there?"

"Oh, I don't know. Seem like a hard working bunch."

"Then why are the locals so opposed to them?"

"Oh. Well, of course, one reason would be the obvious. That building of theirs. Too damn big for these parts. Then there's their hiring practices. In my opinion that's what really bothers the locals, the fact there are more outsiders working and living here now than those whose families have been here for centuries. Mind, most of them don't live in town as such. Several years ago, about the time they expanded the factory into what you see today, Delacon built housing for its employees in an area just outside Duffield, including a small number of upscale homes for the executives. Exclusive and all that, so they wouldn't have to mix with the commoners. I'll tell you, that certainly didn't help Delacon's image. Didn't help one bit." Dr. Edgerton's secretary placed a folder on his desk, then left. "Ah! Here we are..." He read through the file. "Twenty-fifth of March, nineteen ninety-three. Quite a difficult birth...in labor over seventy-two hours—Oh! Oh, dear!"

"What is it?"

"I do remember something. Yes, it was quite difficult indeed. If I remember correctly, both she and the baby were at great risk throughout the delivery. We were in danger of losing them both, and on more than one occasion. I remember, she was so terribly frightened. We couldn't get her to follow any of our instructions. She was so completely unprepared for childbirth. Didn't seem to know what was happening to her. I don't think we've ever worked so hard to deliver a baby. Then to have things end up as they did...Tragic. That's what it was. Tragic."

"What do you mean, tragic?"

"Her baby. It was stillborn."

"Stillborn? What about Mrs. Conover?"

"Well, of course our first priority was to save her. Once we had her stabilized, we worked on the baby. But it was too late. As I recall, the poor thing didn't stand a chance. By the time she came here there was nothing I could have done for the child. It was more than the poor woman could bear. She was so distraught. Even after we'd sedated her she still carried on like nothing I'd ever seen. And that husband of hers was certainly no help. You know what he did while his own wife was delirious with fright trying to deliver his baby? He left. When his wife needed him most, he just up and leaves. Gave her no support whatsoever. It was the nurses saw to that."

"The baby...Was it a boy or a girl?"

Dr. Edgerton consulted his notes. "Hmm...Doesn't seem to be here. I'm afraid my record keeping wasn't quite up to snuff back then. We didn't have anyone to transcribe my notes, so anything beyond ten or so years ago is often incomplete." He handed Ann the file, then pulled out an assortment of chocolate bars from the top drawer of his desk, set them in a neat row in front of him, then began to devour the first one in line.

"What about a birth certificate? I don't see one here. Or a death certificate."

"Those would be at the registrar's office. When a baby is stillborn we issue a Medical Certificate of Stillbirth, which the parents take to the registrar and are given a Certificate of Registration of Stillbirth."

"There's no mention of that in your records."

"Isn't there?" Dr. Edgerton mumbled as he took the file back from Ann. "Odd," he said after extracting the chocolate from his mouth. "There should be some record of it. Oh, well. Probably just been mislaid."

The door flew open and a nurse said, "Doctor! It's Miss Bostock!"

"Right!" Dr. Edgerton said as he lept to his feet. "If you'll excuse me, Inspector. Miss Bostock. Hers is an interesting case. She'll be the fourth unwed virgin to give birth here this month." Dr. Edgerton stopped himself with a hand on the door jam and said, "Inspector. Why all this interest in a case nearly twenty years old?"

"Thank you, doctor. You've been quite helpful."

Duffield was a small village but it conducted business as tediously as any large city. Ann had spent the last hour at the local registry being shuttled from one clerk to the next. Finally a middle-aged woman approached down the hall.

"Inspector. I've located the information you requested. If you'll come this way." Ann tried to keep pace with her back down the hall. "Claire Conover. Lovely woman."

"You knew her?"

"Yes–Well, not so much knew her as knew of her. I often eat lunch in the park in summertime and there she'd be, every day, sitting in the same spot with that pram," she smiled fondly.

"Did you ever see the baby?"

"Oh, yes," the woman said as she led Ann to a small room. "Mrs. Conover let me hold it. I asked, and she said I could."

"Was it a boy or a girl?"

"A girl. A beautiful little girl." She was interrupted by another woman who rushed up and frantically relayed news of some impending disaster in reception. "Sorry, Inspector. I have to see to this. The register is on the desk. Just turn out the light when you leave—Yes, yes, I'm coming! God sakes!"

The register included the entire nineteen nineties. Ann turned to the page covering nineteen ninety-two and found the entry for the Conover's child. The first thing she noticed was that there was no first name. Understandable. It would have been difficult for a woman in a normal frame of mind to name her child under such circumstances. Then Ann saw the date of death: the third of May. That was more than a month after the date in Dr. Edgerton's records. If the baby had been stillborn on March twenty-fifth, how was that possible? Had the clerk who claimed to have held the baby gotten Claire mixed up with someone else? Then Ann saw an even more glaring error. In the column marked 'Sex' there was an 'F' written in, but on closer inspection under the glare of the lamp Ann could see the faint image of an 'M' underneath.

"Excuse me. Can you tell me why this entry has been altered?" Ann asked the registrar, a Mrs. Esmine Vandagrift, a plump, fiftyish woman with gray in her short hair. She spoke with a vibratto in her voice that gave her an air of dignity.

"Altered?"

"Yes. You see? The 'M' on the line indicating the sex of the child has been changed to an 'F'." Mrs. Vandagrift took the register from Ann and looked at it under a lamp.

"This is most irregular."

"Do you know who might have changed it?"

"I would have no idea who did this."

"Apart from you, who else has access to the register?"

"All of our employees are authorized to make entries in the register."

"Was that true twenty years ago?"

"Yes," Esmine said.

"How many employees are there?"

"Counting myself we currently have five full-time employees and a handful of others who fill in when needed."

"How well do you know them?"

"Why, I know all of them quite well," Esmine said with offense. "We all attend the same church, the fill-ins as well as the full-timers."

"Would any of them have had reason to alter an entry?"

"Certainly not," Esmine replied. "I've been here twenty-six years and in all that time, no one has ever tampered with a register. I simply cannot imagine anyone doing such a thing. It appears someone has, but I'm afraid I haven't the faintest idea who, or why. But I assure you, Inspector, I mean to find out."

The shadow cast by Delacon Industries over this area – both literally and figuratively – became apparent to Ann as she drove back to Leeston to see what she could learn about Scott. She tried to navigate around the building and was swallowed up by its immense silhouette, which was so large it turned daytime to dusk, and she better understood why the locals objected to its presence. The building was so out of place it was offensive to its surroundings. Ann gazed up at the steel monstrosity framed by the overcast October sky which was as cold as Delacon's monument to itself. It wasn't even a very imaginative use of architecture, a gray rectangle that utterly lacked for character.

Inside the main entrance was the reception area which was dominated by a huge circular desk where three young, attractive women were seated with their backs to each other. All of them wore thin headsets and were engaged in directing calls to various employees.

"May I help you?" one of them finally asked.

"I need some information about a former employee," Ann said while showing her her warrant card.

"One moment, please." Ann couldn't tell if the receptionist was taking a call or making one. "Mr. Stricker will be with you presently."

While she waited, Ann explored the massive lobby. In contrast to Delacon's all-out assault on the environment outside, inside they had created a tribute to nature. There were plants everywhere, from ground covering moss to full grown trees which extended through skylights in the ceiling where they were undoubtedly being choked to death by the black smoke that billowed out of the chimneys. In the center was a multi-tiered waterfall that cascaded into a pond from which emanated gravel paths leading to several mini-gardens, each of which depicted a different type of vegetation that used to be indigenous – pre-Delacon – to the area.

"Malcolm Stricker, Vice-President, Public Relations." Ann turned to see a man in his mid-forties, hand extended, wearing a dark suit with red pin-stripes. The similarity between Malcolm's suit and his hair, which was dyed black and streaked with red highlights, was not lost on Ann, who couldn't help from thinking that she had never seen anything quite like it on anyone either living or dead.

"I'm inquiring about a former employee. Scott Conover?"

Malcolm's eyes darted nervously around the lobby. He took Ann by the elbow and said discretely, "I think we should continue this in private." He ushered Ann into his office down a hallway to the right of reception, then stuck his head out and looked in both directions before closing the door. "Scott Conover, you say?" Malcolm rubbed his hands together as he sat at his desk and Ann sat opposite.

"Yes. I understand he was transferred here from America. Texas, I believe, some twenty years ago."

"Well, let's have a look, shall we?" Malcolm smoothed his hair with his left hand, typed something into his computer, then waited. He did that a few more times until finally, "Ah! Here we are. Scott Conover. You're correct, Inspector. He did work in Texas. San Antonio, to be precise. Transferred here to our plant in Leeston August, nineteen ninety-two. Promoted once, to senior project manager in February nineteen eighty-seven, then again to head up our Middle East operations when we opened a branch there in June of that same year."

Ann felt Malcolm wasn't being entirely forthcoming, so she decided to prod him along. "I'd heard he'd been abducted not long after he received his last promotion."

"Yes." Malcolm leaned closer to his monitor. "You're right. Reported missing July, nineteen ninety-three."

"And?"

Malcolm tapped a few more keys. "Still being held by some unnamed terrorist organization somewhere in the Middle East."

"Ransom demands?"

"According to our records, there weren't any. It's as if he's disappeared off the face of the earth."

"What about family?"

"Family...," Malcolm again consulted his monitor. "Wife: Claire. Children: None. Parents: deceased—"

"No children? Are you sure?"

"What? Oh, yes. Yes, of course there was a child." Malcolm squinted at the monitor. "Born: Nineteen ninety-two."

"A boy or a girl?"

"A girl."

"Does it say what happened to her?"

"Erm....," he checked the screen again, "....Afraid not. Why? Did something happen to their daughter?"

"And Claire? Did she stay on in the Middle East after Scott was kidnapped?"

"There's no record of her beyond that. In fact, no one seems to know what's become of her. I had heard she returned to England soon after Scott disappeared, but I can't say for certain whether that's true or not. We just assumed that, since she was originally from America, she went back there to await word of her husband's fate."

"Hasn't anyone from Delacon tried finding her, kept her apprised of the ongoing search for her husband? There *is* an ongoing search, I presume?"

"Yes. We even hired a private investigator to try and locate him. We no longer employ her, but it's my understanding local government agencies have taken over the case."

"Her? You hired a female investigator to make inquiries in that part of the world?"

"Delacon does not discriminate in the hiring of its employees, whether it be on a permanent or temporary basis. As for Claire, I'm sure someone has kept her informed of any progress that's been made, only I'm afraid I wouldn't know just who that might be anymore. Since it happened such a long time ago, it no longer falls within the realm of current business. Rest assured, we are just as anxious to find him now as we were twenty years ago."

Ann wondered why. "I'd like to see Scott's file, if I may."

"Certainly. I'll print you a copy." Scott's record had few details of his kidnapping, but that wasn't what caught Ann's eye. He had let his paperwork on the day-to-day operations of the company's newest branch slide, but he did manage to file a detailed expense account. It said that on the eighth of June he went to Geneva for two days, then made a return trip a week later. Which begged the question, what sort of business would an executive of a company that manufactures parts for oil rigs have in a country which produces no oil?

"It says here Scott went to Switzerland twice in June of Nineteen ninety-three. Any idea why?"

"Hmmm, no, not specifically. But I'm sure it was business related. Otherwise his expense account would not have been approved."

"Was it approved?" Malcolm looked at the expense account on his monitor.

"Yes, it was."

"By who?"

"Austin Marsh, more than likely."

"Does he still work here?"

Malcolm smiled. "Austin Marsh is the founder and president of Delacon Industries. When he's in town he lives at Number Four Marsh Road."

MALCOLM HADN'T BOTHERED SEEING ANN to the door, which was a lapse in manners on his part but would prove beneficial to Ann. While most of the executives on his floor were in their second hour of lunch, Ted Garrison – a confirmed brown-bagger – was in his office across the hall from Malcolm's.

"Inspector!" Ted whispered, his slight body half-hidden behind his door. Ann cautiously approached. Ted poked his head into the hallway and looked both ways, apparently a common practice at Delacon. "Try Fitzroy Harrison. Number six, Stovey Hill Road."

"Who's Fitzroy Harrison?"

"He can tell you what you want to know. And don't tell anyone that we spoke." He closed the door and Ann heard it click shut.

"I won't."

CHAPTER 15

FITZROY HARRISON, VICE-PRESIDENT OF ACCOUNTING. That meant he would have some knowledge of past employees, like Scott Conover. A convenient six miles outside Leeston, Stovey Hill Road was located in the exclusive community of DelMarsh, built by Delacon and consisting of mansions that were so large there were only a dozen or so in the entire village. Fitzroy's was a modified yet still impressive Elizabethan. It sat in the middle of a formal garden with stone work the ancient Romans would have been proud of.

Ann waited in the large, circular foyer while the maid informed Fitzroy he had a visitor. Moments later an average sized gentleman in his sixties appeared. He wore a brown double-breasted suit, had thinning gray hair, a ruddy complexion and heavy eyelids.

"Fitzroy Harrison. I understand you're with the police?" His voice was calm and even, mellowed by a steady drinking habit.

"Yes. I'm here regarding a former Delacon employee."

"Why don't we go inside." Fitzroy led Ann into the sitting room directly off the foyer to her right. The room was furnished with a maroon Regency sofa and matching chairs arranged on a large tapestry rug in front of the fireplace. To the right were French doors leading out to the garden, and to the right of the doors were built-in shelves filled with what looked to Ann to be pricey collectibles. Next to that was the focal point of the room, a small yet well-stocked bar.

"Please, have a seat, Inspector." Fitzroy poured himself a brandy, then positioned himself in front of the fireplace. "Now then. Who is it you're inquiring about?"

"Scott Conover. I believe he worked at Delacon in the early nineteen nineties. Did you know him?"

At the mention of Scott's name, Fitzroy's grip tightened around his glass. He stared into his drink and said, "Has he been found?"

"No. You do remember him then?"

"Yes, I remember him. I remember him quite well, in fact. But why would you be inquiring about someone who has been missing for nearly twenty years?"

"What can you tell me about him, his wife, their baby?"

"I'm not aware of any baby, Inspector."

"You didn't know then that Claire had given birth just before they left for the Middle East?" Fitzroy hesitated, but it was no use. As a businessman, he always got right to the point. As a failed liar, he really had no other choice.

"I'm not sure where to begin. When I first met Scott, soon after he arrived from America, I knew we had a winner. He was bright, hard-working, the sort of chap who would do anything for the good of the company. Others noticed it, too. Simon Maskrey for one. He was a vice-president when Scott arrived. He'd been with Delacon for well over forty years and had remained a bachelor most of his life. Then, when he was about, oh, sixty, he married a woman more than twenty years his junior. Priscilla," Fitzroy said with a measure of fondness. "I still don't know why. He had a reputation for being quite the ladies man even as he grew older and I never saw anything that would indicate he cared enough about her to change his ways. But marry her he did and, five years later, they had a baby. Another mistake. Simon was never keen about having children and his wife becoming pregnant did nothing to change his mind.

"He found his escape in his relationship with Audrey Belden. She worked at Delacon for a short time just after Simon and Priscilla were married. When Priscilla became pregnant Simon spent more and more time with Audrey and less time with his wife. He was always off on some business trip, which of course gave him an excuse to take Audrey along. It was never said, but we all knew he had taken up with her. No one really gave it much thought because, quite frankly, he wasn't the only executive who had a mistress.

"Anyway, they had a healthy child, Simon and Priscilla, and Priscilla was delighted. She was so proud of her daughter." He smiled at the memory. "It gave her something decent in her life after five years with Simon. Oh, she knew he was being unfaithful to her, but she never wanted to admit it. The baby was something she could turn all of her attention to so she didn't have to think about what Simon was really doing all those nights he was away. The marriage was dodgy from the start but I think deep down she thought the baby would make him want to stop his straying. But of course it didn't. It only pushed him further away."

"What happened to Priscilla and the baby?"

"Just days after the baby arrived, Priscilla learned she was gravely ill. She had gone in for a routine examination and the doctors found something in her blood. Whatever it was, it was incurable. I never saw much of Simon and Priscilla once they stopped going to business functions, but my wife stayed in touch. I remember her telling me how despondent Priscilla had become, not for herself, mind, but for her child. She worried what would happen to her baby once she was gone. She knew Simon wouldn't care for her properly."

"What did Priscilla do?"

"Her illness had a powerful effect on her. It took away any fear she had of confronting Simon. She told him she knew about his affairs, but she would forgive him his infidelity if he promised to look after their baby."

"Did he agree?"

"Even in Priscilla's condition, Simon wasn't keen to fulfill what amounted to her dying wish. But she begged him with what little strength she had left until he finally consented."

"Why wouldn't he want to look after his own child? He had the money. He could have hired someone to take care of her."

"Because he was only a few weeks away from retirement and he'd already bought a villa on some Caribbean island for himself and Audrey. A child would have only complicated things. He never had any intention of looking after his child. He only said that to humor Priscilla. To be honest, I don't know why she tried so hard. I know she was desperate – from what I understand, she had no family of her own left – but surely there were others who were better suited to raise the child than Simon."

"And Priscilla?"

"Priscilla." Fitzroy's eyes lowered. "She died soon after. Alone, of course. Simon was off with Audrey, or perhaps one of his other tarts, the night his wife died. He grudgingly took custody of the child and hired the first nanny who walked through the door. A hurricane or some such thing delayed completion of his island home so they stayed here another month. My wife dropped by a few of times and said the baby was crying while the nanny was on the phone or taking a nap. After that she came by every day to do what she could for the child, but Simon soon put a stop to that. She explained to him the reason for her visits, mistakenly thinking he would care that the nanny he had hired was so utterly incompetent. He listened to my wife, humored her, but did nothing to put things right."

"Surely that can't have gone on for long. He didn't seem the sort who would put up with the inconvenience of a baby."

"He was not," Fitzroy bit off the words. "It didn't take him long to realize it wasn't going to work."

"What did he do?"

"He turned to Scott. As I said, we all thought him a winner when he first arrived. But he hadn't been here long before he gained the reputation of being a ruthless climber, someone who would do anything to get ahead. Simon decided to use that to his advantage. He had Scott meet him at the Twelve Arms, at the time the only pub in town. You can imagine what Scott must have thought. Drinks with a senior vice-president? And after only five months in his new job? He must have thought he was going straight to the top. He couldn't have been more wrong."

"What did Simon want with Scott?"

"He presented him with a proposal. Scott was young with a wife and no children. Simon told him that if he would take the baby off his hands, he would see to it that Scott would get the promotion he had worked so tirelessly to obtain. What Simon didn't know was how ideally a baby suited Scott's purposes at the time."

"What purposes?" Ann asked.

"None of us had met Scott's wife, Claire, yet but we'd heard through the grapevine that she was not well. Mental problems, that sort of thing. When we finally met her, those rumors appeared to be true. Like Priscilla, Claire was also desperate to have a child. Like Simon, Scott was not as keen. But apparently they were, shall we say, careless one night. Inevitably, Claire became pregnant."

"How did Scott react to that?"

"Predictably. As yet another rumor had it, Scott retaliated by not allowing her to see a doctor during her pregnancy. He didn't want to take the chance of someone finding out about her condition. When the time came for Claire to have her baby, Scott insisted she go to the less-known clinic instead of a proper hospital, which would have been better equipped to handle any problems that may have arisen. Of course, problems did arise. The child died at birth. Given Claire's mental state, finding out her baby had been born dead was devastating. It only added to the poor woman's distress, which was considerable." Fitzroy fortified himself with more brandy before continuing.

"I should mention, even before she became pregnant, Claire was quite fragile. She was having difficulty coping with the transition from America to a small, prefabricated English village like Duffield. The other wives did what they could to make her feel more comfortable, but she was still homesick. At least, that's what we all thought. But there was more to it than that. There was a sadness about her that was heartbreaking. Scott, the one person who should have known, didn't seem to be aware of her unhappiness. He was so completely focused on his career. The baby was the one thing Claire had been holding onto all those months. It was as if everything, her whole life, depended solely on that child. It made it possible for her to cope with all of Scott's neglect and indifference towards her. Now even that had been taken from her. Not only that, but Scott didn't even have the decency to stay with her during the delivery."

"Where was he?"

"Off at another party, this one given by the president of Delacon for the executive staff to celebrate another successful quarter. I was one of those in attendance. I was shocked when I saw him there. It wasn't my place, but I asked Scott why he wasn't by his wife's side at such an important time. He said he had checked with the clinic and they told him his wife was fine and that he wasn't needed there."

"Was that true?"

"Not a word of it," Fitzroy said with disgust.

"Didn't anyone think it strange he wasn't with his wife?"

"Seeing that most of them didn't have the decency to be with their own wives during the births of their own children, that Scott would be out carrying on while his wife was in labor didn't seem out of the ordinary. Not at Delacon."

"What was Scott's reaction to the death of his baby?" Ann said.

"I'd say he could best be described as relieved. He believed that a child would have held him back professionally. They might not want to promote someone with too many family obligations, so he wasn't all that upset when he found out his baby hadn't survived. But Scott's fears over how this would effect his career proved unfounded when he received his first promotion. That was before Simon approached him, so apparently someone at the company liked his work, which I thought average at best. But it didn't take long before Scott again became concerned about his future. He had gotten one promotion, but would he get another? That's the problem with people like Scott. They're never satisfied with their present status. He knew what he wanted and what he had at the time wasn't it. But then Simon invited him for those drinks."

"How did Simon convince Scott to take his child?"

"Simon told Scott his wife was dying and he didn't want to keep the baby. Didn't even try to hide it. He told Scott that if he would take the baby, Simon would see to it he got another promotion. It was as simple as that. Of course, Scott immediately agreed. He still didn't want a child, but he saw this as a way that would benefit him on two counts: He would be doing a favor for a very influential member of the board, and a baby would soothe his wife's longing for her own dead child and complete the perfect family picture Scott was now striving to convey so he could continue his climb up the corporate ladder unimpeded."

"I thought he felt a baby would hold him back."

"That was Scott. He'd change his mind in a heartbeat if he thought that's what the brass wanted."

"So Simon gave his child to Scott, just like that? No legal agreement, I presume?"

Fitzroy raised a brow over one of his droopy eyelids. "That sort of deal does not come in writing, Inspector."

"But, surely Claire would have known it wasn't her child."

"By then, Claire was losing her mind over the death of her baby. She had become so distraught, she had lost touch with reality. Scott decided that with a little bit of convincing and the right amount of drugs, he could easily get Claire to believe Simon's child was her own. We know this to be true because when my wife went to visit her shortly after she came home from the clinic, she said Claire was taking pills. When my wife asked her what they were for, Claire told her Scott had given them to her, that the doctor prescribed them for all women after they had a child."

"What sort of pills were they?"

"My wife managed to get hold of one and had it analyzed. Turned out to be some sort of hallucinogenic. When my wife visited her a few days later, she said Claire didn't even recognize her."

"Then she certainly wasn't fit to care for a child."

"Hmmph! As if that mattered to Scott." Fitzroy finished off his brandy and went for another.

"Mr. Harrison, weren't you or your wife or anyone else for that matter curious as to where this baby had come from? Everyone knew Claire's baby was dead."

"I didn't. Not at first. When I learned of it I offered my condolences to Scott for his loss. He said, 'What loss?' I told him my wife was under the impression their baby had been stillborn. Scott said it wasn't true, that the baby had been born with some complications, none of which he was very clear about, but that the child had survived and was doing quite well. He assured me the baby Claire was wheeling around town in that rather elaborate pram was indeed their own. But my wife is not easily fooled, Inspector. She has wonderful instincts when it comes to such things. But after Scott swore it was his own child, well, we didn't know what to think. We wondered if we had been wrong, if perhaps their baby hadn't died, so we didn't say anything more about it."

"What about Priscilla's baby? Didn't anyone wonder what happened to it?"

"We never put two and two together until it was too late," Fitzroy said after returning to the mantel. "By then, Scott and Claire were on their way to the Middle East."

"Mr. Harrison, do you know for certain that Claire's baby died at birth? Was there a funeral?"

"No, I don't think there was. That's another reason why I believed Scott when he said his child had some sort of problem but that death wasn't one of them."

"But now you suspect you may have been right all along?"

"Yes. Even though it's been nearly twenty years, my suspicions haven't gone away. My wife used to volunteer at the clinic. She knew all the nurses."

"Could the Conovers have adopted another baby, through an agency or a solicitor, perhaps?"

"Babies were hard to come by back then. The red tape would have taken months. He might have gotten one illegally, but the fact Simon had dismissed his child's nanny just before he left for his tropical paradise and the Conovers were seen with a baby around the same time—No, it's just too much of a coincidence, Inspector."

"Could Audrey Belden have taken charge of the baby?"

Fitzroy scoffed at the suggestion. "Mistresses aren't usually interested in caring for children, especially those belonging to their lovers' wives. Audrey was in this relationship for the money and nothing else. We all knew of her dubious character. That's why she didn't last very long at Delacon, at least not on the official payroll. Her skill with a keyboard couldn't match her prowess in bed. I remember, I was the one who told her she was being let go. Normally I dislike firing people, but not on that occasion."

"Did anyone actually see Priscilla's baby?"

"Oh, yes. There's no doubt Priscilla gave birth to a normal, healthy child. She brought it round to the office a few times even though it seemed to make Simon quite uncomfortable. Poor Priscilla. It wasn't easy seeing her grow weaker. Toward the end she could hardly even hold her own baby."

"What about Claire?"

"She instantly took to the child as if it were her own. Poor woman. She believed it *was* her own. She looked like she did all those months when she was expecting, so excited that she was about to become a mother. That's all she ever wanted, really. She no longer had Scott. He was now married to Delacon, to his career. Nothing else mattered to him, not even his own family. With Claire out of the way he was free to go about his business of relentlessly chasing one promotion after the next without interference. It didn't take long before he landed his dream job, the one that would take him overseas. Stupid bastard. I wonder if it ever dawned on him that he already *was* overseas."

"Why was Scott so keen to get this particular job?"

"Because whoever got it would head up the entire middle eastern operation. It meant power, prestige. It would be like running his own separate company. He would only have to report back to Leeston once or twice a month, and it was a sure bet none of the higher ups would visit that part of the world unless they absolutely had to. In effect, he was completely unsupervised, meaning he could get away with murder if he wanted to. It was the job Scott had been waiting for, the one he had worked so hard, so unscrupulously, to get. But Scott was a worrier and he began wondering if Claire might somehow sabotage his career."

"If Scott viewed Claire as such a detriment to his career, why didn't he divorce her?"

"You have to understand how things were back then. Not all of the executives had children, but being married seemed to be a prerequisite if you had ambitions of aspiring to something higher than the first rung. Made it easier at parties or entertaining clients. Scott felt that having a wife was just one more requirement of the job, an accessory to give the appearance of conformity. As for getting a divorce, well, that would have cast doubts upon the stability of his private life, which in turn would have left them less than confident about his ability to take on more duties at Delacon."

"What part does Austin Marsh play in all this?"

"Marsh?" Fitzroy's head snapped in her direction. "Why? Is he involved?"

"I was just wondering why he didn't do anything about Scott since the party Scott attended the night his wife gave birth took place in Mr. Marsh's home."

"He may not have known Scott was there. It's rather a large house, Inspector. It's on the hill overlooking DelMarsh so he can look down upon us underlings in our stately homes which the great man rents to us at less than reasonable rates." Fitzroy set his rancor aside and said, "I don't know why he didn't do anything, but it's not always easy to know what's going on in his head. He's an odd duck."

"How odd?"

"Oh, about as odd as any man who becomes a multi-millionaire before the age of thirty-five and all but retires at the age of forty. But I'll give him his due. He worked hard to build Delacon into what it is today. He didn't come from money. Everything he has, he's earned. He's been kind to my wife and myself over the years."

"Is your wife home, Mr. Harrison? I'd like to speak to her if I may."

"Mrs. Harrison is away at her mother's for at least a fortnight. Old girl's not doing well, I'm afraid."

"Sorry to hear that," Ann said. "Would it be possible to ring her?"

"Ring her? I don't see why not. Except, I'm afraid I don't have the number. My wife's helping her mother move into a residential care home and will be staying with her until she gets settled."

"But you do expect to hear from Mrs. Harrison soon?"

"Yes. Yes, of course. She rings me nearly every afternoon, just before dinner."

"Right. I'll stop by later today. Hopefully she'll have rung by then."

AUSTIN MARSH WAS WELL INTO his eighties but still quite sharp. When he wasn't at the office or his country club, he could be found at his palatial home, a Tudor Revival-style mansion combining old world charm with all of the modern conveniences a man whose net worth was approaching a billion pounds could desire. The drawing room was a masterpiece of carved woodwork and paneling filled with imported furniture, antique tapestries and artwork, some of which Ann suspected might not be copies. Austin was sitting at a mahogany desk checking out the latest in outrageously expensive foreign sports cars when Ann arrived.

"Mr. Marsh. I'm Inspector Treadwell."

Austin took a long, hard look at her over his bifocals. He was a bulldog of a man both in appearance and demeanor. He had olive skin, sloppy lips and brown eyes that glistened in the glare of the green

Tiffany lamp on the corner of his desk. "Do you invest in the stock market, Inspector?"

"No, I don't."

"You should. You can make a damn sight more in one day than they're paying you in a year's time. There's no trick to it. All it takes is a few minutes each day to keep up with the current trends."

"Mr. Marsh, I'm not here about investments," Ann said with respect. "I'm here regarding one of your former employees. Scott Conover?"

Austin lowered the catalog. "Are you now."

"We have reason to believe he was involved in the kidnapping of a baby, possibly the child of another Delacon employee." Ann hadn't been invited to, but she sat down on the cream colored French Bergere chair opposite his desk.

"Conover, you say?"

"Yes. I'm also looking into the whereabouts of his wife, Claire."

"Scott and Claire. I haven't thought about them in years," Austin said while rubbing his chin.

"What about their baby"

"What about it?" he hardened.

"Do you know what happened to her?"

"I've no idea."

"What about Claire?"

"Nope. Her either."

Ann sighed, then said, "Mr. Marsh, I've been working on this case for nearly a fortnight. In that time I've had more people lie to me than I can put a number to. If you know something about Scott, Claire and their baby, I'd appreciate it if you would tell me."

"I can tell you quite a bit. Mind, that's not to say that I will."

"Why? Have you something to hide?" Not accustomed to being spoken to that way, Austin opened his catalog and buried his head in it. "Mr. Marsh, do you know what happened to the Conover's baby or don't you?"

"Of course I know what happened to their baby!" he snapped. "Everyone knows! Everyone who was here at the time. Their baby was born dead. The child the Conovers left with belonged to my brother, Simon Maskrey."

"Simon is your brother?"

"Was," he said with a modicum of nostalgia. "He died some years back. He was my half-brother. We had different fathers."

"And that's why you want the child back?"

"Yes. Our mother died when Simon was only four and both our fathers were long gone by then, so we were all we had. Neither of us had managed to find the time to have children. We viewed family quite differently, Simon and I. When I learned Priscilla was pregnant, I knew Simon wouldn't want to keep the child so I told him I would take it and raise it as my own. The child need never know who its real father was. But Simon said he'd already made other arrangements. I asked what those arrangements were, but he wouldn't say. I persisted until he told me he had all but given the baby away. To Conover. Hmph! Never did care for him. I don't mind ambition, but I detested the way he went about it. He thought I didn't know what he was up to, but I knew. I know all about the people who work for me. I would have stopped him, but before I found out what Simon had done, Conover had already been given his promotion to the Middle East. By Simon, I suspected."

"Did you try to get the baby back?"

"I sent word telling Conover to return immediately, but he never received the message. Or he ignored it. Then we learned he had been kidnapped. We did think for a time that Claire had also been kidnapped, but their maid said Scott left the house alone that day. Said she hadn't seen Claire for several days before Scott went missing."

"Did she say where she might have gone?"

"No. The woman hardly spoke any English. She was hysterical when the British authorities questioned her. Claire just seemed to have vanished. To this day no one knows where she is, or if she's still alive for that matter."

"Mr. Marsh, this is Scott's expense account from his time in the Middle East," Ann said, handing him the report. "It says he made two visits to Switzerland, one just a day after arriving in the Middle East and the second a week later. Why would he go to Switzerland, and why were these expenses allowed if it wasn't business related?"

"I don't know why he went to Switzerland, Inspector. We have no business dealings there. Never have. These expenses should not have been allowed."

"Yet someone did allow them."

"Yes. There should be a signature here of the person who approved it. Who the devil authorized this? Four thousand pounds of the company's money lost. I should at least like to know what for," Austin said, fretting over an expense his company incurred twenty years ago as if it had happened yesterday.

"Mr. Marsh, you said you were keen to get your brother's child back. Are you still?"

"Yes. Of course."

"Did you ever offer a reward?"

"No, but for some damn reason there's been a rumor circulating for years now that I would pay a small fortune for information leading to the child's whereabouts. I never made such an offer. I don't believe in such things. Only leads to more trouble. You'd have every fortune hunter in the country bringing me one child after another. But someone started the rumor and it's only grown over time. Some of my own people do nothing else but speculate as to who it might be."

"What about you? Do you ever speculate?"

"No," he said as he set the catalog aside. "Not any more."

"So you didn't start the rumor, but you've done nothing to dispel it?"

"Why should I? If one of them thinks they can do better than a team of highly paid private investigators, they're welcome to try. If they want to waste their time trying to locate the child for reward money that doesn't exist, I've no quarrel with that. Just as long as it isn't on company time."

"And in all this time you've never had any solid leads?"

"Not a one. Unfortunately, the only ones who know where she is are either missing or dead. I no longer have any hope of finding my brother's child." Austin's hands shook as he rose and carefully examined the orchids on the window sill to the right of his desk.

"Mr. Marsh, was Simon's child a boy or a girl?"

"A girl," he said, his eyes sparkling. But sentimentality was quickly pushed aside. "You know where she is, don't you?"

"We've located someone who may be Simon's child, but we can't be certain."

"Let me see her! I'll know!"

"Mr. Marsh, if it turns out that she is Simon and Priscilla's child, she has no idea who her parents are. She knows nothing of her past. She won't know who you are."

"She will! I'll tell her!" Austin's face changed color and his shaking became more pronounced.

"We still have some checking to do. However, if it turns out she *is* Simon's daughter, I think it should be up to her to decide whether she wants to meet you. I should warn you, she hasn't been well, either mentally or physically."

"Dear Lord. Because of what Simon did to her? Because he gave her away to Conover?"

"It's a bit more complicated than that, but yes, that has a lot to do with it."

Austin closed his eyes and lowered his head. He wasn't crying. Men of his stature rarely did. But they could become consumed by guilt, at least until they delegated it to someone else.

"I should have stopped him. I should have tried harder to find Conover."

"Thank you, Mr. Marsh," Ann said as she stood.

"Inspector," Austin stopped her. "I did try to find her. All these years, I've never stopped searching."

CHAPTER 16

"HELLO?" ANN SAT IN HER car just outside of Austin's home almost expecting Owen's call.

"Inspector Treadwell. In case you have forgotten lo these many days you've been away, this is your boss, Chief Inspector Clarke. Just checking in to see who it is that murdered Terry Royce. Surely you've been at it long enough to have learned that much."

"Not yet, sir."

"I see. Does that mean I should be breathlessly awaiting your arrival back at the station, say, sometime today?"

"Perhaps not that soon."

"Can I assume then that you have taken up residence in Leeston and are now looking into transferring up there?"

Ann rubbed her forehead with her thumb and forefinger. "No, sir. I'm just finishing up with my enquiries. I'll be back, erm, tomorrow. Afternoon. At the latest."

"Tomorrow afternoon, is it? Well then, in the meantime, perhaps you can tell me what you *have* learned on department time during this unscheduled holiday of yours." Ann proceeded to tell him about the discrepancy in the date of death, Scott and Claire, Simon and Priscilla, Fitzroy and Austin. "That's all quite compelling. What I'd like to know is, what the devil does any of that have to do with finding Royce's killer?"

"It doesn't tell us who murdered him, but it does give us an insight into Melinda's past and how she came to be with him. That in turn may ultimately help us find his killer," Ann stretched.

"I fail to see how any of that has anything to do with Royce's murder. You're no closer to solving it now than you were before you left." She heard him grumble something to someone. "You're not a social worker, Ann. I understand your wanting to help her sort out her life, but that is not your job. You've already spent far too much time on this as it is. I want you back here and I want to see what you've got on the assault case by tomorrow afternoon."

"Yes, sir."

"Oh, and I've sent DS Dillon to assist you. Perhaps he can help you speed up your enquiries so you can get back here that much quicker."

"That's really not necessary."

"He's already on his way. Where shall I tell him to meet you?"

Ann bit her lip. "By the church, near the center of town." With her time up north growing short, Ann drove back to the registrar's office. Mrs. Vandagrift reluctantly agreed to compile a list of names of employees covering the last twenty years, including two part-timers – Randall Ryerson and Darla Ingersoll. Mrs. Vandagrift said Randall was desperate to hold onto the family farm he had inherited while Darla always seemed to be at loose ends.

Ann drove back to town and waited in her car in front of the church. She tried the radio, but it kept shorting out to the intermittent strains of high-frequency static.

"Temperamental bastard," Ann remarked.

The CD player was even less reliable. A sharp blow with the heel of her hand, that's what the man who sold it to her said. Ann had yet to try that technique since shopping for CDs was on her ever-growing list of things to do. Her head pounding, Ann let it fall back against the headrest at the exact same moment the radio cut out for good, and she wondered if the two weren't somehow related. Her thoughts were interrupted by the sound of a light tapping on the window. She looked to her left and saw DS Dillon peering in. He opened the door and said, "Sorry, Inspector. Wasn't my idea."

"I know, Sergeant."

Damian got in and closed the door.

"So. What can I do to help?"

Ann filled him in on what she had learned so far. "I've been thinking. I think Scott changed the date of death in the registry, but he couldn't have done it alone. I want to find out who helped him."

"Any suspects?"

"A few." Ann paused. "Sergeant, if I said 'red eye' to you, what would you think?"

"Red eye? I should think I should get myself to the nearest doctor to see if I wasn't coming down with a very contagious disease."

"That's *pink* eye. Does it conjure up anything else?"

"Why? What's red eye?"

"I don't know. Melinda's mentioned it a few times but she hasn't said what it means."

"Red eye...Red eye...Isn't that what cowboy's drank in those westerns? Old Red Eye? Or, could be it's from one of those horror films. All sorts of strange lookin' eyes in those."

"I don't think Melinda's seen too many films. Probably none considering the life she's led."

"What about contact lenses? They have 'em in all sorts of colors these days. Could be one of those men she remembers was wearin' 'em."

"What on earth for?"

Damian shrugged. "Just a theory. Don't suppose it would do any good to check local Optometrists and the like."

"It might. As you say colored lenses are fairly common these days, but I don't imagine there are too many red ones about. First, let's find out what Miss Ingersoll and Mr. Ryerson know about all this."

They headed off in different directions, Ann driving to Randall's farm and Damian making the short walk to Darla's cottage.

Darla Ingersoll stood five-feet tall, her figure spilling over her skin-tight black stretch pants topped with an oversized blouse. Her hair was ash blonde, wavy and covered one eye. She used her face as a canvas, splashing vivid reds and blues and greens around her lips, eyes and cheeks. Such a color scheme was intended to make her look younger, but it only enhanced her age. By now, her flirtatious gyrations had become habit. Darla led Damian into the living room, which in contrast to Darla's youthful spirit had an aged look to it. He sat on the couch and Darla offered him tea, which he politely declined. Darla started out by the window, but she never stayed in one place for long.

"Miss Ingersoll, how long have you worked in the registrar's office?" Damian began.

"Twenty, twenty-two years it's been. Off and on, really, when I've been between jobs." There was a hard edge to her voice, a bitterness that came from years of searching for love in seedy bars.

"Must be difficult trying to make ends meet on part-time wages."

"I've always been able to manage. Oh, I've had to borrow a few quid from family and friends now and again, but I've always paid them back." She paused. "If that's what this is about...Is it? Has someone said I owe them money? Who was it? One of my no-good relatives? Well, I don't owe anyone anything! I've paid back everything, me, every last penny!"

"I'm sure, as you say, you've been quite diligent about repaying loans, Miss Ingersoll." The kind words of an attractive gentleman had a calming effect on her. "I wonder, have you ever heard of a man called Scott Conover?"

"No, I don't know anyone by that name."

"He was an executive at Delacon some twenty years ago. He may have asked you to help him in your capacity as an employee at the registry. He may have even offered you money."

"No, I was never offered money by anyone," Darla said coyly.

"Would you know if anyone else at the registry was approached about changing an entry?"

"It was so long ago..." Darla suddenly felt the need to straighten the fringe on the lampshades, then the doilies on the chairs. Damian followed her with his eyes as she worked her way past the mantel and a group of framed pictures including one of a man with his arm around a much younger Darla.

"Is that you?" Damian asked.

"Yes."

"Your husband?"

"No, not my husband. My fiance."

"When was this picture taken?"

"Twenty years ago, it was. Such a long time ago," Darla said sentimentally.

"Did you ever marry?"

"No, Sergeant. We never did marry," Darla replied with equal parts bitterness and sadness.

"Forgive me for asking, Miss Ingersoll, but why not?"

"Because he left me," Darla said, more hurt than angry. "I never did get over him. I reckon that's why I never married. After him, no man could ever compare. Silly, isn't it?"

"What did you do?"

"I got a bit wild," Darla said with some pride. "Started goin' to bars, seein' other men. Lots of other men."

"Forgive me again, but was one of those men Scott Conover?"

Darla considered his question for a long moment. "Yes."

"Did you help him change the register? Miss Ingersoll?"

"I missed my fiance so much," Darla said, her hard exterior cracking. "I was so lonely without him. I thought, if I sent him money, he would come back to me. But I couldn't do it. I intended to, but when the time came, I just couldn't go through with it."

"Then if you didn't help Scott change the entry, who did?"

"I reckon it was someone else at the registrar's office, wasn't it?"

"Who do you suspect it was then?"

Darla took the handkerchief that was stuffed inside the cuff of her blouse and wiped her nose with it, then said, "I can't prove it, mind, but I'd put a tenner on Ginny Ambrose."

Gray coated the stubble on Randall's craggy face, perfectly accenting his dirt-stained blue jeans and red plaid flannel shirt. It was late October but he had been preparing a small plot of land reserved for growing vegetables for the season ahead. Until he received financial assistance, the bulk of his land would remain a bleak, uninviting patch of dry, cracked earth for as far as the eye could see. Ann sat across from him at his faded green kitchen table, two cups of coffee between them.

"So you started working at the registrar's office twenty-five years ago? You must have been quite young, Mr. Ryerson."

"Seventeen, I was. First job I ever had. Only job apart from this place."

"You must have a keen loyalty then. You would of course report anything of a suspicious nature?"

"Aye." His thick brows came together. "What's that mean, suspicious?"

"There was an incident several years ago. An entry in the registry was altered. Would you know anything about that?" Randall got up and walked to the stove to freshen his coffee.

"What has she told you?"

"Who?"

"You know who. What did she say?"

"I'm afraid I don't know what you mean."

Randall stared out the kitchen window at the patchwork of weeds and grass struggling to survive in the rock hard ground. "She lies, you see. She lies about everything."

"Mr. Ryerson, to whom are you referring?"

"Don't play me for a fool, Inspector!"

"I'm not. I just don't know who you mean."

"Darla. Darla Ingersoll."

"Darla?"

"It were all her idea, that. I didn't want any part of it." He took a drink of the hot brew. "We were the only ones there that day. It was early, just after the place opened. In walks this man, wearin' an expensive suit. I knew straight away he was one of 'em. They all dress alike, that lot."

"What did he want?"

"To change the date of his son's death in the register. Said he'd make it worth our while. Neither of us knew what to say. We'd never gotten a request like that before."

"Did you agree?"

"Before we could answer, he pulls out an envelope. Looked to be thousand pounds inside. I turned him down flat. Things were a fair bit better with the farm back then. But Darla, she had more urgent financial needs."

"Such as?"

"Her boyfriend." He took another swig and swallowed hard. "They'd been seein' each other for nearly a year and planned on gettin' married. Then one day, he rings her at work. I don't know what was said, but it upset her so, she up and left. Didn't come back 'til days later. When she did, she told me she was gonna do it. She was gonna accept Conover's offer."

"Why did she decide to help him?"

"Her fiance. Said he was leavin'. Said he wouldn't be comin' back, not unless she sent him enough money so he could start plannin' their life together. I saw it for the lie that it was, but Darla was so bloody naïve. Believed anything he said."

"But you went along with it. Why?"

"Because, Inspector – back then, anyway – I rather loved Darla. I've never told anyone, never said it out loud, but I was right chuffed when her fiance left. I knew from the start he was no good for her. I knew he wasn't comin' back with or without the money. But she was in love with him and I knew I couldn't change that. Looking back on it, we were both so young. I wanted to marry her, but I never did work up the nerve to ask. Foolish of me, I reckon, but I thought, if I helped her carry out his plan, maybe I'd finally have a chance. But it didn't work."

"Why?"

"Because of him. Because of Conover. He never did come back with that envelope."

"You're saying you and Darla didn't change the entry?"

"We did not," he said unequivocally. "I never saw him again after that day. Should've seen what that did to Darla. But that didn't stop her from tryin' to get her fiance back. She scrimped and saved and did without so she could get enough money to send him. Even borrowed from her family."

"And?"

"And she's still waitin' to hear from him. Funny thing is, Darla's always blamed herself, but that ain't why Conover didn't come back. Wasn't her fault."

"Whose fault was it then?"

"Hers. That other woman."

"What other woman?"

"That nurse. The one at the clinic. Ginny Ambrose."

"How was it her fault?"

"I saw 'em together, her and Conover."

"Are you saying they were having an affair?"

"I'm sayin' I saw 'em together. Put one and one together and what do *you* get, Inspector?"

CHAPTER 17

"Headache, Inspector?"

Ann smiled when she saw that it was Damian who had joined her on the stone bench beneath a leafless tree in the well-lit park in the center of town. She was slumped back against the tree, rubbing her forehead just above her closed eyes. It was late, past ten o'clock on a day that, for Ann, had begun at five in the morning.

"Just tired, Sergeant."

"Dillon."

"What?"

"Sergeant Dillon. I wasn't sure you knew my name." Ann smiled again. She didn't realize she hadn't been using his name, or that it bothered him. "I hope it went better for you than it did me."

"Miss Ingersoll wasn't very helpful?"

"Oh, she was helpful, alright. Just bloody naïve, to put it politely. She and Randall were approached by Scott, agreed to help change the entry but at the last minute, she had a change of heart."

"Randall had no such conflict," Ann added. "He intended to go through with it for Darla's sake. Seems he's been carrying around twenty-plus years of unrequited love for our Miss Ingersoll and couldn't have been happier the deal fell through. That way her fiance wouldn't come back, leaving Randall a clear path to her broken heart."

Damian smiled at her phrasing. "Poor Randall. Apparently Darla doesn't know about his feelings for her. At least she never mentioned it. But she did say she had an affair with Scott."

"Scott. I'd sure like to know if he really was kidnapped."

"You think he might not have been?"

"Just thinking out loud, Sergeant. Sergeant Dillon." Ann sat forward. "So. Apparently Scott planned on sleeping his way through Duffield until he found someone who would help him."

"Well, I doubt he propositioned Randall the same way he did Darla. Doesn't seem the type."

Now it was Ann's turn to grin. "Randall said he doesn't know who changed the entry."

"Darla, either. But she did mention someone, a woman called—"

"Ginny Ambrose?"

"Yeah," Damian said with mild surprise.

"Randall mentioned her as well."

"Who do you reckon she is?"

"Someone with even less resistance to Scott than Darla. According to Mrs. Vandagrift's list, she also worked at the registrar's office nineteen years ago. Randall blames her for their deal with Scott falling through."

"I wonder why."

"We won't know until we speak to Miss Ambrose."

* * *

S HE REMEMBERED IT AS IF it was the most important day of her life. She saw him before he saw her, but she didn't let on. He was young, not more than twenty-six or seven, and immaculately groomed down to his fingernails. His dark hair was parted on the side and framed his hypnotic blue eyes. She was even younger at twenty-two and engaged, to Douglas Ambrose, who in his thirty-eight years had amassed considerable wealth through a series of fortunate deaths. He hadn't so much proposed to Ginny as did her aunt, who knew Douglas' grandmother, and the two women conspired to get them to the altar. It didn't matter that Douglas had no desire to get married and no ambition in life beyond securing a season ticket to Duffield United, the local non-league football team.

Throughout their courtship Douglas would spend all day every day watching sports on television, his frequent requests for beer and bags of crisps promptly filled by his mother or grandmother. Ginny would sit, smiling blankly as conversations sprang up around her, never involving her but often about her. She didn't know what any of it was about until one day her aunt and his grandmother announced to a small gathering of family and friends that negotiations had finally ended and Douglas and Ginny were to be married. Ginny kept smiling and Douglas didn't stir from his television. But as the din in the room – a mix of well-wishers offering congratulations and the match commentator exulting over an equalizing goal – grew, Ginny began to understand the implication of those words. She didn't know why her aunt brought her to Douglas' house every night and she never suspected he wanted to marry her since he had shown absolutely no interest in her from the day they were introduced. When his grandmother asked him for confirmation of their engagement Douglas replied, 'Bloody fouled him!! Where's the bloody card?!', and the plans for the wedding got underway.

For the first time Ginny took a good, hard look at Douglas slumped on the couch. His T-shirt was stained and too tight for his ever expanding stomach, and his track suit bottoms were torn in the crotch. His bulky sweat socks were like new since he never had to get up for anything except to go to the loo. She didn't know why, she just knew she didn't want to sit like this with him every night for the rest of her life.

It was decided that the wedding would take place in late summer, to give the older women a chance to make it the social event of the season in Leeston, a town so small that the biggest event up until then had been when Delacon arrived. Scott came later, at just the right time for Ginny.

Time seemed to stand still. There he was, sitting by himself at a table in the Twelve Arms. He looked lonely. Worried. Ginny had a soft spot for troubled souls. She felt other people's sadness. She just wasn't bright enough not to feel it too deeply. She couldn't have known it was no coincidence that Scott happened to be in the pub that day at exactly that time, or that he had been looking for someone just like her when he found her that day in the park enjoying the first nice day of spring by eating lunch on a bench, tossing pieces of bread to the pigeons. She was perfect.

She was dressed in the style she preferred to this day, a pastel dress with a matching ribbon in her hair, which was the color of the sun, thin and straight, just right for her delicate features. She didn't always catch on to what others said or pick up on innuendo, but she was intelligent and had a good heart. Scott would soon discover those qualities in Ginny, but it wouldn't matter how good she was or how smart she was. It wouldn't have mattered if she split atoms in her spare time. All he needed was for her to do one thing without questioning him. Ginny could do that. She was an expert at blindly following instructions. She was absolutely perfect.

He glanced at her provocatively, no longer pretending to read the newspaper he had folded and propped up in front of him. Ginny tried to ignore him, but Scott was sending powerful signals her way and she wasn't sophisticated enough to see through them. They pulled her toward him, into his aura, this handsome stranger who for some reason had taken an interest in her from the moment she walked into the pub. If she had even the slightest bit of sense she would have looked at the engagement ring on the third finger of her left hand and thought about the promise her aunt had made to Douglas' grandmother. But even if Ginny wouldn't allow herself to think about how cold Douglas was toward her, she knew it inside. In spite of her engagement to him, she had never felt anything for Douglas.

But there was no denying what she was feeling now. She had never felt this way before, but it didn't scare her. They continued to exchange glances, though Scott's had turned into a stare as he let his natural charm do the work for him. Before she knew it Scott picked up his drink and seemed to glide across the room and onto the chair across from her. He began by asking if they hadn't met before, just the other day in fact, in the park. She hadn't seen him there, but it didn't matter. His seduction of her was already underway and for the next three days he spent as much time with her as he could.

On the fifth day he finally convinced her to go away with him. They drove to a small village several miles away, where no one knew them. He had prepared a picnic lunch, which they ate in a far off meadow while he encouraged her to talk about herself. No one had ever asked her to do that before. It made Ginny feel special and gave Scott the information he needed to carry out his plan. After lunch they got into his car and drove several more miles until they came to an inn in a small town Ginny had never been to before. True to her nature, she didn't resist when Scott registered them as Mr. and Mrs. She also didn't protest when she saw there was only one bed in the room, or when Scott began undressing her. Even as he did he was starting to use the information he had gathered from Ginny to his advantage. He had not only found out how business was conducted at the clinic, he also discovered that Ginny's fiance had emotionally neglected her. Douglas hadn't even touched her yet, not so much as a kiss, so Scott made sure that everything he did that night was for her. When they awoke the next morning after only a few hours sleep, she was his. She was grateful to him. She would have done anything for him. Scott wasn't flattered by that. He was counting on it.

ANN AND DAMIAN EACH GOT rooms for the night. The next morning Ann went to see Dr. Edgerton on a particularly busy day at the clinic. There were injuries from a car accident, annual physicals for Delacon employees, and babies to deliver. There were always babies to deliver. Never comfortable sitting, Ann wandered around the waiting room until she was approached by the doctor's secretary.

"Inspector. We found this after you left." She handed Ann a folder, then disappeared back down the hallway.

Ann noticed the file was marked 'Conover', only the handwriting was different than on the Conover file she had seen during her first visit here. Inside were documents, including a copy of the Medical Certificate of Stillbirth, signed by Dr. Edgerton, that had been missing the last time. It confirmed Claire's son had died at birth, on March twenty-fifth, nineteen ninety-two, giving Ann more proof that the entry at the registry had been altered.

"Inspector. Good. I was about to ring you," Dr. Edgerton, still in his scrubs, said as he rushed past Ann. He led her into his office, then sat behind his desk and toweled the sweat off the back of his neck. "I've given this case a good deal of thought since you were last here and I remember, there were some irregularities."

"Such as?"

"Well, you asked if Mrs. Conover had been abused. As I recall, she did bear scars of recent beatings. Older ones as well."

"How can you be certain they were from beatings? Could they have been from something else?"

"I've treated abused women before. No doubt about this one. Textbook case."

"Did you notify the police?"

"You have to understand, Inspector. Back then, it just wasn't done. Not in such a small town, anyway. I did ask her about the bruises, but she was too afraid to answer. The way she behaved when her husband was about, well…"

"Doctor, is it possible Claire had another child?"

Dr. Edgerton dug through a stack of papers on his desk. "Where is it? I know I left it—Ah! Here it is." He read through his notes as his secretary placed a tray with a cup of coffee and a cup of tea on it on his desk. "No. There were no signs of any previous pregnancies. The baby I delivered was the only child she had. The only one she *could* have had."

"What do you mean?"

"After the difficulties with her pregnancy, she was no longer capable of having children of her own." That added credence to Fitzroy and Austin's versions as to where the baby Claire had been seen with had come from.

"Doctor, I have a photocopy of the entry of the baby's death from the registrar's office. You see this line here, the one indicating the baby's sex? It's been changed."

"Has it?" He leaned forward to get a closer look. "So it has. Who did it?"

"I was hoping you could tell me."

"I assure you, I have no idea who might have done this."

"Could Scott have changed it?"

"Why on earth would he want to make it appear as if his child wasn't stillborn, or that it was a girl and not a boy? Doesn't make sense. Anyway, it wasn't his fault. It's not as if he killed the child."

"Doctor," Ann said as she reached for the cup of tea, "who fills out the certificates of stillbirth?"

"I do. Or used to. Since Delacon expanded, I no longer have the time. The nurses see to that."

"I'd like to speak to them, if I may."

"Alright, although I can already tell you the only one who's still here from that time is Ginny Ambrose."

"How long has she been working here?"

"Ever since the place opened."

"Is she reliable?"

"Reliable? Why, she's the most dependable nurse we have. Don't think she's ever missed a day."

"I'll start with her then."

"Alright. But before you do….," he put his hands together prayer style. "Ginny is a very caring person. She's a good mother to her two children and looks after her husband better than my own wife looks after me. And my wife is a wonderful woman, Inspector. Tells me so every day. As a nurse, Ginny's different class. If I were to leave here and could take just one nurse with me, Ginny would be the one."

"But?"

"But...Well, I'm afraid Ginny wasn't blessed with an abundance of common sense. Subtleties escape her. Never seems to understand any of my jokes. Don't get me wrong. She's quite bright. Tops in her class at university if I remember correctly. But, well, you have a word with her. See what you think." He stuck his head out the door. "Ginny? Could you come here for a moment?" The door opened and a woman with the spring in her step of a twenty year old entered. A slight thickening around her waist was the only outward sign of a woman who had lived forty-plus years. "Ginny, this is Inspector Treadwell. She has some questions she'd like to ask you." Ginny smiled pleasantly, radiating the kind of warmth that instantly endeared her to everyone, then sat on a chair by the door.

"Mrs. Ambrose, would you know anything about this?" Ann showed her the altered entry. Ginny didn't seem to understand. "You see? The 'M' has been changed to an 'F'." Ginny examined it closely.

"Yes. It has," she said with genuine surprise.

"Do you know who might have changed it?"

"No. I can't imagine who would do something like this." Ginny looked anxiously at Dr. Edgerton. "Doctor, was their baby a girl? Did I make a mistake?"

"Mrs. Ambrose, were you the one who filled out the Medical Certificates of Stillbirth back then?" Ann asked.

"No. I believe Dr. Edgerton did." Ginny's voice trailed off, as if she had in that instance accused the doctor of committing some unknown crime.

"Then why would you think it was you who had made a mistake?"

Ginny again turned to the doctor, who quickly averted his eyes.

"If it's been changed, I don't think it was me. Perhaps someone at the registry changed it."

"We're looking into that possibility as well," Ann said. "Did you know Scott Conover, Mrs. Ambrose?"

"Mr. Conover? Yes, I believe his wife was a patient here."

"Did you know him well?" Dr. Edgerton's ears perked up.

"No. It's not wise to get too close to patients or their families. No respectable nurse would."

"Would you consider yourself a respectable nurse, Mrs. Ambrose?"

Ginny appeared hurt by Ann's words. "Why, yes. I always try to do my best for my patients. They mean a great deal to me."

"Would you have done anything for Scott?"

"Scott?"

"Conover?" Ginny opened her mouth, but nothing came out. "So you didn't know Scott apart from the clinic, never saw him anywhere else, by chance, perhaps?"

"No. I never saw him once his wife left here."

"With their baby?"

"Certainly. That's how these things work, Inspector. The wives have the babies, then the husbands come to collect them when it's time to take them home," Ginny said in an attempt at levity. "Is that what's troubling you? I can assure you, the baby left here with its mother. We rarely keep them."

Ann smiled and said, "Thank you, Mrs. Ambrose." As the door closed behind Ginny, Ann said to Dr. Edgerton, "She's lying."

"I know, Inspector. I know."

CHAPTER 18

"INSPECTOR. HOW'D IT GO WITH Ginny Ambrose?"

Damian caught up with Ann at the clinic, but she felt light-headed the moment she stepped out into the cool October air. She placed her hand against the wall to steady herself and closed her eyes as everything started to spin.

"You alright, Inspector?"

"Yes," Ann said.

"I'm a bit peckish myself. Wonder if there's some place to eat round here…" Damian said rhetorically as he headed for Ann's car and got in on the driver's side. He waited until Ann finally gave in to her symptoms and got in, then Damian drove to the first restaurant he saw. Ann ordered tea, to which Damian added eggs, bacon, tomatoes, sausages and fried bread, then ordered the same for himself. The stare he got came from as far back as the women's movement of the seventies, but Damian was prepared to defend himself.

"Sorry, Inspector, but I thought you might be hungry. I've been here…" He checked his watch. "…goin' on eighteen hours now and the only thing I've seen you put in your mouth in all that time were two chips you nicked from my plate at dinner last night."

"I appreciate your concern, but I had something brought to my room this morning."

"What, room service in that place?"

"It may not be five-star, but they don't mind making their guests feel at home. Anyway, I'm perfectly capable of looking after myself." Another wave of dizziness swept over her before she could conceal it

222

from him. "Alright, perhaps I have been forgetting to eat lately. My clothes are fitting a bit looser—"

"You look alright to me." Damian was too busy devouring his food to see Ann's reaction. They ate, with Ann finishing less than half her food, but it was still enough to revive her.

"Sergeant," Ann said as she sat back, "what is your opinion of Stropman and Roschine's whores?"

"What's my opinion?" Damian said while nicking some of Ann's sausages.

"I mean, would you sleep with any of them?"

"Really, Inspector. I've never paid for sex. Never had to."

"But if you were to, would it be with any of the women who work for them? Or would you prefer Melinda?"

"Well, strictly from a theoretical standpoint, mind, I'd much rather have Melinda in my bed than any of those old slags that work for Stropman and Roschine."

"But most of them are Melinda's age. Some even younger."

"Yeah, but that sort of work ages them beyond their years, doesn't it? I know most women who become prostitutes are forced into it by circumstances, but it's still their choice. They can get out whenever they want. Melinda didn't have that choice. She was about to be sold. She would've been more a slave than the others."

"Is that part of her appeal? I'm just trying to understand what there is about her that would make them go to such lengths, perhaps even murder, to acquire her."

"Well, could be her appeal was that someone else wanted her."

"Roschine wanted her because Stropman did, Stropman wanted her because Roschine did."

"That's it. And because she belonged to Terry." Damian wiped his mouth, then said, "What did you think of Ginny Ambrose?"

"Ginny. I think I should like to find out one day what it was about Scott she found so captivating that she was willing to risk her future for him." Ann stared out the window for a moment. "I don't think there's much more for us to do here, Sergeant. I'll stop by the Harrisons and see if his wife has rung yet. Why don't you go back to the station, see if you can't learn what red eye means. I'll be along as soon as I've finished here."

"You're sure you don't need me?"

"I think I'll be alright without you by my side for a few hours." Ann didn't intend to be so short, but she was tired and she hoped he understood. Ann thought Damian sensed something about her, but as long as she kept her secrets to herself, he could suspect all he liked.

While Ann waited in the foyer of Fitzroy's house, she observed his household staff cleaning and straightening with the precision of a military unit. Moments later Fitzroy arrived, telephone number in hand.

"Here you are, Inspector. My wife said she'd be in and out all day, and I'm afraid there isn't an answer phone just yet."

"Thank you, Mr. Harrison. I appreciate your cooperation."

"Well, we all liked Claire, especially those of us who found Scott intolerable." A maid breezed by, nearly sloshing water from her scrub bucket onto Ann.

"Spring cleaning, Mr. Harrison?"

"This? No. We're having guests for the weekend."

"We're? You and your wife?"

"My wife? No. As I've said, my wife is away, looking after her mother."

"But you did say 'we're'."

"I often refer to myself as 'we', Inspector. After so many years of marriage, I don't suppose I can think of myself any other way." If it was as simple as all that then why, Ann wondered, did he suddenly not know where to put his eyes?

"Where did you say Mrs. Harrison's mother lives?"

"Darlington. Has for years. Won't live any place else." That was only about twenty miles from Leeston. Close enough for Mrs. Harrison to return home to help arrange for weekend guests. Or whenever else she wanted.

"If I may ask, what sort of ailment does your mother-in-law have?" Ann asked.

"Why?"

"Just curious."

"I'm not sure. My wife doesn't like to bother me with such things. I'm afraid I'm not very good when it comes to family crises."

"You're quite fond of your mother-in-law, aren't you?"

"Yes. We get along quite well. Not all mothers-in-law are meddling shrews, Inspector."

"No. Of course not. Well, thanks again for the number."

What was Fitzroy so nervous about? If he hadn't been so jittery, Ann wouldn't have given it a second thought. Just a slip of the tongue, that's all it would have been. But he reacted in a way no one should in front of a cop, not unless they had something to hide. And that's just what Ann thought he was doing. But hiding what? While she pondered that question, several miles away Sally Harrison was going through a dilemma of her own.

THERE WAS NOTHING UNUSUAL ABOUT the fog this morning because it was always foggy down by the docks. It was chilly, too, so chilly that even pulling the collar of her coat up wasn't enough to ward off the cold. How much longer? That seemed to be the question of the day. How much longer before the ferry arrived? How much longer before this would finally end? The woman was ill, there was no question about that. But was it her and Fitzroy's responsibility to look after her? And for how long? Sally looked out over the choppy water. She would give it a few more minutes. No more than fifteen. Twenty at most.

She checked her watch again. She was sure she had the time right but so far the ferry from Zeebrugge had not yet arrived at King George Dock in Hull. Alright. If she sat in her car, maybe she could hold out a little longer. Twenty-five minutes. Thirty, but not a second more.

While Sally continued her vigil, Ann returned to the station only to learn that the lens theory turned out to be a dead end. The few pairs of red lenses that existed had been made mostly for movie and theatrical productions and were all accounted for. While Ann tried to think of what else red eye could mean, her concentration was broken by the sound of a chair scraping loudly across the floor of her office. She looked up to see an enormous woman, well over two-hundred pounds and easily more than six feet tall, sitting across from her, straddling the chair which she had turned backwards. She had stuffed herself into a black T-Shirt with Biker Chik written across it in red letters made to look like dripping blood. The sleeves were torn off to reveal massive, untoned arms. The barbed wire tattoo, meant to highlight a well-defined bicep, sagged and meandered through the folds of fat each time there was a shift in cellulite. She also wore several symbols around her neck including a German cross, a swastika and a peace symbol.

For most women, that amount of jewelry would have been more than one chest could accommodate. But there was ample room on the woman seated before Ann. Momentarily blinded by the light reflecting off all that metal, Ann soon noticed Owen standing behind the woman, his hands lightly on her shoulders.

"This is Miss Tansy. Poor Miss Tansy was attacked yesterday and, well, very nearly sexually assaulted. Fortunately, she was brave enough to fight off her attacker before anything, erm, unfortunate took place. She has graciously consented to help us find the man who has been terrorizing women on Canavan Street these past few weeks. Miss Tansy, if you're up to it, I'm sure Inspector Treadwell here will be happy to take down the details of your ordeal. Well. I'll leave you ladies to it." He smiled smugly at Ann, then warmly at Miss Tansy before exiting. Ann got his message loud and clear. She watched him leave, then got an earful from the imposing Miss Tansy. But Ann wasn't the only one dealing with an irate woman at the moment.

"SHE WASN'T THERE!" SALLY SAID as she angrily undid the buttons on her coat upon returning home.

"What do you mean, she wasn't there?" Fitzroy met her at the door.

"What do you think I mean? She wasn't there! I don't know how I can say it any plainer than that!"

"Did you wait to see if she was on another ferry?"

"There's only one boat a day, Fitz. And even if there was another, I wasn't about to stand out there any longer. Frightful out there." She tossed her coat over the bannister.

"Where could she be? Where is that letter?" Fitzroy went to his study and took a plain, white envelope out of the top drawer of his desk, then caught up to Sally as she was about to ascend the stairs. "Here...'I shall be arriving on Thursday, the twenty-eighth of October, at King George Dock on the eight o'clock ferry from Zeebrugge. I shall be staying in England for only a short time and would be most grateful if you could arrange accommodations for myself and my secretary.'"

"It's not even signed. We don't even know if it was written by her."

"Oh, it's her alright. Who else would write such a letter?"

"Who? That letter could be from almost anyone."

"It's handwritten. With a quill pen."

"Alright. Assuming it is from her, then where is she?" The answer to that could be found several miles to the east where a chauffer sat in his car, heat turned up high, and waited anxiously for the ferry to arrive. Fifteen minutes later it finally appeared in the distance. The chauffer stood on the pier holding a small sign with the name of his passengers written on it. As the number of passengers began to thin, two women approached him.

"So sorry we're late. Nasty storm along the way," the younger woman said as the older woman stood silently by. The chauffer escorted them to the limousine and put their bags in the boot. He started the car, then looked over his shoulder and said, "Have you in Leeston in no time, ladies."

* * *

S HE MOVED AROUND THE HOUSE like an apparition, appearing with hardly a sound before disappearing again. She still had on her long, black coat, her head scarf and dark glasses. She hadn't said a word since they started their trip four days ago. By now, her secretary was used to that. Their host, however, was not. He went to the bar and poured himself a double scotch and did his best to tolerate this ghostly presence as she wandered aimlessly from one room to the next. He sat in his high-backed, dark green leather recliner and clutched his glass tightly, indifferent to the condensation marks it was making on the arm of the chair, and watched the younger woman, who had placed their suitcases on the sofa and was sorting through them one article of clothing at a time.

"Is she alright?" he chafed. "Can I help her find something?" Her secretary looked up from her unpacking.

"No, she's fine. Just acclimating herself to her surroundings. She always does that when she's some place unfamiliar."

"It's just a house. An expensive one, granted, but I don't see the need to investigate it so thoroughly."

The secretary just smiled as she went about her business. She had gotten used to most of the woman's eccentricities. As far as that went, this didn't even rate.

"I'll have the maid show you to your rooms," he said, his desire for both women to be out of his sight getting the best of him.

"Thank you, but she doesn't usually retire until after midnight. Would it be possible for her to have a rocking chair? She's much less restless if she has a rocking chair."

"I believe we may have one in the attic. I'll have it sent to her room."

"Thank you."

He drummed his fingers impatiently. "When do you think I might be able to speak to her?" The younger woman craned her neck to the right, then to the left.

"I should think it will be at least another half hour."

"What?! A half an hour?" His fingers dug into the arm of the chair.

"Trust me. When she's like this, there's no point even trying. She'll settle down in time."

"Bloody hell!" he mumbled, then flipped open a panel on the arm of the chair and turned everything on: the heater, massager, the classical music piped in through tiny speakers hidden in either side of the headrest. Then he spent the next twenty minutes watching the woman float to strains of Vivaldi as her secretary unpacked, packed, then unpacked again. He couldn't decide which of them was more maddening.

"Do you think I might be able to speak to her now?"

The younger woman again craned her neck.

"She seems to be winding down. I'll get her for you."

"Thank you."

He stood and wiped his forehead with the handkerchief he had removed from his breast pocket and did his best to calm himself. The younger woman entered and announced, "Madame will see you now." He bit his tongue. *She'll* see *him*? The older woman entered and stared at him for a long moment. Then finally, she spoke.

"Who is this man?"

"This is Mr. Harrison, the man you wrote to." The woman walked up close to him and took a long look at his eyes through her lorgnette.

"This is not Fitzroy Harrison. This is Austin Marsh. Lydia, why are we here?"

All the years of searching, all of the private investigators he had hired, Austin had never given up hope of finding his niece, though at times that hope had been no more than a thread. He was at just such a low point when he stumbled upon the biggest break he had gotten in years. It was just luck that he found the letter on the receptionist's desk at Delacon. He never bothered with the mail, but one of the envelopes caught his eye. It was handwritten, unusual in this day, and it was addressed to Fitzroy. Austin slipped it in his coat pocket, then retired to his office.

The letter didn't say much, only that they would be coming to England for a visit. They couldn't give the exact date because ships were so unreliable these days, what with pirates and other scoundrels awaiting unsuspecting travelers. At the bottom of the letter was a P.S. written in another hand stating they would be arriving next Thursday on the ferry from Rotterdam to Hull. The letter wasn't any more specific than that, but it was enough to convince Austin that this was the woman who could help him locate his niece. He returned the letter to the pile but first he carefully cut off the P.S. and rewrote it, substituting Zeebrugge for Rotterdam. While Sally waited for the ferry from Zeebrugge, Austin's chauffeur awaited the one from Rotterdam.

"Please, sit down," Austin said. The woman stood motionless and continued to study his face. "I need to talk to you. About your daughter."

"Madame Peto has no children," Lydia replied.

"Yes, she does!"

"I have been in her employ nearly two years and in all that time she has never once mentioned a child."

"Claire Conover did have a child," Austin fumed. "A son. He died at birth, but her husband brought her another child. A girl. That girl belonged to my brother, Simon Maskrey. That means she is my niece. I want desperately to see her again. That's all I ask, for you to tell me where she is so that I might see her one last time."

The woman stood there for a long moment, then left through the front door. Austin went to the door and called after her, "Wait! Where are you going?! Please! Tell me where she is!" Her secretary caught up with the woman, who stopped at the end of the drive.

"Lydia, have you summoned our driver?"

"Yes, Madame. I shall do that now." Lydia rushed past Austin into the house.

"What did she say? Is she coming back inside?"

"May I use your telephone?"

"What for?"

"Madame wishes to go elsewhere. I'm sorry, but she's quite set in her ways." While Lydia called for a taxi, Austin rushed to Madame Peto and said, "Why won't you tell me where she is?" She didn't acknowledge him in any way. His patience exhausted, Austin grabbed her by her arms. "Where is she?! Where is my niece?!" Lydia came running out and freed Madame Peto from Austin's grasp, then stood between them.

"What do you think you're doing?! I'm sorry for your loss, but as I've said, Madame Peto has no children."

"Yes, she does! She has my niece!" Just then, a cab pulled up. The women got in and Lydia told the driver to take them to Fitzroy's house.

CHAPTER 19

UNDER THE CARE OF DR. Horgaarth, Melinda was beginning to break free of the hold Dr. Stanton's constant overmedication had on her these past couple of weeks. She was awake now, the sterile walls and distinct smells making it abundantly clear where she was. So as soon as she found her clothes, she left.

At the same time, Juan was also about to have a revelation. He had finally regained enough of his senses to resume his search for Melinda. If only he knew where to begin. There was Terry's flat, the location of which would be easy enough to find out from Roschine's men. If only he could remember where Roschine's men were. That was clearly one part of being a hit man Juan was going to have trouble with: actually finding the people he was supposed to kill. So much to learn, so few resources to work with.

At the station, Ann had just finished listening and cringing to the many creative ways Miss Tansy had devised to exact revenge on her assailant if she ever ran into him again. After escorting her out of the station and leaving her with a carefully worded suggestion that pressing charges against her attacker would be that much easier if he was still in one piece, Ann returned to her office. Damian entered moments later and placed a large paper bag on her desk.

"What's this?"

"Some of Melinda's things. Mack dropped 'em off. Thought she might want 'em."

The bag contained only a comb, a toothbrush, a pair of trousers and a jumper. Ann remembered the jumper. It was the same one she had seen in Terry's flat. She held it up. It had been folded for so long the creases were deeply embedded. It was light blue and had a complex cable pattern, and Ann wondered how Melinda had acquired such an expensive, handmade item when the rest of her clothes were at least second-hand. Hanging from the sleeve was a small tag which said it had been made in Austria. It wasn't much, but combined with Scott's visits to nearby Switzerland, it was too great a coincidence to ignore. But it didn't make sense that he would have bought something for a child he didn't want, who, for all he knew, was already dead. And in a size for a girl much larger than the one he gave away to Karl. Ann still wondered why Scott was allowed to write off his trips to Switzerland. Maybe he went there to convince the Swiss government to drill for oil in the Alps so he could sell them some very expensive equipment. Or maybe he had some other reason for going there.

"It's not going anywhere, Inspector."

"What?"

"The door?" Ann didn't realize she had been staring at Owen's door until Damian snapped her out of her spell.

"No," she said, self-consciously turning her attention back to her desk. "I'm sure it isn't." But Ann couldn't ignore the door for long. She gave it another look, then rose. Before she could take a step Damian held a file folder in her path. Puzzled by the gesture, Ann nevertheless took the file and knocked on Owen's door, then entered on his command.

"Ah, Ann. How did things go with Miss Tansy then?" Owen said after exhaling. He sat sideways, the broom handle he had just been pressing with all his might into the inside of the right leg of his desk still in his hands.

"She's been quite helpful, sir," said Ann, who considered it, but decided not to comment.

"Splendid. I assume then that you'll have some new information to share with us soon?"

"Hopefully."

"So," Owen relaxed his grip, "did your time up north shed any light on who killed Royce?"

"No, it didn't."

"I see. I must say, I'm rather surprised that inquiring miles from where the killing actually took place, where there are no known suspects or anyone else associated with the crime, would turn out to be a dead end." He leaned the stick against the wall behind him. "And the assault case? Should I even bother asking what progress you've made there? I mean, apart from what I've provided you." This is where Ann should have confidently handed him what she now knew was the Canavan Street file, but she placed it meekly on his desk instead. She hadn't even had a chance to look at it, but she had no choice but to trust a partner she had no reason to trust yet. Owen eyed her skeptically as he opened the file.

"So. You believe it's one man and one man alone who is carrying out these attacks?" he said without looking up.

"Yes," the word caught in Ann's throat. "Yes, sir."

Owen read further. "And you believe that man to be Colin Thompson?" Thompson? Ann had arrested him before, but for arson, not assault.

"Yes. I do." The tension hung in the air for a few more moments, then Owen closed the file. "Well done, Ann. I've suspected him myself. Now then. Where are you on the murder investigation?"

"I'm getting closer to identifying a suspect."

"Are you? I want it wrapped up soon. It's dragged on far too long as it is. I've broken entire crime rings in less time."

"Yes, sir." Ann wrestled with a moment of indecision, then said, "Sir, I may have some new information regarding Scott Conover. I think it's possible he may still be alive."

"Do you now?" Owen said without surprise as he got to his feet with the help of the stick. "And what has led you to that conclusion?" Ann told him about Switzerland, Austria, the jumper. "I see. What do you suspect was his reason for disappearing? How did Scott stand financially twenty years ago?"

"According to his employment record, he instantly rose to the top of the wage scale as soon as he was promoted."

"Then he was in no need of money."

"Apparently not. He was making a good wage and living rent free. He had no responsibilities beyond himself, his wife and, quite possibly, a child."

"If not money, why else does someone disappear?", Owen pondered as he strolled by the window. "Perhaps he was having an affair and wanted to keep it quiet so it wouldn't hurt his chance for promotion."

"I don't think so, sir. It seems having a mistress was virtually a prerequisite for employment at Delacon."

"What about a secret life? Something more sinister than hiding a mistress, perhaps selling company secrets to the competition?"

"Delacon sells parts for oil drilling equipment. They don't develop new types of technology. Nothing to go to such lengths over."

Owen stared out the window. "You know what I think? I think you're right."

"You do?"

"Yes. As a matter of fact, in light of all this, perhaps you should go to Switzerland and see if you can't find him."

"Sir?"

"Well, someone gave her those things. Why not Conover? Perhaps he never was kidnapped by a terrorist group. Perhaps he's been living in some secluded village and has blended in with the locals. Or, could be he lost himself in one of the larger cities, like Salzburg, or Innsbruck."

"That's in Aust—Right. I suppose he could have done."

"Then it looks like it's you off to Switzerland. Pack your bags. I'll have someone arrange your tickets."

"Yes, sir." Ann slowly rose, then stopped. "You're not having me on, are you, sir?"

"Certainly not. And take DS Dillon with you. Might be of some use."

"Right," Ann said, still not completely convinced of his sincerity.

"Oh, Ann," Owen said as he handed her the Canavan Street file. "Don't forget to thank young Dillon."

Damian, however, wasn't waiting for praise. It had been twenty years since Scott disappeared. There wasn't much to celebrate in some of those countries harboring terrorists, but the kidnapping of a western businessman would certainly be one of them. Damian turned to his computer to follow up on Ann's suspicions and soon found what he was looking for. He printed out the front page of a Middle Eastern newspaper featuring a large photo of a thin man with a full beard, his face drawn, his eyes hollow, and presented it to Ann, who had just returned to her office. Ann couldn't read the caption, but she did recognize the man in the photo: Scott.

"Where did you get this?"

"Internet. They've got newspapers from all over the world."

"When is this from? What's the date?"

"June of this year. It's to mark his twentieth year in captivity, countin' the year he was kidnapped. The newspaper he's holding appears genuine." Ann continued to study the photo. "That eliminates Scott, eh, Inspector? He couldn't have been the one who sent the books or the jumper."

"It would appear not. The question now is, who did?"

"Perhaps Audrey Belden can tell us."

"Audrey?"

"I took the liberty of contacting the authorities in the Caribbean," Damian said. "They can confirm Simon and Audrey did live there for a time. And get this. They said Audrey also had a baby some twenty years ago."

"Simon's?"

"They didn't know, but we can ask her ourselves. She's back in England now."

Audrey Belden lived in a fairly affluent town with a strong medieval core. When Ann and Damian arrived Audrey was in her back garden wearing a long, tan coat, a wide-brimmed hat secured to her head by a green scarf tied under her chin, and gardening gloves which she swiped against each other as she led her guests into her living room.

"I was putting seed out for the birds. They have a dreadful time of it if we don't help them during the winter."

"Miss Belden, we'd like to talk to you about Simon Maskrey," Ann said. Audrey paused for a moment, then removed her hat and coat, revealing light brown hair and a fair complexion. Ann noticed that her house was in sharp contrast to the staid traditionalism of the Harrison and Marsh homes. Audrey's was quaint and splashed with color, with each room having a different theme. This one was in shades of blue with bold wallpaper featuring bird motifs. There were flowers everywhere, in vases, pots, on needlepoint pillows. Audrey sat on the blue print sofa while Ann and Damian sat on matching chairs.

"I understand Simon's wife, Priscilla, had a baby shortly before you and Simon left for the Caribbean, yet no one seems to know what happened to her child," Ann said.

"I'm not aware of any baby Priscilla might have had." Audrey opened a wooden box on the coffee table, removed a Rothman Royal and lit up.

"You yourself had a baby some twenty years ago, didn't you?"

Audrey hesitated before blowing out the match. "Yes. I did."

"Was the baby Simon's?"

"Who else would it have been?" Audrey conceded.

"Simon gave Priscilla's baby away, didn't he? To someone at Delacon? Or, was it your baby he gave away?"

Audrey took a puff while she sized up Ann and Damian. "About five months after Priscilla learned she was pregnant, I found out I was as well. I knew about Priscilla, but I don't believe she knew about me. Oh, I'm sure she knew Simon had someone on the side. They all did, all those fine, upstanding family men at Delacon. Anyway, I didn't show and didn't have any symptoms, so I didn't know until I was halfway through my pregnancy. Then, when Simon told me Priscilla was pregnant as well, I was mortified. I thought he was going to tell me he was going to call off our plans and go back to his wife. But that wasn't the first time I had underestimated Simon. He assured me he still intended to take me to the Caribbean. I was delighted, of course, but I told him I didn't want to take a baby along. He told me not to worry, that he would put things right."

"Did putting things right involve Scott Conover?"

"Scott," Audrey sniffed. "Simon saw right through him. Everyone did. Simon used to come round to my flat and tell me about him, about his desperate attempts for promotion. It was one of the few things that made him laugh. Simon made him some outrageous promise which he didn't intend keeping if Scott would take the baby off our hands."

"And you had no objection to giving your child away?"

"I knew how Simon felt about children. I wasn't too keen, either."

"What about Priscilla's child?"

"When the time came, we both had girls, Priscilla and I. Then one day Simon told me he had given Priscilla's child away. It was just after she died. But I noticed him looking at our child rather strangely, as if he suspected something. Then he admitted he didn't know which child he had given to Scott."

"How could he not know?"

"There were a number of times during our last days in England when both babies were together. Simon would bring Priscilla's baby when he came to my flat because Priscilla was too weak to care for it and she wouldn't allow Simon to hire a nanny. I was never certain myself which baby was which. There they'd be, in their playpen, making odd noises at each other, never knowing the sordid circumstances of their existence. When the time came to give the baby to Scott, Simon just picked one up and drove off. I wasn't there at the time, but I assumed he could tell them apart and had taken Priscilla's. The thought that the child we kept wasn't mine never even occurred to me until much later. By then, I didn't care anymore."

"What happened to the other child?"

"Simon said not to worry, he would take care of it. Except there we were, in our tropical hideaway, with a baby," Audrey said with mild disgust. "Simon knew I wasn't pleased so he again turned to Scott. He had already agreed to take one baby, so why not two? Wouldn't be any more bother, he told him. But Scott had already received his promotion and said he couldn't manage it. He could easily explain one child, but how would he explain two?"

"What did Simon do?"

"He told me to place the blame on Scott. Bastard. It wasn't Scott who fathered those two girls. But I didn't care who was at fault. All I knew was I didn't want to retire to paradise with a child in tow. To me, that wasn't paradise even if someone else was changing the nappies. There was still the smell and the crying and breaking things—"

"Who looked after the baby?"

"Simon hired a local woman. I was a young woman back then, Inspector. I had my whole life before me. If I was going to follow a man all the way to the Caribbean, it was to have fun, not play mummy to a child who might not even be mine. I could have walked out on Simon any time I wished, and I would have had he been a bit younger. He was alright as far as lovers go, but I could have done a lot better. But I knew he was in poor health so I stayed and waited for the inevitable to collect the money I'd earned."

"When did Simon die?"

"Two years after we left England. Shortly before, we discussed the child's future. Over time he had grown quite fond of her. Even started carrying pictures of her in his wallet and showed them to everyone he met. If he was gone for more than a few hours, he would ring me and ask about her. He told me he had set up a trust fund for her. I didn't mind, really, because I thought he'd still leave the bulk of his estate to me as he had promised when I agreed to go away with him. That included several million pounds and homes in England, Switzerland and France. But when his will was read, the bastard left me virtually penniless. I discovered he had sold the majority of his property in the last year of his life and that he intended all along to leave most of what he had left to a daughter whose mother he couldn't even identify. I had to sell the villa and take a flat in a part of town littered with alcoholics and drug addicts. Not exactly what I had signed up for."

"Have you been living in the Caribbean all this time?"

"No. After a few months of living in squalor I wired Austin. He sent some money, enough to move to a more suitable flat, though it was still below the standard I had been promised. To cut expenses I fired the nanny and took charge of the child myself. I did the whole mother bit, cooked her meals, washed her clothes, cleaned up after her. But as she got older, I decided I didn't want her educated in the Caribbean. We moved into Simon's home in Switzerland and I enrolled her in the finest school I could find, again with Austin's assistance."

"You lived in Switzerland?" Ann asked.

"I didn't want to send her away to school as Simon requested in his will. I knew what he was up to. He wanted to take her from me, away from my influence. I was alright for him to sleep with, to have his child, but I wasn't good enough to raise her. For all either of us knew, she could very well have been mine. By the time we arrived in Switzerland, I wanted to be her mother whether she was the child I had given birth to or not." Audrey filled her lungs with smoke, then became sentimental. "I suppose I grew to love her. Love, or just gotten used to her. One of the pitfalls of growing older, I suppose. Old, and lonely."

"Weren't you ever curious to find out if she was your child?" Ann said.

"What would I have done had I discovered she wasn't? Given her back? Trust me, it was much easier not knowing." Just then a slim man of average height entered the room. He was much younger than Audrey with small, round glasses framing his large brown eyes. His dark hair was slicked back and he had on a white cotton shirt and khaki trousers. His skin was dark, though it was difficult to tell if that had come from his parents or the sun.

"Peter. These people are from the police. We shan't be much longer." Peter kissed the back of Audrey's hand, then left the room as silently as he had entered.

"Your husband, Miss Belden?" Damian asked.

"A friend. We're off shopping this afternoon and I'm afraid he's a bit impatient."

"Miss Belden, how long did you live in Switzerland?" Ann asked.

"Not long. Less than a year after we arrived, Austin had his solicitor sell the house along with everything in it, so I took the money that was left from the sale of the villa and rented a flat in a small village in Austria. After living in London most of my life I didn't fancy such a quiet, secluded place, but it was all I could afford. I planned on staying only until my daughter finished her schooling in Switzerland."

"When did you return to England?"

"Just last year."

"Is your daughter still in school?"

"No. To my great disappointment, she left school a couple of years ago."

"Why?"

"Because she's under some misguided notion that I can't be left alone. She's taken it upon herself to devote all of her time to looking after me."

"Why does she think that?" Damian asked.

"I'm sure I don't know. Utter nonsense. I'm perfectly capable of looking after myself. But...she has been a great help. I do forget sometimes...she's such a great help..."

"Miss Belden? Are you alright?" Ann asked as Audrey's face suddenly went blank. She sat motionless, the cigarette falling from her fingers. Damian snagged it just in time, then snuffed it out in the ashtray on the table.

"Shall I get an ambulance?" he said quietly to Ann.

"I don't think that will be necessary," Ann said just as softly. "Why don't you go upstairs and see if Miss Belden's daughter is here." Damian took the stairs two at a time and did a quick search. A short time later he returned and shook his head. "Miss Belden? Do you know what happened to the other child, the one Simon gave to Scott?"

"Who? No, I don't think so."

"Thank you, Miss Belden. We'll see ourselves out—Oh, do you know the Harrisons?"

There was a look of faint recognition in Audrey's eyes. "Fitzroy and Sally? Yes. I know them quite well."

The door closed behind Ann and Damian. Peter looked in from the kitchen as Audrey sat crying. He finished his sandwich, then rushed to her side. He knelt on one knee and held her hand as if he was about to propose.

"My darling, what is it? What has happened?"

"It—It's my daughter."

"She is alright, is she not?"

"I don't know. I don't know where she is."

"But of course you do. She is upstairs, in her room."

"No, that isn't her."

"No? Then who?"

"I don't know. All I know is, that girl is not my daughter."

"But you told me she left school in Switzerland to be with you, here, in England."

"She never went to school in Switzerland. She was taken from me ages ago."

"My darling, don't be silly. Who would take her from you?"

"Simon. Or rather some people Simon hired to take her from me," Audrey bristled.

"But why?"

"When Simon became ill and knew his time was short, he became worried. He never thought I cared as much about her as he did. I did care, but I couldn't have matched his affection for her. No one could.

So he made arrangements to have her taken from me upon his death. I went to the authorities, but they refused to help after Simon's solicitor produced a copy of his will. It contained the results of blood tests which proved he was the girl's father. The police told me I would have to prove I was her mother or the letter of Simon's will would be carried out. But I was afraid, afraid that if I were tested it would show I wasn't the girl's mother, that the child we kept was Priscilla's. Then I would be left with nothing. When I refused, Simon's wishes prevailed over mine. Even in death, he had gotten his way."

"But, I do not understand. The woman who is staying with you, she is your daughter, no?"

"Woman? There's no woman staying with me."

"But of course there is. I have seen her myself."

"I don't know who she is."

"Then why did you invite her to stay with you, here, in your own home?"

"Did I? I don't remember—"

"Then it *is* your daughter, the woman upstairs?"

"Yes. My daughter," Audrey said, the faraway look returning to her eyes.

"Then why do you search for her if she is already here?"

"We were going to have such a wonderful time, Simon and I. Just the two of us, living on the beach, golfing, sailing. But there she was, crying, making a mess, constantly demanding all of our attention."

"Oh, but she was just a little baby. She was helpless. She needed you."

Audrey brightened. "Yes. She needed me. She still needs me."

"You love her then."

"Don't be silly."

Peter held her hand between both of his. "You do. You always pretend you're so hard, but you love her."

"Yes, I suppose I do. She's all I have now, and I can't lose her again. I searched for her for so long, ever since those men took her from me that day in the park. I'll never forget her screams as I watched her face disappear through the car window. She didn't know what was happening. I begged them not to take her, but they just laughed."

"But...that is her, no? The girl, the one upstairs?" Peter said, pointing upward.

"She reached her arms toward me, begged me to come for her. But I couldn't! I couldn't stop them!"

"My poor darling!" Peter gave her a long, comforting hug as Audrey again dissolved into tears. This was not only beyond Peter's comprehension, it was also beyond his job description. He wasn't required to deal with the personal problems of the women he accompanied, but he soon learned that women were suckers for a man who was sympathetic, who listened and pretended to care about their emotional upsets. Usually, that would be followed by some small gift of gratitude. To be presented with something more substantial, he would have to make love to them. "My darling, what about the police? Here, in England? Surely they would help after you told them Simon kidnapped your child."

"No, they wouldn't! She was taken from me in the Caribbean, not here!"

"But you told me Simon also arranged for his other baby to be taken, kidnapped, by someone he worked with. Surely the police would do something about that."

"What other baby?"

"The other one, the one Simon had with Priscilla? The one the police were just here inquiring about?"

"There was no other baby," Audrey dried her tear-stained face with a lace handkerchief. "Just mine. Mine and Simon's."

"Yes, of course. But if you told the police Simon was a British citizen, of course they would try to find her."

"Or they would blame me for not reporting her disappearance sooner. I can't search for her if I'm in jail. And I must keep searching. I can't tell you how my heart aches!" Audrey began crying again and Peter gently pulled her head to his shoulder. Then suddenly, Audrey stopped crying. She rose and announced, "I have to go now. My daughter and I have a long drive ahead of us." She put her coat on and tied a blue print head scarf under her chin. She removed a pair of sunglasses from her coat pocket, carefully slid them in place, then left.

"DROP ONE MORE OF THOSE, Sergeant, and you'll be the one cleaning it up."

Ann's mock anger wasn't lost on Damian, who was having a devil of a time holding onto his chips. They had stopped for lunch and were eating in Ann's car before heading back to the station. Damian's mind was somewhere else and the seat covers were suffering for it.

"Sorry, Inspector. I was just thinking about what Audrey said. You reckon Melinda might be her daughter?"

"Melinda can't be the girl Audrey raised. That girl's been living abroad or in boarding school since she was an infant. As far as we know Melinda has been here, with Karl, then Terry, since she was a year old." Ann ate a chip, then said, "Melinda seems quite bright for someone who's been so isolated, whose only real education has been limited to the history of one particular country and whatever books Karl allowed her to read. I wonder why?"

"Maybe she just comes by it naturally. Some people are like that. Could be she inherited it."

"From who? We know Simon was probably her father, but we don't know anything about him apart from the fact he was a self-centered womanizer. Audrey seems of average intelligence at best. Then there's Claire. There's a person I'd like to meet one day."

"Maybe you already have."

"What do you mean?"

"Audrey Belden. Maybe she's Claire."

"How can she be?"

"They both had babies at about the same time. They've both been out of the country for the better part of twenty years, and no one seems to have a clear and continuous accounting of where they've been or what they've been up to all that time. All we have is the word of a few people who knew them back then. Maybe they're protecting someone, like Audrey. Only, why would they, unless she's Claire? They saw the way Scott treated Claire. Audrey was a tart, someone who broke up families. It doesn't make sense they'd go out of their way to protect her."

"True, although I have my doubts about Audrey being Claire. Scott and Simon left England at about the same time. It would have been difficult for her to have gone with both of them."

Damian washed his food down with a large gulp of coffee. "So if we can prove the child Audrey raised was in fact her own, that's the end of her part in all this."

"Not necessarily. Priscilla couldn't have done anything about the fate of her child, but Audrey could have saved both girls if she had wanted to. So could Simon, who seemed destined to father half the population of Leeston if he hadn't left the country."

Damian grinned. "The CPS will think they've gone on holiday when this one's over."

"I shouldn't worry about that. There's still Melinda. She's had enough crimes committed against her to keep the courts busy for years."

Damian muffled a burp. "Who do you reckon Peter is? Audrey's Caribbean lover?"

"How ironic. The former mistress now has the male equivalent, whatever that is," Ann said. "It seems to me the question now becomes, where is Simon's other daughter, and which of them is her mother?"

"Pardon me for asking, but do we really need to know that? I mean, does it really matter which girl belongs to which mother?"

"It might matter to Melinda, and whoever her half-sister is."

"Well, as far as who's to blame, Simon would be at the top of my list. He's the one arranged for his child to be taken from his dying wife, then tried to give the other one away as well."

"Let's concentrate on people who are still alive, Sergeant. That's the problem with this case. Everyone seems to be either dead or missing."

"Except Melinda. Then there's Fitzroy Harrison and Austin Marsh. And Fitzroy's wife, Sally."

"Yes. Sally. She seems to know everything that's happened in Leeston the past twenty years. Perhaps she can shed some light on Simon's family tree."

CHAPTER 20

ANN AND DAMIAN ARRIVED IN Leeston just past three the following day. Damian parked the car across the street from the Harrison's house and reached for the door handle, but Ann stopped him.

"Let's wait here a moment, Sergeant."

"Wait? What for?"

"Sally Harrison."

"Why don't we just ring the bell?"

"Because I've been here twice and each time the elusive Mrs. Harrison seems to be out. Only I don't think she's been in Darlington tending to her ailing mother. I think she's been here all along. She just doesn't want to talk to us."

"But why?"

"That's what I intend to find out."

"But, how do you know she hasn't already left?"

"I don't. I only know there are two cars in the drive and, since as far as we know there are only two people living in that house, I'm going to assume one of them belongs to Mrs. Harrison. Unless, of course, they own a fleet of cars or Sally doesn't drive, in which case my theory has just been shot to hell." Another ten minutes passed. Just as Ann began to consider giving up, her patience was rewarded. She was coming out of a yawn when she happened to catch a glimpse of someone moving in front of an upstairs window. She sprang from the car and Damian followed. Ann rang the doorbell and waited.

"Inspector? What on earth are you doing here?" a stunned Fitzroy said.

"May we come in?" Ann said as she and Damian pushed past him.

"See here, what's this all about?"

Ann looked toward the top of the staircase and said, "Your wife... You said she's away caring for her mother?"

"Yes, that's right."

Ann turned to face Fitzroy. "Then who is it in your guest room?" Fitzroy's eyes lowered. "You did say you were expecting guests?"

"Yes." Ann waited for more details, but none were forthcoming.

"That's your wife in the guest room, isn't it, Mr. Harrison?"

"Yes, it is."

"Then she hasn't been away at her mother's?"

"No—She was, but, her mother was feeling a bit better so my wife returned early this morning."

"I'd like to speak to her, if I may."

"I'm afraid I cannot allow that. She's had a long, tiring week and she's simply not up to it. Now if you don't mind, I was about to—"

"It's alright, Fitz." Ann, Damian and Fitzroy turned in unison to see a woman too youthful in appearance to be in her early sixties standing at the top of the stairs. Her makeup was impeccable, as was her blonde hair, which was neatly swept back and pinned into place. She wore a beige skirt and jacket over a white chamisol blouse and jewelry befitting the wife of an executive of a very successful company.

"Mrs. Harrison. I'd like to ask you a few questions," Ann said.

"Now? No, that's simply not possible. I'm meeting friends in town and I—"

"I promise this won't take any longer than necessary." Sally sighed, descended the staircase with suitable dignity, then entered the sitting room. Ann and Damian sat on the maroon arm chairs while Fitzroy sat on the sofa next to his wife, but there was an icy distance between them. He struck Ann as being a troubled man, no doubt made that way by the women in his life. Sally tilted the crystal of her watch, then said impatiently,

"How can I help you, Inspector?"

"We're inquiring into the whereabouts of Claire Conover."

"Claire? Why, I haven't seen her in years."

"I understand, Mrs. Harrison, you saw Claire with a baby just after she left the clinic, after her own baby had supposedly died at birth."

"You don't have to answer that," Fitzroy interrupted.

Ann stared darts at him. "Mr. Harrison, are you aware that the recorded date of death for the Conover's son was changed at the registrar's office? And that we believe Scott is the one who changed it?"

"No. Why? I mean, when?" he fumbled.

"I assume he did it after he acquired one of Simon's daughters. He obviously needed to change the sex of the baby in the register, but he also saw fit to change the date of the baby's death as well."

"But why? It makes no sense to change the date of death of someone who is still alive."

"Unless he was planning on killing the child later and wanted to cover it up by making it seem as if the baby had died of natural causes shortly after birth. Did you know that? Did you know Scott was planning on having the second baby, the one he acquired from Simon, murdered?" Sally gasped while Fitzroy went to the bar for a whiskey.

"My God, Inspector. Of all the terrible things Scott did, I never thought him capable of something like that," said Fitzroy, who raised his glass to his lips, then froze. "Did he do it? Did he kill the child?"

"No. He didn't."

"Thank God for that," said Fitzroy, who felt relieved enough to partially empty his glass.

"What of the child, Inspector? Where is she now?" Sally asked as Fitzroy brought her a G&T.

"We're not certain. That's why I need your help. Mrs. Harrison, your husband said you thought Scott was drugging Claire?"

"Yes."

"Did you ever see her take drugs?"

"No. Scott was too clever for that. I don't know if he was putting them in her food or somehow tricking her into taking them, but I know he was drugging her into making her believe anything he wanted her to believe."

"What did he want her to believe?"

"I don't think I should say."

"I would be very keen to hear your thoughts."

"Well, I think Scott drugged Claire so she wouldn't protest when he took her child from her."

"How do you know he took the child?"

"Because one day she had the baby and the next day she didn't. I saw her pushing the pram one morning, heading toward the park. She looked absolutely exhausted. Didn't answer when I made general inquiries into her health, and the baby's. Then I looked inside the pram. It was empty."

"She was wheeling an empty pram?"

"Yes. I asked where her baby was, but again she did not respond. I told her to come inside and I'd make her a cup of tea, but she said no, she had to take the baby to the park. I didn't want to upset her, so I let her go on her way."

"Do you think she knew her baby was gone?"

"As she walked away, I could hear her crying. She knew, Inspector. And, I daresay, she had to have known who had taken it from her."

"But surely getting rid of the child would have raised suspicions, especially among Delacon executives."

"You didn't know those men. Wives and children were mere formalities, something you were encouraged to have so people doing business with Delacon would see the company as one big, happy family. That's the image Austin Marsh wanted to portray and the men who achieved success in his company were the ones who played along and fulfilled that fantasy."

"You and your husband don't have children, do you?" Damian asked.

"No, but we disagreed with the company's policy. I knew it would eventually cause trouble with women like myself who couldn't have children."

"Forgive me for asking, but if it was so important to your husband's career, why didn't you adopt?" Ann asked.

"Because in the eyes of Delacon, an adopted child was not the wholesome family image they wished to convey. They wanted women in all stages of creation, from innocent bride to expectant mother to doting parent, all nicely fitted into the artificial ideals of their artificial community. We could have adopted, but I didn't want a child merely to use as a device to advance my husband's career. Even though we were childless, my husband managed to hold onto his job for no other reason than Austin liked him. And his work, of course." Fitzroy thanked her for the faint praise by raising his glass in her direction, then emptying it.

"What about Scott's trips to Switzerland, Mr. Harrison? Do you know anything about those?"

"As Vice-President of Accounting, I had seen Scott's expense account. I knew straight away those trips were not authorized. They couldn't have been. Delacon does no business in that part of the world. There was no way to justify such an expense so I disallowed it. But I later learned someone had approved it. Simon, I presumed."

"Did you ever find out why Scott went there?"

"After it was approved behind my back, I decided to look into it before Scott found out. He refused to tell me, but I threatened to go to Marsh. I don't think he believed I would, but he couldn't be certain so he reluctantly told me of his plan after I promised I would keep it confidential and wouldn't try to stop the expense account from going through."

"What was his plan?"

"On the flight to the Middle East, Scott said he became concerned about Claire's mental state. Not as it affected Claire, mind, but how it might harm his career. He thought about what it would be like attending parties and other business functions with Claire along and her losing control and making a scene, which he claimed she had done in the past. He decided getting rid of the child wasn't enough. So, before he even had a chance to unpack his bags, he was off to Switzerland."

"Why Switzerland?"

"He decided to have Claire committed to an asylum in some far off place where she would eventually be forgotten. He was afraid if she was found she would tell them everything, what he had done to her, the baby. If only he'd realized, she didn't know herself what he had done to her or the baby. I later learned Scott knew of a number of reputable institutions that could have given Claire the care she needed. Instead, he chose the most secluded place he could find. Needless to say, it wasn't one of Switzerland's finest. Hell, absolute hell. A week later he returned with Claire and left her there. Just left her. Then he got on a plane and was back in his office that afternoon, entertaining clients as if nothing happened."

"But if he didn't want anyone to find her, why did he put Switzerland in his expense account? Surely that was bound to raise suspicions, as it obviously did with you."

"Hard to know what went on in that head of his. Perhaps he thought Simon would be the only one who would see it and cover for him, as he had done in the past. Only this time, I saw the expense account first and confronted him with it."

"I assume Claire did not go willingly?"

"Willingly? Would you go willingly if you knew you were going to be locked away in an asylum in a country you were unfamiliar with, where you didn't even speak the language? No, she did not go of her own accord, Inspector. Scott never told her."

"How did you know the asylum was hell, Mr. Harrison?" Damian said.

"My wife is a very caring woman, Sergeant. When I told her what Scott had done, she insisted we go to Switzerland and bring Claire home. I learned long ago there's no sense arguing with Mrs. Harrison so I took a few days off and, without telling anyone, we flew to Geneva. After quite a long taxi ride we found the asylum in some fly speck of a village. I tell you, I've never seen such deplorable conditions. The place was filthy. It smelled damp and musty in some places and strongly of urine in others. It was unbearably hot and the patients wore tattered and soiled night clothes. Some wandered about aimlessly, muttering incoherent ramblings that made sense to no one but themselves. Some were even bashing their heads against walls until they bled. No one bothered to stop them."

"Did you find Claire?" Ann asked.

"It took quite a substantial bribe before we were finally allowed to see her. We were told to wait and a male nurse escorted Claire to the visitors room. We were horrified at what we saw. As dreadful as Claire had looked before, it didn't compare to what had become of her in the short time she was there. She didn't recognize us. Couldn't even speak. We demanded to see a doctor. Hmmph! That man was no more a doctor than you or I. We told him we wanted to take Claire with us, that we'd pay to have her sent to an asylum here, in England, but they refused. They said her husband was the one who signed the papers to have her committed and only he could have her released. I rang Scott immediately, but it was too late. His secretary said he'd already left. No one's heard from him since. As they drove down a quiet road, they were ambushed. The two businessmen who were with him were released after their employers paid their ransom, but Scott remains missing to this day."

"What did you do, Mr. Harrison? Did you go back to England without Claire?"

Fitzroy stared into the bottom of his glass. "That was one of the most difficult things I've ever had to do. We assured Claire we would do all we could, through legal and diplomatic channels, to get her out.

We returned home and did just that, but we ran into red tape after red tape. I consulted lawyers, both here and in Switzerland. I even got the United States consulate involved since Claire was an American citizen, but no one was able to help. I finally convinced my wife to go away on holiday. At that point we both needed to get away for awhile. But as we were about to leave for the airport, the private investigator I hired rang and said Claire had gone missing."

"Where had she gone?"

"We didn't know. We didn't hear anything more about her. We just got on with our lives. We hadn't forgotten her, we just didn't know what more we could do. Then one day, we got a letter. It wasn't signed, but we soon realized it was from Claire."

"What did the letter say?"

"That she wanted us to contact her. Seems she had been living in Austria. Of course we were delighted to hear from her. We flew out there as soon as we could and we were amazed at what we saw. Claire had escaped the asylum, but she had built a whole new life for herself completely devoid of reality. Her clothes, everything in her flat was from at least one hundred years ago."

"How did she manage it?"

"Even after Scott disappeared, Austin still paid his wages. Once a month he sent a check to a numbered bank account in Switzerland, and each month the money would disappear."

"Then Austin knew Claire was living in Austria."

"If he didn't, he must have strongly suspected it."

"Were you ever able to confirm it was Claire who was withdrawing the money?"

"Who else could it have been?" Fitzroy scoffed as Ann and Damian exchanged uneasy glances.

"But why would he send Claire money?" Ann said. "It wasn't out of a sense of duty, of loyalty to Scott, was it? It was because he believed she knew the whereabouts of Simon's daughter, the one he had given to Scott."

"Yes."

"Mr. Harrison, if Austin was so keen to find his niece, why didn't he go to Austria himself, or hire a private investigator? Surely he had the resources if he wanted to."

"That's just it, isn't it?"

"Are you saying he didn't want to find his niece?"

"Not at first, no."

"But now he does?"

Fitzroy answered with a smirk before lowering the level in his glass. "When the child was born, Austin was indifferent towards her, to say the least. But over time, his interest in her grew along with the rumor."

"Right," Ann sighed. "So Austin didn't want his niece at first, but now he does. Are there any rumors, real or otherwise, as to the reason behind this sudden change of heart?"

"Rumors? At Delacon? Well, *rumor* has it Austin's real reason for wanting the girl is because of Simon's money. Austin owns the company, but there are those who believe that Simon had a huge stake in Delacon as well, which would now belong to his heirs."

"Any of that true?"

"Your guess is as good as mine, Inspector," Fitzroy said, then lit up a cigar.

"How could Simon own more of Delacon than Austin? He founded the company," Damian said.

"Because Simon was a crafty devil. He bought out several minority owners, but to keep Austin off the scent he arranged for their shares to go to dummy accounts Simon set up under a false name. Totted up, I believe Simon's estate now controls the majority interest in Delacon."

"Any idea if *that* rumor is true?" Ann asked.

Fitzroy puffed on his cigar, admired the smoke and said, "One never knows at Delacon, Inspector."

"What did Claire want to see you about in Austria?"

"Her daughter. Even though Claire had buried herself in a bygone era, she never lost hope of finding her child. I think the memory that she did once have a baby, that for a brief time she held it and fed it and put it to bed, had remained with her. When we went to see her, before we had a chance to ask how she was or how she came to be living in such a place, Claire asked if we knew anything about the girl. We told her we didn't. We talked for a while, then Claire began acting strangely. She didn't move, didn't even blink. We thought she had become ill or perhaps was having some sort of spell, but she said she was fine and we returned home the next day. A week later, we received a letter saying she would be arriving on the ferry in Hull in two days time and could we put her up for a few days."

"She came back to look for her child?"

"While she was here she would go out every day by herself. Never a word as to where she was going or when she would be back. My wife and I assumed she was out searching for the girl, but we wondered how she would even know where to look. But I found out later she did have a clue. A single, solitary clue. For years Claire had kept boxes containing Scott's possessions, but she had never given them so much as a look."

"What was in the boxes?"

"We didn't see them, but Lydia told us they were filled with ledgers and files that Scott had kept."

"Lydia?"

"Lydia Wilding. She was there, in Claire's flat. It was explained to us she was Claire's personal secretary."

"Did Claire hire her?"

"Yes. Well, I assumed she did. Lydia told us that one day Claire, at Lydia's urging, went through the ledgers when she discovered an entry in the amount of ten thousand pounds to be paid in equal parts to a Karl Wagner and Terry Royce. It meant little on its own, but the date of the entry was the same as the day Claire's child disappeared. One day, after she had come back from one of her solo jaunts, she asked me to contact this Royce fellow and arrange a meeting with him and the girl.

I asked Claire, who's Terry Royce? But she didn't say. With virtually nothing to go on apart from his name, I managed to track him down. He agreed to meet me in a dilapidated shack just outside of town."

"How did you get him to agree?"

"By offering him a rather large sum of money. Claire and I drove there the next day and waited. He arrived nearly an hour late with that poor girl in tow. Wretched creature. Even at a distance I could tell she hadn't been properly cared for. She was dirty and her clothes were in tatters."

"Did she appear to have been abused?"

"She did not look to be a happy child, Inspector."

"What about Claire?"

"She remained inside the car. I went inside the shack with Royce, who ordered the girl to stay outside. She did as she was told, as if she had been trained to obey his every command."

"What did the two of you talk about?"

"When I agreed to go along with this Claire told me all she wanted was to see the girl. If, upon seeing her Claire determined she was her daughter, I was to offer him money for her."

"She wanted you to buy her from Terry?"

"Yes, I suppose that's what it amounted to." Fitzroy sat on the arm of the couch next to Sally, cigar and drink in hand. "Before I went into the shack I looked at Claire. The tinted window came down just a bit, which was Claire's signal that she was satisfied it was her child."

"She didn't understand that wasn't possible?"

"She doesn't understand that to this day. Once we were inside the shack, I asked Royce what he wanted for the girl. He just laughed. Said she wasn't for sale. I told him I had been authorized to pay a substantial amount of money in exchange for her. He again laughed. Said he wouldn't let her go at any price. I tried to persuade him, which only seemed to amuse him more. When it became apparent we weren't going to reach an agreement, I had no choice but to leave without her.

Before I did I gave him a package as Claire instructed should he refuse her offer."

"What was in the package?"

"Some personal items."

"A handmade jumper?"

"I believe that was one of the items."

"How long did Claire stay with you after that?"

"The following day, she announced she would be returning home immediately. That came as a complete surprise. We never thought she would leave without her daughter, not after she seemed so certain she had found her."

"She gave up?"

"On the contrary. As I was about to learn, it was only the beginning."

"What do you mean?"

"True to her word, she left that night. Then, this past July, we returned home one day and, there she was."

"No letter this time?"

"No. We had no advance notice she was coming."

"She just showed up at your door?"

"Yes. Well, not the door, actually. At the airfield about four miles from here."

"Why had she come back?"

"She didn't stay long enough for us to find out. She was gone the next day. We didn't hear from her again until earlier this month when we received a letter asking if we could meet her ferry in Hull and put her up for a few days."

"When was it, this last visit?"

Fitzroy looked with uncertainty at Sally, who said, "The ninth, tenth and eleventh of October." Ann could feel Damian's eyes on her.

"Mr. Harrison, does Claire own a gun?" Ann asked.

"Certainly not," Fitzroy replied with indignation. "Even if she did, I doubt she could have gotten it through customs. But I own several firearms, and I did notice one of my handguns was missing during her last stay. A thirty-eight."

"Did you report the weapon stolen?"

"There was no need. It was back the next day."

"Had it been fired?"

"I don't know. I suppose I should have, but I didn't examine it."

"Apart from the one that went missing, can you account for the rest of your guns while Claire was here?"

"Yes, I can."

"No, Inspector. He can't," Sally said. "He sent five of them out to be serviced. The man rang us the next day and said one of the boxes was empty."

"Was the gun ever found?"

"Yes, Inspector. It was." Fitzroy refilled his glass with an unsteady hand.

"Would you mind if I had a look at it?" Fitzroy threw back his drink, then went to the oak gun cabinet and unlocked it. He removed a small cherrywood box, brought it to Ann and opened it. She believed the look of shock on his face was genuine.

"Where's the gun, Mr. Harrison?"

"It—It was there! I know it was there!"

"When was the last time you saw it?"

"Last month. I was going to polish it up a bit—"

"Do you own any other thirty-eight or nine millimeter handguns?"

"Yes. I own six thirty-eights and a couple of nines."

"And they're all here?"

"Yes. All present and accounted for." Fitzroy checked each box, determined not to be proved wrong a second time.

"I'm afraid we're going to have to take them with us," Ann said.

"Whatever for?"

"Just routine tests. I promise they'll be returned in good order." Fitzroy could only watch as Ann and Damian placed his gun collection in the boot of Ann's car. Damian closed it and said, "He's lying, isn't he?"

"Sergeant," Ann leaned against the back of the car, "every last one of them is lying, everyone involved in this case. They've been lying from the start."

"But why?"

"You were right. They're protecting whoever it is who killed Terry. Or perhaps who they believe killed him."

Damian leaned on the car next to her. "So it was Claire who gave Melinda the jumper, not Scott. That means the photo's genuine. Scott's still being held captive." Ann was deep in thought, trying to work out in her mind what it actually did mean. "What about the missing gun? Where do you reckon it is?"

"I'm not so sure it *is* missing."

"But there are eight boxes and only seven guns," Damian said.

"That doesn't necessarily mean the gun is missing. It just means it's not in its box."

"So what's next?"

"We have the guns tested, though I have little hope that any of them will turn out to be the murder weapon. I think that will be the one that has conveniently been misplaced."

"What about Claire? You reckon she killed Royce?"

"He mistreated the girl Claire thought to be her daughter, but there's also Stropman and Roschine. Terry double-crossed both of them. Then there's Karl. Terry's refusal to give Melinda back to him would be motive enough to make him a prime suspect."

"Then there's Melinda herself."

"Yes. No one had more reason to want Terry dead than her," Ann conceded.

"Could it have been an accident?"

"Eight bullets are no accident, Sergeant. Until we find the guns those bullets came from, we can't even begin to know who fired the fatal shot."

Damian scratched his five o'clock shadow. "The Harrisons, Austin, Audrey…They didn't know Terry, did they?"

"As far as we know. And none of them appear to have had reason to kill him. But you never know, Sergeant. "This case is filled with contradictions and things that are hidden just beneath the surface." Ann got in the car and Damian followed suit. Before starting the motor Ann said, "Why do you suppose Claire didn't come by ferry the second time she visited?"

"I don't know. Maybe she changed her mind and decided to fly."

"Seems a bit odd, what with her mind so firmly set in the nineteenth century, that she would get on a plane. Unless Lydia somehow persuaded her."

CHAPTER 21

AN ATTORNEY BY TRADE, ROBERT Mason could never find enough hours in the day to read everything he needed to read in order to practice corporate law. Faced with another long night with the mound of papers stacked up next to him on the passenger seat of his Jaguar, Robert was using the evening rush to get caught up, which is why he never saw the lorry directly in front of him until his face was inches from it. The front of his car disintegrated and he was wedged somewhere underneath it, creating a traffic jam that included Ann and Damian.

Because of the hour, it was taking forever for the ambulance to get through. While she waited for the street to be cleared, Ann wiled away the time by having a look around. The shops drew her attention first. It had been so long since she'd gone for a day of shopping. Then she noticed the people. Some had stopped to gape at the accident but most went about their business. One group in particular caught Ann's eye. On the pavement to her right a paunchy, middle-aged man held a video camera in one hand and waved his other arm wildly at an equally animated group consisting of three children and a woman.

"What are they doing? It's freezing out there," Ann remarked.

"They're tourists," Damian replied.

"Tourists? Who goes on holiday in the dead of winter, unless it's some place warm?"

"It's off-peak. Have you never heard of it? Me and my mates went off-peak to the Bahamas a few years back."

"The Bahamas? What's off-peak in the Bahamas?"

"It only means there's less tourists. They also don't gouge you as much on hotels and restaurants and the like." Ann watched the energetic group flitting between lamp posts, standing in front of shop windows, posing and making odd faces as the smiling man recorded their every move.

"What are they doing now?" Ann wondered out loud, her impatience over the delay growing.

"Touristy things. It's where everyone gets to make fools of themselves so they can show everyone back home what a smashing time they had while they were stuck home leading their dull, ordinary lives."

With nothing else to do, Ann continued to watch as the children and the woman ran to pose by a phone box on the corner behind Ann's car. All Ann could see was the man waving and smiling gleefully as he pointed his camera at them. Even though she couldn't see what he was filming, Ann was able to follow their movements by watching where he aimed his camera. To the left. Down. Straight ahead. To the left again. Now to the right. When he swung the camera around toward the street to capture the arrival of the ambulance, Ann finally saw it. The light flickering on the front of the camera. It followed its subjects everywhere they went. And it was red. A red eye.

IT HAD BEEN STUCK IN the back of her mind ever since Ian said Karl must have hated Melinda. Ann knew Karl had probably abused her. He had every opportunity. But what would Ian know about it? Karl was asleep when Ann came to see him in his cell this afternoon. It didn't escape her that, even in these conditions, he was sleeping more soundly than anyone who had committed the sort of crimes he was suspected of had the right to.

"Wake up, Doctor!"

Karl stirred, then quickly sat up. Even in his semi-awake state he had the presence of mind to try to make himself presentable.

"I hope you've come to tell me my lawyer has arranged my bail."

"Dr. Wagner, did you know Ian Harding and Melinda were having an affair?"

"An affair?" he said as he stretched his glasses around each ear. "I'm afraid you're mistaken, Inspector."

"Then you didn't walk in on them while they were making love?" Karl's jaw quivered and his face turned red. "You're not helping your case by remaining silent."

"Oi! Inspector! If he won't tell ya, I will!" The last thing Ann wanted to do right now was talk to Roschine, but she thought hearing him spout his usual array of lies might help loosen Karl's tongue. Ann had the guard open the door to Roschine's cell. He was lying on his back on the bed, knees up, staring at the ceiling.

"What could you possibly know about this?" said Ann, who stood by the door, arms folded.

"What, me?" Roschine sat up. "I was there. I saw everything."

"Mr. Roschine, is there any significant event in the past one hundred years at which you haven't been present?"

"Alright. Maybe I wasn't there. But I know who was."

"Who?"

Roschine smiled, the spotlight once again shining brightly on him. "Way I heard it, it weren't a private affair, if ya know what I mean. Wasn't just them two in Stroppy's barn, that lass and that gardener."

"Stropman's barn? What are you saying?"

"That it was more a party than a date. More a, more a orgy."

"What do you mean, an orgy?"

"Have you never been to one? You really have led a sheltered life, Inspector."

"I'm getting tired of this! If you don't tell me what you know, if you don't tell me the truth this time, you can sit here and tell your little stories to yourself the rest of your life!"

"Alright, alright. Don't get yourself in a state. Mind, I can't give ya names and such, but I can tell ya certain things that may have taken place."

"Why can't you give me names? Is it because you don't know any?"

His smile faded and his tone became serious. "Because it's safer that way."

"So what happened at this so-called orgy?" Ann asked.

"There's a certain individual…Makes videos, him. Films."

"What sort of films?"

"What sort? Erm, educational films, they are. My, my, Inspector. I never cease to be amazed at how little you know. For instance, I'd wager you think me and Stroppy, all we care about is drugs and whores. My, my. How little you know."

"Enough games, Mr. Roschine. What else does Stropman care about?"

"Sex. Stroppy loves sex. I mean, *loves* it. In fact he's so obsessed with it, he makes tapes. Sex tapes, they are. Sells 'em on internet. I've only seen a few of 'em meself. Well done, mind, but a bit rough even for a bloke like me who's fulfilled a few fantasies of me own." Ann's eyes began drifting toward his misshapen organ, but she caught herself in time.

"How rough?"

"Well, they weren't quite snuff films, but they weren't far from it. I mean, girls were still alive, but just barely."

"Was Melinda in any of these films?" Ann managed to get out.

"Melinda…Melinda…Hard to say. Wasn't their faces the camera was aimin' at."

"Who else was in these films?"

A wide smile came across Roschine's face.

"I can tell ya who was in one of 'em. That bloke there." He nodded toward the door. "The doc."

It could turn out to be nothing more than another one of Roschine's lies. He knew he wouldn't be getting out of jail any time soon, so why not have some fun by leading the police into one dead end after another? Ann couldn't talk to Karl right now because his lawyer finally arrived and refused to let his client answer questions, so Ann turned her attention to Stropman. First, Damian led a raid on Stropman's house. He confiscated everything in the media room, the DVDs – none of which were marked - and all of the equipment. Then he rounded up whoever he could find at the station to help him go through the discs while Ann got to work on Stropman, who was picked up in an herbal shop buying incense and aphrodisiacs.

"All those women you've got working for you. Why Melinda?" Ann said as she sat across him in interview room four. Stropman, dressed in a paisley print caftan, smiled smugly. "Don't bother to deny it. I've seen your pornography collection."

"Really, Inspector. If that's how you choose to see them, then I can only conclude that you must be sexually repressed. I make artistic films, films that transcend the limits of one's creative imagination in the art of sexual performance." His eyes sparkled with intensity.

"You can knock off the art crap. You hire other sexual deviants to rape and torture women, film it, then sell them to perverts like yourself."

"What a pity you choose to see it that way."

"It would be an even greater pity if you didn't tell me what you did to her."

"Am I not cooperating? I thought I was."

"Yes, you are. In fact, Mr. Stropman, I wonder why you're being so forthcoming."

"Because, Inspector, I feel my rights would be violated if I were to be arrested merely for artistic expression. I have every confidence my solicitors will have me out of here before the day is out. I have documents, release forms, which everyone who takes part in my films are required to sign. It's all quite legal."

"You expect me to believe Melinda signed a form consenting to this?"

"I can produce such a document with the girl's signature on it, if you like."

"I don't doubt that. What I do doubt is whether the signature would actually be hers." Stropman sat back and folded his hands on top of his ample belly.

"Tell me about this film you made, the one with Melinda."

"Melinda?" Ann held a photo of Melinda in front of him.

"There was no film with this Melinda, Inspector."

"Then what was she doing at that so-called orgy?"

"Nothing."

"What do you mean, nothing?"

"I mean, quite literally, nothing. As I recall, she failed her screen test and was deemed unacceptable."

"You're telling me Melinda wasn't in any of your films?"

"That is exactly what I am saying. As I said she did do a screen test, just a few head shots, but I'm afraid she was a bit lacking when it came to acting ability."

Ann studied him for a few long moments. "Who else was in your films?"

"Who else? Do you know how many of these I've made? The cast changes from film to film." They were interrupted by a knock on the door. It was Damian, who asked to see Ann out in the hall.

"Roschine was right. Not a lot of visible faces," said Damian, who held half a dozen DVDs in his hands. "I haven't found one with Melinda in it. Even so, judging by what I've seen so far, Stropman's solicitors have their work cut out for them this time."

They used the DVD player in Ann's office. There was a long leader, then the crudely made opening titles appeared with all credit for this production attributed to Stropman. Then the screen went black and for the next ten minutes they watched footage of Stropman's version of artistic expression. Damian spoke from time to time, trying to identify various people, while Ann fought the urge to press the stop button on more than one occasion. She could feel herself drifting away. The horror of what she was watching was no longer registering. Damian himself had reached his limit and fast-forwarded through the rest of the disc until the screen again faded to black.

"Inspector?"

"What?" Ann said as she felt Damian's hand on her shoulder.

"Are you alright?"

"Yes," Ann said, then cleared her throat. "Yes, I'm fine."

"Bit difficult to watch something like that."

"Not as difficult as it was for the victims," Ann said, then quickly, "What about the other tapes?"

"They were every bit as graphic. Haven't been able to identify any of the other victims as yet."

"Have Garzecki help you. I'm sure they can spare someone for this. Try to identify them, then see if any of them are still alive. It could be Melinda is our only living witness."

CHAPTER 22

BUSINESS HAD PICKED UP SINCE Mack bought the Black Knight, but it was quiet now. There was less than an hour left before closing and the place was practically empty. Mack was biding his time drying glasses behind the bar when the door slowly opened. He did a double-take at the figure standing in the doorway. Melinda had always been slight, but she looked absolutely lost in the dark brown jacket, gray top and black trousers she took from the hospital. She appeared pale, as if all the life had drained out of her, as she made her way to where Terry's table used to be and sat, her back to the bar.

At the same time, after several failed attempts Juan finally found his way to Waterpool Road, the same street where the Black Knight was located. It wasn't his uncanny sense of direction or remarkable power of recall that got him there. He had been inadvertently redirected a number of times by people he bumped into as he aimlessly wandered the streets. He had only been down this road hundreds of times in his life, which began and still continued for no apparent reason in this same town. He didn't know it yet, but he had completed phase one. He had found the pub. Now if he could only get his eyes to focus.

It was night time again, the only time Juan seemed to be able to function anymore. At the moment he was propped up against a lamp post, engaged in another battle with his senses. He drove the heel of his hand into his forehead to try to make the confusion subside, then shook his head from side to side like a wet dog. But it didn't alleviate his discomfort even though he had enough painkillers in him to prevent him from feeling the full effects of the aneurysm that was undoubtedly developing in his brain and would probably kill him one day, if his other self-destructive habits didn't do it first.

He came out of one of those head shakes and the light from the pub aligned perfectly with his eyes. Even if it was one of the many establishments he had been banned from, he had gone nearly an hour without putting an addictive substance in his system, an unprecedented amount of time in between reinforcing his perpetual high. He peeled himself off the lamp post and dragged himself toward the pub, staggering under the strain of such an endeavor. He steadied himself with a hand against the wall, his forehead resting against the pub window. He mustered enough strength to roll his head up until his face was flush with the glass. When he finally opened his eyes, they locked on the table in back. After so many days of searching, he had stumbled upon his prey. He would now take the first step on the path toward immortality. He would begin to make his mark in the annals of crime. It was all there before him.

The gun nearly fell from his right hand, which he held at his side. He adjusted and readjusted his grip in his suddenly sweaty hand as he moved toward the door. A deep breath, and he flung the door open. He took a step inside, held the gun with both hands, aimed it at the girl sitting alone in the corner, closed his eyes, and fired.

The noise filled the room, freezing everyone in place except for Mack, who ducked behind the bar. The bullet hit Melinda squarely in the right shoulder, but she didn't flinch. The wisps of smoke began to dissipate, revealing a stream of blood slowly making its way down the back of her jacket. But why hadn't she moved? Was she dead and just hadn't fallen yet?

A barely audible gasp escaped from Juan's lips as Melinda stirred, but still she didn't fall. Instead she looked over her injured shoulder straight at him. The hatred in her eyes was so intense it caused him to take a step back. His hands lost their grip on the gun and it dropped to the floor with a thud. Instincts dictated that he should run, but the only thing that moved was his left hand to his right side as the sound of a second gunshot registered in his mind. He looked down at his shirt, at the small spot of blood that quickly spread. Moments later, he had no recourse but to crumple to the floor. Just before he lost consciousness the silhouette of a dark figure walked past the door, then disappeared.

The sounds of the gunshots made their way down the street to the café where Lydia and Peter were sitting. Lydia jumped to her feet and hurried to where a small crowd had gathered in the doorway of the pub. Peter followed and caught up just as Lydia was wading through the onlookers until Juan's lifeless body was visible, sending her and Peter off into the still, dark night on a frantic search of the streets.

"It wasn't her, was it? Do you think it was her?" Peter said, holding onto his panama hat as he tried to keep up.

"I don't know, but we have to assume it was. We have to find her before the police. If we don't, this might not be the end of it. It won't be until she reclaims her child. Or who she believes to be her child."

"Why do we need to be caught up in all of this? Why do we not go back home, let things fall where they may?"

"We can't do that."

"But why?"

"We just can't."

He again struggled to catch up. "What about the girl? Who do you suppose she was?"

"What girl?"

"The one in the pub. The one who was shot?"

Lydia stopped dead in her tracks. "I thought it was just him that got shot."

"No, there was a girl in back. Did you not see her?"

SHORTLY AFTER LEARNING MELINDA WAS missing from the hospital, Ann received word about the shooting at the Black Knight. When she and Damian arrived Juan was lying on the floor in a pool of blood, Mack was still cowering behind the bar and Melinda was sitting with her back to the door, indifferent to everything that had just taken place. Ambulance sirens wailed in the background as Ann kicked the gun from Juan's hand, checked for a pulse, then said to Mack, "What the hell happened here?"

Mack peered over the bar and said, "He dead?"

"No, but he's not far from it." Ann then went to see about Melinda. She hadn't seen the blood at first against Melinda's dark jacket but she could see it now, dripping down the length of Melinda's arm, off her fingertips and onto the floor at a rapidly increasing rate.

"He—He shot her!" Mack managed to say. "Aimed his gun right at her, then shot her!"

"Juan shot Melinda?"

"Aye!" Mack wiped his forehead with a bar rag.

"Who shot Juan?"

"Don't know! All happened so fast! He shot her, then someone, someone out there, shot him! Down he goes in a heap!" Damian rushed out of the pub and looked up and down the street while Ann sat across from Melinda.

"Melinda?" Melinda's eyes were open, but they were unfocused. It might have been from shock, or a loss of blood, or from pain. But it was none of those things.

"He was nice to me," Melinda began, her voice soft and emotional. "He talked to me, took me places I wasn't allowed to go—"

"Where did he take you?" Ann asked.

"A barn."

"Why?"

"So we could be together."

Ann noticed the tears welling up in Melinda's eyes. "Something happened, didn't it? Something you didn't want to happen?"

"It was late. I wanted him to take me home…He—I wanted him to help me, but he held me down…let them do things to me—"

"Who did things to you?"

Melinda swallowed hard. "Ian. Stropman. And my…my fath—"

"You're father? You mean Karl Wagner? How do you know it was him?"

Melinda looked Ann in the eye and said, "I remember." A paramedic arrived and began treating Melinda while another team worked on Juan. Ann surveyed the scene before her and helped keep onlookers out of the pub and off the evidence until the paramedics were finished.

"How is she?" Ann asked a medic off to the side.

"Lucky. Bullet went through her shoulder, out the front," he said, illustrating on himself. "You'll probably find it somewhere in that wall. She's lost a lot of blood. Really should go to hospital, have a doctor look at it to make sure the bullet didn't damage anything on the way through. Could probably do with a stitch or two as well."

"What about him? Is he gonna make it?"

"Hard to say, but my money's against it," the medic said, then left to help load Juan into an ambulance. Mack took Melinda into his office to rest while Ann joined Damian by the bar.

"Not a soul out there," Damian said.

"Who do you think shot him, Sergeant?"

"I don't know, but there's got to be loads of people wouldn't mind seein' him on a slab in the morgue. Could be a drug dealer he owed money to."

"Perhaps. But why would Juan shoot Melinda?"

"So she can't testify against him, I reckon."

"But, where did he get the gun?"

Secure in the knowledge that Melinda was safely in Mack's care, Ann and Damian drove to the Harrison's to see if the answer to that question might be found there since guns seemed to disappear from Fitzroy's cabinet with the ease and frequency of books leaving the lending library. Mack, however, had turned to the bottle to calm his nerves and was by now too drunk to have seen Melinda leave. She didn't sneak out. She simply got up and left through the back door.

They arrived at the Harrison's just after eleven. Ann was about to ring the doorbell when she heard raised voices.

"I'm fed up with it, that's why!" Sally shouted.

"She just needs time. She hasn't bothered anyone," said Fitzroy, whose volume couldn't match that of his wife's.

"Hasn't bothered anyone? Have you forgotten already?"

"No, I haven't. But may I remind you that it's nothing more than speculation on your part. On *our* part. No one's ever been able to prove she was involved."

"Proof? How much more proof do you need? Now I want this to be the end of it!" There was the sound of footsteps on the stairs, prompting Ann to ring the doorbell.

"Inspector. What on earth—?"

"Please, Mr. Harrison. I haven't the time!" said Ann, who didn't wait to be invited in. "Who is staying with you? Is it Claire?"

"Yes, Inspector." Fitzroy's eyes shifted downward toward the ever-present drink in hand. "She's been staying with us the past few days. But she isn't here now."

"Where is she then?"

"I honestly don't know."

"Was she here earlier tonight, around ten o'clock?"

"Yes."

"You're certain of that?"

"No, but she was here when I left at eight."

"Is there anyone who can vouch for her whereabouts at ten o'clock tonight?"

"No, there isn't. My wife was with me. There was no one here except Claire. And Lydia, of course."

"Is Lydia here now?"

"No. She left shortly after my wife and I."

"Mr. Harrison, at approximately ten o'clock this evening a man who was recently involved in the kidnapping of a young woman was shot. Moments earlier, he shot that same woman. And we believe that woman to be one of Simon's daughters."

"My God," Fitzroy's head popped up from his drink. "Is she alright?"

"For now."

"And you believe Claire shot this man? No, I know her, Inspector. She wouldn't have done such a thing."

"But she's been staying here, with you, and one of your guns has gone missing. By the way, have you found it yet?"

"No, but I'm certain it will turn up soon. What, you think Claire stole my gun, then used it to shoot that man? Nonsense. She doesn't even know how to use a firearm."

"That's enough!" They turned to see Sally coming in from the library. "It's time to tell the truth, Fitz. All of it."

"What do you mean, my dear? I've just been telling the Inspector and the Sergeant here all I know. All *we* know."

"The truth," Sally reiterated in a tone her husband knew all too well.

Fitzroy rubbed his brow and said, "Come through, Inspector. Sergeant." The four of them went into the sitting room and all but Fitzroy sat. "It isn't Claire who's been staying with us. It's Priscilla."

"Priscilla? But I thought she died just after her baby was born," Damian said.

"She nearly did. As her condition worsened, her doctor approached her about testing a new drug that had recently been developed. He never expected it to work. Even told her as much. But he said if she tried it, it would help them eventually perfect it. She agreed and, well, it turned out to be more than they had hoped. She made a complete recovery. However, her joy at regaining her health was short-lived once she learned of Simon's betrayal."

"That's also what made her want to take revenge against those involved, isn't it?" Ann said. "Her and Claire both?"

"You have to understand, these are desperate women, and it's a desperation not of their own making. There are many similarities between Priscilla and Claire. Claire has been abused in one way or another since she was a child. She once told me she had been made pregnant by an uncle but lost the baby soon after. She was just twelve years old. That was just one incident. There were others, each more sordid than the last. The final obscenity forced upon her was Scott. Their families knew it was an arranged marriage. Claire hardly even knew him when they married. On their first date he forced himself on her. I don't know, she may have consented—"

"Fitzroy!" Sally said with indignation.

"And Priscilla?" Ann intervened.

"Priscilla," Fitzroy again turned his gaze downward. "While Claire has been deliberately, systematically destroyed by the people closest to her, Priscilla's downfall was more a matter of neglect. First Simon, then Austin. She was certain she was going to die when they told her they couldn't cure her. Had last rites more times than I can count. Even when they approached her with that experimental drug, she had a priest come see her after the first treatment. That's how certain she was that it wasn't going to work."

"But it did work."

"Yes, but it didn't give her a sense of relief. Instead, it changed her. She became morbid, more fearful than ever of death. Then, on top of that, Simon had given her child away. Poor Priscilla. She couldn't cope."

"What did she do?"

"She devoted herself to finding her daughter. I always thought it would have been better if she knew one way or another what happened to her child, but not knowing drove her to the brink of madness. She asked Austin for help but he refused. In the end, she went to the Caribbean to talk to Simon and Audrey in the hope they would tell her what they had done with the child, but by then Simon was dead and Audrey had become a hopeless alcoholic. One more victim of Simon's neglect."

"What *had* they done with the girl?"

"When he learned his time was short, Simon made plans with an acquaintance to have his daughter put in her care upon his death. When Austin found out, he had the child taken away."

"But Audrey claims her daughter has been with her, in Switzerland, the past nineteen years."

"Someone's daughter may have been with her, Inspector, but I doubt it was the same girl Austin had taken from her. He put that girl in boarding school as soon as she was old enough. Don't think he's seen her since."

"Is Audrey's daughter – or the one she believes to be her daughter – with her now?"

"Audrey seems to think so."

"Then why is she still searching for her? She *is* still searching, isn't she?"

"Yes. I thought she'd given up, but each time she seems to have put it behind her, something compels her to go off again."

"Audrey's daughter – her *real* daughter…Where is she now?" Ann asked.

"She's with Priscilla. Has been the past couple of years," Fitzroy said.

"Lydia?"

"Yes. She's the one Austin had taken from Audrey."

"How do you know?"

"Nothing more than a guess, really. She's quite bright, Inspector. Has quite a high IQ. It wasn't long before she began wondering about her mother and father. Once she began looking into it she learned everything, about Scott, Claire, Austin, Audrey, her half-sister. She became obsessed with finding her family."

"How did she find Priscilla?"

"As she searched for her mother, Lydia learned that Audrey was living in Austria. She left school and went there to see if Audrey was indeed her mother. She didn't tell Audrey who she was. They soon became friends and through that friendship Lydia met Peter. I don't know if you've met him, Inspector, but I believe he's what you would call a gigolo. He was, among other things, Audrey's escort, accompanying her to parties and what have you. It was at one such party that Peter met Priscilla and was, for a time, her companion as well. Then, this time through Peter, Lydia met Priscilla."

"What was Priscilla doing in Austria?"

"She followed Audrey there. But all Audrey knew was that Austin had taken one of the girls. She knew no more of either girl's whereabouts than that."

"How has Priscilla managed?"

"She hasn't. While Audrey found a way to cope at the bottom of a bottle, Priscilla—well, that's a different matter entirely. As she became more distressed over her daughter, her fantasies began to take over. She started to believe she was living in another era, in Austria during the eighteen-sixties."

"I thought it was Claire who believed that."

"No. That was Priscilla. We don't know why she chose that era other than she studied history at university."

"Mr. Harrison, why did you tell me it was Claire you visited in Austria and not Priscilla?"

"Because I thought Priscilla was the one who stole my gun. I was trying to protect her."

"Then you don't know where your gun was, where Claire or Priscilla were, on the tenth of October?"

"No. I don't." Fitzroy steadied himself with a drink before continuing. "Poor Priscilla. She's become quite delusional. That's where Lydia has been such a great help. She became Priscilla's personal secretary and has done her best to see to it Priscilla stays out of trouble. I know it's difficult to understand, but Priscilla doesn't know of modern conventions. She's nearly been run over by automobiles half a dozen times. She only knows of horse-drawn carriages."

"Did you try getting her some help?"

"Yes, but she didn't respond to treatment. I believe the only thing that will put her right is finding her daughter."

"Where has Claire been all these years since escaping the asylum? It *was* Claire in the asylum, wasn't it?"

"Yes. No one seems to know," Fitzroy said. "A few years ago she just turned up at our door. Since then she appears from time to time, never staying long or saying why she's come back."

"When did Audrey return to England?"

"In July. She stayed with us for a few days, but then she said she intended to stay for an extended period so we arranged for her to live in one of Simon's homes."

"So it was Audrey who came to visit, not Claire? She's the one who flew instead of taking the ferry?"

"Yes. Both Claire and Priscilla are afraid to fly. The only way they'll travel is by car, boat or train."

"How did you come to know Audrey?"

"She, erm, worked for Simon, but she also worked for me for a time when my own secretary was in hospital. We would, erm, chat upon occasion. In spite of her reputation, I found her to be a rather interesting woman."

"Fitzroy...," Sally warned.

"I, erm, we – Audrey and I – we, erm, as I said, got to know each other. Quite well, in fact." Fitzroy turned a shade paler as he again imbibed, then kept his eyes aimed at his constant companion. "We had an affair. It was just the one time, the one and only time I've ever been unfaithful to my wife." Then, directing his words at Sally, "I deeply regret it. I regretted it then as I do now. If it's any comfort to you, I shall be regretting it for the rest of my life."

"Sorry, Mr. Harrison, but I have to ask," Damian said. "Is there a chance you're the father of Audrey's daughter?"

Fitzroy's eyes met Damian's. "No chance, Sergeant. My relationship with Audrey ended more than a year before her daughter was born."

"So you helped Audrey, as you had done with Claire and Priscilla?" said Ann, mindful of the growing tension between the Harrisons.

"I felt I owed it to her. Not because of our affair, mind, but because of the way Simon treated her."

"You said Claire had access to your car. What about Audrey?" Ann asked.

"Audrey doesn't drive," Fitzroy replied. "But Claire took the car nearly every day as I recall."

"Do you know where she went?"

"No, I don't."

"Mr. Harrison, did you know that the man Melinda was living with, the man you spoke to in that shack, intended to sell her into prostitution when she was just fifteen years old?" Sally gasped while Fitzroy appeared stunned.

"No, Inspector. We didn't know," Fitzroy said.

"Then you also wouldn't know that that man, who had been part of a scheme to kidnap Melinda when she was a baby and had been abusing her for years, was shot and killed recently?"

"Surely you don't suspect Claire."

"A missing gun, Claire's rather odd habit of disappearing for hours on end without explanation as to where she'd been, a man she had you arrange a meeting with turning up dead while Claire was here, staying in your home. None of that set off any alarm bells?"

"I didn't know Royce had been murdered. If I'd known, I'm sure I would have had my suspicions," Fitzroy said as he walked a well-worn path to the bar.

"Could Claire have known?"

"That Royce had been murdered? No. How could she?"

"If she's the one who had you arrange that meeting with Terry, she might have. When he refused to sell Melinda to her, Claire may have thought her only option was to kill him."

"Dear Lord," Fitzroy uttered as he continued his assault on the liquor cabinet.

"Was one of those days Claire went off on her own the tenth of October?"

"Yes," Sally replied. "It was a Monday. I remember because we planned on going for a drive in the country but by the time I woke up, she had already gone."

"As near as we can tell, Terry Royce was killed on Monday, the tenth of October," Ann said. "He was shot dead in an alley, the same alley from which Melinda was kidnapped that very same day."

"Are you saying Claire killed Royce? And with my gun?" a shaken Fitzroy said.

"I'm saying she had the means, the motive and the opportunity."

"I can't believe that, Inspector. I've known Claire for years. She's not capable of such a thing. None of them are."

"Aren't they?" Sally contradicted. "All of them were here at about the same time and all had access to your guns."

"Sally, please!" Fitzroy pleaded. "You make it sound as if they were gunning for him. I've read up on this Royce fellow. He was a despicable character. Any number of people could have wanted him dead."

"Why are you still protecting them?" Ann said. "Is it because you know which of them killed him?"

"Because they all need protecting," Fitzroy said. "How could I have turned my back on any of them?"

"Just who is it we're looking for?" Damian braced himself with a hand against the dashboard as Ann showed the Astra's accelerator pedal no mercy.

"All of them. The streets are filled with prospective mothers and daughters searching for one another. It's as if someone's opened the door to the nut house and let everyone out all at once."

"Which of them do you think did it? Shot Juan," Damian asked once he began breathing again following a near-miss with a lorry parked on the verge.

"They all had their reasons. They wanted revenge for their daughter. Or who they believed to be their daughter."

"Then it had to be Priscilla. Her child is still alive while Claire's isn't."

"Yes, but Claire doesn't know that. In her mind, her child is still very much alive."

"What about Lydia?" Damian said. "According to the Harrisons she knows either Priscilla or Audrey is her mother, and that Melinda is her half-sister. That would be reason enough for her to want Terry dead. Juan as well." Ann remained strangely silent. "What do you think, Inspector?"

"I think we ought to find out where Lydia was tonight."

At the moment, Lydia and Peter were still searching for Madame Peto. They finally spotted her, walking down a street in a residential part of town, bedecked in her usual modified nineteenth-century costume.

"Madame. We've been sent to find you," Lydia said as she approached, her head bowed respectfully.

"Sent? By whom?" Madame Peto stood erect, her eyes hidden behind dark glasses.

"Why, the Emperor himself," Lydia replied. "He's requested your presence at the royal court in anticipation of the arrival of distinguished dignitaries."

"Dignitaries? From where?"

"Persia, as well as heads of state from Siam and Prussia."

Madame Peto stood silent, then said, "Lydia, is this your young gentleman?"

"Yes. This is Peter."

"How do you do, Madame," Peter said, then kissed the back of her hand. A commoner may have been struck by his manners, but a woman of class never betrayed such feelings. Instead, her status reaffirmed by his gesture, Madame Peto again looked off into the nineteenth century.

"If the Emperor himself has summoned me, then of course we must leave at once. Lydia, fetch my cape. We mustn't keep his majesty waiting." Madame Peto started down the street and Lydia and Peter followed.

"I hate to bring this up," Peter whispered in Lydia's ear, "but where is the gun?"

"What?"

"The gun. If she is the one who shot that fellow, then where is the gun?"

"Madame, have you a weapon?" Lydia asked as she caught up to Madame Peto, who didn't break stride. "Madame, you know the Emperor does not allow firearms in the palace. If you have one, it might be best to leave it with me before we arrive."

"I have no weapon, my dear."

"Might you have had one earlier tonight and perhaps forgotten where you left it?"

"I haven't used a firearm in ages. Not since I was a young girl."

"But, if she has no gun, then how could she have shot that fellow?" Peter again whispered to Lydia.

"Madame, you're certain you did not fire a gun tonight?" Lydia asked.

The corners of Madame Peto's mouth turned upward. "Of course not, my dear. I leave that sort of thing to others." Suddenly, Madame Peto stopped dead in her tracks. Puzzled, Lydia walked around in front of her.

"Madame? We must hurry. The Emperor is waiting." Madame Peto stood motionless for a long moment, then looked to her right.

There, silhouetted by the moonlight, was a woman standing in the passageway between two buildings.

"You may come out now," Madame Peto said.

"Madame, who is she?" Lydia asked as the woman emerged from the shadows. She wore a full length coat, and a scarf covered her head.

"She has waited such a long time to meet you," Madame Peto smiled.

"But…Why does she want to meet me?"

"Because she is your mother."

Lydia looked at the woman for a long moment. "No, I am not her child."

"But you are. You were taken from her when you were but a baby. And now that she has found you she has come to help me find my own daughter."

"But—"

The second woman approached Lydia and said, "I know it's difficult to understand, my dear, but you are indeed my child. There can be no doubt." She had tears in her eyes as she gently cradled Lydia's face in her hands.

"I'm sorry, but I cannot be your daughter," Lydia said calmly, her years with Madame Peto teaching her patience in the face of extraordinary circumstances.

"You are her daughter, and Melinda is mine," Madame Peto insisted.

"That's not possible. Her child – her son – died at birth."

"No, that isn't true!" the second woman said. "They took my baby from me, but she came back! *You* came back!"

"No, it wasn't—"

"My baby didn't cry at first, but he put you in my arms and I heard you cry." The woman smiled as a tear rolled down her cheek. "But then he said he had to take you away again. I begged him to let me keep you, but he said that wasn't possible. I didn't know what he had done with you, but I knew I'd find you one day. And now I've come to take you home."

"I'm sorry you lost your child, but it wasn't I Simon gave to Scott. It was Melinda."

"You're right. You are not her child," Madame Peto said in an ominous tone. "You're mine."

The tension between the women grew as the implication of their alliance set in. Lydia was about to try to diffuse the situation but in the short time it took her and Peter to become distracted by police sirens, the women disappeared. Lydia and Peter set off in different directions, and Peter's search led him straight to Ann and Damian who had just returned from the Harrisons.

"Inspector. To what do I owe the pleasure?" A smiling Peter asked, hat literally in hand.

"Where's Audrey?" Ann asked as she and Damian got out of the car.

"Audrey? No, I am afraid, she is gone. Back to Switzerland."

"Why didn't you go with her?" Damian said.

"Me, I cannot take the cold."

"Gets cold in England," Ann pointed out. "Are you planning on staying then?"

"For a little while. Then I go back home, to Jamaica."

"How long have you been with Audrey?" Ann asked.

"For a long time. I meet her in Jamaica, on holiday, many years ago. I go back with her to Switzerland, but there it is quite cold, especially in winter."

"How many winters have you spent in Switzerland with Audrey?"

"Ah, I would say, four. Four winters."

"What about her daughter? Have you ever seen her?"

"Yes, of course. On her holidays from school."

"I was under the impression she lived with Audrey."

"No. Only Audrey and me."

"How do you know she's Audrey's daughter?"

"Because that is how we were introduced. 'Peter, I would like for you to meet my daughter.'"

"Did she say what her name was?"

"No. Names are not necessary for me. My memory, I am afraid, I am no good at names."

"But she's been staying with you and Audrey, here, in England?"

"Yes. She left school and is now always with her mother. Never leaves her side."

"Did she come to England with you and Audrey?"

"Yes. The three of us come here together on a boat."

"She wasn't another one of your little flings, was she? A mother-daughter threesome, perhaps?"

"To my great disappointment, no."

"You wouldn't happen to have a photo of her daughter, would you?"

"Me? No. I do not photograph my work. Videos, perhaps, but they are of course extra."

Naïve or just plain stupid. Ann wasn't sure which. "Does her daughter resemble Audrey?"

"To me, Inspector, all women look the same with their clothes off."

"How about with their clothes on?"

"I do not know. Perhaps."

"If I put you with a police artist do you think you might be able to come up with a description of her daughter?"

"For how much?"

"How about we do a deal: a description of Audrey's daughter in exchange for overlooking prostitution charges against you."

"But of course, I would be most happy to help."

Chapter 23

I T HAD HAPPENED INNOCENTLY ENOUGH. A telephone conversation was overheard and a new voice formed, one that seemed to be acting independently from the rest of her. One that risked Terry's wrath as it prodded her, pushed her, implored her to convince him to let her help him with his latest dilemma. And what a dilemma it was. Kill Stropman, or be killed. After nearly four years of total isolation Melinda had found a way out. She had found a way to escape the hell she was living, the nightmare that had followed her from Cumbria and was given a new twist by Terry, who saw her as a fitting outlet for his rage. A harder side emerged and she stood up to Terry, and he rewarded her by sending her out on trial runs before the real thing. Trial runs that were, by all accounts, tragic failures.

In spite of her brief taste of freedom, the scope of Melinda's life had become very narrow. But getting shot had a profound effect on her. The return of one memory had, as Ann once predicted, brought back others. For the first time, Melinda could remember everything about that night in the barn. She could see them. Hear them. Smell them. A bullet in the shoulder? The pain didn't compare. The events of this night also allowed her to experience a new emotion: anger. She didn't know what it was, but it didn't frighten her. It freed her, consumed her, caused her to lose track of her surroundings. It was late now. The shops were all closed. She had no idea what street she was walking down. All she heard were voices from the past. But one voice sounded too real to be a memory. Someone said her name. She stopped and looked to her left. She heard a rustling sound, then out of the darkness and into the light of the full moon stepped a solitary figure.

Only the bottom of the woman's dress was visible under her tweed coat. A scarf covered her head and she seemed to glide along the pavement. She stopped a few feet away from Melinda, just close enough to the street light to be partially illuminated.

"It's you. I knew it was you," she smiled as she reached out a trembling hand and tears spilled down her aging face. "They took you from me. When you were just a baby, they took you away. I've been searching for you ever since. I've thought of nothing else." Melinda was unmoved. "I know you know who I am. The bond between mother and child is much too strong to be broken by time or distance." The woman came a step closer. "You must come with me," she said ominously. "I fear for your safety! There are those who mean to harm you!"

She took another step forward but was stopped by a glint of light reflecting off of Melinda's jacket. Without any stitches, her wound had begun to bleed again. The woman gasped. Her daughter had been injured. What if she bled to death? Would their reunion end before it had even begun?

Just then a figure appeared in the middle of the street, also wearing a long, dark coat, its head concealed by a hood. Was it the angel of death? She was convinced it had been following her for years. Had it finally found her, now, just as she was about to be reunited with her daughter? She had known so many cruelties in her life, she should have expected this. If this was death coming for her, she would not go quietly. But what if it was here for Melinda? That must be it. Melinda's blood must have summoned it here.

The air was more than just still. It was as if a vacuum had sucked most of it away. Then the hooded figure started moving toward them.

Lydia's search led her down a quiet street where, several yards ahead on the opposite side the women stood facing each other. Before Lydia could move, their right arms raised and they aimed guns at each other. And in the middle of it all was Melinda, who seemed oblivious to being in harm's way.

Meanwhile, Damian waited at the station while the police artist finished the sketch of Audrey's daughter, then met Ann outside.

"Anything?" Damian asked as he got into her car.

"No, no sign of any of them," Ann replied as she kept her eyes on the street. "Was Peter able to give a description of Audrey's daughter?"

"Yes, but I don't think it will be of much help." Damian showed her the sketch.

"It looks like Audrey."

"It is." Ann started the car and they resumed their search. Minutes later they came upon the standoff between the two women, prompting Ann to shut off the headlamps and park the car just down the road. At the same time Melinda quietly withdrew into the shadows as Lydia slowly crossed the street and stopped where Melinda had stood just moments before.

"Mother. Please. Don't shoot her." The women turned their eyes to Lydia, who took care not to raise her voice or look at either of them. "Please. I don't know what I'd do if something happened to you." After several long seconds, both women lowered their guns. Lydia had been successful in appealing to their maternal side, a quality that was abundantly clear due to their devoted searches for their daughters. It was less clear to Damian, who started to get out of the car only to be stopped once again by Ann.

"Not yet, Sergeant."

"But Lydia's life may be in danger!"

"I don't think so." As if on cue, Lydia reached her hands out to either side. Neither woman moved at first, then they started toward her and each took her hand. Then Lydia led them away, her eyes still avoiding theirs.

"Are we just going to let them go?" Damian said.

"No, Sergeant, we aren't. They'll be picked up once they reach the end of the street. Then we'll have their guns tested but my guess is, nothing will come of it."

"Nothing will…? Inspector, which one of them shot Juan?"

"Do you mean was it Priscilla, Claire or Audrey?"

"Yes."

"None of them."

"What? Then who?"

"Darla Ingersoll. That's who the other woman is," Ann said, nodding toward the woman in the hood.

"Darla? But how? Why?"

"Because it was her baby Scott stole and dumped somewhere in the Middle East."

"But, Darla never had any children."

"Oh, but she did."

"How do you know?"

"Her file at the clinic. You'd think people would know better than to leave a copper alone in a room full of files."

Damian grinned. "Yeah, quite careless, that. But how do you know it was Darla's baby Scott took to the Middle East?"

"Just a guess. We know where Priscilla and Audrey's daughters have been. That leaves Darla's unaccounted for."

"What about Ginny Ambrose? She had an affair with Scott. Could be she's Melinda's mother. Or Lydia's."

"I don't doubt Ginny had an affair with Scott, but it's unlikely she had a child with him. She's lived in Duffield her entire life. She has two children with her husband, both of whom Dr. Edgerton delivered. She's never missed a day of work. Never gone on holiday. If she had an illegitimate child, someone would have known about it."

Damian scratched his head. "What do you suppose it was about, this confrontation tonight?"

"The only thing that would bring those women together: Melinda."

"But, where *is* Melinda?" Before Ann could answer Damian bolted down the street, to the constables escorting the women to a panda car. He peered into the back seat, then hurried back to Ann's car.

"It's not her!," Damian said through the open window.

"What?"

"The other woman! It's not Darla!"

"Who then?"

"Priscilla Maskrey. It was her and Claire pointing guns at each other." Momentarily caught off-guard, Ann quickly recovered and started the car.

"Let's go, Sergeant." Ann started to drive before he finished closing the door.

"Where to?" he asked.

"If that other woman is Priscilla, that means Darla is still out there. And so is Melinda."

MINUTES BEFORE REACHING THE HOSPITAL, Juan's heart arrested. The paramedics got it started again, but it soon became apparent he hadn't arrested as a direct result of the bullet wound to his side. His eyes told the doctors all they needed to know, and a toxicology screen confirmed it. It revealed a lethal level of alcohol and too many drugs in his system to count. The doctors stabilized him and began pumping out his stomach, then took him to the operating room to have the bullet removed. For some, it might not seem fair that he should be getting the best care available while Melinda was still bleeding from the bullet he put in her as she stared into the face of yet another mysterious stranger.

But this time, the woman kept her distance. She kept her eyes on Melinda as she pulled a cigarette out of nowhere and lit it. She placed one hand on her hip and took a long drag, then blew out an angry stream of smoke. She took another drag, then let the cigarette fall to the ground and snuffed it out hard with her heel. She forced the corners of her mouth up, but even she didn't believe its sincerity and it soon vanished.

"Well?" she said with contempt. "Don't you have anything to say me? Your mother? That's right. I'm your mother. And your name is Melinda. Melinda Ingersoll."

Just then Ann came upon the latest act in this high drama and brought her car to a slow stop. Damian put his hand on the door's handle and was about to pop out, but he looked at Ann first, who got out without a word. Ann motioned for Damian to go through the alley.

"Well? Aren't you happy to see me? I've come to take you home...." Darla lit up another cigarette, "....back where you were before that bastard took you for the weekend and never brought you back." She blew out the match and looked at Melinda. "Does that surprise you? Did you think you came out of one of those other women? Well, you didn't. You belong to me." Melinda didn't react.

"Is it proof you want? You were born on the twenty-fifth of March, nineteen ninety-two, in Leeston. I wanted you to come into the world there, where I myself was born. There have been Ingersolls in Leeston since eighteen-twenty, when the first Ingersoll left Sweden to seek his fortune. Poor bastard thought he could do it farming that gray bit of land we Ingersolls have struggled to survive on the past two hundred years. Don't go thinking it was all fun and games...," Darla said before going for another taste of nicotine.

"I had just gotten you home. Had to sneak you back in the dead of night so no one would know about you. But Leeston is a small town. By the next day, everyone knew. But I didn't care. You were mine and that's all that mattered." Darla took a long puff, the end of her cigarette lighting up brightly, then exhaled as she looked wistfully into the distance. "I don't know why I said yes. Scott rang me, said he wanted to come for a visit. I should have known he was up to something. Bastard wasn't even there when I gave birth to you. Said he just wanted to come by to see you, that you were his child every bit as much as you were mine. I was young back then, young and naïve. Too naive to say no. He was so good with you. Just like a proper father.

"Just the weekend," he said. "Wanted to show you off to his friends, his family. I was against it at first. Then I told him I'd come along, but he said that was impossible, him being remarried and all. So I agreed. He was to bring you back that Monday, but he didn't return. I tried ringing him, but he had given me a false number. I went to his house, but he had given me a false address as well. I even went to Delacon, but they wouldn't help me. No one would."

"That's not entirely true, is it, Miss Ingersoll?" Ann said as she appeared behind Melinda. Darla slowly, instinctively pulled a gun from her coat pocket and held it at her side. "Is that the gun you used to shoot Juan tonight? Looks to be a Derringer, isn't it? Forty-five caliber, I believe."

"I didn't shoot anyone. I don't know anyone called Juan."

"You didn't have to know him, you only had to see him pointing a gun at your daughter. That's why you shot him, isn't it?"

"As I said, I didn't shoot anyone. My gun has not been fired."

"Then why are you carrying it? Do you intend to use it now?"

Darla kept silent, but that didn't matter since gleaning answers was not the point of this little exercise. "Why have you come here, Miss Ingersoll? Is it to reclaim your daughter?"

"Yes."

"Why now? Why not twenty years ago? Oh, I don't doubt you tried getting her back when Scott first took her from you, but why did you give up the search?"

"I had exhausted every possibility. What more was I to do?"

"I think it would be best if we continued this discussion at the station," Ann said just as Damian appeared behind Darla and easily slipped the gun from her hand.

CHAPTER 24

"DILLON! WHAT IS ALL THIS?"

Owen's ire over the state of the interview rooms, all of which were currently occupied, was directed at Damian, who had picked the wrong moment to step out into the hallway holding what little information he had managed to dig up on the women in custody.

"Sir?"

Owen made a sweeping gesture encompassing all four rooms. "Oh. Well, that's Priscilla Maskrey in one, Claire Conover in two—"

"I know who they are. What I want to know is, why are they tying up all of the interview rooms?"

"Inspector Treadwell wants to question them about the shooting tonight."

"I'm sure she meant for you to put them in cells, Sergeant. We need those rooms. There *are* other cases going on, other suspects to be interrogated."

"Yes, sir. I'll have them moved straight away."

"Hang on. Just where is DI Treadwell?"

"I believe she's speaking to another suspect."

"What, another one?"

"Come, sir. I'll fill in the details."

Karl was already seated in interview room four when Ann arrived. She didn't know what else he had to say for himself but she did learn from the guard that Karl had again allowed himself to fall victim to Roschine's taunts. From the information he had given Ann, Roschine knew the subject of Ann and Stropman's conversation would be Stropman's filmmaking. Roschine played it for all it was worth until Karl couldn't take it anymore and asked to see Ann. Stropman insisted there was no rape of Melinda, and Ann had yet to find any proof of such a crime. But how much did Karl know about it? Perhaps, with a bit of bluffing, Ann might finally learn the truth this time. Karl sat wringing his hands, his lower lip quivering.

"You wanted to see me, Doctor?"

"Yes. I want to unburden myself. I want to tell you the truth about that day. I don't suppose the courts will show any leniency towards me…"

"If I have anything to say about it…," Ann said under her breath.

"I—I don't know where to begin. Could I have some water, please?" Ann nodded at the guard, who then left the room. "From the day Melinda was old enough to understand, I made it clear she was forbidden to leave the house or let anyone in," Nearly in tears, Karl gave emphasis to his words by tapping his index finger on the table. "I know it was unfair to her, but there was simply no other way." The guard returned with a clear glass of water and Karl drank half of it. "I remember, it was very hot that day."

"When was this?"

"Shortly before Terry came for her. We had a problem at school, an electrical problem, and classes were cancelled. I arrived home around one o'clock. I didn't notice at first that Melinda wasn't in her room. The house gets quite hot on days like that so I went outside to sit in the garden. I saw McQuaid's truck parked out back, then I noticed the knot garden hadn't been trimmed. Harding had forgotten it twice before so I went looking for him to remind him. He wasn't by his truck, but the door to the barn was ajar. I looked inside and couldn't believe what I was seeing. Until that day, I had no idea Melinda and Harding even knew each other. I suppose I should have suspected something, her being home all day and him coming by so frequently during the summer. When Melinda saw me she was rightfully embarrassed, though I don't know if it was because of what she had done or because she had been caught, but she quickly gathered her clothes and ran to the house."

"What did you do?"

"Naturally, I was quite upset. She had disobeyed me. As for Harding, I fully expected to wring the young man's neck. But I didn't. I began seeing him not as a problem, but as a solution."

"To what?"

"As you know, Terry and I had a deal. I would raise Melinda until she was twelve, then he would take her until she was old enough to be on her own. I know I told you I didn't want her to go, that when she turned twelve and every year thereafter I lived in fear that Terry would show up on my doorstep one day and take her away. But," he swallowed hard, "that's not exactly true. The truth is, I was the one who kept calling Terry. But he didn't want her and by then – God forgive me – I didn't want her, either. I had no life because of her. I managed to go away on the odd weekend with a lady when I could, but there was never any hope that any of those relationships could become serious, not with Melinda around. I could have explained her away as a relative, but I didn't want to start a new relationship with a lie, so I had to be satisfied with our arrangement.

"Another year passed, then another. Coincidentally, I had just spoken to Terry the day before I found Melinda and Harding together. He had again refused to take her and I wasn't in a very good mood. I had just met a woman. A very special woman. We only had lunch together a few times but I began picturing my life with her. The hopelessness of that ever happening, then catching Melinda in the barn– well, it just got to me all at once."

"What did you do?"

"After Melinda went in the house, I asked Harding what his intentions were. It was my hope that he was fond enough of her to see this as something that might lead to marriage or, at the very least, living together. But he said he wasn't ready for that kind of commitment, that it was just some fun on a summer afternoon. I even offered him money, but he turned me down. I thought that was the end of it, but I'm afraid it wasn't."

"What do you mean?"

Karl had more water. "You have to understand, Inspector. By then, I was desperate. Everything was going wrong all at once. Terry was the last straw. When he wouldn't take her either, I turned to Stropman."

"Why Stropman?"

"Because I knew he and Terry were rivals. I told Stropman that Melinda belonged to Terry and if he would take her off my hands, there would be no questions asked."

"Even though you knew Stropman was involved in prostitution and pornography?"

"I knew, but I just didn't care anymore. All I could think was, once she was gone she would no longer be my problem. I could do whatever I wanted, date whoever I wanted. In other words, I would finally be able to live a normal life again."

ANN INTENDED TO TAKE A moment in her office before interviewing Darla, Priscilla and Claire, but she was interrupted by an unexpected visitor.

"I've come to collect Mrs. Maskrey." Standing in front of her desk was Lydia who, despite being a young woman, was dressed much older. Ann took note of her maroon print dress and red wool coat with barrel buttons, her minimal makeup and plain hairstyle and instantly understood. If her appearance were any more modern it would break the fragile line between fantasy and reality that Lydia dared not cross without risking what little remained of her mistresses' sanity.

"Miss Wilding," Ann said. "I have a few questions I'd like to ask you first."

"Is that necessary? I've only come for Mrs. Maskrey. I've already begun making arrangements for her return."

"If you wouldn't mind." Ann gestured toward a chair to Lydia's right. Lydia sighed, then relented.

"Miss Wilding, where was Mrs. Maskrey on the tenth of October of this year?"

"Why, she was with me," Lydia said, prim, proper and professional.

"And where was that?"

"Here, in England. Visiting the Harrisons."

"Why had she come back?"

"Madame Peto told me she had some personal business to attend to. She said no more than that."

"Excuse me for asking, but why do you call her that?"

"When Peter introduced me to her he explained she would only answer to that name. That is the only way I have ever addressed her."

"You've never wondered why, never asked her?"

"It is of no concern of mine why she chooses to call herself Madame Peto instead of Mrs. Maskrey."

"Were you with her the entire time she was here?"

"I am not her jailer, Inspector. I look after her, see to her everyday needs as best I can. But if you're asking was I with her every moment, no, I was not."

"Then you don't know where she might have gone on the tenth?"

Lydia took on a serious expression. "I remember, I left early that day. When I returned, just before noon, she was gone. That in itself wasn't unusual, but then Mr. Harrison mentioned one of his cars had gone missing."

"Could Mrs. Harrison have taken it?"

"No. She was home at the time."

"What did you do?"

"I waited. Madame's days are quite regimented. She eats lunch at twelve-thirty every day. When she hadn't returned by then, I became concerned. I borrowed Mrs. Harrison's car and went looking for her. I knew how desperate Madame was to find her child."

"Desperate enough to kill someone?"

"Certainly not! Madame Peto is not capable of such a thing."

"She had access to a car and a gun. She went missing the day Terry Royce was murdered. If she didn't kill him, who did?"

"I don't know, but it couldn't have been her."

"Why not?"

"Because I went to that man's flat."

"Terry Royce's?"

"Yes. I rang the bell but no one answered, so I went to the pub the private investigator Mr. Harrison hired wrote of in his report and spoke to the barman. He said he hadn't seen anyone matching Madame's description, but as I left the pub I noticed Mr. Harrison's car parked down the road. As I started toward it I heard a sound. A gunshot. Then I heard a terrible commotion coming from the alley. Ordinarily I wouldn't have gone into such a place, but until Madame was found, I had to."

"What did you see?"

"It was quite dark between buildings, but I saw a rather large man leaning up against the wall. He was barely able to stand. He turned his head and I caught a glimpse of his face. It was Mr. Royce."

"Did you see anyone else?"

"My only concern was Madame Peto. I heard guns being fired and saw flashes of light coming from the alley. I wanted to find her before something happened to her."

"Where did you find her?"

"I didn't. I looked everywhere for her but she was nowhere to be found. I had no choice but to return to Leeston. When I arrived at the Harrison's I found Madame in the study, sipping tea. That's how I knew she had nothing to do with what took place in the alley."

"Did you ask her where she'd been?"

"One doesn't ask such things. It would be pointless. If I had asked her where she'd been, she would have replied that she had gone to the

Schloss Schoenbrunn for high tea with Elisabeth, the Emperor's wife. Or that she had been on a carriage ride with Franz Josef himself."

"Did she seem different to you?"

"Did she seem as if she might have just killed someone? No, Inspector. Madame could set an entire town ablaze and not even have smelled the smoke."

Ann sat back. "Miss Wilding, did you see anyone else near the alley or passageway?"

Lydia thought for a moment. "There was a man. He ran in front of me, on the pavement. Nearly knocked me over."

"Did you get a good look at him?"

"No, I didn't. Inspector, if I could just see Madame Peto. This is no fit place for her."

"I'll see what I can do." Curious, Ann said, "Miss Wilding, if I may ask, do you know who your mother is?"

"Why, yes," Lydia said with some surprise. "Priscilla."

"How do you know it's Priscilla?"

"Well, look at me, Inspector. Which of them do *you* think I resemble?" Ann didn't know what to say. To her, she didn't look like any of them.

ANN AND DAMIAN WERE ABOUT to enter interview room one to speak to Priscilla when they were cut off by a portly man who appeared to have started dressing somewhere between his car and the station. He remembered his manners and stopped in the doorway to let Ann go first, causing an even greater traffic jam. He clumsily apologized as Damian pointed him in the right direction with a firm hand on his shoulder. After they were all safely inside, he introduced himself as George Wiley, esquire, sent by Fitzroy to represent both Priscilla and Claire. Priscilla's reddish hair was parted down the middle, combed over the top of her ears and pulled up in back, a common day style among women from her preferred era. The lines in her face were visible through her thick pancake and splash of rouge. The dark glasses were, as always, in place.

"Mrs. Maskrey. I understand you prefer to be called Madame Peto," Ann began. "Mrs. Maskrey?"

At the sound of her name Priscilla inflated herself into a regal position and said, "My secretary has returned to Austria. She has gone on ahead to see that everything is in order for my return at the end of the week."

"Your departure may be delayed a bit longer than that, I'm afraid."

"Why?" Priscilla said with alarm. "Has there been another uprising? Have the Prussians invaded again? Or the Huns? Murderers, the lot of them!" Ann sighed. That's all she needed, one more colorful character in this case. Where were the normal suspects, she wondered, the ones who plied their trade in the twenty-first century?

"Mrs.—Madame Peto, where you were at ten o'clock tonight?"

"I do not concern myself with such trivial matters. Lydia, my secretary, has all pertinent dates and times."

"Yes, but Lydia isn't here right now, is she?" Ann countered. "Where were you on the tenth of October?"

"The tenth of October? That would have been the week before the Emperor's Harvest Ball. I remember, I was overseeing the preparations. Two thousand guests from all over Europe. The event of the season—"

"Wouldn't someone else have been put in charge of that? Surely someone of your stature would be busy with more important things."

Priscilla sat perfectly still for several long moments. "Yes, of course. Someone else would have seen to that," she replied. "Then I must have been at my villa, being fitted for my ball gown—"

"Inspector, I think this interview should end here and now. Clearly my client has an important ball to prepare for," George Wiley said.

"Yes, except she's about a hundred and fifty years too late. I shouldn't worry, counselor. I don't think the ball will start without her. Don't think it can, really." Ann again addressed Priscilla. "No, you were not in Austria. You were here, looking for the man who abused your daughter, right? You wanted revenge."

"Revenge," Priscilla dismissed. "So barbaric. Not something a woman of refinement would take part in."

"But you wouldn't be above hiring someone to do it for you, would you?"

"Revenge is an act of cowardice. Cowards have no place in this world."

"Tell me, if not revenge, then what is it that keeps bringing you back to England?"

"Most of my visits are on behalf of the Royal family."

"Would your duties require you to fire a gun?"

"In these uncivilized times, women have to know how to defend themselves. With the men away so often fighting enemies of the crown, a woman's virtue is always at risk."

Ann placed a photo of Melinda on the table. "Do you know this girl?" Priscilla looked at the photo. "This is the girl you believe to be your daughter, isn't it? The one you've been searching for all these years, ever since Simon took her from you when he thought you were dying?"

Priscilla sat stonefaced, and Ann wondered if she was even listening. But that speculation was laid to rest by a tear that fell from behind Priscilla's sunglasses and splashed onto the table.

"Mrs. Maskrey?"

"That man you mentioned…He was a scoundrel of the lowest order!" Another tear fell. "He took her from me. Took her away…."

"What did he do with her?"

"He gave her to someone, some vagabond!"

"You remember then?"

"She is my child," Priscilla softened. "How could I ever forget?"

"Do you know where your daughter is, Mrs. Maskrey?" Priscilla again sat motionless. "Madame Peto?"

"We've been called in to dine. The food is always exquisite, prepared by the finest chefs in Europe—"

"Mrs. Maskrey, you returned to England in October determined to get Melinda back from Terry. You believed then, as you do now, that Melinda is your daughter, the one Simon took from you some nineteen years—"

"The Emperor will make a royal decree proclaiming the start of the winter season. This truly is a joyous time for the entire empire—"

"Mrs. Maskrey, did you kill Terry Royce?"

"There will be Kings and Queens, Emperors and Empresses, Dukes and Duchesses—"

"Prisc—Mad—Mrs....Did you shoot Terry Royce?" Priscilla didn't reply. The tears ceased, the fantasies stopped, the answers came to an end. And so did the interview.

On her way to speak to Claire, Ann was summoned to Owen's office. Just before the door closed Sergeant Whitcomb stuck his head inside and said, "Excuse me, Chief Inspector." There's a man asking to see DI Treadwell." Peering around Sergeant Whitcomb was Peter.

"I am here for the Madame. She will be leaving soon?" Peter said.

"She may be staying with us for awhile," Ann replied.

"Who the devil is this?" Owen asked.

"But why? What has she done?"

"Ann?"

"This is Peter...erm, Peter...He's Priscilla Maskrey's companion. Among others."

"Because of the shooting? Surely you do not suspect her of such a thing?"

"We won't know until we get the results of some tests we're conducting."

"Results? Hang on...Results, results...," Owen muttered as he flipped through the stack of papers in his hand. "I've got the ballistics report. Had 'em rush it through…Spent too much time on this as it is—Ah! Here it is. Bad news, I'm afraid. Claire Conover's gun is a twenty-two and wasn't loaded. Darla Ingersoll's is a forty-five but hasn't been fired recently. And Priscilla Maskrey's isn't even a gun. It's a bloody cigarette lighter."

"Yes, that one is from me," Peter said. "The Madame, I was afraid, she might hurt herself. So I take the gun and give her that one, as a gift."

"Where's the gun you took from her?" Ann said.

"I throw it away, in the Thames."

"What did this other gun look like?"

"Look like?" Peter gave it some serious thought. "A gun. Yes, I am certain of it. It looked like a gun."

"What kind of gun?"

"What kind?"

"What did the barrel look like? You know, the part where the bullet comes out?" Owen said.

"It was long, like this," Peter said, holding his index fingers six inches apart. "The color, I would say, was a steel color. Except for the handle, which was a sort of a wood color."

"Sounds like a twenty-two to me. Probably some sort of target pistol," Owen said. Too small to be the gun used to shoot either Terry or Juan. But Ann already knew that.

CHAPTER 25

O F ALL THE PEOPLE IN his circle of friends, Juan had always been the least ambitious. Even so, his mother constantly pushed her son to work hard at becoming a success. If greatness came of it, so be it. Except Juan could never decide in which particular field his immortality should be achieved. Perhaps his mother meant for him to excel in something noble, like science, or medicine, or possibly something in the arts.

In reality, she had no higher aspirations for him than to find work, even something that paid minimum wage. If she were here right now, she would tell him that. But she didn't know that he had been shot. She wouldn't until his face appeared in the morning paper accompanied by an article explaining that he was a suspect in the kidnapping and shooting of a young woman. Would she be surprised by that revelation, or would she have known all along that her son was destined for such a fate? Would she be pitied for bearing the burden of having such a child, or would she be reviled as the mother of a monster? It didn't matter. For Juan and all of his dreams, time had finally run out.

THE GUNS WERE LINED UP side by side on Owen's desk. All had been tested and none could be linked to Juan's shooting. But Ann didn't come to hear Owen recite ballistics reports. She came to give him Terry's murderer.

"What? Are you sure? You know who killed Royce?" Owen said.

"Yes, sir." Ann slid Darla's Derringer toward him.

"But, that's a forty-five. According to the ME the fatal bullet was either a thirty-eight or a nine mil."

"That's what he originally thought. But the pellets he mentioned in his report kept bothering me."

"Pellets?"

"Yes, sir. Remember? In his report he said he found five pellets in Terry's stomach. There had to be a reason why they were there. Unless he ate them, I assume someone must have shot him with a shotgun. But the damage wasn't great enough to have been caused by a shotgun."

"Then how did the pellets get inside Royce?"

Ann picked up the Derringer and said, "With this gun."

"How is that possible?"

"It fires forty-five caliber bullets, but it also fires a four-ten shotgun shell which contains five buck-sized pellets."

"Five pellets? That's not enough to kill a man, especially one of Royce's immense size."

"It was fired at close range, most likely with the barrel up against him."

"But how do you know?"

"After reviewing his initial findings, the ME determined the bullet found in Terry's stomach was not the fatal shot. None of the other bullet wounds were serious enough to have caused his death. The only thing that could have are the pellets. All five were embedded either in Terry's heart or aorta, which should have killed him instantly. The ME believes the only reason he stayed on his feet as long as he did was his size."

Owen ran his hand through his hair, then stopped. "What about that girl? I still think she may have killed him."

"With what, sir?"

"Royce's gun, one of his mate's guns…How the hell should I know!"

"I don't think so. For one, the distance is wrong,"

"Distance?"

"The powder burns. From where Melinda was stood in the alley, she wasn't close enough to have shot the pellets into him."

"She could have killed Royce on the street, before she came into the alley."

"Ironically, Stropman is her witness there. He led her into the alley, all the way from the pub. They didn't go down that street."

"Right," Owen reluctantly conceded. "So Darla killed Royce. What about Juan? Any of these guns hiding any little secrets that might tell us who shot him?"

"Not so far. Perhaps Darla or Claire will enlighten us."

TO CLAIRE AND PRISCILLA, THE quest to find their daughters had been a twenty year pursuit. To Darla, the thought had occurred much more recently. But her desire to locate her child was every bit as fierce. She had spent the last hour sitting in interview room three smoking non-stop. She wasn't a patient woman, and making her wait wasn't helping. Making her wait was an old ploy, trying to break her so she would talk. Darla would talk, but what she had to say wasn't what Ann expected to hear. While Damian interviewed Claire in interview room two, Ann spoke to Darla in three.

"Why did you kill him, Miss Ingersoll? Why did you shoot Terry Royce?"

"I didn't."

"We know it was your gun that killed him."

"That doesn't mean I was the one holding it," Darla said in her street-hardened way.

"Who was?"

Darla responded with a defiant stream of smoke. "Miss Ingersoll, unless you can come up with a name, you will be charged with murder." Darla glared at her with her exposed eye through the persistent smoke.

"You want a name? How about Scott Conover?" Ann tilted her head. "That's right. He took my gun along with my child."

"Why would Scott want to kill Terry?"

"Because they'd done a deal, him and Terry, only Terry didn't keep his part of the bargain."

"To kill your child?"

"Is that what he was intending to do with her?" Darla brought her cigarette to her lips with a shaky hand, belying her indifference, and took a long drag. "I don't know all the details, but I believe it had something to do with drugs. Scott took drugs, you see. He wasn't an addict but he was a user, in more ways than one. He used to take all sorts of pills. When I asked him why, he said he was ill."

"Did he have some sort of ailment?"

"I wasn't his wife, Inspector. I only wanted a child from him, not a lasting relationship. His health was none of my concern."

"Where did you get the gun?"

"Scott gave it to me as a gift."

Ann had done enough of these interviews to know when something didn't ring true. "I find it interesting, Miss Ingersoll, that a man who hasn't been seen or heard from in years would be allowed by his kidnappers to return to England just to murder a man who cheated him in a drug deal some two decades earlier."

"He may have disappeared, but he wasn't kidnapped. That was all a lie he made up so he could carry on with his other affairs."

"What other affairs?"

"I'm sure I wouldn't know. But he was always up to something, him."

"Miss Ingersoll, I saw a recent photo of Scott in a Middle Eastern newspaper. There can be no doubt he's still being held hostage."

"Shall I give you the name of the man who took that photo? It wasn't taken in the Middle East, Inspector. It was taken in Cheltenham."

"Cheltenham? You're saying that's where Scott has been all this time?"

"He's been so many places, Cheltenham included."

"How do you know?"

"Scott has contacted me periodically over the years. For the first two he kept promising me that, if I did him just one more turn, he would bring my daughter back. Then one day he told me the child was dead."

"Did he say how she died?"

"Car accident. Bastard said he couldn't show me her body because the car caught fire and she was burnt beyond recognition."

"And you believed him?"

"Of course not. But by then I had done him enough favors that some might consider…illegal, that he had something to hold over me if I refused to help him. Or if I went to the police."

"What sort of illegal favors?"

"Oh, no. You don't get me so easily, Inspector."

"Right. So Scott had his picture taken with, what? Actors dressed as terrorists? How did the picture end up in a Middle Eastern newspaper?"

"Scott wasn't in the Middle East long, but he has a talent of making friends quickly. Or finding ways to make them cooperate. In the short time he was there he made a few contacts. One of them had connections with the editor of a local newspaper. That's how he got his picture in that paper. It was all quite calculated."

"Can you prove any of this?"

"I can prove all of it."

Ann smirked and shook her head. "You think I killed that man? For what reason? My daughter's honor? Please. I admit, I was upset when Scott first took her from me, but I soon got over it. The bars are filled with men, Inspector, men who aren't interested in coming home with a woman who has a child looking over their shoulder. I thought I wanted a child and I acted impulsively to get one. But after seeing how people's lives have been ruined by children, I knew I was well rid of her."

"If you weren't keen on getting her back, why were you out looking for her tonight?"

"Austin Marsh. He wants her too, but not because she's his niece. As one of Simon's heirs, she's worth a fortune. Austin would do anything to get his hands on her, just long enough to have her sign away her share of Delacon."

"But your daughter isn't his heir, is she? If Scott's her father, then she would have no claim to Simon's estate."

"But Austin doesn't know that, does he? He's keen to find her, and I'm just as keen to get something in return for all I've been through."

"Is that why you aimed a gun at her tonight, to persuade her to tell Austin she's his niece?"

Darla pointed the two fingers holding her cigarette at Ann and said, "I did not fire that gun."

"You were arrested holding the gun that has now been positively identified as the weapon used to murder Terry Royce. Unless you can prove to me that Scott is still alive, and that he was the one who shot him, you will be charged with Royce's murder."

Darla expelled another lung full of smoke. "I can prove it, Inspector. I can take you to Scott Conover."

Ann had to get away for awhile. She went to the vending machines in a less busy corridor on an upper floor, bought a bag of crisps and went through them one by one as she leaned back against the wall between the machines. It gave her time to think. What if it was true? What if Scott did kill Terry? It never made sense, his kidnapping. To Ann, it had all the earmarks of a man wanting to disappear so he could start over. And now she was getting a better idea of what that fresh start entailed. She thought about the path of destruction he had carved through so many lives spanning so many years. All of the women who ever had anything to do with Scott and Simon shared a similar trait: varying degrees of insanity.

"Oh, Inspector. I've been looking for you," said Damian, who nearly walked past her.

"Have you?" she said with indifference. He handed her an envelope. "What's this?"

"A surveillance photo of Darla taken at the bank in Duffield on the tenth of October. She made a withdrawal that day at half three, all conveniently captured on video tape."

"Which means she couldn't have been here when Terry was killed."

"Oh, I don't know, Sargent. Have you checked Cheltenham yet?"

"Inspector?"

"Go on."

"Oh. Alright. Well, we also have the gun that was used to shoot Juan. A thirty-eight. Belongs to Fitzroy Harrison. I also don't suppose it will surprise you to learn it's not as simple as all that."

"As what?"

"As finding the gun."

"What do you mean?"

"All of their prints are on it. Priscilla, Darla, Claire, Audrey. And get this: Lydia's as well."

"So any one of them might have used it, Fitzroy and Sally as well. The question is, which of them pulled the trigger?"

"There's another partial print. They haven't been able to identify it as yet."

"Partial?"

"Yeah. Must belong to one of the suspects, I reckon." Damian leaned against the wall to Ann's left. "Lydia and Melinda, Simon and Scott. Scott fathered Darla's daughter, Simon was the father of Audrey and Priscilla's girls—"

"Not a Y chromosome between them," Ann commented.

"Except Claire's baby."

"Claire. I wonder what part she played in Terry's demise," Ann said before having another crisp.

"None, according to her. But, I thought Darla was the one who shot him."

"The gun is right. I'm just not certain we've got the right shooter."

WHEN SHE TOOK THE GUN from Fitzroy, she intended to use it to kill Terry, then return it. But she lost it. It was found, pawned, then bought as a gift to help smooth over a misunderstanding. The gift was accepted and immediately put to use.

Juan wasn't his preferred target. The bullets in the gun were meant for Roschine, but getting to him was impossible since he was still in jail. But if Stropman couldn't get to Roschine, he would kill the man Stropman believed Roschine had sent to kill him. The only problem was, Stropman was now also a guest of the police. So, like Roschine, Stropman had to turn to someone on the outside. Someone who now slept soundly underneath a quiet bridge, his meager belongings and a half dozen empty wine bottles scattered nearby, a brand new set of false teeth resting comfortably – painlessly – in his mouth.

"Ann! Dillon!" Owen stood outside his office, ever-present file in hand. "Sit, sit," he said as they entered. "So. I see we have half the population of Leeston in our interview rooms. Have you gotten round to speaking to any of them yet?"

"Yes, sir, we have," Ann said.

"Well? Which of them is our murderer?"

"We haven't been able to determine that yet. We're still in the process of—"

"Of what? You said you've spoken to them."

"Well, they all had motive and opportunity—"

"What about this Lydia?"

"She does seem to be the only one of the lot with enough mental clarity to find Melinda and plot revenge against Terry and Juan," Ann acknowledged.

"But why kill Terry and not Karl?" Damian said. "If Lydia knew about Terry then surely she must have known about Karl." He paused. "Priscilla wouldn't know about Karl, would she?"

"She would if Lydia told her," Ann said.

"What about Claire? She had just as much reason to want Terry dead as the others."

"Claire, Lydia, Priscilla. What is it, not enough suspects for you?" Owen said.

"Until we find out who shot Terry and Juan, I don't think we can have too many suspects," Ann said.

"Hang on. Didn't you just tell me it was Darla that shot Royce?" Ann told him what Darla told her about Scott.

"The only drawback is, we don't have any proof that Scott was here at that time," Ann said.

"But you're keen to find out, is that it?"

"I think we should at least look into it. The problem is, after all these years, where do we start?"

Chapter 26

"WHAT'S THAT?"

"That," Ann said after placing a piece of paper on the table in front of Darla, "is your free ticket out of jail. Now. Where is Scott Conover?"

Darla looked over the agreement, folded it, then slipped it in her ample cleavage. "You'll find him at the Inn in Alvord. If he's still there."

"He'd better be, or that paper you're…holding will be worthless."

"Oh, he'll be there."

"What makes you so sure?"

"Because he's waiting for me. You're probably thinking what would he want with an old tart like me? Why not someone younger, prettier? Because he knows I'm safe, Inspector. He knows I won't go to the police."

"But you have gone to the police."

"No, you came to me. Besides, I don't owe him anything. If it's a choice between him or me, it'll be him going to jail, won't it?"

"How did you get mixed up with him?"

"When I met him, he said he was an executive at Delacon. Didn't matter to me. He was young, handsome and in desperate need of a favor."

"Changing the entry at the registry."

"I told him what he was asking me to do was illegal. I'd lose my job. He promised me I wouldn't, that he'd use his influence. Said all I had to do was get the register, leave him alone with it for five minutes, then put it back. I told him I wouldn't, not unless he made it worth my while. What I had in mind was money and lots of it. He said he didn't have any, so I told him the deal was off. Then he said he'd make it worth my while in other ways."

"He offered you sex?"

"With a bit of coaxing from me." Darla took a cigarette out of its pack and reflected. "Perhaps I shouldn't have given him such an ultimatum. But at the time I very much wanted a child, and I didn't want to raise it without a father. When my fiance left me, I still wanted a child, but who the father was didn't seem quite so important anymore. I knew from the start Scott was only using me, so I decided to do the same. I told him I would give him the register and turn a blind eye to whatever he did with it, and I wouldn't say anything if the authorities came round. In return, he would give me a child. I knew that would be the last I ever saw of him, and I didn't care."

"Where is your child now, Miss Ingersoll?"

"Honestly?" Darla said, her reply muffled by the cigarette she finally placed between her lips. "I don't know. I suppose it could be Melinda. Does it really matter?" Darla lit up, blew out a cloud of smoke, then mellowed a bit. "I know he never loved me, and I was still in love with my fiance. I regretted what I had done. Still do."

"What did you do?"

"In the end, I didn't help him. I didn't get the money, didn't get my fiance back, and I didn't have Scott's attention anymore. I was left with what you see now, Inspector. Nothing."

THE INN HAD STOOD FOR more than four hundred years without so much as a single complaint being filed. Nothing improper had ever taken place, not as far as the proprietors were concerned. The current one, the one who had been there the last thirty years, believed Scott and Ginny were husband and wife for no other reason than that's the way Scott registered when he brought her there as he drew her deeper and deeper into his plan. If Ginny were to appear before Scott now, he wouldn't know her any more than he would the countless other women he had slept with in order to get what he wanted. So far, it had worked like a charm. His success in his current field of endeavor had given him a feeling of invincibility. He took chances. Ignored risks. And like so many mercenaries before him, it would prove to be his downfall.

He didn't know it yet, but they were all around him Not just the police. Not just Interpol. Not just the various agents of his many enemies. He had successfully eluded all those obstacles before. This time it was his past that was catching up to him, a past that had left so many ruined lives in its wake. They were there, all those anguished voices from his past. He just couldn't hear them yet.

CHAPTER 27

ANN AND DAMIAN WOULD START for Alvord in the morning, but instead of going home and getting some much-needed sleep, Ann had another matter to attend to. She was back at St. Pritchards tying up one more loose end.

"Melinda, I know this may be difficult to understand, but we have reason to believe Karl isn't your father. In fact, we don't believe he's related to you at all."

"But he...No, he raised me! He took care of me!"

"Then who was Terry?"

"He-He's my father."

"I thought Karl was your father. You can't have two fathers, can you?"

Melinda's eyes again searched for answers as Ann tore away at her belief system. Ann had to make her understand but she also knew that facing the truth would be difficult since Karl and Terry were everything to Melinda, the horribly misshapen foundation upon which her entire life had been based.

"Was I adopted?"

"No, not adopted." Ann showed Melinda a newspaper photo of Simon. "We believe the man in this photo is your father. Your *real* father. His name is Simon Maskrey." Melinda studied with blank expression the photo of the man staring down the camera, his eyes glistening intensely as they pierced through the lens. "I'm afraid he passed away some years ago."

Ann could see the fear on Melinda's face as the false reality to which she had clung to for so long, to which the thin thread of her sanity was so loosely attached, appeared to be fraying. Ann doubted this version of Melinda could cope with this. Her harder side could, but for some reason it had deserted her again. It would be left to whatever incarnation of Melinda sat before Ann to try to understand, and understanding wasn't this Melinda's strong suit.

"Do I have a mother," Melinda asked

"Yes. We're not sure who just yet. We're still sorting through a number of sus-erm, a number of possibilities."

"Will I have to go with her?"

No. I only told you because I thought you had a right to know," said Ann, who knew that by putting Melinda together with any of those women would constitute the standard by which all dysfunctional families would forever be measured. Ann expected to see some expression of relief, but all she saw was more sorrow.

"It's never going to end, is it? It's never going to go away." Then Melinda looked Ann straight in the eye and said, "You know, don't you?"

HE WAS NEARLY EIGHT FEET tall, his face accounting for at least two feet of that. His teeth were filed down to sharp points, blood dripping from each of them. There were dark, black holes where his eyes should be, holes so deep that no light could penetrate them. At times, they were all she could see. Rodney didn't really look like that, but that's how he seemed to Ann. She knew terror. She knew fright. She knew what it was like to be so paralyzed by it that you couldn't function. And not just for a day. For weeks, months, years. Ann understood fear. And she knew she couldn't tell Melinda that one day it would get better. Because that day didn't always come.

CHAPTER 28

IT HAD BEEN ALMOST THIRTY-SIX hours since Ann had slept. She had never been the type who could just nod off whenever she wanted to, but it had never concerned her until recently. It was all she thought about as she sat, her legs curled up next to her, in her darkened living room. The only light came from the kitchen where, from force of habit, she had put the kettle on as soon as she came home on another gray, rainy evening. She treated her headache with a couple of aspirins, which she washed down with a glass of orange juice as her contribution to her daily health regimen. She could feel some of the juice coming back up as it met the acid churning away in her stomach.

The next morning, at the break of dawn following another restless night, Ann went to the cemetery. She didn't want to go but as an only child she felt it was her duty to visit her parents' graves as often as she could. She brought flowers and stayed a few minutes each time, never really knowing why she had come. She knew these visits were supposed to make her feel better, that she should reflect upon her parents' lives and all the positive things about them. But all she ever felt was sadness. Unbearable, heart-wrenching sadness at the suddenness, the needlessness, of their deaths. Lost in the past, she didn't hear the sound of leaves being crushed under the feet of the man approaching until he was next to her, causing her to jump.

"Sorry, Inspector," Damian said. "I've got news."

"Good or bad?" Ann replied, looking as tired as she felt. Too tired to ask him how he knew she was here.

"It's Juan. He died earlier this morning."

"Well. That'll make the trial a bit shorter."

Damian read the names on the tombstones. "Only been one person in my family's ever died. An old uncle. Natural causes. That how they went?"

"Yeah. Natural causes," Ann said as she tried to wipe away a tear before Damian could see. But it was too late.

"It's funny, the things you hear," he said.

"What do you mean?"

"Before I was transferred here, all I'd heard was how difficult you were to work with, how cold-hearted you could be. But it isn't true, is it?"

"Oh, I don't know. Even the hardest of hearts would surely shed a tear at their parents' graves."

A long, awkward pause followed. "Since we're working together, I want to be honest with you," Damian said as they walked toward their cars. "The Chief Inspector—When he assigned me to work with you, he told me to keep an eye on you. Said he was concerned you'd lost sight of this case, that you seemed distracted by other aspects of it he felt had no relevance to the kidnapping."

"I was only trying to solve a murder," Ann said defensively in an attempt to hide how much that hurt her. "And what were you supposed to do? Stop me before I found out who killed Terry?"

"To be honest, I wasn't sure what I was meant to do. He never actually said." Ann resented Owen for questioning her judgment. At the same time, it meant something to her that Damian trusted her enough to tell her.

"So," Ann said after they reached her car. "How am I doing, Sergeant?"

"Eh?"

"What is your opinion of my work?"

"I'm not really one to judge such things. I've never been asked to critique a fellow officer's performance. I've also never informed on another officer and I've no intention of starting now."

"You haven't answered my question. What is your opinion of the way I have conducted this investigation?"

"Well, you've got four suspects behind bars, a signed confession from one and verbal confessions from two others. If my opinion counts for anything, I'd say you'd done quite well."

Ann smiled. "Thank you, Sergeant."

"Dillon. Sergeant Dillon."

ACCORDING TO DARLA, SCOTT WOULD be staying at the Bluebird Inn for three days, starting today. Unable to secure any back-up from the cash-strapped department, Ann and Damian were on their own.

"How are we going to go about this?" Damian said as Ann drove to Alvord. "We can't just walk in there and arrest him. Surely he's too clever for that."

"I got word from Interpol last night. He's high on their wanted list. Illegal arms trade, drugs, slavery, prostitution. If it pays, he's got a hand in it. We were right. He never was kidnapped. Staged the whole thing. A man who's avoided capture as long as he has, he won't go quietly. That's why we'll need a bit of deception."

"What sort of deception?"

"Well, to begin with, I've called ahead for reservations."

"Do you think that was wise?"

"I think it would be much less conspicuous for a couple to call ahead than to pop in unannounced."

"A couple?"

"Yes, Sergeant. You and I."

"Well, why don't we just storm the place?" Damian said, wiping his suddenly clammy hands on his trousers.

"With what? Two lightly armed detectives and an inexperienced local police force of three? If Darla's right, Scott's come back to do a weapons deal. For all we know, he might have an arsenal in there with him."

"OK. We don't storm the place. Right," Damian said, adding a slight forward-and-back rocking motion to his list of nervous ticks. "What if one of us stays with the innkeeper while the other finds Scott and arrests him?"

"He's been wanted by the police for twenty years," Ann said as calmly as he was jittery. "If we march in there and try to arrest him, he'll be gone before we show our warrant cards. He knows the inn, the area. That's probably why he goes back there, because it affords him protection."

"Right. We go undercover then." Damian took a deep breath. "Luggage! What about luggage?"

"I've an overnight bag in the boot." Ann glanced at him. "You seem a bit on edge, Sergeant."

"Yes, well, it's just that I've never actually gone undercover before."

"Nothing to it. Just behave normally and everything will be fine."

"You've done this before then?"

"Sergeant—"

"I mean, don't you think we should at least rehearse what we're going to do, to say?"

"I think it would be better if we were spontaneous."

"Yes, but, shouldn't we at least have some sort of plan? You know, just in case?"

"Alright," Ann said, amused at his uncertainties. "How about… We're a couple, and we've come to the inn to try to sort out some problems we've been having with our marriage."

"What sort of problems?"

"I don't know. I've never been married. What sort of problems do married people have?"

"I don't know. I've never been married, either. Right. So that's it then. We're a couple having marital difficulties, except neither of us has ever been married so we don't exactly know what sort of difficulties they might be."

"Could work to our advantage. If we knew what our problems were, we wouldn't need to come to the inn to sort them out."

"Right. So how does that help us with Scott?"

"When we get to the inn I'll strike up a conversation with him, try to gain his confidence."

"His confidence?"

"Yes. Perhaps he'll even be sympathetic once he learns our marriage is in such a shambles."

"And then what? He'll try to save you from your unhappy marriage by coming after me? Then we arrest him for assaulting a police officer, I reckon."

"I doubt he would allow himself to be arrested for something as simple as that. According to Interpol Scott has been prosecuted twice, both times in absentia, both times found not guilty. Too much reasonable doubt. Too much influence is more like it."

"If he's been tried twice, why didn't we know about it?"

"Because we've been looking in the wrong place, Sergeant. We thought he was still a hostage, not an international criminal, so there was no reason to check with Interpol until now."

"So in order to make the charges stick this time, we'll have to catch him red handed."

"That would help."

"Yes, but how are we going to do that?"

"If I can get him to trust me, perhaps I can learn what it is he's selling and to whom. That should make it a bit more difficult for him to get the charges dismissed this time."

"I don't know, Inspector. Sounds a bit risky to me."

"If we stay calm and keep our nerve, there shouldn't be any problems. Trust me." Damian had no reason to, and if he hadn't been so consumed by his own doubts he would have noticed that Ann wasn't as confident as she appeared to be, either.

THE TINY VILLAGE OF ALVORD sat in the middle of aging barns and ancient trees that stood like islands, marking off the edge of one farmer's property and the beginning of another. Scattered throughout the rolling countryside were remnants of stone walls, some crumbling, some with large sections removed decades earlier for private use. Not many tourists knew about Alvord or the inn, which was a four hundred year old cob and thatch building consisting of twelve rooms.

Ann was right to have made reservations. Those who dropped in without any were cast in a suspicious light by Tom Overbeck, the burly innkeeper with a large paunch and square head topped with a bristly crewcut, and Scott, Tom's most faithful guest. Scott paid plenty for the privilege of Tom's silence, and his instincts. If Tom didn't trust someone, Scott knew about it. Tom had no reason to be suspicious of Ann and Damian, who arrived late this afternoon, overnight bag in hand. He checked them in, then led them upstairs to their room, his boots scraping heavily on the steps. It was a cozy room with white lace curtains framing a bay window on the wall opposite the door and plush white cushions underneath. There was a king-sized bed to the right of the door covered with a light blue duvet and large pillows near the antique headboard. There was a bureau along the wall to the left and a full bath just beyond that. Damian placed the bag on the bed while Ann took in the view from the window.

"Now what?" Damian asked after Tom had left.

"We go downstairs, and I'll try to make contact with Scott."

"Do you know what he looks like?"

"With the photo Karl provided and the one from the newspaper, I shouldn't think it will be too difficult to find him. Now, if you'll excuse me, Sergeant, I think I'll change into something a bit more appropriate."

Ann grabbed the overnight bag and went into the bathroom. Damian sat on the bed and rummaged through the pockets of his jacket looking for gum or sweets or anything else that might help him work off his nervous energy. A short time later Ann emerged wearing a tight-fitting, low-cut black dress that not only changed her appearance but Damian's perception of her. Ann was too preoccupied with finally meeting Scott to be nervous. Her make-up was more dramatic, erasing the tired lines and smoothing out her skin tone. Her lipstick was a not-so-subtle shade of red, and her hair had been brushed and now shined.

"Sergeant, why don't you go on ahead," Ann said as she fastened a silver bracelet onto her wrist. "Might make us look a bit more at odds if we didn't arrive together." Dumbstruck by Ann's transformation, Damian gave up trying to find words and simply headed downstairs.

Scott didn't have a care in the world, and why should he? He had come back to England many times and had never drawn the attention of the police. He knew a cop the instant he saw one. He suspiciously eyed the woman wearing the sexy black dress as she descended the stairs and headed for the bar, but conquests were part of his mystique. He had charmed women in every part of the world. Here was a golden opportunity, and at just the right time. His latest deal wouldn't take place for two more days. Plenty of time to work a little romance into his schedule. And, cop or no cop, he had found just the right woman for the occasion.

Ann had already ordered her first drink by the time Damian came downstairs. He sat alone at a table in the corner of the dining room and reluctantly continued the ruse of fretting over his unhappy marriage while Scott made a move on Ann. He sat next to her at the bar, then lit up a cigarette and eyed her while she ignored him.

"Whiskey. And one for the lady," Scott said to the bartender. Ann slowly turned her head, the scotch already in her system keeping her from showing her true reaction to finally coming face to face with such a ruthless criminal. He didn't overwhelm the room but he was hard to miss. He was in his late forties but years of being on the run had left him trim. He had almost as much silver as black in his full head of hair, but his dark eyebrows and matching stubble made it look premature. His eyes were an intense blue that a woman could get lost in. He wore black slacks, a black jacket and a white shirt open at the neck. There was a Rolex strapped to his left wrist and a couple of rings on his right hand, one gold and the other encrusted in diamonds. Ann sat so close to him that she felt intoxicated by his scent, one part musk, the other part purely male. Their drinks came, but Ann didn't touch hers. She had managed to water down her first one but she knew one more and she would start to lose control.

"You here all by yourself?" Scott asked.

"You don't waste any time, do you?"

"I'm not a man who usually has a lot of time," he said before having a sip of whiskey. Ann started to roll her eyes but stopped herself in time. "So. Are you alone, or....?"

"No," she said, a slight nod of her head in Damian's direction. Scott took a longer look.

"Your husband?"

"So the courts tell me."

Scott smiled as he turned back. "Where's your ring?"

"I don't wear it anymore," Ann quickly covered. "He's...We're not on the best of terms these days."

"Then why come to a place like this?"

"A pathetic attempt at resurrecting our marriage. Go someplace romantic and it will put everything right again. His idea, not mine."

"And has it? No, I suppose not, if he's sitting all the way over there." Scott had another sip. "This your first time in Alvord?"

"First, and last."

"Oh, don't let him ruin it for you. It's a charming old place. Not much to it, but what there is can be very romantic. I'd be happy to show it to you....," he glanced at Damian, "....if, that is, you don't have anything else planned."

Ann hesitated, then said, "No. I don't have anything else planned."

RODNEY WASN'T HER FIRST LOVER. That was the boy her wealthy friend Constance introduced her to on one of their holidays to the French Riviera. Viscount something-or-other. Or maybe it was Vincent something-or-other. It didn't matter to Ann. It was a spur of the moment decision aided by the champagne she had been consuming since she boarded the plane. The mood was right and they made love on a well-hidden section of beach near a wall of boulders. They rarely did anything else the rest of the week.

It would have been a memorable experience for Ann if only she could remember it. Since then, she did her best to keep a clear head when it came to men. But she hadn't with Rodney. Why hadn't she seen it? Had he suffered some sort of illness that turned him into a monster overnight, or had he become a master at hiding that side of himself? It didn't matter anymore. None of it did. Rodney hadn't brutalized her for four days, he had brutalized her for life. How could she have been so wrong about him? How would she ever be able to trust her judgment with men again?

WHATEVER HIS MISGIVINGS ABOUT ANN's behavior and Scott's growing interest in her, Damian would have to be content for now with his role of spurned husband, a role which required him to stare daggers at Scott while keeping a close eye on Ann. That got a bit more difficult when Ann and Scott left the dining room through the double doors and started down the path into the garden, over the Georgian brick and stone footbridge that rose above a large pond. Scott put his jacket around Ann just before they disappeared into the woods. Damian wandered onto the flagstone patio and sat on the stone ledge circling the large fountain and waited.

Their walk lasted nearly an hour. Scott told one lie after another about himself while Ann made up the details of her life as quickly as he asked about them. It was obvious to Ann that he was after a relationship lasting no longer than an evening, and she rejected his initial advances. Then gradually – calculatingly – she stopped fighting him. She wouldn't let him go too far, giving him just an idea of what was on offer. When they emerged from the woods, she thought their date was over. But without warning he pulled her close and kissed her, and she let him.

"No, I shouldn't," Ann said as she made a feeble attempt at freeing herself.

"Why not?"

"Because…My marriage. I want to try to make it work."

Scott brushed up against her and said softly in her ear, "You know, if your marriage is already a wreck, this place isn't going to fix it. If your husband was interested, he wouldn't have let you go off with someone you just met. He'd at least be looking for you." Ann looked to her left and saw Damian by the fountain, wishing he would show just the slightest bit of concern for her instead of skimming dead leaves out of the water.

"Despite our difficulties, I love my husband. And he loves me."

"Does he?"

Ann again glanced at Damian, who at the moment was mesmerized by the way the flow of water streaming out of the lion's mouth changed when he stuck his fingers in it.

"Alright. Things haven't been going well," Damian made it necessary for Ann to concede.

"Since?"

"The honeymoon, really." Scott kissed her again, and she again offered no resistance as their kiss became more passionate.

"That wasn't the kiss of a woman trying to save her marriage." His eyes were working their magic. "Look, I'm in number ten, on the top floor. Why don't you drop by tonight, say, after dinner?"

"Erm…No. No, I shouldn't. Really."

"I promise I'll make it a memorable evening for you." Ann looked once more at Damian, who was now drying his hands on an oversized leaf from a low-growing shrub behind him. "I'm only here 'til tomorrow. I don't want to leave without being with you for at least one night."

Her hesitancy only seemed to make Scott more eager. "We can spend tonight together, or you can go back to your husband wondering if you passed up an opportunity to find out if your marriage was meant to be." Ann wondered how many women had been won over by that line.

"But...I don't even know you."

"What do you need to know? You can't deny there's an attraction between us." Scott again glanced at Damian. "You and your husband... How long has it been?"

"Sorry?"

"How long has it been since he made love to you?" Scott asked as he gently caressed her face. Passion stepped in before reason could intervene and Ann let her eyes close. Scott wasted no time and gently kissed her neck, then her shoulder. "I promise you won't regret it." In spite of what she knew about Scott, Ann was also intrigued by him. He drew her in, excited her, cancelled out common sense and made her forget Claire and Melinda and Darla.

"You'll be there all night?" Ann said.

"I'll leave the door open. Come whenever you like. Whenever you can get away."

He kissed her again, then deliberately walked past Damian on his way inside. Damian waited until he was out of sight, then walked over to Ann and said, "Well? Did you learn anything?"

"Hmm?" Scott's influence lingered. "Yes. Quite a bit, in fact. He wants me to meet him in his room tonight, after dinner."

"Are you?"

"Yes."

"Why? I mean, why his room?"

"Because that's where he wants to meet."

"Yes, but if I'm to search his room—"

"Shit! Right. I'll take him to our room instead. Christ! What was I thinking?" Just then Scott came out onto the second story balcony overlooking the patio, cigarette in hand. He leaned on the wrought iron railing in full view of Damian.

"You don't think he'll become suspicious, do you?" Damian asked as he and Ann strolled to the fountain.

"He hasn't so far. He hasn't had reason to. He loves danger, what could be more dangerous than being with a married woman right under her husband's nose?"

"And what do I do while you and him are—I mean, just what is it I'm supposed to be looking for?"

"You'll know when you find it."

Damian shook his head. "I don't like it. Excuse me for saying, but you've had quite a lot to drink. You've been coming on to him all afternoon. And that dress! What sort of woman dresses like that in the daytime?"

"The sort of woman I'm supposed to be. Now look. I want you to get hold of yourself. Then I want you to check out the grounds. I don't think he'd be stupid enough to hide whatever it is he's selling here, but you never know."

"Where will you be?"

"Keeping the man of the moment occupied." Damian looked skyward and sighed hard.

"You'll be in there all alone, without a wire, without enough back-up should anything go wrong."

"I'll be alright, Sergeant," Ann said, intending to sound reassuring but allowing just enough doubt to creep in.

"You've never done this before, have you? Gone undercover?"

"Sergeant—"

"I knew it!" He flung his arms in the air and turned away. Ann glanced up at Scott. To him, this must look like one more fight in their ever-crumbling marriage.

"The Chief Inspector couldn't give us any back-up. We can't rely on the local police. According to Darla, Scott's been coming back here for years so could be they're in on it as well. What are we supposed to do? Let him escape?"

"We could tell Interpol where he is, let them deal with it instead of putting yourself at risk." Damian quickly spun toward her. "That's it, isn't it? You want to catch him yourself, for what he did to Melinda and Claire and all the rest."

Damian sat on the edge of the fountain and held his head between his hands. Ann sat next to him and said in a conciliatory tone, "This case, it's important to me."

"Inspector, I may not have spent as much time on it as you, but I want him to pay for what he's done just as much as you do."

"I know."

Damian sighed. "I reckon it's partly my fault. I haven't been much help. I mean, it's not as if I have all that much to do. Just play the jilted husband."

Ann took another quick look at Scott. "I don't think this would be the best time to reconcile, Sergeant." Damian quickly got back into character. He stood up, repeated the gesture of throwing his arms in the air, then stormed off, putting Ann in mind of a silent film actor making a dramatic exit.

Ten o'clock and Ann still hadn't shown up. Scott went downstairs to look for her and found her at the bar nursing yet another watered-down drink.

"I thought you were going to meet me," he said after settling next to her.

"My husband and I had a terrible row."

"Then you should have come to my room. I'd've made you forget all about him."

Ann had a drink, then said, "I don't want to go to your room. I want to go to our room."

"*Your* room?" Scott smiled. He offered her his arm and said, "Shall we go?" They went upstairs and Damian came out of hiding down the hallway. He waited until the door closed, then made his way quickly, quietly up the stairs and, with the help of his credit card, entered Scott's room. While he rummaged through Scott's belongings, Scott poured more scotch into Ann. She thought she could manage one more, but he kept refilling her glass.

"I think I've had quite enough for one day," she protested.

"Ah, you're on holiday. No restrictions on holiday. On anything." Not wanting to give herself away, Ann took just one more sip. That was enough to push her to the next level of intoxication. Scott threw back his scotch, then took her hand and led her to the bed. He held her close and began kissing her. His hands kept wandering and Ann kept finding ways to slow their advance. She tried to pull away, but he was too strong and she was too drunk.

All she could think was, how long would it take Damian to search Scott's room? Would he return in time, or was she destined to get to know Scott more intimately than she cared to? In her zeal to catch Scott, Ann now realized there were a few things she hadn't thought all the way through. Like this. She didn't want to sleep with Scott, but if she kept resisting him, he might catch on that this was a set-up. She also knew she shouldn't have drunk so much. She was becoming drowsier and he was becoming more aggressive. One minute she was kissing him and the next, she heard a loud knock on the door.

"Darling, I've forgotten the key." That startled Ann, but not as much as the realization that she was lying across the bed in her slip, her arms out of the straps, her dress hanging off the end of the bed. She saw Scott coming out of the bathroom drying his face with a towel. His trousers were on but his shoes and shirt were off.

"Shall I climb out the window, or should we just fight it out for you?" Scott said matter-of-factly.

"What?"

"Your husband. He wants in." Ann hurried as best she could to the door and opened it. Her consternation paled in comparison to the shock registered on Damian's face when he saw the state of undress Ann and Scott were in. He reacted by throwing an off-balanced punch that just grazed the side of Scott's head. Scott laughed as he grabbed his shoes and shirt, then casually walked out the door. Damian kicked it shut behind him.

"Are you alright?"

"Yes," Ann replied.

"What the hell happened? Did he—Did you—"

"What did you find in his room, Sergeant? Anything useful?" Ann said as she quickly put on her robe.

"Erm, yes. Some papers that say he's doing a deal with an Iraqi ship in the North Sea in four days time."

"Four days. That's one more day than we thought. Must be moving a lot of weapons."

"Inspector, what exactly—"

"We've got to ring the Chief Inspector, let him know what we've found. Could be drugs, too."

"The CI…Right."

CHAPTER 29

ANN MADE THE CALL TO Owen the next morning.
"A ship, eh? Why would he leave that sort of information lying about?"

"Perhaps because he feels invincible. He's never had reason not to."

"Or could be he planted it there in the event someone broke into his room," Owen countered. "Right. Let's assume what Dillon found is accurate. Give me that information again."

Ann did, then said, "If you can free up some help we can be there in two hours."

"That won't be necessary. I'll pass this along to Interpol. I'm not having the two of you traipsing off to some heavily guarded arsenal. That's best left to the experts."

Ann and Damian returned to the station the next morning. The information Scott left behind was indeed false, though only partially. His meeting took place not on a ship but just fifteen miles from the city centre. Interpol saw through the parts of his plan that didn't ring true and for the first time they had enough advance information on one of his deals to enable them to set up a sting and finally catch him. They brought him to the station – it was the closest one with suitable facilities – until they could arrange extradition to the first of many countries that were interested in prosecuting him for his numerous crimes. Ann didn't know that until she heard a commotion by the front entrance. She turned to see several Interpol officers escorting Scott, his wrists and ankles chained. As he walked past Ann, Scott looked into her eyes and said in a voice only she could hear, "Inspector. All those scars…Who would do that to you?"

"Ann? Ann?"

The last thing Ann remembered was watching Scott being led away. In the time it took her to turn her head, she was sitting across from Constance in a restaurant. She didn't know where she was or how she got there. She saw Constance's mouth moving, then looked around the room slowly and saw others speaking as well, but she didn't hear a sound. The whole room bustled with activity, yet it was dead silent. Then, as if someone flipped a switched, Ann could hear voices, music, dishes and silverware clanking together.

"You haven't been listening to a word I've said," Constance mildly scolded her.

"No, I have. Every word," Ann said unconvincingly as her eyes discretely scanned the room.

"Really, Ann. You've been acting so strangle lately, ever since you returned from Alvord. By the way, you haven't told me what happened. Did you and your new partner strike up, shall we say, a more intimate collaboration?"

"We went there strictly on business, to catch a criminal."

"And did you?"

"Yes." Constance took a bite of food, prompting Ann to do the same. But when Ann looked at her plate, all she saw were escargot.

"Yes, I was wondering about that as well," Constance said. "A bit adventurous, aren't we?" Ann's fork hovered over her plate. "Ann, is everything alright?"

"Yes. Why?"

"Oh, I don't know. The silence, the staring, the snails—"

"Everything's fine. Really."

Constance kept a watchful eye on Ann as she resumed eating. "You know you'll feel a lot better if you tell me what's troubling you."

Ann had no intention of eating snails and set her fork down.

"Tell me about Scott."

Ann didn't recall mentioning his name to her. "There's nothing to tell," Ann said as she tore a roll in half and started eating it dry. As she did, she noticed Constance's wristwatch was the size of a wall clock. And it read nine-forty. *a.m.*

"Really? I should think it must have been quite exciting, meeting him face to face."

"Well it wasn't," Ann said firmly. "He's just another con artist who thought himself smarter than everyone else. Nothing special about him. Nothing at all."

"I see," Constance said, then had another bite. "Where did you and Damian go after you left the inn?"

"Go?"

"Yes. You told me you left Wednesday, yet you only just returned Sunday. That's three days time unaccounted for." Wednesday? Had it been that long? Ann remembered leaving the inn, that Damian insisted on driving. He got behind the wheel...Scott was being led to a cell...And she was in a restaurant, eating dinner at nine-forty in the morning. What happened to all that time?

"We didn't go anywhere. We left the inn and came straight back to town."

"I don't mean to pry, Ann. I only ask because you seem so preoccupied."

"I'm not. A bit knackered, perhaps. Been a long week...or two." Ann knew she wasn't fooling Constance, but she was more concerned about her memory loss. Was it the alcohol? She drank more than she should have in Alvord, but was it enough to cause a blackout? Was it the start of a pattern, or had Scott put something in her drink? She wanted to find the cause of this, and at the same time she didn't. It might lead her to places she didn't want to go, to questions she didn't want answers, to answers that were better left unknown.

HOME AT LAST. FOR SOME reason Ann's flat was dark, much darker than usual. She turned on the light but the bulb blew with a distinct pop. "Shit!" Ann didn't fancy the prospect of balancing on that rickety step stool again to change it. She went to the kitchen first to get some water, but she felt dizzy and rested her forehead against the refrigerator door as she waited for it to pass.

"Hello again." Ann's breath caught at the sound of the voice coming from the living room.

"Who is it? Who's there?"

"Forgotten already?" Stepping out of the darkness was Scott, dressed as Ann saw him last, trousers only.

"How did you get in here?!" Ann said, her adrenalin racing.

"I've come to finish what we started. You promised me the whole night, but your husband cut the evening short." His body pressed up against hers, pinning her against the refrigerator, and he began kissing her. She tried to get away but to her surprise, she didn't have the strength to fight him off.

"Inspector?" Scott's voice startled Ann. Her eyes did a quick search of her surroundings. She was in her office. And it wasn't Scott leaning toward her, it was Damian.

"Yes, Sergeant?" said Ann, who tried covering her blushes by tidying things on her desk.

"It's the boss. He wanted to see you twenty minutes ago." That was the first Ann had heard of it. She noticed the clock on the wall behind Damian. Three-forty-five. *p.m.* "Shall I tell him you're coming?"

"I'll be along presently," Ann said as she filed a random handful of papers in the bottom drawer of her desk. "Can't be all that important. This case is over and—" When Ann came back up, Damian was gone, and she was sitting in Owen's office. The room was pitch dark with the exception of a bright light aimed at Owen, who was seated at his desk. The clock behind it, according to Mickey's hands, said it was eight-twenty, *p.m.*

"Inspector. So glad you found the time to join us." Us? Then Ann noticed the men standing to either side of Owen, visible only from their shoulders to their knees. Owen walked around to the front of his desk and sat on the edge closest to Ann. "Inspector, are you satisfied that this case has been resolved to the best of your ability?"

"Sir?"

"Simple question, Ann."

"Well," Ann said warily, "we've got those three for kidnapping Melinda, we've got Danny's confession for the murder of Wallace Thornton, Scott has been arrested for—"

"Yes, yes. That's all well and good, and don't think we don't appreciate having that lot off the streets. What I meant was, are you happy with the methods that were used to catch them?"

"Methods?"

"For instance, do you think it was necessary to go off on those wild goose chases, first to Duffield, then Leeston, then Alvord? Cost the department quite a bit of dosh in case you're interested."

"I believe the results justify the expense, sir," Ann replied with some trepidation. Owen walked back behind his desk and stood shoulder-to-shoulder with the other men. His voice seemed to be coming from the walls, the ceiling, and it echoed.

"You failed, Ann. You have no proof they committed any crimes. We can't hold any of them. The prosecutor is quite upset with you." As if on cue there was the sound of a switch being thrown and a light shone on the face of the man standing to Owen's left. It was the Crown Prosecutor, and he was indeed angry. The light went off and the entire room was plunged into darkness. Then the switch sounded again and Ann was bathed in an intense white light.

"They're all going free, Ann," Owen's disembodied voice continued. "And they know where you live. We had to tell them. They're suing you for false arrest. It's their right to know." Stropman, Roschine, Karl, Danny, Pablo? They all had her address?

"Sir, I—"

"The Complaints and Discipline Department has already met to decide your punishment. You will be allowed to remain on the force. However, you shall be required to meet with the Deputy

Chief Constable and comply with whatever conditions he deems appropriate."

The light went out again, then quickly on to the man to Owen's right. Scott. And on his lapel was a large badge with the handwritten words Deputy Chief Constable. Ann's heart was racing. She wanted to get out. She *had* to get out. But as she tried to get up, she discovered her wrists and ankles were tied to the chair. As she struggled to free herself she heard their laughter. Loud, maniacal laughter that grew until Ann's panic became so great, she passed out.

"Well? What do you think of my design?" Constance and Ann were sitting on the couch in Ann's flat, Constance's sketches for her latest project between them. "Perhaps this is a bad time."

"No," Ann said urgently as she stopped Constance from gathering her things. "I-I want to see them." Ann was desperate for some sort of distraction as she tried to make sense of what was happening. She picked up a drawing and noticed Constance's now normal sized watch. Two-twenty. *a.m.,* judging by how dark it was outside. She didn't remember when Constance arrived, or letting her in. Or why she was here at this late hour.

"I'...sorry, Ann. I know I should have rung first, but I simply had to stop by and show you these sketches. A police station. Can you believe it?" Constance said gleefully.

"A police station? I didn't think they ever got remade."

"Oh, no, I'm turning it into a studio. For an artist. Wants to make some sort of statement. Quite cheeky, some of his ideas." Ann couldn't suppress a yawn. "Have you been here all day? I thought you were going to try to enjoy your day off. Ann didn't recall having a day off.

"I, uh, was going to go out, but I..." Constance lit up a cigarette, took a few puffs, then rested it on the ashtray on the coffee table. Constance didn't smoke. Ann had no ashtrays. And Constance's watch now said eleven-fifty. *a.m.*

"Ann," Constance took on a more serious tone, "there's something I must tell you. Something I should have told you years ago. It's just that you seemed so certain at the time." Constance took another puff, then snuffed her cigarette out in the ashtray. "When Rodney kidnapped you, you told the police that he tortured you."

"Yes?"

"How much of it do you actually remember?"

"What do you mean?"

"I mean, what do you remember?"

"Are you saying it didn't happen?"

"No, of course not. I'm just saying it may have happened a bit differently than you remember."

Differently...Different...

"According to the doctor who treated you in hospital, there were no cuts or burns. All they found were abrasions from the rope."

The blade...it pierces through my skin...

"No, he did! He cut—he burnt me!"

"I believe you, Ann. I'm just telling you what the doctors told me."

"Miss Livingstone, you'll be pleased to learn Miss Treadwell was not seriously injured."

"Then why is she in hospital? Why is she bleeding so?"

"She's suffered a few minor abrasions. Nothing serious. But it isn't her physical condition we're concerned about."

"I thought you knew, Ann. Don't you remember?" Suddenly, Constance was a million miles away. Nothing existed except Ann and her deepest, most disturbing memories. Her mind was transporting her back in time, letting her senses revisit her ordeal: the smells of that night, his car, the woods, the stale air that had been trapped inside the abandoned restaurant freezer for months, perhaps years; the roughness of the walls and the stinging of her raw, bloodied fingertips as she desperately tried to claw her way out as hours grew into days; the deafening silence while she lay exhausted on the floor in what she was certain would become her tomb. She saw Rodney. Then, nothing. Her mind wouldn't let her go any further, but it was merely a cruel pause. Like an avalanche, it all came back to her all at once: the pain of the knife as it cut into her, not once, not twice, but dozens of times, sometimes reaching bone. The look on Rodney's face as he ignored her cries of pain, her pleas for him to stop. And through it all, she heard his insane laughter.

She saw it. Felt it. Lived it. Why was Constance telling her it didn't happen? Why was she bringing it up again when she knew how hard Ann had fought to cope? Didn't she realize what this was doing to her, or was she intentionally trying to destroy her? No, Constance was her closest friend. She would never do something like that.

"No! It isn't true! He tortured me, over and over again—"

Constance squeezed Ann's hand. "It's alright. No one would blame you for trying to get a bit of attention. After the way your parents treated you, you deserve some sympathy."

"Miss Treadwell, do you know where you are? Can you hear me? She's not responding. I'm afraid she's gone into shock. A serious mental trauma."

"How long will it last?"

"That we don't know, Miss Livingstone. It could be a few days, a few weeks, perhaps even permanently."

"No, it happened!" Ann insisted as she pulled her hand away from Constance. "I was bleeding, and the doctors...the doctors said..." What *did* the doctors say? Ann had never experienced such fright, and maybe her memories had changed over time, but she knew what Rodney had done to her. Could she have imagined it? No, she was certain she hadn't. She had the scars. Didn't she? She started to check but as she did, she noticed Constance was gone. The room was dark. All that was visible was the clock on the end table. Ten-twenty-five. *p.m.*

Afraid to sleep, Ann came into the station early the next morning. She got started on her paperwork, but she couldn't concentrate. Had she been tortured? Had she slept with Scott? Why was Constance doubting her? Then there was Damian. He was acting strangely and

Ann knew why. When he came to work this morning, Ann spoke to him in her office.

"I just wanted to commend you for the job you did in Alvord."

"All I did was search his room."

"Still, I wanted to thank you for backing me up in such…For backing me up."

I didn't though, did I? I let him go with you when I knew you'd had too much to drink."

"That was our job, Sergeant, to get enough evidence to put Scott away."

"It's alright with you then? Being alone in a room with a man you hardly know, letting him have his way with you just so you could solve a case?"

"Is that what you think happened, that Scot took advantage of me?"

"The thought had crossed my mind."

"Nothing happened, Sergeant. He saw me in my slip. That's all."

"You're certain?"

"I think I'd know if anything more had taken place."

"Well, I'm glad nothing happened, that he didn't—that you're alright."

"The only reason I'm telling you this is to remove any doubt from your mind. But if we're to continue working together – *if* we continue working together – it's important you understand what I did, I did for this case. That's all you need to know. Otherwise, my personal life is my business and mine alone."

"But it wasn't your personal life, was it?"

"WELL? ARE YOU GOING TO order or not?"

"What?" In an instant, sights, smells sounds all came alive to Ann. She was again sitting in an unknown restaurant holding a menu while Constance, the waiter and a couple sitting at the next table stared at her. Ann glanced at the waiter's watch. Twelve-thirty-five. *p.m.*

"Yes. Of course." Ann opened her menu but her mind was too busy trying to find something that made sense for her to peruse today's specials.

"Ann, is something wrong?"

"Did you come to my flat last night?" Ann asked.

"Last night? No. I was in London showing my designs to that new client I told you about. Why do you ask?"

"You're remodeling a building?"

"Yes. That's what I do."

"A police station?"

"Police station? No, a warehouse. We're turning it into a loft." Her hand in a loose fist, Ann tapped the knuckles of her first two fingers lightly against her lips. "Ann, what is it?"

Ann moved her hand and leaned closer. "What—When I was in hospital after Rodney...What did the doctors tell you he had done?"

"What? You don't want to hear all that again, do you?"

"What did they tell you?" Ann asked firmly, her voice low.

"Very well. That Rodney had tortured you."

"How?"

"Really, Ann. I don't want to talk about—"

"How did he torture me?"

Constance shook her head, then partially relented. "All I know is what the doctors told me. You suffered serious burns – I can't remember what degree they said they were – and most of the cuts were so deep they required surgery." That's the way Ann remembered it, but which version was true? "Ann, what's this all about?"

"And you didn't come to my flat last night?"

"No. I haven't seen you in a fortnight. Remember?" Constance sat back and looked at Ann with concern. "It's just stress, Ann. You really should find a more relaxing job. I can find you something in my office if you'd like."

"I'm fine. Really."

"You look a complete wreck. What you need is to get away for a bit. I'm spending the weekend in St. Moritz. I have a client who has a home there and he's letting me use it while he's away. You're welcome to come."

Ann's first inclination was to decline, but she found herself smiling at the thought. "I'll, uh – Yeah, if I can get –"

"Oh, sorry! I hope you don't mind. I'm running behind schedule on one of my remodels and I've arranged to meet my client here. I'll only be a minute." Constance waved at someone, then left. Ann was grateful for a few minutes alone to think, but a loud crash in the kitchen abruptly ended that. She felt relieved enough to butter a piece of bread and take a bite. If she had been eating lately she wouldn't have been surprised at how good it tasted, but one of the effects of being deprived of food was that even the flavor of something as pedestrian as bread and butter became magnified.

Ann finished her bread, then checked her watch and saw that twenty minutes had gone by. She sighed, then heard a loud conversation at a table to her right. It was Constance, animated as ever, sharing a laugh – and lunch – with someone out of Ann's view. Suddenly feeling self-conscience Ann decided to leave, but she was overcome by dizziness the moment she got to her feet. The floor seemed tilted as she made her way to the door, but she couldn't move her feet fast enough to escape Constance's attention. "Oh, Ann! How lovely of you to join us!" Constance called out, oblivious to Ann's distress. "I'd like to introduce you to my newest client, Mrs. Emily Parsons." Ann looked at the woman sitting across from Constance: Ophelia Stanton.

"But you...You're not..."

"Oh, but she is, Ann. One of my most valued clients," Constance enthused. "She's got some absolutely marvelous plans for an old farmhouse. Here. What do you think?" One half of Constance's sketch showed a hotel with a swimming pool, luxury suites and a restaurant. The other half featured a row of beds, a nurses' station and an isolation ward. There were two doors, one marked 'Awards' and the other 'Electro-Shock Therapy'. "Isn't it wonderful? It's the latest in holiday resorts."

"Yes, and I'd love for both you and Miss Livingstone to be there for the grand opening," Emily said pleasantly as she handed Ann a card. It entitled the bearer to a free weekend at the resort, including a complimentary electro-shock treatment. Ann felt her knees go weak.

"What is it?" Constance asked, then took the card from Ann. "How wonderful!"

"What?!"

"Free use of pool and free massage! Well, you'll certainly be taking advantage of that, won't you?" Ann took the card back and read it: Free use of pool and free massage. Ann looked at Constance and Emily, who both smiled knowingly at her. Ann read the card again and when she looked up, both of them were gone.

The phone rang. And rang. And rang again. The watch Ann held in her hand read nine o'clock. At night. And the phone kept ringing. It was Owen. Or Constance. Or a telemarketer. It didn't matter. Ann wasn't going to answer it. She was concerned about the time she had been losing lately and she was trying to work out where it had gone. What happened to those days between the time she left Alvord and arrived home? What happened between the time Scott kissed her and Damian came to her rescue? As she sat curled up on her couch, those questions consumed her. And the phone kept ringing.

SEVEN-FIFTY. A.M. ANN HAD TAKEN to looking at her watch frequently the last few days. As she was about to enter the CID office, Damian was exiting.

"Oh, Inspector. You got a visitor." Damian nodded towards Ann's office. There, like a black T-shirt-clad wall, was Miss Tansy. As imposing as ever, Miss Tansy also appeared to have brought a healthy amount of anger with her this time. She was biding her time by alternately grinding her fist into her palm, massaging her biceps and rubbing the ring inserted through her nose.

"Not again," Ann said as she rolled her eyes. "Christ! She must weigh fifteen stone. You'd think someone her size could deal with a mugger, for God's sake."

Damian did his best not to smile. "I'll have a word, if you'd like."

"Thanks."

Damian erased his smile, cleared his throat, then bravely headed for Miss Tansy. At the same time Owen exited his office, his palms pressed tightly together, his face turning ever deepening shades of red. He let out a gush of air and said, "Ann. Got a minute?" She didn't, but she knew his question was rhetorical. "About this case," Owen said as he stretched. "Perhaps you can tie up a few loose ends. First, do we know who killed Royce? Was it Scott, or was it Darla?"

"Scott. This new business of Terry's wasn't exactly prostitution, it was the white slave trade. Ironically, he was going to sell Melinda to Scott, who wasn't aware she was the same girl he gave Karl to kill all those years ago. Seems it was Terry's way of getting revenge on Scott for not paying the extra three-thousand pounds that was to go to the person who killed Melinda. That's according to Darla, anyway, supported by Terry's meticulous - if rather vague – record keeping. Scott was the man who nearly knocked Lydia down when she went looking for Priscilla at the pub."

"Stupid bastard obviously didn't know he had a small fortune locked away in that flat of his all those years. Marsh surely would have paid whatever Royce asked in order to get Melinda back. And Juan?"

"My guess would be either Claire or Lydia, though we can't rule out Darla or even Scott."

"Got it narrowed down that far, have you? What about Darla's baby, the one Scott took with him to the Middle East?"

"Near as we can tell, Scott sold her to someone just after he had Claire put away in that asylum. Where she is now is anybody's guess."

"Any idea why he staged his own kidnapping?"

"The businessmen who were with him. Their companies paid their ransom, money that went to Scott."

"I see. Anyway, what I wanted to say was, well done. For the most part, that is. However, in future, I trust you can see your way clear to conducting an investigation without exhausting valuable resources which we simply do not have at the moment."

"Yes, sir."

"So," Owen said as he lowered himself onto his chair, "I suppose you'll want to get on to Juan's murder."

"With your permission, I'd like to start—erm, continue—with the assault case."

Owen raised an eyebrow. "I'm surprised at you, Ann. I should think you'd be champing at the bit to get onto another murder instead of a simple assault."

"It's not all that simple, sir."

"Isn't it?" He eyed her dubiously. "You were quite keen to work on this case to the exclusion of all others. Now you want out. Why?" She could tell him the truth, that she was still suffering the lingering effects of this case and the similarities between it and her own ordeal eighteen years ago, but she knew he already had his doubts about her and she didn't want to add to them. "Well? Which is it to be?"

"Juan's murder," Ann said, drawing Owen's approving smile.

* * *

S HE HAD RECEIVED HER INVITATION to the Emperor's ball, the most anticipated social event of the season. It had taken months to plan, with only the very elite receiving the gold-embossed cards, hand-lettered by the Emperor's personal staff on the finest woven paper. Her search to find her missing daughter hadn't suddenly become unimportant to Priscilla. Rather, it had been overtaken by her need to survive. Twenty years ago, Priscilla Corbett had a well-paying job at a public relations firm and had planned on continuing her education in the hope of advancing her career. But all that changed when she met

Simon. He was an expert at finding flaws in people and a master at exploiting them. Even his own wife wasn't immune to his destructive manipulations.

Teetering on the brink of madness after the cruelest of his betrayals, Priscilla saved herself by becoming Madame Peto. A woman of means. Of importance. If she was recognized by someone as significant as Emperor Franz Josef II, if she could gain the acceptance of his wife, Elisabeth, then the rest of the empire would treat her with the respect she so richly deserved.

An invitation to the ball would clinch it. She would arrive at the palace gate, her carriage drawn by majestic white horses. A footman would open the door and offer his hand as she descended the steps onto the cobblestones below. She would take the arm of her escort for the evening, a man of nobility, and they would walk down the cobble stone path past rows of sixty-foot tall Italian cypresses standing like soldiers forming an honor guard, then through the grand arbor into the main palace garden. She would be announced to the Emperor, in full military regalia, who would kiss the back of the woman's hand. Then a bit of socializing with Europe's elite until they were called into the dining room to feast on a ten course meal prepared by the finest chefs in Europe.

Then, after the men had retired to the smoking room for cigars and brandy, the women would be left to discuss the events of the day. Dancing would be the next order of business. The orchestra, which had rehearsed for weeks on end for the occasion, would play until dawn. Guests would slowly filter out as the sun came up over the stables. Their carriages would be brought, one by one, as each guest departed after expressing their profound appreciation for their host's generosity, hoping all the while they would be invited back next year.

Sitting next to her on the long train ride back to Austria, Lydia knew Priscilla was again lost in the past. During these times, there was only one way to communicate with her. She handed Priscilla a white envelope and told her it had arrived by royal messenger. Priscilla placed the envelope on her lap, then peeled off her white gloves a finger at a time and slipped them inside her satin bag so as not to get any ink on them. She pushed her reading glasses into place, then picked up the envelope and ran her finger over the blank seal. She opened it carefully, read the paper inside, then placed it back in the envelope. The paper, like the envelope, was blank.

CPSIA information can be obtained at www.ICGtesting.com
Printed in the USA
LVOW121712100313

323419LV00004B/7/P